Thirty Minutes to Heartbreak

Volume One:

Paramount

By Nadia Scrieva

ISBN-10: 1477618392
ISBN-13: 978-1477618394

This is dedicated to everyone who encouraged me to keep writing this story during its humble beginnings:

I would like to thank Melody Bernal, Maggie Stroud, Brittny Anmylica Cain, Katelyn Francis and Jasmine Brown for their lengthy discussions with me about the subject matter of the story. You girls were always so passionate that you made me more excited about my own creations, and got me all fired up with unlimited writing mojo!

Also special thanks to Arian Lopez, Melissa A. Chitwood, Danielle Hall, Shaheda Choudhury, Holli Farrell and Katie-Ann Foster for their constant encouragement!
I received such insightful responses on this story and I will always treasure every single review. Even more so, I will hold dear the lifelong friends I have made along the way.

TABLE OF CONTENTS

Chapter 1: Defying the Laws

A feminine hand clad in a fingerless leather glove pulled a hard left on the steering wheel, maneuvering to avoid a car that had swerved into the way at the last second. The woman's face remained emotionless, but she felt anger rise up inside of her at the other driver's reckless act. She raised her hand, palm facing forward and fingers spread apart as she breathed deeply.

"Oh, I could just…"

She could see the flow of heat emanating from her volcanic center, obliterating the other car and its driver in mere moments—and then, perhaps, continuing on to clear out the highway for the next few dozen miles. Her windshield began to crack. *No.* She abruptly stopped visualizing the gratifying havoc she could wreak if she released all the pent up power which hummed at her fingertips. The temptation was too great, and she immediately closed her fist and returned it to the steering wheel.

She grimaced, fighting to control her twitching fingers, and forcing them back down onto the Jeep's steering wheel placidly. Regret coursed through her, and she acknowledged that she would need to replace her windshield again. A foul smell reached her nostrils, causing her forehead to crease. She glanced down at the bruised, tanned knuckles visible through little oval holes in her worn gloves. Smoke was drifting up from between her fingers as her heated palms burned into the rubbery-plastic material of the steering wheel. She felt sick at the stench.

Thorn. How could you?

The heart of her anger wasn't caused by reckless drivers. It was the lingering sting of betrayal. Startling her, a cell phone buzzed against her hip, and she fought the instant urge to crush it like a pesky insect. Was it *him* calling? She hadn't answered her phone in weeks. Why would anyone still bother to call?

Thorn in my side, thorn in my brain.

The sections of the steering wheel she gripped had finally melted completely. Yet another part of the Jeep would need to be replaced. Luckily, her mechanic no longer asked questions. She removed her hands from the wheel and tried to wipe the sticky substance off her gloves. Giving up, she interlocked her fingers together before resting them in her lap. She continued steering with only her mind. She enjoyed driving with just her thoughts. She liked the idea that her body was flying through the air, and direction was controlled by her mere intent. It reminded her of what made her special: this inherited telekinetic ability. The ability she had promised her family never to use. The phone rang again.

The feminine posture of having her hands clasped demurely in her lap brought a sardonic smile to her face. The only thing which had ever been feminine about Pax was her long black hair. She had taken great pride in being able to sit on the lustrous mass, and had enjoyed the competitive factor of being able to say that hers was longer than that of any woman she knew, and almost all women she met. (In retrospect, tying her ego to the length of a physical extension of her body had not been completely feminine.) Even then, it had always hung in tangled, messy waves which she had hardly ever brushed.

It was only a month ago that she had shorn it all off. She still felt awkward when she turned to check her blind-spot and did not have a pound of tresses rolling over her shoulders comfortingly. She still felt like something was missing when the window of her Jeep was open, and the harsh wind did not whip unruly strands into her eyes. She felt naked without these little luxuries. Pax had not realized that her hair had been her security blanket—and once she did realize this, she had quickly introduced it to a pair of garden shears.

Pax wanted to stop depending on external substances for strength. She was sure that she could find a greater confidence inside her that had nothing to do with her hair, her car, or her lover.

She had depended far too much on him.

Her phone was still pulsating against her hip annoyingly. She did not want to look at the name on the caller ID, but her mind was already sliding the phone from its holster and lifting it to hover at her eye level. She glanced away from the road for a moment to warily read the letters. *Amara Kalgren.* It was only half of the name that she most feared seeing. It was the sister of the man who betrayed her.

She had no wish whatsoever to speak to the blond woman. It was a pity really, since she loved and respected Amara. The two had been very close when they were younger, and in recent years they had occasionally double-dated since Amara was also seeing a relative of hers. Pax felt a bittersweet smile tug her lips as she thought of her silly uncle Asher. Their families had grown up together, and the Kalgren kids had always been loyal friends. When families shared secrets such as theirs, they tended to stay together. Pax had not spoken to her favorite couple in far too long, because her uncle was exceedingly close to her ex-boyfriend. She could endure no reminders of what she had lost. Any contact with Amara or Asher would be chock-full of painful reminders and would inevitably lead to contact with exactly what she was trying to avoid.

Releasing her focus on the phone, she allowed it to fall against her thigh. She looked ahead at the highway, and cursed when she saw the sea of red brake-lights appearing. She willed the dial that controlled the volume of her speakers to turn up the music to the maximum. She closed her eyes and let the sound bombard her ears as she sat still in traffic. Pax did not really have anywhere to go, but driving endlessly along the highway made her feel like she was going somewhere. It made her feel like she was getting away, although she was quickly finding that the continent was not large enough to escape the older Kalgren sibling. She had been sleeping in her car and on uncomfortable motel beds as she tried to escape her disgrace, but her rest was littered with fitful nightmares while her waking hours were tormented with frequent involuntary memories.

A vibration against her thigh caused her to peer down. She scowled at her phone. Amara hardly ever called at all; this was an old signal from their youth. Double-calling. Twice in a minute was a true sign of emergency. Pax jabbed her canines into her bottom lip, chewing as she considered taking the call. There might be a crisis. Something could have happened to her uncle Asher. She turned off the music telekinetically. Unlocking her hands and sliding her pinky finger tentatively across her thigh, Pax used the tip of her nail to press the green button.

"Yes?" she asked curtly. For a moment she was seized by an intense panic that it might be Thornton calling from his sister's phone. She held her breath, reassuring herself that he would never stoop that low. But then, there was precious little she knew about the depths to which he would stoop.

A small voice on the other end whispered a usually-upsetting diminutive of her name. "Paxie…"

Pax slammed her skull back into the headrest and cursed. Although she had not been especially close to Amara in the past decade, she could recognize the helplessness and despair in her friend's soft plea. They had been infants together, followed by childhood playmates. She knew Amara's every emotion as though it were her own, and although she had no inkling of what happened, she instinctively knew that this must be the worst kind of disaster. Her heart leapt into her throat as she imagined the worst case scenario—had her foolish Uncle Asher somehow gotten himself killed?

"I'm on my way," Pax said into the phone before hanging up. She glanced at her GPS to get a sense of her location, and cursed again. Her aimless, wandering circles had taken her three states away from Amara's beachfront home. Three states and at least fifteen hours. An idea struck her: the Jeep was a mess anyway, so perhaps she could abandon it and travel with her mind.

Pulling over into a ditch, Pax took several deep

breaths to concentrate. She had only successfully done this a handful of times in her life—usually in emergencies when it was most necessary. This was an emergency, and surely she would be able to focus enough to move her body across the distance instantaneously. It was only one small body—she could lift much larger objects without any effort. She reached into her passenger seat and slipped her wrist under her purse before beginning.

Pax placed the palm of her right hand firmly against her solar plexus. She took a deep breath, visualizing her destination. She placed her left hand beside her right hand, forming the shape of a heart with her fingers. Her head begin to spin as her body begun dematerializing, starting at her core. For a moment, she was immaterial, and floating in nothingness.

A tickle of fear caused her to gasp, and she immediately found herself falling butt-first onto the hood of her Jeep.

"Shit! I suck at this," she muttered, looking around to see if anyone had noticed her blunder. Grumbling, she rolled off the hood of her Jeep, wiping the dirt off her pants. Many insects had been slain with her speed in the past few days, and now their corpses were decorating her jeans. Pax swore repeatedly as she picked up her purse from the mud near the wheel of her car. She considered traveling by air, but there were too many people nearby. She climbed back into her Jeep, and slammed the door, upset with herself for her own inadequacy at using the technique which was supposed to be her birthright.

It was often her downfall that she tried to obtain

everything she desired instantaneously.

Digging her key into the ignition, she jammed her foot on the gas pedal and began driving on the rough, potholed shoulder. She flew by the stopped cars on the highway, disregarding the dozen rules she was probably breaking. If she could not be successful in bending the laws of nature, then at the very least, she could satisfy herself in defying the laws of the road.

* * *

"Mara! Where are you? Is everything okay? *Amara!*"

Pax felt sick. It had taken ten hours, but she had driven directly to Amara's waterfront home, stopping only once for gas. Seeing her friend's Jaguar in the driveway, she had let herself in. Now, as she moved from room to room on the hunt for the blonde woman, she was growing alarmed. She considered calling, but it was faster just to lift the palm of her hand.

"Pilot me to thine light," Pax chanted softly. The incantation was not necessary, but it helped her to focus. Soon enough, she found herself being subliminally led to her friend's bedroom. Amara was still nowhere to be seen, so she continued to follow the guiding energy to the ensuite bathroom.

Upon touching the doorknob, Pax recoiled as the strong scent of her uncle overwhelmed her senses before the door was even fully open. Terror flooded her breast as she imagined Asher's corpse sprawled out on the floor. Her gloved hand flew to cover her mouth before she had even seen a body. A déjà vu swept over her as she recalled finding her dead mother when she was just a teenager. The scent was familiar—it was not only Asher, but his blood.

Pax felt her heart skip a beat as it ached with love for her uncle. She expected to see him lying there dead, but she still moved into the room with determination. Asher was nowhere to be seen, but a small blonde woman was huddled in a corner of the shower stall. Amara was completely naked. Pax swallowed back her fear before she took in the surroundings. Amara's fashionable clothes were strewn all over the floor, and there was dark blood which had dried as it had been dripping down the glass doors of the shower stall.

"Amara, are you hurt?" Pax immediately moved to comfort her friend, crawling into the shower stall and crouching beside her. Pax spotted Amara's cell phone sitting in a pool of water nearby. It was amazing that the thing hadn't short-circuited, but then again, it was Kalgren technology.

"Mara?" Pax asked in a soft voice, reaching out to brushing her friend's hair off her face. She was surprised to find that Amara's hair was perfectly dry. Her skin was perfectly dry. There was hardly any water in the shower stall, except for a few small pools gathered at the bottom. It must have been hours since the shower was used.

"How long have you been like this? Amara! Talk to me!" said Pax firmly. Hearing no response she desperately sent her message directly into her friend's mind. *Has something happened to Ash? Please, please, Mara. Please tell me that my uncle is fine. I hardly have any family left. Is he…*

Amara snapped out of her little daze and looked up at her friend. "Ash?" she asked dumbly. "He's fine."

"Thank Sakra," Pax said, referring to the god of gods. She allowed herself to fall from her raised position on her ankles to a seated position on her bottom, ignoring the pools of water beneath her. She released a gush of air. "Is this your blood?"

The blonde woman stared forward for a moment silently.

Pax began to frown as her worry began to be replaced with anger. "Did Ash hurt you? Because if he…"

"No," Amara responded softly. "When he touches me, he is always gentle. So tender. He wouldn't hurt a fly."

Pax rolled her eyes at this description. Were they talking about the same man? Her annoyingly powerful uncle who had wrestled her toys away with his mind before she could even walk? "Maybe he wouldn't," Pax agreed, "but he certainly could. Did he?"

"No."

"Sure. He didn't hurt you. That's why you've been sitting naked in the corner of a blood-soaked shower stall for god-knows how many hours!"

Amara looked at her friend for the first time. "Oh, Paxie. Where's all your beautiful hair?"

Pax was already reaching up to search for it before she remembered. She scowled. "Don't call me that, Amara. We're not five anymore. And don't change the subject. What the hell happened?"

Amara's eyes lowered again. "I did something bad."

Glancing up at the bloody shower walls in confusion, Pax frowned. "What did you do?" She knew that Amara was not strong enough to harm her uncle, physically or psychically. She reached out to grasp the girl's shoulder and give it a firm shake. "Mara. Hey, hey! What did you do?"

"I don't know. He left me."

"He *what?*" Pax repeated in shock. Asher and Amara were the most solid couple she knew. Every birthday and holiday, she and Thornton would always… she could not finish the thought. Her anger at her own lover was beginning to seep into thoughts of her uncle by extension.

Amara turned to Pax with wounded innocence in her clear blue eyes. "He said he just wanted to… have me one last time. Then he walked away."

Pax felt comprehension dawn on her as she took in the state of the bathroom. "So… he fucked you and then he left you?"

The blonde woman was as still as death. "Do I deserve this? I don't understand."

Rage flushed Pax's body with warmth as the anger blossomed inside her again. She clenched her fists. Even after all this, Amara refused to say a negative thing about Asher. She refused to condemn him for hurting her, and she chose to believe that it was somehow her fault. While Pax loved her uncle to pieces, she could not make sense of his actions. Asher often followed the wrong company (Thornton) and this has often influenced him negatively and gotten him into all kinds of trouble.

"You didn't do anything wrong," Pax reassured her friend. She reached out to rub her gloved hand over

Amara's naked back. "I'll stay with you, okay? We'll get through this together."

Amara felt the familiar waves of heat radiating from Pax's hand and lifting her hair. She felt a small smile touch her lips. She hadn't realized that she had been so cold. The warmth of the dark haired woman's angry energy surrounded Amara's skin like a comforting blanket. As her lips curled they cracked, revealing how dry they had become from the salty tears that had been running over them for so many hours.

"Thank you, Pax," said Amara softly.

"What for?" she asked.

"For being here. I needed you."

Pax felt guilt wash over her when she remembered that she had been ignoring Amara's phone calls. *It's partly my fault she's like this. If I had been a better friend… Gah! I should have flown here instead of driving when my teleportation didn't work.* As she stared at the small blonde woman who was deathly pale, Pax began to form a vow in her mind. Uncle or not, she would not allow Asher to hurt her friend like this and get away scot-free. She would find a way to make sure that he was the one sitting on the floor and broken. She did not realize that she was fusing her own pain with Amara's and transferring it to a different man. *Asher will regret the day he did this to her. She's the last person who deserved this. Amara is so sweet and loving—not bitter and vengeful like me. She was always so true and devoted. I'll make Asher pay. I'll hurt him so deeply, and so terribly that it will ruin his already ruined life. Damn you, Thorn! I mean Ash...*

Pax saw a single tear run down Amara's face and it snapped her out of her guilt and anger. She put her arms around the blonde woman and held her close, ignoring that she was naked. Amara leaned against Pax's shoulder and let the tears fall freely.

Chapter 2: Neither, yet Both

"This is why we made that pact," Thornton was saying as he crossed his arms across his chest and leaned back in his chair. "Family was supposed to be off limits." It was very rare that his friend came to visit him during his office hours.

"I know," Asher said, "but you broke that pact before I did. Way before I did, man."

"And that makes this fine? She's my baby sister," Thornton said. He rose to his feet and slammed the palms of his hands down onto the mahogany desk. "You promised you wouldn't hurt her."

"Come on, buddy. You really want to get into this with me? You really want to talk about *hurting* someone, because I can dig up some real sweet-smellin' shit…"

"No. Just explain yourself."

Asher laughed bashfully, reaching up to scratch above his ear. "You know how it is. Mara was great, but I don't think I was ready for the kind of commitment she expected. I was starting to feel real old. I couldn't stand the marriage hints. I shouldn't have to explain this to you, man. Look at what you've…"

"Well, why shouldn't you have married my sister? You've been with her for over five years and things seemed to be going swell." Thornton reached up to rip his glasses away from his face and began to polish them nervously.

"I don't know," Asher shrugged. "I guess when I saw that you were free and living the life again I felt jealous. I know that we're not kids, but I still feel young and… I want things to be like they used to be. Fun and no-strings. I want to party with you."

"Don't blame this on me!" shouted Thornton. His mahogany desk drifted a few inches off the floor. "I'm not 'living the life,' Ash. I'm trying my best to stay sane. My company is falling apart, and I am up to my neck in friggin' lawsuits here. If I go out clubbing at night to blow off some steam, it doesn't mean I'm reliving the glory of my college days. It means I'm working my ass off and going fucking insane!"

Asher pointed at the desk with two fingers and forced it back down to the ground. "Relax, Thorn. Look, I know running Kalgren Tech isn't easy, but you gotta keep your cool if you want to keep the building standing, okay?"

Thornton lifted his hands in apology. "Sorry. I just—I know that Mara really loves you. She used to scribble your name in her notebooks when she was a little kid." The businessman slid his glasses back onto his nose with a sigh. "I told her that she was dumb and you were a jerk, but would she listen?"

"Do you really wanna go there?" Asher asked. "Because if we start talking about Paxie…"

"No. Don't even say her name," Thornton said, sitting down abruptly. He groaned and rested his elbows on his desk, shoving his head into his hands and beginning to aggressively knead his temples. "I made some major mistakes recently. I have royally screwed myself beyond the point of unscrewing. But you didn't have to follow my example. You could have been better than me, Ash."

"When in our entire lives have I ever been better than you?" Asher sent his friend a gloomy grin. "Face it, Thorn. In every test I aced, you scored a little higher. In every race we ran, you timed a little faster. I've always been the shadow and the sidekick. You're the big time CEO, and I'm your unemployed best friend. Got me a few nifty superpowers, but still. Never gonna be the bigger man."

Thornton glanced up in disbelief. "So if I accidentally happen to act like the world's greatest asshole…"

"It is my time-honored duty to intentionally be the world's second greatest asshole," Asher joked. Seeing the lines around Thornton's eyes soften, he continued to push his luck. "We made another pact when we were kids, remember? We said we'd never let a woman come between us." When his friend nodded, he declared with emphasis, "Bros before hoes!"

Thornton looked up with his blue eyes suddenly stormy. "You're talking about my sister, man."

"Yeah, I'm talkin' about her. I'm also talkin' about my niece who you *babysat.* My niece who lost her mother when she was thirteen, and looked up to you as her hero. Paxie fucking worshipped the ground you…"

"Okay. You win." Thornton lifted his hands in surrender. "It will never be mentioned again. Buds before broads, and bitches, and whatever the kids are saying. So, forget them. It's you and me, Ash. Just like old times. Let's grab a pitcher tonight at the Oleander Lounge."

"I can't afford that place!" Asher said, wincing.

"I can." Thornton looked down at his Rolex and

saw the new scar running along his forearm. He reached down to finger it gingerly. "Just one more thing before we stop talking about it altogether. You'd better be careful. Your niece has a hell of a temper on her, and she's a lot more powerful than you think. So if she gets wind of what you did to Mara…"

"She's going to take out her anger at you on me?" Asher asked cheerfully.

"Yeah. Sorry, man, but this isn't a joke."

"I know what she's capable of," Asher said with a shrug. "But we're family. She won't do shit to me."

Thornton began rubbing his temples again. "This is so messed up. I need that beer now." Reaching for his phone, he pressed his intercom. "Nina, cancel my meetings. I'm calling it a day."

"Yes, Mr. Kalgren."

Asher smiled down at the phone. Once his friend's finger had lifted, he sent him a knowing look. "So now that you're single, have you tapped Nina yet?"

"I hadn't thought of that," Thornton admitted. "Good idea. What are secretaries for?"

*   *   *

Pax concentrated on a silver handle to slowly mix a spoonful of honey into chamomile citrus tea. The scent that wafted up from the ceramic mug was divine. She somehow recalled that it was Amara's favorite. Cupping the mug with both hands, she sighed and tried to calm her insides. How could she console the youngest Kalgren sibling when her own emotions were scattered and unfocused? She made her way from the kitchen into the living room, holding her freshly-boiled panacea.

Amara was curled up in a corner of the sofa. She was still hunched over, her posture just as Pax had found her in the shower. Pax pulled a bathrobe around her friend's naked body and all but carried her down to the sofa. Amara had remained somewhat oblivious as Pax spoke to her and covered her with a blanket. Sometimes she spoke to Pax, but most of the time she buried inside of her own mind. Pax knew she needed to drag her out.

"Okay, Amara. I need you to get yourself together," Pax insisted. Receiving no response, she tried again. "Mara? I want you to be angry at him."

The blonde woman didn't respond. Pax sent the thought at her, with a wave of her own anger. *Mara! You need to be pissed at him.*

Amara looked up then, her eyes meeting Pax with confusion. "No."

"Why the hell not?" Pax asked with a frown. "You are above taking crap from anyone. Your dad is a demigod. The King of Devas. You're a Kalgren. One of the most respected, powerful, and beloved families in…"

"Only because of magick."

"And technology. Your mother is a genius. Your family has always used their power for good…"

"So has yours."

"Not in the same way." While Pax had great pride in her ancestors, she was happy to belittle them for the sake of her friend. "My grandfather might have died fighting the Asura, but my mother destroyed herself by using magick she couldn't control. My dad ran away to the mountains because he couldn't handle the pressures of modern city life. We're not blessed like you Kalgrens. Asher is weak and stupid—all the power of a deva and he couldn't even graduate from college! How can you let inferior scum treat you badly? He's not even worth your pain."

"I love him."

"He used you. He strung you along like a puppet for years. If your dad knew…"

"No," Amara whispered. "Don't tell daddy."

"Fine. But you have to say you hate Ash or else I won't give you this steaming hot delicious tea." Pax circled the cup under her friend's nose. Injured or not, there was no way her delicate nostrils could avoid this point-blank tease.

Amara cracked a small smile, taking the cup with her hands through the blanket, "Okay. I hate him."

She sipped on the tea. Pax silently said a prayer of thanks for that little smile.

I think I do kind of hate him, Amara spoke telepathically as she sipped her tea. The blonde woman stared at her reflection in the amber liquid. *I thought things were fine. Better than fine. I thought we were going to get married. I had my dress picked out and everything. My favorite designer was working on the design for me. I wanted to have his babies—Ash was so good with kids and he would have made a great dad.* Tears began to gather in Amara's eyes. *Do you know how badly I want babies, Paxie?*

Pax stood up rather suddenly and took a deep breath. "Excuse me," she said apologetically. She ran over to Amara's sliding glass doors. Unlocking the latch carefully with her trembling hands, Pax exited onto the exquisite patio overlooking the ocean. She walked briskly across the patio and down the stairs, almost bolting to the edge of the cliff. She concentrated in order to levitate her body a few meters into the air before guiding herself forward off the cliff and out over the water.

She stared down at the dark waves crashing on the rocks far below, her chest heaving with deep breaths. Pax involuntarily arched her back, bringing her hands to her sides. Opening her mouth, a murderous scream ripped forth from her chest, causing a physical manifestation of her rage to escape her body. A huge beam of blazing red *prana* escaped with her scream, traveling forth into the night sky where it exploded like celebratory fireworks. Pax panted, watching the reflection of the explosion in the dark water below. She did not even understand this new power.

Pax, come back here! That looks dangerous. Please…

Hearing Amara's worried thoughts in her mind, she obediently turned around and levitated back to the cliff. Once there was ground beneath her feet, she stopped concentrating and allowed herself to fall to her knees in the grass. She balled her hands up into fists and pounded the ground as she felt her energy suddenly depleted. When was the last time she had slept? It felt like she had been driving nonstop for days. There was a ringing in her ears from the echo of her own scream, and her head ached.

Pax saw a pair of bare feet in the grass before her, and she looked up to see that Amara had followed her outside. It seemed that her natural fireworks had startled the blonde woman out of her daze.

"What was that?" Amara asked, holding the

blanket around herself tightly. "Does it make you feel better?"

"A little bit. No. Not really, I guess." Pax sighed, pushing herself off the ground and wiping the grass stains off her already ruined jeans.

"Why did you leave my brother?"

Pax froze. "What?"

"Sorry if it's rude to bring it up. I could just see that you were upset and I don't know why," Amara said softly. "I have been so selfish, focusing on my own problems when you're unhappy too."

"What have you heard?" Pax asked slowly.

"Not much. Ash wouldn't say anything." Amara shrugged, wiping a few blonde strands out of her eyes. "Thorn has been acting really weird since you left. Blowing loads of cash. Clubbing and partying every night like he's nineteen instead of thirty-nine. What gives?"

"Mara. Your brother cheated on me."

Amara's eyes widened. "No! Are you sure?"

Pax decided to sit back down in the grass abruptly. She stretched her arms backward and rolled her head from side to side to crack her neck. "Yeah. I went to his office to surprise him with lunch. Fried rice and pork chops. I found him…" Pax swallowed and began laughing a little bit hysterically. She could not think about this too much. She spit out the rest of the words very quickly. "He was on top of a woman who was lying on his desk. A redhead in a pinstriped business suit. Her skirt was bunched up around her hips. He was… enjoying himself."

Amara had dropped her blanket as both of her

hands raised to her lips. "Thorn? *Thorn* did that?"

"Yeah. I tried to turn around and walk away. I tried to focus on how good the pork chops smelled, and on the pleasant thought that I wouldn't have to share them. But before I could step out of that room… I blacked out."

"Oh, no, Paxie…"

"I don't even know what I did. When I came to, your dad and Uncle Ash were physically restraining me. My whole body was glowing and I didn't feel human. I've never totally lost control like that. My first thought was horror that I might have killed him. It doesn't matter what he did to me, but I could never live with myself if I killed the man I love. That moment of not knowing what I'd done, not knowing whether he was dead or alive—it was possibly more awful than the moment I saw him with that woman." Pax smiled and shrugged, trying to play it off as nothing. "Possibly."

Amara had been rendered speechless. She shook her head from side to side in disbelief.

"But everything was fine. Thorn was mostly fine. I apologized to your dad for whatever I did to his son, and I got in my Jeep and started driving."

"Where did you go?" Amara asked.

"I don't know. I pretty much drove in circles all over the continent."

"Paxie! What about your job at the hospital? Why didn't you call me?"

"Why *would* I call you?" Pax asked venomously. "He's your own flesh and blood—he can do no wrong in your eyes."

"That's not true," Amara whispered. She knelt

beside Pax in the grass and began to sniffle. "I didn't know. It's so unfair. I'm so sorry." Tears began to spill down her cheeks again. "Look at us both! What a mess. Ash was the only man who ever loved me for me. Everyone else was after my family's money. The Kalgren heiress, what a great catch! I really thought… oh, *god!*"

"Well, crying isn't going to solve anything," Pax said in disgust.

"And neither is violence!" Amara shot back, between sobs.

"I know," Pax said, "but it's all I have."

The two women sat in silence for several minutes. Pax idly ripped at the grass.

You know what I wish? Amara asked telepathically as she wiped the wetness from her lashes. *I wish I could somehow make Ash feel exactly the way I feel right now. He didn't hurt me physically—I want to hurt him inside.*

That thought clicked somewhere in Pax's mind, and she frowned as she studied the blonde woman. *Keep talking,* she encouraged.

Amara's blue eyes drifted over to lock with Pax's chocolate irises. *I want him to suffer just like I am right now. Maybe he never loved me, but I pray to Sakra, Lord of the Devas, and all the gods and demigods who live and ever lived that Asher should fall deeply in love with someone, his soulmate. I wish it could be me—I wish he could somehow fall back in love with me, except this time I wouldn't be good to him. I would rip his heart out in the worst imaginable way, just so he can feel the way I feel right now!*

"Do you really want that?" Pax demanded out loud.

Yes. But it's impossible.

A slow smile spread over Pax's features as she rose to her feet. ""It's not. What are you willing to sacrifice for this?"

"Anything. Anything at all."

"What about everything?" Pax pressed.

"Yes. That too," Amara said with quiet determination.

"Fine. I have a plan," Pax said, putting her hands on her hips. "Do you still have my books?"

"Um." Amara searched her memory, trying to think of the last time Pax had given her a book. They had surely been children. "The bestsellers?"

"No. The Babylonian texts."

Amara's eyes widened. "Don't you remember? We locked those up in a safe in the attic and vowed never to touch those vile things again."

"I believe it's time to dig them out."

"You can't. You can't practice magick, not after what happened to your mother…"

Pax crossed her arms and glared down at the blonde girl. "Tell me something: why did you call *me*, Mara? Why didn't you call one of your fancy socialite friends?"

"Paxie… I know we haven't hung out in a while. I'm sorry for that."

"Honestly, now. Did you call me here because Ash is my uncle, or because you wanted *me?"*

"If I needed fashion advice I would have called the socialites," Amara said, obviously hurt. "But I felt like I was drowning and I needed someone to save my life. Forgive me, but you're the first person who came to mind."

Pax tried to ignore the flattery. "And why do you think I came to mind? Because I was your childhood friend way back before we both developed breasts? Or because I have power, and unlike you, I know how to use mine?"

Amara was quiet for a moment. "Maybe it's a bit of both. Or maybe it's because whether you're dating my brother or not, I've always considered you my sister."

"Very touching, Mara." Pax levitated a few inches off the ground. "Well, if you really want to hurt my uncle, I can help you. You know you couldn't manage it on your own. You haven't got the experience or the strength."

"Would you really do that for me?" Amara asked, looking up at the dark-haired woman pleadingly.

Pax pressed her tongue against the tip of her canines. "If you agree to help me in return."

"Of course," Amara said instantly. "What do you want, Paxie? I know you don't need money…"

"Your brother."

Amara hesitated. "You want him back?"

Pax lifted her chin as a laugh rumbled forth from her throat. "No. I want his penis to rot and fall off. Metaphorically speaking."

"I understand, and I would love to help. But what can I do? My skill with magicks is limited. I stopped studying when you did."

"I never stopped studying," Pax admitted. "I only stopped practicing… to some degree. But my power seems to be naturally fighting its way out of the cage. Lately I can't seem to stop using *prana* to do every little thing."

"That's dangerous. You could get addicted."

"I know. I need you to keep me in check. And I need your blessing—I know you love your brother, and I don't want an enemy in you. I can only take on one Kalgren at a time."

Amara paused. She thought of Asher. He had come home to her, sweet and kind as usual, and unexpectedly made love to her in the shower. He had held her protectively and passionately—it had been blissful. It was the way she wanted the rest of her life to continue. But as soon as he had finished, as soon as he had found his release, but before he had even pulled out of her, he was telling her apathetically it was over. She could not understand. Where was this coming from? Asher had pulled out of her body and ripped her heart out as he turned his back.

Her eyes became cloudy as she thought of her brother. She could not help but feel that the blame should fall on Thornton. The older man had always been a role model for Asher. Why had Asher never mentioned the reason why Pax had skipped town? Did Asher condone what his friend had done to his niece? Amara felt her insides churning with the questions.

She knew one thing for certain. She understood why Pax had fled the state, leaving behind her job and her family. She understood why Pax had enough anger to blow up a decent chunk of the globe every few minutes. This anger was generated to mask grief. Amara appreciated that her friend had returned to help her in her moment of need. She also appreciated that Pax had spared her brother. The twenty-seven-year-old woman hovering before her was also a descendant of a demigoddess, and if she had wanted Thornton dead, Amara was sure that her brother would be. No, there was a much more complex game that Pax wanted to play.

"You have my blessing," Amara said. "I would like to make him suffer."

"Who?" Pax asked. "Thorn or Ash?"

Amara smiled cryptically. "Neither of them, and yet both of them."

Chapter 3: Babylonian Instruction Manual

"This shouldn't be so difficult," Amara said as she rushed around in her pink lab coat with a mortar and pestle. She huffed and wiped her forehead with the back of her hand. "Goddesses shouldn't need to sweat in order to make something out of the ordinary happen."

Pax smiled as she looked up from her Babylonian instruction manual. "That's what we get for being mostly human. I bet our ancestors could have done this type of thing with a sneeze."

"Of course," Amara said as she dusted a powder into a small bowl, "and it takes me days just to gather and prepare the materials. Deuterium? Pyroelectric crystals? Classic! Had to be the only things I didn't have in my lab."

"You had the palladium," Pax reminded her. "Frankly, this place is so well-stocked that I'd be shocked if there was *anything* you didn't have. I'm just about finished with this translation."

"There better not be a single other ingredient…"

"Nope. And once we activate the process once, we won't need any ingredients. Just the incantation and our own *prana.*"

"Well, that's swell. That's just peachy. That's ten kinds of…"

"Nervous, Mara?" Pax asked with a chuckle. She gently closed the old volume and picking up her translation, moved over to sit cross-legged before the bowl.

"I won't lie. I'm having second thoughts." Amara's eyes darted nervously to the materials that were spread out over their workspace.

Pax pulled her lips into a grim line. "Well, I can't do this without you. You can't do this without me. So decide."

Visualizing Asher's smiling face, Amara quickly dropped into a seated position on the other side of the bowl. "Go. Do it now before I change my mind."

Pax nodded and began to peel off her leather gloves. She never removed her gloves. Not even when she slept. She felt naked without the layer of security and feeling of normalcy they provided—they served much the same purpose her lengthy locks had. When the grotesque scar tissue of her burned palms were uncovered, she extended them outward.

"This may take a few tries to get it right," she told Amara. "You'll have to touch my hands."

Amara shuddered at the thought.

Pax noticed the subtle motion. "Look, I'm trying not to whine about it, but imagine how I feel. Your brother was probably the only person strong enough to bear my touch."

"Oh, Paxie."

"Stop calling me that, and do this damn spell with me," Pax barked, repulsed by the pitying tone.

Amara nodded, reaching out hesitantly. "Are you sure about this?"

"No," Pax said, "but I don't have anything to lose. Do you?"

She thought of Asher again and sighed. "I suppose not."

"If you want to back out, do it now," Pax advised sternly. The dark-haired woman began to chant softly as she extended her fingertips above the bowl. A dark magenta glow began to emit from her palms. It ignited the powder in a small inferno of energy.

"Shit, Pax! That's powerful. I thought you said you haven't been practicing!"

I haven't been. Pax communicated telepathically as she rhythmically continued chanting. *You can thank Thorn for this—it's like he awakened something primeval in me. The rage has me constantly throbbing with energy. My insides are ablaze and I feel like I'm going to disintegrate. I need to do this, Amara. I need to channel it outward. I can't live with this smoldering inside of me anymore.*

Then let's do it, the blonde woman responded purposefully. Amara gritted her teeth before extending her own hands into the magenta glow until her fingertips barely brushed against Pax's. She flinched, feeling the hotness rapidly travel through her until it burned her core. Instantly, empathy overwhelmed her at the glimpse of what her childhood friend was feeling. She felt guilty for burdening Pax with taking care of her, when the younger woman was obviously dealing with her own demons.

She had not touched Pax's hands in over a decade, and now she remembered why. The heat was too intense. She could smell her own skin singeing, and wanted to withdraw her neatly-manicured fingers to save them from being scalded. But she couldn't. For along with terrible tremors of fear, the vivid magenta flames sent the delicious thrill of power through her. It reminded her of something she had known long ago, and something she had long since forgotten.

The fuchsia glow began to gradually spread from their knuckles to their wrists. Amara was trying to be strong, but she could see that even the tough Pax was grimacing at the pain. The energy was moving along inch by inch, and when their hands were fully engulfed by the radiant blaze, Amara began to hyperventilate. It seemed that the whole basement laboratory under her house was rumbling with the newly invoked power. Amara visualized her beautiful house crumbling into ruins around them.

"We shouldn't be doing this!" Amara shouted. She cringed at the sensation of her perfect skin beginning to bubble under the high temperature.

"Silence!" Pax hissed in a dark voice that sounded nothing like her own. She immediately resumed chanting. The magenta fire was spreading steadily to their elbows.

"Is my skin going to be boiled too?" Amara screamed over the thundering sound of the energy. She could no longer feel her hands and forearms. There was only heat. She imagined losing her limbs altogether and how awful she would look in a sleeveless dress as an amputee. If Ash hadn't wanted her before…

Maybe. Pax continued chanting, swept away in the magicks and paying no attention to her friend's fear. She naturally transitioned to chanting in English, her voice mounting to a furor as the air fizzed with crackling energy around them, electrifying their skin. Pax repeated the chant with such passion that Amara felt nausea. The words were so sharp that they penetrated her body:

Be in me. Be of me. Be with me.

Only but fragments, let us be whole.
Seamlessly we unite, soul to soul;
My heart is half yours, this half hour.

"I can't do this," Amara moaned as her body trembled. "It's killing me. It's killing me!"

"You said you'd pay any price," Pax spat upon finishing her chant. She tightened her grip on Amara's hands, interlocking their fingers. "Be strong."

"I'm not cut out for this! I'm not a goddess! My dad and brother might have power, but *not me*. The god genes must have skipped me—Pax! Stop! Stop this!" Amara tried to rip her hands away from the inferno as it approached her face. She could not move. "It's too hot!"

"It's not heat," Pax whispered. "It's life"

Amara was surprised that she could hear her friend's voice over the crashing of what was surely her house collapsing. "Life! Where's it coming from? Whose life?"

"Mine. Ours. The *prana* surrounding you is coming from me, and the *prana* surrounding me is coming from you," Pax was shaking from the strength of the spell. "It's part of the coalescence process."

"Why is the life killing me?" Amara gasped.

"Life and death are one. The same force which creates also destroys. Can you feel it?"

"Yes! I don't want to feel my life outside of my body." Amara began to sob as the energy began to surround her chest. "Paxie! I'm being turned inside out."

"That's right. It's so good!" Pax threw her head back and allowed the magenta flames to wash over her. Her jaggedly-cut short hair was tossed around in the violent maelstrom of energy. Her eyes turned upward, and her usually dark irises began glowing golden.

"Pax!" Mara screamed, seeing that her friend had lost control. As their bodies became completely engulfed with energy she tried desperately to pull away, but it was futile. She felt the atmosphere suddenly become very pressurized, and she instinctively knew that there would be an explosion. Pax felt this too and turned her golden eyes down toward Amara's frightened blue ones.

For a quiet moment, the two women exchanged an alarmed look. As debris floated all around them, frozen in suspension, they shared the same terrified thought. They knew that they had gone too far and destroyed themselves by channeling mystical forces beyond their capability for control.

But it was not the last thought they would share.

Chapter 4: Too Much Woman

"I need a drink pronto," Asher said as he clutched his head. "Still way hung over from last night."

Thornton sighed and leaned forward to open the minibar in his limousine. "I told you to pace yourself with water. We're not teenagers anymore."

"What's the difference? With the yearly rejuvenations, our bodies are as young as ever." Asher reached out to take the scotch his friend had poured for him. "Thanks, man. Where we headed tonight?"

"Tryst Lounge," Thornton said, fixing himself a drink as well before leaning back in his seat.

"Are you *crazy?*" Asher asked, choking on the liquid he was generously gulping. "That's even more expensive than the last five places we've been to. I can't afford that!"

"I can."

Asher shook his head in amazement. "This really is the life. You have it made, Thorn."

"Sure. Of course I do," Thornton said, extending his glass. "To the life."

With a grin, Asher clinked his glass against his friend's and returned it to his mouth. "So," he said, once it had been emptied. "What are we on the prowl for tonight? More delicious fresh fruit?"

"I'm in the mood for something exotic. Dark skin and a thick accent—maybe Spanish or Brazilian," said Thornton.

"Amateur," Asher said with a chuckle. "Those are easy. Hasn't it gotten boring yet when they fall into your lap without a chase?"

"I thought the whole point of this hedonistic binge was to have a pretty young thing on my lap at all times. Or two, or three. In various positions." When Asher laughed at this, Thornton grinned and jostled the ice cubes in his glass in a circular motion. "What pleasures are you seeking, my friend?"

"You know I have a taste for local dishes. Just a sweet, normal, completely naïve chick." Asher smiled as he stretched out his legs on the ample seating room in the limousine. It was his innate duty as a man to take up as much room as physically possible. "I'll feel out their energy, and I'll find the purest soul. I'll tell her everything she wants to hear; everything she's ever prayed to hear a man say to her. Then I'll rock her world hardcore."

Thornton raised his eyebrows at this description. "So you're looking for a keeper?"

"Nah. I just get a kick out of finding the most virtuous human girl around and corrupting her. They always fall in love. Bang her good, and she's yours. Then you can disappear, breaking her heart and her innocence. You can feel the energy change from pure to perverted."

Thornton shook his head. "You're twisted, man."

"Said the pot to the kettle!" Asher accused. "Admit it, Thorn. There are mega-kicks to be had here. You get a rush from it too! It makes you feel powerful, doesn't it?"

"It makes me feel better for a few minutes," Thornton said. "It makes me hate myself so much that I forget how much I hate myself underneath that."

Asher frowned. "You should talk to…"

"It looks like we're here," Thornton said, grateful

for the timing of the limousine stopping. He slapped his knees and turned to his friend. "Ready to go be a sick fuck?"

"I learned from the best," Asher said, watching as his friend slipped on sunglasses and ran two hands through his dead-straight blonde hair. Asher knew that there was no hope in styling the wavy black mop on top of his own head. Besides, the ladies liked it messy just as much as he did. Thornton's perfect center-part and always immaculately-styled coiffure seemed unnecessary to Asher, but then he did not know what the grooming etiquette was for being a businessman.

When the driver opened the limo door, Thornton exited in a fluid motion. He waited for a moment for Asher to join him before he began to walk through the crowd waiting outside the club. The people parted like a sea of admiration as they began to recognize the blonde man's confident gait, even beneath his sunglasses. Asher groaned as the excited whispers and pointing began. He could almost hear the thoughts in all of their minds: *Look! It's the rich CEO of that tech company and… some other guy!* Yes, he was just some other guy. With the pressure Thornton was always under at Kalgren Enterprises, he almost preferred it that way.

Asher observed as his friend worked his magic on the hostess to allow them to bypass the stampeding hordes eagerly awaiting entrance to the club. He could not help rolling his eyes when Thornton gave his full name and rank along with a handful of hundred-dollar bills.

"Thornton Vincent Kalgren the third. Esquire."

This somehow worked, and Asher waited until

they were inside before he hit his friend in the arm and insulted him telepathically. *Man, can you be any more pretentious?*

"Don't complain. It gets us where we need to be. It gets *you* access to a bunch of quality babes you can bone. Smile and say thank you."

"Thank you, your royal highness, Mr. CEO, esquire, fancy pants…"

Thornton grinned as they made their way to the VIP area to order bottle service. *Shut up, Ash. You and I both know that all of those titles are garbage and don't mean anything. We're both the sons of demigods, and underneath all of these human hierarchies, we're equals.*

Nah. You'll always be the bigger jackass in my eyes, bro.

Thanks. Thornton was barraged by the usual throng of admirers as the men made their way over to the shadowy, more secluded area of the club. Asher received his share of attention too; generally from cougars who assumed that he must be wealthy if he was Thornton's wingman, but also from a few timid girls who wanted to be in the CEO's spotlight, but were too shy and inhibited to approach him directly. Asher didn't mind being fussed over, but he politely turned away everyone who approached him as he waited for the right victim.

Just getting to their seats had been exhausting. Asher collapsed in the soft leather couch while exhaling blissfully. "It's like they knew you were coming, Thorn. It's like they were waiting around to attack you. Do you have people anticipating your every move?"

Thornton nodded, reaching up to pull off his sunglasses as he sat down. "Money will do that."

"Sometimes I understand why my family went to such great lengths to live privately," Asher remarked. "This could drive anyone insane."

Thornton shrugged. "You get used to it. See anyone you like?"

"Nah, not yet. Let's get drinks first."

The men signaled a waiter to order their usual bottle service, along with a sampling of everything on the menu. While most people in clubs did not eat much, Thornton and Asher were plagued by voracious appetites due to their special heritage. The men were almost constantly eating. Although the food was ridiculously overpriced, Thornton had shrugged indifferently and ordered a normal person's feast. For him and Asher, it would amount to little more than a light snack.

While they waited, they lounged and chatted in a combination of their voices and telepathy to conquer the loud music blaring around them. At the same time, their eyes scanned the crowd discreetly, like predatory hawks seeking out their prey. For perhaps the first time in their lifelong friendship, their gaze settled on the same woman.

"Hey, Thorn. What do you think about *her?*"

"Honestly? I think I saw her first. I call dibs."

The woman in question was sitting all alone in the darkest corner. There was no question that she was breathtaking. An aura of calmness hung around her, as if no one dared approach. She wore a slender silver watch on her wrist and glanced at it furtively.

"She's not your type—let me take a crack at this," Asher suggested. "You said you were looking for an exotic woman. She doesn't seem like she has an accent."

"I changed my mind," Thornton said, already standing up. "What about you? She doesn't have that naïve thing going on, does she?"

"No, but I do like the feel of her energy," Asher said, standing and moving to block his friend's path. "It's special. Different than any other person in this place. Sweeter, yet grittier. Like honey and granola. I want. Gimme!"

"No. She keeps checking the time. Think she's waiting for someone?"

"Either that or she has to leave." The two men glared at each other.

"We'd better move in fast, Ash." Thornton extended his fist. "Rock, paper, scissors?"

"No way! She looks kind of conceited, so this might be a challenge. Let's both go talk to her and see which one of us she likes better," suggested Asher.

"You're just saying that so you can use my fame and fortune to your advantage," said Thornton, but he agreed with his friend and they moved over to the woman together.

Her posture was indeed arrogant as she reclined luxuriously in her chair. She had deep indigo colored hair—so dark it was almost black, but not quite. When the club lights danced over her, the unusual color became illuminated. Her midnight tresses swirled over her shoulders and far past her bottom. Her hair would likely go down to her knees when she stood up. Was all of that natural? Both the length and the color of her hair were unreal. She was swathed in a tasteful silver dress with matching gloves and strappy heeled sandals.

She was sipping on a martini thoughtfully as the two men approached her. They moved cautiously but confidently as they zeroed in on their target.

"Good evening, miss," Thornton began politely, and the woman's head snapped around to glare at him. She had the annoyed expression of a woman who was often approached by men, and exhausted with the sheer volume of rejections she had to dole out. The look in her fierce eyes gave Thornton pause. There was something familiar about her.

"Hey! Have we met before?" asked Asher, who had been thinking the same. "Did we go to school together?"

The woman smiled slowly, assessing both Thornton and Asher from head to toe. "Spare me. I hope you can do better than that."

"Oh, it wasn't a pick-up-line," said Asher, with a sheepish grin. "I was really asking… you just remind me of someone."

"Oh, really? Who might that be," she murmured, leaning back in her chair and sipping her martini. She could not have appeared less interested.

The men looked at each other in confusion. This was the first woman they had encountered in days who showed no signs of warmth or invitation. Instead she was almost dismissing both of them. Thornton frowned. He was unsure of how to process this new situation.

Asher's eyes slowly consumed every inch of the woman's body, digesting the curve of her breasts straining against her silver gown. He allowed his hungry gaze to travel over her toned arms and legs. The creamy skin visible through the thigh-high slit in her gown sent his imagination spinning down dusky avenues.

Thornton cleared his throat, trying to cover up his friend's blunder innocently. "He's probably thinking of my sister. Even though she's blonde, like me, she has a similar facial structure to yours. She's also very beautiful. Perhaps you've heard of her: Amara Kalgren?"

"Oh, sure," said the woman, apathetically, "the ditzy socialite."

"She's actually not like that," Asher said defensively, surprising himself. "That's just the media's version. She's a brilliant scientist, a freelance inventor."

"Whatever." The woman slipped the rest of the martini down her throat. "It was nice meeting you boys, but I have to run."

"Wait!' said Asher, throwing his arms out as if he were trying to block the other team from scoring in his net. He hadn't been blown off like this since... ever. "I'm sorry, have we done something to offend you?"

"Not really," she said, shrugging and glancing at her watch. "You just haven't done anything to impress me either. For starters you were too busy gawking at me to introduce yourselves properly. In case you haven't noticed, we're not in high school."

"Please, forgive our rudeness," began Thornton in his most suave and sensual manner. He slid his fingers around the wrist of the girl as she tried to pull away. She looked back at him in surprise, her dark eyes flickering from Thornton to Asher with something akin to alarm in them.

"My name is Thornton Kalgren," he said as he lifted her gloved hand to his lips to plant a kiss. While maintaining intense eye contact, he allowed his lips to linger there for far too long. "I'm the CEO of Kalgren Technological Enterprises."

"So I gathered," she said, observing his actions without enthusiasm. She looked disappointed, as though she was on the cusp of yawning.

"I'm Ash Burnson," said his companion, taking her other hand and giving it the same gentlemanly treatment. He sent her a goofy smile to ease the tension in the atmosphere. "Also known as 'that other guy.' Being friends with Thorn is sometimes like a full-time job."

Thornton and Asher glanced at each other smugly, knowing that no woman could resist this double-attack of magnetic charisma and wit. It was a finely-honed and expertly-coordinated technique from their college years.

Nice one, man. Thornton was already congratulating his friend telepathically.

We haven't done that in a while, thought Asher wistfully. *So which of us do you think she has the hots for?*

Let's see. My money's on the first person she looks at.

The woman ripped her hands away from the men and turned her slender wrist over to glance at her watch. "How charming. Well, it was nice meeting you both, but I really need to go."

Did she look at you or me? asked Asher in confusion.

Neither, you fool! She looked at her goddamned watch.

The woman had reached out with her silver-gloved hand to grab her small purse before darting directly between the men to leave.

"Wait!" shouted Thornton, panicking at the unbelievable rejection. He was floundering to keep his cool in the unusual circumstance. "You didn't even tell us your name."

"You didn't ask," she said, attempting to slip through the crowds. Asher caught her wrist this time.

"Please," begged Asher, attacking her with his most adorable pleading puppy dog eyes. "We might never meet again. What is your name?"

She looked at him, hesitating. She glanced back at her watch. "I don't think…"

"Why do you need to rush away? Stay for a moment," Thornton insisted. He moved close to her, placing the palm of his hand lightly against her lower back. It appeared to be a gentlemanly guiding touch, but what no one could see is that he sent the tiniest amount of energy into her body, warming her insides. It was one of his signature moves, guaranteed to get any woman in the mood. There was no point to having access to ancient power unless it could produce some sort of pleasure.

However, this indigo-haired beauty simply scowled and yanked his hand away from her body as though she knew exactly what he'd done. She turned her back to them, determined to leave this time, but she could not resist throwing a final glance over her bare shoulder condescendingly. Midnight blue-black eyes burned into them both like fire.

"Give it a rest, boys," she advised with a sweet smile touching her full reddened lips. "Unfortunately, I'm too much woman for the both of you to handle."

She drank in their shocked reactions for a moment, savoring their speechlessness before her watch began to beep and she turned and disappeared into the crowd.

"What the *hell* was that!" asked Thornton angrily. "I used my *prana* trick on her!"

"You did! No wonder," said Asher frowning. "You probably used too much and hurt her. Great job in scaring her away."

"No, it wouldn't have hurt her. She was strong. There was something unusual about her energy. Didn't you feel it? She might be an athlete or a spiritual woman…"

"A spiritual woman? How many spiritual women you know with cleavage down to *here?!*"

"I can't believe we didn't even get her fucking name!" complained Thornton. "I'm handsome—all the magazines say so. I look years younger than I am thanks to magick. I have shitloads of money. How could she just walk away from this?"

"You forgot the endless vanity and snobbery," Asher added. "No, she obviously wants a more down-to-earth fella like me. She seemed like a woman with morals."

"Morals," Thornton muttered as if in agony. "Who has those anymore?"

Asher stared after the woman's path of retreat. "She was hands-down the most gorgeous girl I've ever seen," he declared earnestly.

"I agree. Damn, you and I *never* have the same taste in women. But that body! That hair! Those eyes!" Thornton cleared his throat as he noticed that their bottles and food were being delivered to their booth. "I just hope you know that eventually she'll choose me."

"If she's into bigheaded, egotistical narcissists, she definitely will," Asher said with a smile. "If she's a nice girl looking for a nice guy—she's going to be underneath me, moaning my name before you can say 'Hallelujah!'"

*   *   *

Meanwhile, in a dark alley a few blocks away, the indigo-haired woman was leaning against a brick wall and laughing hysterically. Part of her was concerned about ruining the designer silver dress, so she tried to contain herself. Another part could care less, and let the hilarious mania take control of her body.

"Too much woman for the both of you to handle!" she said, mimicking herself and throwing her gloved arms up in the air. "Too much woman for the both of you to handle!"

I'm too great, too amazing, too devious, she thought in delight. *Definitely far too much to handle! Too much power and brains packed into one gorgeous body! I'm better than I ever was.* Her watch started beeping extremely loudly and she realized that she had to get away from the area. She opened her silver purse and pulled out a key as she lifted her skirts and began running through the alley. Finally, she came upon a black vehicle with the windows tinted so dark that it was impossible to see inside. The girl quickly slid into the driver's seat. Instead of having a normal console in the center separating the driver and passenger seat, the car had a single bench.

She looked at her watch again. "One minute."

She began to drive, intending to get as far as possible from her current location. When the minute was nearly complete, her watch began beeping faster and faster. She pulled over to the side of the road and put the car in park before leaning back and waiting.

It happened then. With a flash of light, her body separated. Two girls sat in the vehicle where there had only been one.

"Ow! I hate it when that happens," said the one who had been flung against the passenger door. She moved her hands up to touch her face, running her fingers through her blonde hair.

"No kidding," said the dark-haired one who had put the car back in gear and was already pressing her silver strappy high heel down to accelerate the vehicle. Once the car was moving, the driver sighed. She looked down at herself, using one hand to feel her legs and body. "The more often we join together, the less complete I feel when we separate."

"I know. It's nice to be someone else… while still being myself. Para is me too."

"I know what you mean."

"Of course you do."

The two girls laughed, but there was a hint of sadness in their voices.

"Should we have told them our name?" Amara asked. "Is it safe to call ourselves Para?"

"I don't think so," Pax responded. "They might figure out it's us. I don't know if they have heard of this specific incantation—but even if they haven't, their parents might put it together. We have to find a pseudonym. How about Unity? Or Harmony?"

"Ugh," said Amara with disgust. "Does Para look like a Harmony?"

"No. She looks… otherworldly. There's more goddess in her than in either of us combined. It's like the spell takes the most powerful aspects of each of us and amplifies it exponentially. When I'm Para I feel like I can do anything! She deserves a legendary alias. Why don't we let her decide?"

"That sounds good. I can't believe they didn't recognize us!" Amara said with a happy sigh. "Jeez, Thorn is such a dweeb! 'You look like my sister, except she's blonde, and I'm going to hit on you anyway!'" She had comically lowered her voice to imitate her brother.

Pax tried to laugh at her friend's mimicry, but she could only manage a pained smile. "That's my Thorn. He'll chase after anything that moves."

"I'm sorry," Amara said, "but it works in our favor this time. Phase one of this crazy plan has been initiated. Do you think this will all work out?"

"It's too soon to tell. I guess we have to make every thirty minutes count."

Chapter 5: The Leaky Pipe

At last, I have found you. Granddaughter of the Fire Deva.

Pax was sleeping when she heard the booming voice echoing in her mind. It was an unfamiliar masculine baritone. She would have ignored it as a figment of her imagination, or a random creation of her dreams, if not for what happened next.

A sledgehammer was smashed down onto her chest. The heavy iron mallet knocked the breath out of her, and her eyelids flung themselves open in shock. A demon with massive teeth was grinning down at her with copious saliva dripping from its pointed teeth. The fluid was a vivid red color, contrasting sharply with the creature's yellowed fangs. It looked as though it had just feasted on small busload of people. When Pax felt the warm saliva dripping down onto her lips, she knew it was real. She tried to punch her fist into the demon's face, but she could not move. She mentally cursed, pressing her lips tightly together so that she would not taste the creature's bloody saliva.

Now, now, dear. Lie still and be willing.

Pax realized that it was not a sledgehammer that had connected with her chest, but the creature's massive hand. She winced as its sharp claws began digging into her breasts, puncturing directly through between the bones of her ribcage. Pax used her mind to pick up the largest piece of furniture in the room (a massive dresser with eight drawers) and she slammed it directly into the creature's back. The demon began to cackle as the wooden missile splintered apart against his back as though she had tossed dandelions.

I am outside of the physical dimension, young fire maiden. You cannot harm me.

She felt sharp searing pain permeate her chest as the demon's claws clenched around her heart. *Who are you? What do you want?* Pax mentally screamed. She feared for Amara who was sleeping in the next room. Since beginning their plan, Pax had decided to move in with Amara for the time being. The blonde woman was not strong enough to take on a demon of this caliber. Amara could already have been killed.

Your heart has been weakened, fire maiden. I have come to feed upon the holes in your soul. Your power seeps out through the wounds—ah, yes! You are a delicious leaky pipe from which I can suck.

Pax began to move another piece of furniture, but then she realized that it was useless. Instead, she concentrated on the air itself around the demon. *So you're here to suck my power?* Pax asked, piercing the creature with her dark eyes. Her fingers twitched as she lay frozen on the bed, imagining the air around the demon compressing and boiling. As she imagined it, she forced the atmosphere to bend to her will, and was gratified when the demon began gasping. More of its red saliva dripped down onto her cheeks and nose as the creature struggled.

Beginning to feel a smug sense of victory, Pax used her mind to push the creature away from her body until its hand exited her chest. The crushing pain on her heart eased. *You don't know anything about my power. Better luck next time.*

I know all there is to know. You are the weakest of the half-breed devas, and the power leaking from you is too precious to forfeit. Your energy comes from a place of purity, and you have already allowed filth inside! Now, it is only left for us to suck you dry. Night after night, little by little.

Uh huh. Pax smiled as she concentrated and rotated her wrist to violently crush the demon's skull. *And I'm just going to sit around and watch while you stick your claws in me. Very likely.*

Red saliva poured down onto Pax's face as the demon writhed. *Even if I fail, they will send another incubus to you at night!*

Pax felt a small wave of delight in having gained the upper hand. She enjoyed the cracking sound as she twisted the demon's limbs. *Who do you work for?*

I am sent by the Asura.

A chill ran through her. The thrill of torturing the demon disappeared as terror flooded her shoulders. The Asura had attacked her family several times in her youth, always with calamitous results.

Not smiling now, are you? the demon asked. We have already planted the seeds of destruction in your lover. *Oh, the young prince of devas is so easy to manipulate! How quickly he falls from grace and tumbles from his throne.*

Pax stopped struggling with the demon abruptly. *What about Thorn? What did you do to him?* She completely forgot that she was angry at the blond man as she worried for his safety. The Asura had been responsible for the death of her grandfather. The awful rival demigods were just as powerful as her own ancestors and the Kalgrens.

Nothing is beyond the Asura. They will destroy all the remaining devas, beginning with you.

Feeling her anger return, Pax glared at the creature boldly. *Bring it on. I'll take all of them on at once.*

The incubus lunged forward with a piercing shriek. Its claws dug back into Pax's chest and began crushing her heart. When Pax began to gasp desperately for air, the creature snickered. *You are weak to the call for vengeance, fire maiden. Even if we cannot fully suck the power from your soul, we can make it our own. We will steal the goodness from your heart, and replace it with anger. Soon you will join us.*

Bet you ten bucks I won't.

What?

Pax closed her eyes and clenched her fists, unleashing a wave of hot energy into the creature. Its body began to stretch and distort while its eyes bugged out monstrously. Finally, it disintegrated. Quite suddenly, Pax found that she could move again.

Her vision cleared, and it was rather like awakening. She sat up abruptly and immediately began to unbutton her pajama top. She looked down at her chest, and saw no claw marks. She rubbed her fingers over the smooth skin in confusion. Looking across the room, she saw that all the furniture was intact. It had just been a dream.

She exhaled as she tried to clear the intense images and emotions from her mind. The nightmare had been unusually realistic. It was surely born of the guilt from using magick to create Para. She lifted her hands to cup her face, sliding her fingers under her bangs and massaging her scalp. It still surprised her how short her hair was. Everything the creature said had been false. If there were any Asura remaining, they certainly had no interest in her. She was mostly human, and hardly a threat. She was hardly of importance on the hierarchy of power in the world.

Yet it made sense that performing the spell to create Para would attract the Asura. It made sense that such a massive output of energy would seduce her enemies into sending demons to mess with her already messed up head, and play on her weaknesses. It made sense, but it was not real. It had just been a nightmare.

Pax flung the covers off her legs and levitated out of bed. She picked up her purse, and dug for her phone. Although it was the middle of the night, she speed-dialed her father. He was in a different time zone, on the other side of the world. When there was no response, she closed her eyes and tried to contact him with her mind.

Papa? she asked, searching for him.

Paxie! How's life in America?

It's fine, she responded. *I just had a nightmare about the Asura.*

I'm sorry, sweetie. It was just a dream—don't worry. I'm training with Sakra, and we would know if there was any trouble amiss.

Pax immediately felt better. *Thanks, Papa.*

Is everything else good? No exciting news for your old man?

Nothing important is happening, Pax answered.

How's Thorn doing? That boy still treating you well?

Pax lowered her chin miserably, grateful that her father couldn't see her facial expressions. *Yes. Everything is fine. I have to go now. I love you, Papa.*

Take care, kiddo.

Rubbing her hands along her arms to ease the gooseflesh created from her nightmare, Pax exited her room and walked into the corridor. Her bare feet padded against the ground gently as she headed to the bathroom, intending to soothe herself with a hot shower. She flicked on the bathroom lights and looked at her face in the mirror.

There was a spot of red liquid smeared on her chin. Pax frowned, reaching up with two fingers to wipe off the smudge. She used her thumb and forefinger to test the sticky consistency of the liquid before bringing it to her nose to sniff it. Blood and saliva.

In a panic, she exited the bathroom and ran down the hallway to Amara's master bedroom. Throwing the door open, she saw the small blonde girl curled up in her bed. Pax ran over to her friend and wiped the gunk off her hands before feeling Amara's neck for a pulse.

"Paxie?" Amara mumbled in her sleep. "What gives?"

Pax breathed a sigh of relief. Amara was completely unharmed. "I had a nightmare," she told her friend. "There was this demon with bloody saliva, and then I thought I found some of it on my chin…"

"Was just a dream, silly," Amara said sleepily. "You probably bit your lip."

"That was probably it," Pax said, nodding, "but he mentioned the Asura…"

"You can sleep here if you're freaked out," Amara suggested.

Pax normally would have been too prideful to accept an offer like this, but she was not only afraid for herself. "Thanks, Mara," she said, climbing into the gigantic bed with her friend.

"Remember, we have to do Para stuff tomorrow," Amara said with a yawn. "You need to get more sedatives to make her seem more weak and human."

"Sure. I will." Pax was having difficulty thinking about Para at the moment. The dream was still haunting her. She lay on her back and crossed her arms, imagining the demon and trying to remember the things it had said, even though they were slipping away. The chilling aftermath was beginning to fade, and she realized that she had been foolish to believe it was real. The memories were all becoming hazy as they were overpowered by the onset of new dreams.

Chapter 6: Some Unfinished Business

Asher rose to his feet quite suddenly, knocking over their bottle.

"Hey, watch it!" Thornton said with annoyance. "Just because you didn't have to pay for this stuff…"

"Thorn, it's her. She's back." Asher's voice carried undertones of reverence.

Thornton turned to look in the direction that Asher was staring. The woman with the knee-length indigo hair had entered the VIP lounge again. She was wearing a stylish black number with rhinestone details on the straps and waistband. Once more, black gloves extended all the way up to her elbows. Her style was muted, but elegant.

After days of aimless club-hopping, the men had confined themselves to Tryst in hopes of encountering the woman who had rejected them again. They both felt the pressing need to take care of some unfinished business, and it had just arrived.

"Do *not* screw this up, Asher," Thornton warned in a low voice as he followed his friend's lead.

Asher seemed to already be doing exactly that. He had reached out to place a hand on the woman's shoulder to gain her attention, and Thornton felt that this was far too familiar a way to address a lady who seemed so uptight and formal.

When she turned to face him, her face displayed surprise and pleasure. They saw the ghost of a smile play across her mysterious features. She lifted her gloved hand to snap her fingers as if trying to recall something. Finally she pointed upwards in recognition.

"Ash Burnson," she said.

"You remembered my name," Asher said with a huge smile.

"How could I forget a name like that?" she said with a mischievous smirk. "It's very… hot."

"Go on, make your jokes!" Asher said, raising his hands in surrender. "I heard them all when I was growing up. Someone turn on the air conditioning! Burnson just walked into the room. Ashes to ashes, eat my dust. Can I cook my dinner on your ass, Burnson? Oh Ash! I'm just burning with desire…"

"I think I could probably come up with a few new ones if I gave it some thought," she said with a bit of a flirtatious tone.

Thornton frowned as he approached the pair. The woman was certainly acting friendlier than the last time they'd encountered her. She noticed his approach and nodded slightly in acknowledgement. "Mr. Kalgren. I fear I was a bit rude the last time we met."

"Please. My friends call me Thorn."

"Thorn. I like that," she said with a smile. "Are there any jokes about your name?"

"Every rose has them," he answered without missing a beat. Now this was the casual flirting that he felt familiar with. He felt his confidence returning. "I must apologize if my friend and I were a bit forward with you the last time we met."

"I'm really sorry, miss," said Asher, inclining his head in a gentle bow. "I didn't mean to make you uncomfortable."

Please. Like they mean these apologies, thought Para, but she only smiled and let her eyes shine at them trustingly. "It's quite alright."

"Can we buy you a drink?" asked Thornton, gesturing to the corner booth where she had been seated last time.

"That would be lovely," said Para. "I usually have the chocolate martini."

"Delicious!" said Asher, cheerfully, as he moved to sit in the booth.

I think I'm less sexually attracted to the guys when I am merged together, Para pondered as she slid into the booth beside Asher, *maybe because I'm partly related to both of them.* Asher made small talk with her until Thornton returned with the drinks and a handsome smile.

"Thanks, Thorn," she said kindly as she accepted the beverage.

"You're very welcome," the blonde man said as he slid into the booth on the other side of Para. "I hope today you will think we are deserving of knowing your name."

Para studied Thornton, holding direct, steady eye contact with him for the first time through her new perspective. Although his baby blues were exactly the same, her own had been altered, and what she saw was consequently new. She tried to fuse her old concept of this man with the man who now sat before her, but it was challenging. *Big brother. I missed this; just sitting beside you and seeing your smile. Disloyal lover. There can be no punishment severe enough to avenge the hopeful parts of me that you have shattered. But I'm going to try anyway.*

"My name is Medea," said Para, after briefly

scanning her mind. She surprised herself with the choice. It was the name of a woman who had been betrayed by her husband in Greek mythology. Perhaps infidelity was a common theme, but what was uncommon about Medea was her capacity for vengeance. In every version of the story, she went to great lengths to achieve revenge on the men who had wronged her. Para could deeply identify with this—she would go to any lengths. The thought brought a lovely smile to her lips, and Thornton smiled back, enchanted.

"Medea," repeated Asher appreciatively, "that's such a striking and unusual name."

"Thank you. Feel free to make jokes about it if you like." She turned to Asher as she sipped on her martini, sending him a playful look. Her emotions combined and twisted quite differently as she observed him through her new lens. Both beings which resided in her body felt overwhelmed with affection for the man, but both were also overwhelmed with anger. *It's not fair to her, Ash. Why? Things were so good, and you were so cruel.* She could not even look at him for a few seconds without feeling despondent, and she turned her gaze back down to the triangular silhouette of her martini glass. She reached out and began to run her finger around the rim of the glass in slow circles to distract her thoughts.

"We were thinking of heading to a cool after-hours place in a bit. It's very exclusive and hush-hush. Thorn's got the hookups," Asher said. "Wanna come with?"

Wow, they move fast, don't they? Para lifted her wrist to glance at her watch. "I wish I could but I can't stay for very long. I have to run to the hospital soon."

"The hospital?" asked Thornton. "Are you a nurse?"

This was the point where Pax would have normally snapped, *Doctor!* She had studied for the profession because of her grandmother's wishes, mostly volunteering wherever she felt the need for her services. "I'm a resident doctor," Para said. "I work on-call."

Amara and Pax had given this some forethought and decided to give Para the same job as Pax. It was the only job that could require someone to be so busy that they needed to be available 24/7 and rush away without warning. Thornton and Asher both knew how exhausting that stage of her career had been on Pax, and how she'd worked an average of far over 100 hours a week. The girls imagined that the guys were more likely to understand Para running off to separate with this excuse.

"Wow, you look far too young to be a doctor!" was Asher's first remark. "I would have guessed you were nineteen when I first saw you, but you were drinking…"

"Now that we know your name, you'll have to let us know if you're legal," Thornton said with a smile.

Of course, Para thought to herself. *I forgot to plan this one. Well, I might as well lie about my age and say I'm a few years younger. I'm lying about everything else, and I can't give any suggestions that I might not be human.*

"I'm 24," she answered, improvising. "I skipped a few grades and graduated early. Crammed my semesters together. You know."

"Ah, you must be really sharp. I know residency

can be very challenging," said Thornton understandingly. He hesitated. His eyes shifted out toward the bar, and he seemed to be staring several thousand yards away. "My close friend is a doctor as well," he said in a quiet voice.

"Oh, is that so? Do I know him?" asked Para, wondering if he would mention one of her halves.

"Her name is Pax Burnson," said Thornton, downing a mouthful of his drink. "You might have heard of her—her mom was a famous actress in the nineties."

What the hell, Thorn? Are you using me as part of your game to pick up chicks? That's sick. You must be getting really old and running out of ideas. Para nodded as she lifted her eyebrows. "Oh yes, I have heard of her. She volunteers in the ICU, right? She's quite brilliant."

"Pax is actually my darling little niece," Asher said fondly. "Thorn dated her for a while. They only recently broke up. It was messy. Very messy."

Thornton glared at Asher to shut up and Asher smiled at him sweetly. "Not quite as messy as your breakup with *your* ex-girlfriend," contributed Thornton. "I believe you bled more than I did."

"Externally," Asher stated solemnly.

"It seems you gentlemen both have a lot of baggage. Troubled pasts?" asked Para. She leaned back against the cushioned seats, trying to keep a frown from her face and trying to keep her anger in check. *Did I really make Thorn bleed internally? Anyway, this is fascinating. To hear them both talking about us without knowing that we're listening.*

"Not baggage," Thornton assured her. "Ancient history."

"Gotta make your mistakes, right?" Asher added. "What about you, Medea? Have you had any recent relationships?"

Mistakes! I'll show you what a mistake I was. Ancient history? Maybe, but things are about to get real *contemporary*. Para hid the pain she felt, and just smiled. "Not recently. I fear that I never really have the time for relationships. All I really have is a few minutes here and there to sit in a nice club and have a drink. Take a little time to fantasize about anything other than work…"

"What do you fantasize about?" asked Asher softly, moving to pick up his drink and brushing his arm slowly against her arm.

She stared down at his arm in surprise. *So obviously intentional, Ash. Yet I feel this body responding to your touch. Dammit, Para, control.* She turned to Asher, letting her eyelids flutter half closed with a sigh. "I dream of sandy beaches and tropical paradises. Staying in bed all day with someone I love, not having to work so hard. I dream of silly things… being rescued by someone strong from some kind of danger."

And I fantasize about hurting you both. A lot. A whole lot. Para opened her eyes and breathed deeply, looking at the men she was pressed in between. Their individual scents surrounded her, mingling to create a new pheromone that was so masculine it made her dizzy. She blushed and laughed lightly, returning to sipping her drink.

"You know, the right kind of man can make all of those dreams come true," said Thornton, moving a bit closer to her and letting his breath move her hair against her ear. "In an instant, all your money problems could disappear, and you could have all the time you needed. Life could be less difficult and filled with more… pleasure."

"Is that so?" she asked, turning to him curiously. She felt a bizarre combination of both disgust and arousal. Her stomach seemed to be doing flip-flops.

"Of course. You just need to know the right people." Thornton reached out to touch her satin-covered forearm, allowing his fingers to caress her slowly. "There's nothing I find anything sexier than a woman wearing gloves."

She wanted to hit him. It took all of her resolve not to. For how long had Thornton been making propositions like this to strange women in bars? She wanted to cry. She wanted to rip off her glove and press her palm to his face, and scorch his skin until he melted. Until there was nothing left of him but a pool of liquid. He was strong, yes, but now that she had the combined power of both Pax and Amara, she was tough enough to take him on. How dare he?

He had always told Pax that he didn't mind her burned palms. He had called them battle scars, telling her that he wanted to be the one person that she didn't have to wear her gloves around. When they were in bed together, he would press her bare hands against his body to demonstrate that she could not hurt him. And now here he was, complimenting a stranger for wearing gloves. Was nothing sacred? She felt bile rise in her throat. *I can't do this. I have to get away from here.*

Her watch beeped and she looked at it thankfully. "Sorry gentlemen, I have to get going. Thanks for the drink and the conversation."

"Already?" asked Asher. He slid his hand onto her bare thigh and squeezed slowly. "Won't you stay a few minutes longer?"

She was surprised by the boldness of the motion, and the feeling of warmth that radiated from Asher's hand, spreading through her thigh. Pax's uncle knew many more advanced energy techniques than she did, and this was evidently how he employed them. She felt another hand placed on her other thigh, but this one slid a few inches higher, with the fingers resting just under the fabric of the hem of her dress. The touch sent shivers through her.

"Come on. Skip work and spend some time with us," Thornton pleaded as he continued to slide his fingers up her dress. Para looked up at his face, reading his expression.

How shameless, Para thought to herself. She read the expressions on the face of each man. *They must be communicating telepathically,* she realized. *They must be actually planning this. Thorn and Ash! What are you guys doing? This is so petty and low. They're probably wondering who I'm going to choose.*

But this is working. You can't touch a woman's upper-upper thighs and send warm energy waves through her body without making her head spin a little. Para could not help it as her imagination created visuals of the men sliding their hands a little higher. She imagined how exquisite it would feel to have both of them touching her at the same time. The thought made her stomach roll over and her arousal intensified. She stretched back and wiggled in her seat a little, imitating discomfort, and they both removed their hands. She hoped that her movement would send the subtle scent of her own arousal to both of them, so that they could be as affected as she was.

What if I choose both of you?

"I'm so sorry. I have to go," she said, looking at her watch nervously, even though there was plenty of time. She acted like she was uncomfortable, and tried to move out of the booth in the direction of Thornton, but he wouldn't budge. "Please, excuse me," she said, pushing her body against his, letting her breasts brush against him, but he still didn't move. He only fixed her with a strange expression. *Boner-face, Thorn? I never knew you liked to put your fingers under the skirts of strange women in bars.*

She then moved to the other side, trying to make Asher scoot over, but she had a similar problem with him. He wouldn't move, so she pressed herself against him in a fake attempt to make him scoot over. She 'accidentally' allowed her hand to brush his groin, and pretended she didn't notice.

"Gentlemen, please. I really need to go to work."

"Stay, Medea," begged Asher, in his innocent childlike way. He reached out and placed a hand on her lower abdomen. Heat spread through her feminine organs, and she felt her body shuddering involuntarily. *How many women have they done this to?* She wondered as her eyes closed of their own accord. *Probably dozens. The women probably thought they were in love, that it was the heat of emotion or a divine sign. Why did they never do this to me? I guess they knew that I understood energy and would figure them out. So they want a clueless woman they can easily control. Well, I'll pretend to be that.*

"I really do want to stay," she said, in a breathless

voice. "But I have my career to think of."

"What if we keep you trapped?" asked Thornton, leaning in with a playful tone.

Casting a magick spell on me, boys? One second you're working against each other as rivals, the next moment together, as allies. Kind of like me, thought Para, *like Amara and Pax working together to get what we want.* Her watch beeped, snapping her out of the train of thought. Now time really was running out.

"I can't afford to be trapped," she said, grabbing her purse. She promptly began to climb over Thornton, sitting in his lap for a second to feel his erection pressed fully against her bottom, before sliding off and leaving the booth. She all but ran from the lounge.

"Wait!" called Asher frantically. When she didn't comply, Asher dematerialized and appeared in front of her. While she easily could have dodged him, stopped herself, or dematerialized to appear on the other side of him, she allowed herself to 'accidentally' run into his body as a human girl would have. He caught her before she could execute a fake fall.

She gasped and pressed a hand to her chest in mock surprise and exclaimed, "My goodness, you're fast!" She said this while mentally commenting. *Pretty slow, Ash. Not using your powers much these days, huh?*

He smiled as he held her. "I couldn't let you leave again without knowing your phone number."

"Sorry," she said, pulling away from him. For a fleeting instant she considered stopping this whole ploy altogether—being around the guys evoked too many painful emotions. Maybe she should surrender her quest for revenge and move on. "I'll tell you another time."

As she backed away from Asher, she ran right into Thornton who grasped both her arms to steady her, his fingers grazing the sides of her breasts. Even this tiny touch was too tantalizing to bear. She wanted to just lean back against him and let him touch her however he wanted. He leaned down and whispered into her ear, "We might never see you again. Please, Medea. Your phone number."

She turned her head, letting her cheek graze his and her giant mass of indigo hair tickle his neck. "Alright, Thorn. Here it is."

Asher grabbed a napkin and pen and jotted the numbers down. Para's watch began to beep frantically. She would be joined together for only five more minutes before the spell wore off.

"I hope we meet again," she said, making eye contact with each of them and smiling her best Burnson smile before leaving. When she was out of the club, she dug into her purse and popped a pill in her mouth quickly. It was a heavy sedative which would lower her energy to almost untraceable amounts. That way, the men wouldn't be able to follow her. She moved quickly through the streets to the secluded spot where she had parked her car.

"That was insane," she said to herself when she was sitting safely behind the wheel and driving away. When the timer on the watch indicated one minute, she pulled over to the side of the road again to separate. Amara's head went crashing into the passenger side window again, while Pax bounced off the driver door and fell right into the seat where she preferred to be.

"It's kind of nice to be myself again, this time,"

said Amara, rubbing her head. She buckled up her seatbelt. The sedative had made her a bit drowsy and she curled her feet up under herself in the seat.

"I know. It's nice that we can talk to each other about what just happened instead of Para just speaking to herself."

"So, she chose the name Medea?" said Amara with a chuckle. "Epic. I like to think I might have influenced that."

"We both did," said Pax with a wink at her friend. She sighed, and leaned back against the seat of the car. "Sweet Sakra. I can't believe they're trying so hard to seduce random women almost instantly after breaking up with us."

"Para's not a random woman. She *is* us," Amara reminded her. Then the blonde woman shook her head. "The way they work together! They must have been doing that since we were toddlers."

Pax shrugged, feeling a bit miserable about the whole situation. "Yeah. Thorn's fourteen years older than I am, and I knew he was a manwhore and a playboy long before I hit puberty. I just thought that after being together for so many years…"

"You guys started dating before you even started college, right?" Amara asked. "I know he took you to your prom. I was kind of hanging out with my own crowd by then, I guess."

Glancing over at the blonde woman, Pax shrugged. "It doesn't matter now, does it?"

"Five years? Six years?" Amara asked.

"Who-cares-years," Pax answered. She released the steering wheel so that it would not melt due to her growing anger. "It was basically a quarter of my life that I can't get back."

"I'm sorry, Paxie."

What Pax was too ashamed to tell Amara was that she had been seeing her brother for far longer than anyone knew. It actually amounted to well over half of her life. "Even if I live longer due to magick, even if I manage to live double or triple the lifespan of a normal person… I'll never get those years back, and I'll never get over this."

"It wasn't all bad though, right?"

"That's what makes it all bad now."

Amara sighed and stared at the streetlights in the distance as the women drove in silence for several minutes. She turned to her friend suddenly. "Everything changes now that we have Para. She's our secret weapon. We've got some unfinished business that we can't deal with on our own—but she's going to take care of it for us. Right?"

"I just hope it works out the way we want it to," Pax answered. "Lies and deception usually end badly."

"They were lying and deceiving us the whole time," Amara said fiercely. "I thought Asher loved me! I saw no signs whatsoever of anything being wrong between us."

Pax glanced over at her friend and sighed, choosing to speak to Amara with her mind instead of her voice. *I know. I can feel the way you feel about him when we're merged. He doesn't deserve that much love, Amara. Not after what he did to you.*

Amara glared at her friend. *By Sakra, Pax! I could say the exact same to you. The exact same. Thorn doesn't deserve your adoration! You should end these feelings. I felt your love and your desire for him as though it were my own. I've never felt so much passion and* need *for my brother. For heaven's sake! I just sat on his goddamned erection for you!*

Pax burst out laughing at the ridiculous image. Amara joined in. The two girls laughed for a moment without being able to stop. *Well, Mara, we're even. I just practically grabbed my uncle's penis for you.*

Amara squealed and let out something between a giggle and a gasp, and they both launched into a fit of laughter again. Pax doubled over, her body shaking so much that her chin hit the horn on the steering wheel and honked it rather loudly, which made her sit straight up with a start. Of course, they both knew that technically neither of them had done those things, and it was the unique combination of both of their bodies and minds which had chosen to initiate those suggestive sexual acts, but it sure was fun to take responsibility for Para's wickedness.

"I guess we should get out of here," said Pax with a smile, beginning to drive them home again.

They had covered a few more miles in a pleasant silence. "Pax," Amara said softly. "I want you to know that even if we don't achieve what we initially intended to do by merging into Para, I've already learned so much from practicing magick with you and doing this whole thing."

"Don't get sentimental on me, Mara. I know."

"No, listen. Sometimes it's rough, and sometimes it's fun—but overall, I have really learned a lot about myself. I didn't know I could ever feel as strong as I do when I'm Para. And if part of her is me—then that's not all your power, is it? Some of it must be mine."

"Of course it is."

"Paxie, what I'm trying to say is that I feel like this experience is healing me a little bit. Maybe I lost Ash, but you've been there for me, and I know that when things get rough you'll always be there for me. I've got my best friend back. And you're helping to make me so much smarter and stronger that I know I will *never* allow myself to be hurt this way again."

Pax glanced at her friend out of the corner of her eye. She swallowed back a lump of emotion in her throat. For the first time in the months since Thornton trampled on her heart, she felt truly happy. She knew that she had done something right. She helped her friend feel better.

She smiled, looking back at the road and thinking, *We're so screwed up, Mara!*

I know, right? Amara grinned, feeling the cheerfulness in the thought. *Whatever happens, at least we're in this together. Let them deal with the monster they created!*

Chapter 7: Welding Things Together

The sound of power tools buzzing caused Pax to groan and pull a pillow over her head. Her fitful sleep had seamlessly bled into an equally nightmarish reality. *I almost prefer the demon,* she thought to herself. *At least he wasn't noisy.* She stretched her legs out slowly as she willed herself awake. *Why do I feel like I've been hit by a truck? Oh yes, the sedatives to make Para weaker.* Amara's guestroom bed was extremely comfortable, especially when slightly sedated. Pax removed the pillow from her face so that she could release a giant yawn. She squinted one eye open before turning her head slightly so that she could look at her surroundings. A panoramic view of the ocean was visible through a giant pane of glass. It was several minutes before she realized she was staring. *So this is why Amara lives on the waterfront. What a spectacular scene.*

Pax pulled herself up onto her knees to better appreciate the view as she stretched out her arms. Except for the incessant roar of what was possibly a chainsaw or a power drill, it was a lovely morning—or afternoon. Realizing how high the sun was in the sky, Pax figured that the sedatives must have knocked her out and caused her to sleep well past noon. Pressing the palms of her gloved hands against her ears, Pax began to move off the bed before she noticed something strange.

There was a drop of blood on her pillow. Pax frowned, reaching up to check if her nose was bleeding. She ran her fingers over her lips to check if she had bitten herself. She glanced down at her pajama pants to see if it was her time of month. Finding no trace of blood anywhere on her body, she grew puzzled. On a hunch, she checked her chest again to see if there were claw marks. The memory of the creepy dream still lingered in her mind. Finding nothing, she shrugged. It was just one drop of blood—it wasn't important.

She levitated herself off the bed and materialized downstairs directly beside Amara. The blonde woman jumped a little, and turned off the power tool she was holding. She pulled her safety goggles off her head and gave her friend a big smile.

"Don't you love the smell of Kalgren technology in the morning?"

"I'd like the smell better if a Kalgren was frying me up some bacon instead of welding metal."

"I'm not that kind of Kalgren," Amara said unapologetically. She pointed one of her tools at Pax jokingly. "If you want to be woken up with breakfast in bed, you should go back to living with the other sibling."

Pax smiled. "That's not how he used to wake me up."

"Ew! Too much information. Too early to hear that kind of thing. Especially after yesterday." Amara shuddered theatrically. "Anyway, don't you want to know what my genius mind has generated?"

"What is it?"

"Well… this thing isn't finished yet; it's a surprise. But I've been productive this morning! Here." Amara reached into her pink lab coat and pulled out a phone before tossing it to Pax. "I took your phone and programmed it to emulate Para's voice in addition to your voice. So if one of the boys calls you, and we're not welded together at the moment—see what I did there? Then you can still take the call and just talk normally—it will sound like they're speaking to Para. And if we *are* welded together, we can still sound like our individual selves! I did my phone too. Tell me I'm brilliant."

"You're brilliant. But since when do we refer to two guys who are over a decade older than us as 'the boys?'" Pax asked as she began to play with the phone.

"Since they started acting like children," Amara answered instantly. She pulled her goggles back down over her eyes and returned to welding things together.

Pax smiled, and continued toying with the phone as she walked out to Amara's patio. She slid the doors open and headed past the deck into the grass which was still moist from the morning dew. She shoved the phone into the pocket of her pajama top as she stared out at the scenic water below the cliff. Walking to the edge, Pax could not resist jumping off just to feel the sensation of falling.

As she fell, the wind whipped her short black hair around violently. She was enjoying her own all-natural rollercoaster when her new phone began to ring. She paused in midair, levitating halfway down the cliff. Her hand reached into her pocket, and the vibration against her hand sent tingles of excitement through her.

She wondered whether it was Asher or Thornton calling. They had both called her countless times before, and she had never felt this excited. Whoever it was, he wasn't calling *her*; he was calling part of her, part of her that existed in a dreamlike state. Yes, she might as well be dreaming when she was Para. That was exactly the way it felt. She was still herself, but not totally in control.

Para was a dream of falling. Even though Pax knew fully well in both her conscious and subconscious mind that she could control her energy to create an air-cushion beneath her to keep her from falling, for some reason she simply couldn't fly in some dreams. As much as she tried, she was robbed of her powers. The most terrifying dreams were the ones where she was completely human, and completely vulnerable. However, Para wasn't that type of dream; not the kind that robbed you of your abilities and ridiculed your insecurities mockingly.

Para gave pure power. She was the dream where you could fly endlessly through the open skies without a trace of fear or pessimism. Fly without needing a spaceship through the galaxies to distant planets. She was the dream where you tried to grasp the rainbow and it burst into a kaleidoscope of even more rich and stunning color which you could hold and twist in your hands. She was the dream of being born again, with all the wisdom and joy you ever possessed, multiplied to astronomical proportions.

Para was all of Pax's fondest fantasies rolled up into one ball. The dream that her mother and grandfather were alive and well, that they had not been taken from her over a decade ago, and that their uplifting smiles and warm hugs were something accessible. She was the dream where the Asura gathered in a swarming army, and they were all attacking her family, but Pax somehow had the power to defeat them all—all by herself. Well, not by herself. With her best friend.

Para was mostly made of goddess. Literally. It was so challenging to suppress the energy which radiated from her skin that Pax had raided the hospitals where she volunteered for drugs to accomplish the feat. If not for this, Para would not have been able to hold a martini glass without it bending to her touch as though it were rubber. Pax could only imagine what it would feel like to test Para's powers without restraint. If both girls could let loose and exercise their true strength when their bodies were joined… they would probably be the most powerful female demigoddess who currently existed! It would be incredible.

It was almost a shame that such great potential was being wasted on two foolish boys. On playing a game. *But we deserve this revenge. They played games with our hearts. Why shouldn't we play too?* Pax felt a moment of guilt. *When this is finished, I promise to use Para to achieve something good.* She smiled, and allowed herself to continue falling to the rocks below. She still hadn't withdrawn the phone from her pocket. She almost did not want to know who was calling.

Everything was new. Having always been Asher's little niece, she had never seen him from this twisted, hateful, sexual perspective. She would never think the same of him again. After half a lifetime of belonging to Thornton as his woman, as his girlfriend; it was new once more. He looked at Para with an excitement that wasn't in his eyes anymore when he looked at Pax. He had become too comfortable in knowing that she belonged to him, and always would.

She closed her eyes at the painful recognition that she always would. Even so, she understood the sense of new excitement she recognized in his face because she felt the same. It was not the feeling of falling in love all over again, but more the feeling of retracing her steps to find something she had lost: her individuality. How ironic that she had needed to completely coalesce her body with another human being in order to rediscover her individuality. It was the undoing and unraveling of the fabric of their lives which had been carefully constructed on a now broken loom. It was the demolishing of a fortress, stone by stone.

In truth, theirs had been an unusually friction-free relationship. They had both been abnormally happy. They hardly ever argued, except playfully. Thorn and Pax were both carnal, competitive people who loved to wrestle or pit their mental powers against each other. They had understood each other better than the average couple, and they had been through the lowest of the low moments together. Pax's fingers tightened around her phone, and she considered chucking it out into the sea, never to retrieve it again. She did not want to answer the phone call. She did not want to hear his voice.

The humble beginnings of their relationship had occurred when she was only fourteen. It had started innocently enough—just a stolen kiss here and there. Pax had recently lost her mother, and her father had absconded to the mountains of India. She'd been alone, and she had focused all her need on the twenty-eight year old businessman who was a close family friend. She had chased after him for years, scaring away every other woman who looked his way until he relented. She was now twenty-six, and she recognized that perhaps she should not have been so adamant about pursuing Thorn.

She had been far too young to make such an important life decision about who she intended to spend the rest of her life with. She had been foolish and naïve, and now that she was twenty-six, which was much older and wiser… she would make the exact same decision. She would make it over and over again, a thousand times, for there was no one else for her, and there would never be anyone else.

If she had to assume the disguise of a different body each time, she would keep his love. Every time he got bored of her, she could simply change into a different woman. Every time he hurt her, she could find a way to slide into his heart from a different angle and hurt him back. It was not fair that Thorn had stopped wanting her because he knew she was his. Was there no reason to desire what one already possessed? Why did he want to be with the redhead in the pinstriped business suit he'd had on his desk, or with strange women in clubs like Para? Was the majority of their appeal that they were not Pax?

When she had been a broken-hearted and tragedy-stricken teenager, she had been plenty exciting. There was the feeling of *this is so wrong but I can't stop*, combined with *our parents can never know*, and followed by the good ol' *we're breaking all kinds of laws.* That was all very well, but Pax had believed that there were certain things that would withstand the test of time. Disregarding the connections based on their special lineage, she had expected the *I love you* to remain, and especially the *I respect you.*

But Para had it. Instantly, and just because she was a beautiful stranger, Para had his attention. She wasn't someone Thorn could easily have his way with at any moment of the day, because he was assured of her love. This thought angered Pax, but then so did almost every other thought. How long had Thorn been screwing around on her? Why didn't he think what they had was special and electrifying? Why didn't he think their love was worth keeping? She had.

Pax threw her arms out and levitated out over the water, letting the ocean breeze save her from her train of thought.

Did we just get a phone call? Amara's voice projected into her mind. *I was working. Why didn't you take it?*

Didn't feel like it. Come out here and enjoy the water. This cliff is pretty.

Well, I guess I deserve a small break. Where are you? I don't see you on the cliff.

Near the bottom.

You jumped off it? I can't do that…

Pax rolled her eyes. *Do you mean to tell me that the daughter of the Prince of Devas can't even levitate?* When there was no response, Pax flew up to the top of the cliff, moving so quickly that she wasn't visible to the naked eye. She completely dematerialized, appearing behind Amara to push her friend off the edge of the cliff.

When Amara released a bloodcurdling scream, Pax could not resist a laugh, but she flew after her friend to ensure her safety. She was surprised when Amara was unable to catch herself, and she reached out to catch her under the armpits.

"Seriously?" Pax asked in surprise. "You're twenty-eight years old and you can't levitate?"

Amara only began to relax once Pax had deposited

her safely on the beach. She took several deep breaths before she began laughing. "Ash used to toss me off that cliff all the time and say the same thing. I guess I was always too afraid to learn, but now I somehow feel ready."

Pax shrugged. "I guess it's the deva equivalent of women who are too scared to learn how to drive. So they keep putting it off, saying they'll learn later just to avoid driving altogether. Then the next thing you know, they're twenty-eight, and falling off a cliff, and they can't do anything about it except let their heads get smashed on the rocks."

"I think that analogy got lost somewhere in the middle," Amara said with a grin. "On the bright side, I think my head might be naturally hard enough that even if I did go hurtling down onto jagged rocks, I'd get off with little more than a massive headache. Nothing a little Advil wouldn't fix."

"Shall we test that theory?" Pax asked gesturing up at the top of the cliff maniacally.

"Oh, Pax. I know you're just trying to avoid the phone call. But it's going to take more than almost-killing-me to distract me from the situation at hand. I am very, very upset." Amara sighed and reached up to touch her temple. "Do you think merging together might be playing with our sanity? Give us brain damage?"

"In my professional opinion: absolutely." Pax smiled and stretched out on a rock. "I have considered that it might be slightly altering our physical makeup."

"I guess we'll find out," Amara said as she pulled out her phone. "Okay, enough stalling. It seems we have a missed call from both Thorn and Ash and there's a text from Thorn."

"Ooh, I want to read," said Pax, sitting up and bolting to Amara's side to poke her face over her shoulder.

The text message read:

Medea,

Please allow me to take you out for dinner. I'm nothing like Jason.
Thorn

Pax growled at the phone dangerously. Jason had been Medea's husband in the myth. The husband who betrayed her. "Well, I was having a good morning until I read that. It sounds just like him. Disgusting sweet-talker. You are Jason, Thorn! You *are* Jason. I think I need to be joined with you to think of a reply without exploding into a million pieces."

"Yeah," said Amara with a light nervous laugh. "Ash left a voicemail. Listen."

The phone went to speaker and the voice began to play:

"Hi Medea! Ash here. I can't get the image of you out of my mind, and I keep hearing every word you've said replay in my mind. Unfortunately, I haven't heard you say nearly enough words, so there's way too much repetition. How would you like to help me with this problem? I'd love to treat you to lunch."

Amara moaned, placing her face in her hands. "This is ridiculous. I need to be joined with you just to listen to this without getting depressed. Right now, I'm just Amara, and he's trying his best to have sex with some girl he just met. It's humiliating how little he cares… but when I'm Para, it's a victory, it's just part of the plan."

"I don't want to answer either of them, Mara."

"But we must. Do you want to go to lunch *and* dinner? What do you have time for, aren't you scheduled at the hospital?"

"I'm the famous daughter of a beloved actress who tragically died. I can go into work whenever I choose. What do you want to do?"

"I don't know."

"Let's let Para decide," said Pax. "She'll know whether she's the kind of woman who goes out with Thorn or Ash or both or neither. Get dressed and I'll get some safe doses of sedatives ready for us."

Amara nodded. "I'm going to reconfigure a few more features into the watch so that we don't screw up and split apart in front of the…" The blonde woman twitched when her cell phone suddenly rang in her hand. She frowned, pressing the silencing button. "It's my damned brother."

"You should answer it. Don't let my beef with him become your beef," Pax warned.

Amara shook her head stubbornly. "Too late for that. There's beef everywhere. We're just swimming in beef."

Immediately, Pax's cell phone rang. She pulled it out of her pajama pocket and looked back at Amara. "It's your damned brother."

"You should answer it," said Amara.

"Why me? You hypocrite! I haven't spoken to him in weeks." Pax stared at the phone until it stopped ringing.

"Who are you kidding, Pax? You sat on his lap last night and shoved your breasts against him."

"Not me, we!" corrected Pax, putting her phone back in her pocket. She jumped as it instantly started ringing again, and then growled loudly. *Double-calling! Twice in a minute. Emergency? Someone had better be dying.*

Before she could change her mind, Pax answered the call calmly. "Hello, Thornton."

"Pax… finally." There was a long pause at the other end of the line as both parties held their breath. They both seemed to feel as though a truckload of eggshells would be crushed if either of them breathed too hard. Thorn was the first to break. "Could you and Amara please stop ignoring my calls?"

"No. How may I help you?"

"I haven't been able to reach you in over a month."

"Does that surprise you?"

"Dad is getting worried. He said that he noticed unusual fluctuations in Mara's life force last night, and yours too. He said you both seemed very weak or possibly ill. Have you been practicing?"

"I've been teaching Mara to levitate," Pax lied. Amara nodded to encourage this lie.

"I hope you're not getting her into anything too dangerous. Were you hurt or unconscious? Is everything okay?"

Pax remained silent, holding the phone and staring into space. The sound of his voice caused nausea and nostalgia to overpower her and render her speechless. Amara tugged on her friend's pajama sleeve when she saw her zoning out.

"Paxie, are you there? Please speak to me. Do you know how long it's been since I heard your voice?"

Holding her breath, Pax waved her fingers to telekinetically separate large boulders from the cliff. She spun her fingers around to make the gigantic rocks rotate in a macabre carousel. Amara began to back away from her friend nervously.

"Neither of you have called or visited. I'm used to seeing you both at the breakfast table at least half of the time, so I'm really starting to worry. I nearly flew over there last night to check on you…"

Her grip on the phone tightened and she felt her heat spreading throughout her body, intensifying and consuming her. All of the spinning boulders burst into flame, creating massive fireballs with solid, crunchy centers. Gumballs of doom.

"Thornton Vincent Kalgren, you had better stay away from here," Pax warned in a whisper. The fireballs began to spin so fast that they created a burning ring of flame. "I nearly killed you, so help me."

"Pax, I am so sorry. Sakra himself doesn't know how sorry I am. But I swear I have tried to contact you thousands of times since that night, in every possible way. You blocked yourself off telepathically, and you won't take my calls. I have tried to explain what you saw…"

"I understand what I saw," Pax hissed. "I'm a big girl now, Thorn, and you taught me lots of things. I'd like to hang up now. First I'll say this: your sister is fine, and I am fine. You'll see us when you see us." She moved her finger to end the call.

"Pax, wait… I miss you."

Pax let loose a funny noise from deep in her throat. If there was ever such a thing as a final straw, this was probably a prime example. *Bad move, Thorn. Wrong thing to say right now.* She shifted the phone to her left hand, and let the other one extend out towards Amara. "Thorn, I have something which belongs to you. May I return it?"

The ring of blazing boulders began to descend until they spun around Pax. Amara had been sitting rather close to her friend, and she gasped and scrambled out of the way to avoid being struck by one of the deadly projectiles.

"I guess I left a lot of things at your place, Pax. I have a lot of your stuff as well. What is it? You can come and return it anytime. Pax? I just felt a strange surge of power…"

She hung up the phone, and returned it to her pocket in order to lift both of her hands. She dislodged several more boulders from the cliff and added them to the fiery blaze surrounding her. Many of the boulders narrowly missed Amara who was still scrambling away nervously. The crackling energy in the air sent Amara's blonde hair flying backward and over her shoulders. Amara put her arms up instinctively and crossed them over her head, ready to block any boulders that flew her way.

Amara began to panic a bit when she saw glimpses of her friend's red eyes through the wall of fire. *Pax, you're not going to hit me with that, are you?*

The rock-and-fire missile only grew and Amara found herself sliding away and stumbling back into the cliff. There was nowhere left to run. She was trapped. *Please, Paxie. I can't block that. I'm not joking… killing me won't piss Thorn off nearly as much as you think, trust me.*

When she saw insane flickers of gold in Pax's eyes she frowned. *Can you just not aim that thing in the direction of my house? The property costs a fortune and… just let me upgrade my insurance first!*

Pax closed her eyes and pressed her left hand across her abdomen. She exhaled and pressed her right hand over her left. In an instant she had transported herself through the air and landed right in front of Thornton, with her pre-made ring of fireballs spinning inches from his nose.

This is for you, she told him as she released her carefully collected mini-volcano at point-blank range. She didn't wait for the aftermath as she teleported directly back to Amara. She collapsed on the rocks and curled up, staring dejectedly at her knees.

"Did you hurt him?" Amara asked with concern. The blonde playboy was still her brother.

"He's not dead. He's a deva. Unlike you, he's the actually-tough kind. I think I might have broken every bone in his body and burned every inch of his skin, but for me and Thorn that's basically flirting."

"Pax," said Amara, disapprovingly. "That wasn't part of our plan. We decided not to let them have any physical contact with our individual selves while we're doing this. Not to let them see us so that they won't get any hints."

"He didn't see me," Pax explained, rolling over and putting her forehead flat against the rock. *All he saw was an explosion right in his face. How dare he try to apologize, try to tell me he misses me while trying to have sex with Para? I want to go back to sleep now for the rest of the day. Maybe I'll hide in a dark corner of the basement and never leave again.*

"You can't. We have work to do with… Pax!" Amara shrieked. "Your teleportation thing worked!"

Pax looked up in surprise before frowning. "Yes, I can get it to work sometimes. Usually when I'm teleporting to *him*. Something about his life force. I guess I know it really intimately and I'm used to keeping track of where he is in the back of my mind. For many years, he was the only destination I really wanted to get to, so it became easy to dart across the world and be beside him in an instant. I wish it could work when I was trying to get anywhere else."

Amara smiled. "Joining bodies is really doing great things for our friendship."

"What do you mean?" Pax asked.

"You were able to teleport back to me," said Amara triumphantly. "I guess you must be intimately acquainted enough with my energy too."

Pax smiled in genuine surprise. "That's right. I did teleport back."

"You should practice that skill more," suggested Amara. "I'll help however I can. It could really help us if we ever get into a tight spot as Para."

"That's a great idea," Pax said cheerfully. "I'll work on it as soon as I finish bawling in misery in a corner of your basement."

"What?"

"Kidding, kidding. Sort of."

Chapter 8: I'm Only Human

"This is kind of weird, Asher," Thornton admitted, straightening his bow tie.

"You're telling me? I am not used to having you along with me on my dates. You're going to cramp my style."

"That's actually kind of a lie. We've been double dating since high school, and for the last five years that you were dating my sister…"

"Well, there are usually *two* women present," Asher clarified.

"You see, this is the problem with seeing doctors," Thornton complained, glancing at the menu. "They're always so busy that you have to make allowances for them. I can't believe she asked us both to be here, and more importantly, I can't believe we agreed."

"It was the only time she said she'd be free today," said Asher with a shrug. "I really wanted to see her again."

"As far as I can see she doesn't have a preference between the two of us," said Thornton in confusion. "Maybe that's why she asked to see us both together, so that she can decide."

"Well, how long is she going to take to make her decision? I want to sleep with her already," complained Asher, playing with his cufflinks.

"We'll just see about that," said Thornton with a smirk. Then he noticed the girl and blinked. "Good Sakra."

Heads of both men and women at other tables began turning to see the champagne gown which shimmered with the motion of confident strides. The low-key color was so neutral that it bestowed the effect of making its wearer look almost nude. Her deep plunge neckline exposed ample skin, as her hairstyle exuded sophistication. It was unmistakable to every onlooker that there was goddess in this woman. It was so unmistakable that they could not bear to look at her, and turned away to avoid seeming impolite. By being over-the-top posh, Para had managed to disguise herself as a completely human woman.

It had taken her upwards of four hours to get ready. Pax and Amara had separately prepared for the date before uniting, and their clothes had also merged into a wonderful combination of what they both had chosen to wear. It was a fascinating side effect of the spell—the girls would never have to argue over what Para should wear, because even her garments took on the respective properties of each of her segments.

The spell was so precise with the way it employed its ancient magicks that Pax often wanted to scan through the old books and seek out similar recipes. Amara did as she had promised, although she was also sometimes tempted, and kept her friend in check. *"It's like drugs or drinking,"* Amara had explained. *"When you feel great, you always think that if you take a little bit more you'll feel even better. But there's a maximum, and from that point onward it's all downhill. You'll regret not recognizing the high point, and quitting while ahead—but we always want more than we can handle."* Pax had wondered where Amara had gotten such experience with drugs or drinking; she had not been present for those events.

"Hello gentlemen. I'm so sorry I'm late," she said with a smile. Both Thornton and Asher stood up to pull her chair for her, and glared at each other. Asher won this mini-battle and snatched the chair.

"I'm just happy you returned my call and could make time to meet us today," said Asher, pushing the chair in as she sat down. "You look as stunning as ever, Medea."

"I want to apologize for what happened the last time we met," explained Thornton, taking her hand gently and kissing it in greeting. For the first time, Para was not wearing gloves. Pax's scars were less visible when blended with Amara's perfectly smooth hands, and the girls were beginning to think that it might be suspicious if Para always wore gloves. Thornton was still speaking. "Asher was helping me out with some paperwork at the office yesterday, and it's the end of quarter. It's hectic like you wouldn't imagine at KE. We were both already quite drunk by the time we ran into you, and I know we weren't acting as we should have."

Seriously? Drunk? Para knew how high their tolerance was. *Maybe if you'd both consumed every drop of liquor in that bar and then some.* "Oh, I understand *all* about stressful days at work," said Para, resting her hand on Thornton's forearm. "I'm so sorry that your job brings you to drink. Mine does too. You wouldn't believe the things that I see on a daily basis. The impossible, heartbreaking things that I've seen."

I've seen my two greatest allies turned against me. I've seen the two men I loved more than anything in the world become my nemeses and hurt me more than any demon or Asura ever could. As Para let these negative thoughts about Thornton and Asher seep through her mind, she consciously remembered to keep an expression of sweetness on her face and look sad and distressed about her own job.

When the waiter arrived to take their orders, Asher and Thornton both ordered dishes that Para knew wouldn't satisfy a tenth of what they needed to consume for one meal. She knew this, because her respective parts were used to cooking for both of these men several times a week. *Three can play, my loves.* She ordered a chocolate fondue. When the boys asked her if she planned to eat any more than that she said that it was all she really felt like at the moment. They picked up the conversation.

"You must be a very strong person to deal with the stressful situations that arise from working in the hospital," said Asher.

"I try to be strong, Ash," said Para earnestly, "but the truth is… I'm only human." *Oh, that's a good one. I'm only human. Please, help save and protect me, big strong godlike boys.*

"What do you do to relax?" Asher asked. "I know we mentioned to you that my niece is a doctor. Sometimes the pressures of her job drive her a little crazy."

"No, Asher, your niece is *always* crazy," complained Thornton. "She tried to demolish my face this morning."

Don't laugh. Don't laugh. Wait… tried to? Speaking of that, why didn't it leave a mark?

"She didn't *try to*," said Asher with a smirk and a

grin. "She *did.* Or do you not remember using your emergency vial of Sakra's healing water?"

Para tried to keep from scolding Thorn. *What an idiot! Using Sakra's water which has the power to save lives, just to make himself look good for a date? There's such a limited supply of those vials, and this is just wasteful! Also, if he couldn't take a little explosion like that, he really is getting old and weak.*

"Demolish... your face?" asked Para with a concerned gasp. "What does that mean? Did she try to shoot you with a gun? What is 'Sakra's water'? Are you alright, Thorn? Let me look at it."

Para reached up to cup Thornton's face in both of her hands, turning his head first to one side gently, and then to the other. She ran her fingers along his cheekbones firmly, and then along his jaw. She then ran her fingers lightly around his eyes and eyebrows.

"There's no sign of any damage here," she said knitting her sapphire brows in a frown. "What did that crazy girl do to you, Thornton? I always thought she was nice."

"It's nothing, Medea," said Thornton with a small laugh. He had been enjoying the feel of her soft hands on his face and the sweet concerned look in her cobalt eyes. *I should get hurt more often,* he thought. "Pax is one of those violent types. Which is a bit ironic since she was named after a Roman peace goddess. She often uses both me and Ash as punching bags."

"How awful," she said with a grimace. "If either of you ever need any medical attention feel free to call me immediately. I do sometimes make house calls for my favorite patients."

Para felt an inward tickle of humor as she saw

Asher and Thornton look at each other with wide eyes. *Are they planning to hurt each other now so that I can take care of them? Are they fantasizing about playing doctor with me? Oh, boys! Don't make this too easy now.*

"That could be very helpful, Medea," said Asher with a smile. "I have a hunch that I'm next on Pax's hit-list."

You have no idea. "How could anyone hurt such a sweet boy as you, Ash? Why, I bet you wouldn't harm a fly."

Asher smiled and blushed, casting his eyes downward, while Thornton laughed. "That's definitely Ash! He's always been the kindest person I've known. And I've known him since we were little kids."

"How sweet. It's rare to see such deep, loyal, lasting friendship these days," said Para. *I used to think he was kind too.* Just then her fondue arrived and she almost squealed in delight at the sight of warm chocolate running in rivulets down a small fountain, and surrounded by an appetizing assortment of fruits.

The meals ordered by Thornton and Asher had not yet arrived, so they had nothing to do but watch Para eat. "Oh my goodness. I hope you boys don't mind, but there are some things you just *cannot* eat with a fork. It would be sacrilegious," she said, picking up a strawberry with her fingers. Now she was very glad that she had not worn gloves. She dipped the strawberry in the chocolate and lifted it out, rolling it so that the excess dripped off before bringing the fruit to her lips and closing her eyes as she tasted it.

Damn, Thorn! That is so sexy. The strawberry looks good too. A sexy woman with a sexy strawberry, this is too much for me to handle.

Para opened her eyes. Asher had sent that thought into *her* mind instead of to Thornton. Accidentally giving her information, and telling her exactly what he wanted. As if she didn't already know. How could Asher screw up his telepathy like that? The strawberries and chocolate (and cleavage) must really be affecting him.

"Would you like to try a piece, Ash?" she asked softly, generously coating a strawberry for him. She fed it to him before he could respond and as he took it into his mouth his lips closed around her fingers as well. She tried to pull her hand away but he held onto her wrist gently, and after eating the strawberry he licked and sucked the excess chocolate off her fingers.

"It's delicious, Medea," he said, looking into her eyes as he released her hand.

"Oh," she said, feeling her cheeks flush. She silently cursed within her mind at how much Asher's touch warmed her insides.

Nice one, Ash. Now I'm feeling a bit left out. Except I don't really like strawberries, but that banana would taste delicious from her fingers.

Thorn, man, how can you not like strawberries? Seriously. Bananas are in no way, shape, or form, tastier or sexier than strawberries. Besides anything would taste delicious coming from those fingers. I wouldn't mind licking chocolate off the rest of her either. I swear, man. I'll be licking chocolate off those perfect breasts by the end of the week, you'll see. I wonder what color her nipples are?

Damn you, Bro. It will be me! I don't even need the chocolate. Can you smell her? I already know how delicious she'll taste.

Nothing like a good, ol' fashioned purebred human woman. I'm going to plunge my tongue in her honey soon. I'll tell you all about it afterwards.

Para was frozen. Were they screwing up the telepathy intentionally? Did they *always* talk about women in such an explicit and lewd manner? Why was she able to listen in on this? Was it a new technique that came with the fusion? *So they like my scent. I guess I should let myself go and let my body respond to them. Just let myself go, and try to intensify that scent. Be turned on in order to turn them on, yet maintain control in my mind.* As she planned out her strategy she reached for the piece of banana and expertly dipped it.

"Thorn," she said with a naughty smile. "Something tells me you're more of a banana boy."

He looked at her in surprise before taking the banana from her fingers into his mouth, and the perfect flavor of banana and chocolate and her skin mingled together to create the ultimate aphrodisiac.

"What about you, Medea? I'm going to guess pineapple," said Thornton, smiling like an excited kid, and reaching for the pineapple. He fed it to her in much the same manner that she had fed him, accidentally allowing a small drop to fall onto her shoulder as he brought his fingers back to his own lips to lick them.

"Oops," said Thornton, leaning in. "May I?"

She nodded in surprise as Thornton put his lips on her shoulder and gently kissed and licked the chocolate off. She felt her eyes closing of their own initiative. In addition to the natural tingles she felt at his touch, she felt him send small jolts of electricity into her skin by flickering his energy against her arm as he ran his fingers down it. He was turning on the seduction at full force. It was working too.

How did these two men, with all of their power, make it with normal human women? Para remembered all the times that Asher and Thornton had left her own bodies bruised and sore, and wondered if they wouldn't seriously injure a human girl with their lovemaking. Wouldn't they have to use so much restraint that it would be boring? *All the more reason they'll come back to us, begging on their knees. Stop it, Para! That's against one of the foremost rules of this game: no thinking of reconciliation. Just revenge.*

She knew that she had to push the anger aside and let herself be seduced in order to fully seduce. She could call upon the anger to stabilize herself at any time. She wasn't just one clumsy and insignificant mostly-human girl any longer. She was not one weak girl who would let them win. She was Para. She was the best of two quasi-goddesses twisted together in a glorious fusion. She did not only feel equal to the men at the table, but the newfound arrogance from her merger caused her to feel superior. For a woman, it was always necessary to feel far superior to a man in order to seem barely his equal.

This was war. Even Thornton licking chocolate off her exposed shoulder… well, that was war too. War felt pretty good.

Asher cleared his throat loudly. "I don't know, Thorn. I would have guessed Medea would like kiwi best."

Asher's glare at Thornton clearly seemed to say, *"Why are you hogging our new toy? I want to play too."*

"I do like kiwi," she said, opening her eyes and

looking at him through her thick midnight lashes.

Thornton moved away from Para hesitantly and allowed Asher to dip and feed her a piece of kiwi. Asher very obviously smudged his chocolate-covered thumb against the side of her mouth when he pulled his hand away and smiled at her wickedly.

"So sorry. Not intentional at all," he said with a wink. "Allow me."

He didn't wait for permission before leaning in and brushing his lips against the side of her mouth, almost touching her lips, but not quite. It was somewhere between a chaste kiss on the cheek and a feather-light promise of lusty wet French kisses to come.

I want to be inside of you, Medea, thought Asher, gazing down at her body hungrily.

Para's eyes widened and she almost pulled away at the shock of those words. Did he intend to communicate to her telepathically? Did he intend to say that, or was he just thinking?

What is it about your scent? Asher was staring into her face with puzzlement. There was something of recognition there. *You're so exceptional and out of the ordinary… yet so familiar too, as familiar as… myself. You remind me of home… but at the same time, of a distant place I've never been.*

Fuck you, Asher! Para ripped her gaze away from Asher and looked at the frowning Thornton. She felt her breaths coming quickly, and Asher's thoughts were affecting her far too much. Her chest heaved with the deep intakes and her heart was racing. She had to be careful not to respond to him telepathically. *Can he hear my thoughts too? Did he hear me curse at him?* She looked back at Asher who still gazed at her whimsically and knew that he had not heard.

Her watch beeped. Ten minutes.

"I'll have to go soon," she told the two men, and they were about to object, but the waiters arrived then with the main dishes. Food. The only thing, the only glorious thing that could distract a deva from a woman. Para quickly and ravenously finished the rest of her fruit and most of the chocolate fondue, all the while listening to her stomach growl for more. She ate while the boys were eating so they didn't notice that her particular style of eating was just as piggish as theirs.

Her watch beeped again. She had to get going.

"Thanks for meeting with me, guys. I have to get going. Dinner was wonderful."

She was already beginning to stand up when she felt both boys restrain her by grabbing her arms. She sat back down abruptly. *They move as simultaneously as I do when I'm merged together.*

"I have a question before you go, Medea," said Thornton. "Which one of us do you prefer?"

"This is a bit embarrassing. You boys both seem great. But I hardly know either of you."

"Then get to know us," said Asher. "Why don't you go out with each one of us privately so you can decide who you like best?"

"I don't think I have the time for something serious," said Para hesitantly. "I'm simply too busy these days."

"That's fine. No pressure. But you'd like to spend more time with us, wouldn't you?" Thornton prodded.

She paused for a moment, glancing at her nails in

her lap. *Cool! Even my nail polish is a combination of Amara's French manicure, and Pax's orange nails. Shiny. Okay, that was enough time for a thoughtful pause, time to answer.*

"Yes," said Para, letting a sincere look drift over her features as though she had considered the pros and cons at length. "Frankly, I am very surprised. What I most admire is your loyalty to each other—your friendship is so inspiring. There's something special about you guys. When I first met you I thought you were just another pair of skirt-chasing whores, but I think I was mistaken."

Thornton and Asher looked at each other and began to silently congratulate themselves in thoughts that Para could hear every word of. *You morons. There was an insult in there. You shouldn't be too proud of yourselves.* She glanced at her watch. Five minutes.

"See you guys another time," she said, rising to her feet.

"Such a really busy girl. Always rushing off before things get interesting," remarked Thornton.

"Next time you can show me what you mean by 'interesting,'" said Para, throwing the boys her best Kalgren smirk before pivoting to leave. As she glided by other tables, several couples discreetly turned their eyes to observe her swaying mass of navy-blue hair as she exited the room.

"She's going to be a tough one to break," said Asher, staring after the shapely retreating legs, "but now that she's gone, can we order enough food to *eat*?"

Chapter 9: The Breakfast Table

"Daddy, I hope you don't mind that I've been practicing a bit with Pax recently," Amara said, taking a deep breath. "May I ask you a few questions about devas?"

"Go ahead, Amara."

The blonde woman daintily used her knife to carve a morsel out of her soufflé as she considered how to phrase her question. Her father was not an easy man to address. "Well… is telepathy common?"

"Of course," answered Vincent Kalgren. He did not look up from his newspaper to respond. "Almost anyone can project their thoughts into the mind of another."

"What about hearing the thoughts of another?" Pax asked between sips of coffee.

Vincent did look up from his newspaper then, so that he could scowl at the girls. "Doesn't it seem obvious that if one can project thoughts, the receiver should be able to hear them?"

Amara and Pax glanced at each other.

"Something is obviously troubling you both," observed Vincent. When his wife placed a huge plate of food before him, he smiled at her appreciatively. He touched the plate and all the food on it disappeared, instantly absorbed by his body.

Amara's mother smiled. "Don't you girls worry too much about this deva stuff," said Rose Kalgren, wiping her hands on her apron. "In my research on my husband's blood, we found an extremely high concentration of certain particles that aren't present in the purely human body. There are trace amounts in half-breeds like you girls, of course. I figure the particles generate and store what you call 'prana'— they seem to react and connect with the Earth's magnetic field. It's like your bodies are filled with these little lightning rods that can literally draw energy from the…"

"She's oversimplifying things," Vincent said, waving his hand in dismissal. "Our powers are much more mystical and ancient than your mother's inadequate science can define. Now what was it you girls were curious about?"

"Daddy," Amara began again. "Is it possible to hear the thoughts of others if they don't intend for you to hear them?"

Vincent frowned. "Yes, it's possible for a true telepath. There were a few children of devas, usually females, who had perfected that skill. They liked to use it to control their husbands since they could tell his every desire and every wish."

"That sounds handy, Vince," said Rose playfully.

"They also were expert tacticians, completely invaluable in battle." Vincent had returned to his newspaper. "It was a very rare trait though, and usually only the strongest warriors could use their minds that way."

"Is it one of those special hereditary things?" asked Pax. Realizing that her coffee had grown cold, she waved her hand over the mug, causing it to instantly boil. "Can anyone with power learn the technique?"

"I believe it's a rare trait in certain families, but I

haven't seen enough of it to judge. Why all the questions? Have you discovered this skill, Pax?" Vincent's voice sounded mildly interested, which was a great feat.

Pax chewed on her lip. *I think it's probably yours, Amara. Maybe you need to have access to my power in order for it to work.*

Amara nodded thoughtfully. "Yes, Daddy. I think I have something of the sort developing."

"Impossible," Vincent responded instantly. The newspaper disappeared from his hands as he leaned forward. "You would need to be at least ten times stronger than you are to use something like that, Mara. It would take a lot of energy to manage."

"It's just the beginning stages," Amara said, smiling. *Wow, so Para is at least ten times stronger than I am! Well, that's not surprising—I'm not very strong, and you are. But at least I have something to offer to our union, right? This mind-reading thing could really help things along.*

I agree. But we're going to hear things we don't want to hear. Like last night, but worse.

The advantages outweigh the costs! I want to get stronger.

"Paxie," said Rose with worry. "I trust you, darling, but I need to ask. Are you sure it's safe for Mara to be practicing these dangerous arts? I know you've had issues in the past, and I know that your family…"

"I may have issues with control, but Mara is very responsible with her powers," Pax answered. "She isn't greedy and indulgent like I am sometimes."

"It's my choice, mom," Amara added. "I want to do this to learn more about where I come from."

Rose reached out to touch her daughter's hand.

"You come from Kalgren Tech, darling. A long line of inventers and tinkerers who struck it big. We're the people who move the world forward. Forget the ancient powers that your dad goes on and on about."

"But mom…"

"Other than a few neat tricks in the bedroom, what good is it being a god anymore? The bloodlines are diluted and the powers become weaker and weaker with time. The modern world is about technology. It's about the race to find the ultimate source of green, renewable energy for everyone to use! Who cares if you have excessive amounts of energy inside of you? You're just one person. Who cares if you can make fireworks with your hands, lightning with your eyes, or tornados with your ass…"

"You infuriating woman!" Vincent said angrily. "How dare you insult my heritage like this? My power has always protected my family from harm."

"And my power uses sunlight to keep the television on at night so you can watch your sports channels, Vince! My power keeps the fridge running so you can grab a cold one during the commercials!"

Vincent clamped his lips together tightly. For someone possessing untold supernatural abilities, he did excessively enjoy the sports channels. "Fine. But I, for one, think it's prudent that our daughter should pursue this new path. I am pleased that Mara has finally shown an interest in learning to protect herself—she has already proven that she can tinker with gadgets enough to satisfy you, Rose."

"She's safer that way," Rose said firmly. "When she's in her lab playing with her toys, she's safe!"

"No, mom," Amara said gently, although she would have completely agreed just a few weeks ago. "Life is never safe. As long as I'm living there will be always be multitudes of danger—and they will inevitably attack just when I feel the most secure."

"This is true," said Vincent sternly. He turned to the dark-haired woman, fixing her with a harsh glare. "Pax Burnson, can I trust you to be extremely careful with Amara? You grew up practicing. Hell, I recall your parents demonstrating that you could fly before you could walk. I recognize that you have never been patient, but you will need to be patient with my daughter."

"I will, sir," Pax vowed.

"You need to recognize that it will take Amara longer to pick up even the most basic of techniques since she is beginning so late in her life..."

"Twenty-eight isn't old..." Amara began to protest.

"There is another option," said Vincent Kalgren. The massive blonde man drummed his fingers heavily on the table. "We do have a... rite of passage of sorts which the girls could endure."

"No!" Rose insisted. "*Vince!* Not my little girl. It's bad enough that you forced Thorn and Ash to go to that place..."

"Our daughter has goddess in her blood. All this potential, yet she lives like a helpless human. If she wants to grow stronger (and thank the gods she finally does) there is no better option to test and condition her skill than the Pseudosphere."

"She could be seriously injured or killed," Rose said softly. The older woman tightly gripped a serving spoon.

"Relax, mom. I hadn't even considered going *that* far." Amara shuddered and wrinkled her nose. "I don't know if I can handle… *that place.*"

"I can," said Pax, beginning to tap her toes on the ground rapidly in excitement. "I can! I have wanted to go to the vector zone *forever.*"

"Well, you definitely should, Pax," Vincent said, nodding. "You have been far too volatile lately. You need to work on your self-control."

"I will, sir."

"I can't believe you would endanger the girls this way, Vincent!" Rose was scratching erratic patterns into the tablecloth with her fingernails. "Goodness me, I never thought I'd hear the name of that place again. The Pseudosphere—it makes me shudder."

"You would shudder more if you had actually ever been there," Vincent informed her.

"Well, if the girls *must* go, I will gather plenty of electronic literature for them to read in case they get bored." Rose tried to make this offer casually as she kneaded the tablecloth.

Vincent rolled his eyes. "They're not going to be bored enough to read while they're trying to survive having their bodies being brutalized by the harshest of elements."

Amara hesitated, pushing Parisian potatoes around in circles on her plate. "Mom, I wouldn't worry too much. I wish I could make the trip, but… don't you need to die to enter that realm? I don't think death agrees with my complexion."

"Life and death are one," Vincent said, echoing

the words Pax had spoken when they first joined their bodies together. "There's nothing to it—I've been dead plenty of times."

Amara made a hesitant face. "Yeah, I'll have to give it some thought…"

Pax's head turned sharply to the south and she frowned. "Vince—is there something coming this way?"

"Yes," Vincent answered. "It's my son."

Pax stood up abruptly. "Why is he coming here? I have to go."

"He does live here, Pax. Maybe he forgot something," Rose said with a shrug.

"You said he'd be in meetings all day!" Pax looked around frantically for an exit. *I think this was a set-up, Amara. He knew you and I were waiting for a day he wouldn't be home to visit.* Pax weighed her options. Her car was parked in the garage beneath the building, and if she exited that way there might be confrontation. Hiding elsewhere in the building would be pathetic, even though the Kalgren Compound was a very large building.

"Mom, he didn't call to say he was coming back?" asked Amara anxiously. She dotted her lips with a napkin, preparing to bolt if necessary. *Damn it, Pax, what are we going to do? He can't see either of us, especially not both of us together. He might figure it out. I don't want to deal with this now.*

"No," Rose responded. "When he left this morning he said he wouldn't be home until dinner, maybe later."

"I should leave," said Pax, knocking over her chair as she clumsily moved from the table.

"Why?" asked Vincent, raising an eyebrow. "Are

you afraid of him?"

"I'm afraid of what I might do to him. Or are you going to step in and fight for him like you did last time? Because your mighty son can't defend himself from a weak little quasi-deva female?" These were the words Vincent had often used to taunt Pax when they were training together.

"Pax, please," begged Rose. "No talking of killing my son at the breakfast table."

"She's right! I thought you knew this family better than that." Vincent's voice was a low growl. "Save it for lunch and dinner."

"Aw, Daddy. I love you," said Amara with a giggle while Rose glared at her husband.

"Speaking of which," Pax said quickly, "I miss my own father! I'm going to go and visit him immediately." She was already moving to the windows.

"In India?" Amara yelled. "Are you mad?"

"It's only the Pacific Ocean," Pax said with a gulp as she levitated off the ground. "Thanks for having me over for breakfast, Mr. and Mrs. Kalgren. I'll see you again soon."

"See if you can bring back some vials of water," Vincent said. "My supplies have been running low since my son started getting himself repeatedly mortally wounded."

"Will do." With that, Pax disappeared. A burst of windy energy was left in her wake, rattling the window as it slammed shut. Amara wiped her hands with a napkin and stood up to make a formal announcement. "I have a stomach ache, headache, menstrual cramps, or something of the sort. I'll be in my old room and I don't want to be disturbed by any of your other children."

She turned to leave, but Vincent stopped her. "Wait, Mara. You don't have to leave yet. He's not coming here."

"What? But I thought you and Pax said…"

"It seems he's parked his car in the front lawn, but he completely bypassed the house and is now flying in that direction." Vincent jabbed his thumb west. "Towards India."

"Oh shit… he's going after Pax!"

"Language, sweetie," cautioned Rose.

"I'm not interfering in their business again. If they want to fight until they kill each other, it's none of my concern," said Vincent. He materialized a new newspaper in order to better act like he cared far less than he actually did.

"What's going on between those two anyway?" asked Rose. "I miss Pax around the office—she always used to help out around quarter-end and bring us loads of Chinese food. The last I heard, things were fine between Thorn and Pax."

"It's a long story," Amara said. "I didn't find out until recently either."

"Well, at least you and Ash aren't being immature," Rose said with a smile. "It makes me so happy to know I can count on one of my children to do things the right way. You had better tell me the moment he proposes, because we are going to plan the wedding of the century!"

Amara stared at her parents, feeling the immense love that only a youngest child could feel after being away from home for a while. She wanted to tell them everything. They still didn't know about her breakup, although she was sure her dad had some sort of idea. Vincent always seemed to know everything about everyone—it was like he had a map in his head that always tracked his daughter's whereabouts. Godly powers were not just useful in the bedroom; they were indispensible when one needed to spy on their children. Surely he had noticed that Asher's life force was no longer in her house at night. How could she tell her parents that she'd lost the love of her life? How could she tell them that they were right; she'd been hurt by the man they had warned her about?

"Oh, mom… everything's gone horribly wrong." This was all she could muster before turning and running up the stairs to her old room. When she entered, she was relieved to see that every inch of the décor was exactly as it always had been. She threw herself down on the bed and closed her eyes at the familiar feel of this mattress and these sheets. Somehow, being in her childhood bed made her feel much more protected and secure.

Chapter 10: Pride is Paramount

Pax was already too far out over the ocean to be able to see a landmark on any horizon. This had quickly wiped all trace of a smile from her face, and she was wondering to herself why she had made the rash decision to fly to India. Her altitude wavered with indecision as she considered turning back. While she was rather energized from the large breakfast with the Kalgrens, especially her favorite feta-filled omelet, she wasn't sure whether she was motivated enough to cross such a vast expanse of sea. If she grew hungry by lunchtime and needed to stop for another meal, there weren't even any fast-food joints in the middle of the ocean.

The wind ruffled her blouse, causing it to billow up as Pax paused in her flight to turn around. Yes, she had been hasty. There was no need to fly to India, as much as she wanted to see her father. It had been the first place which had come to her mind as she thought of escaping Thornton, but sometimes a person's second thought was wiser than the first. She was already heading back to California when she felt the sensation that there was something powerful flying towards her.

The omelet in her stomach did a somersault. It was the same life force she had felt approaching the house, and she did not have to ask anyone for confirmation. She hadn't needed confirmation to begin with, really. When it came to Thornton, she just knew. He was following her. Turning back around, Pax felt doubly invigorated for her flight to India. Even if her ex was pursuing her, he would surely give up when he saw how long her trip was going to be. He probably thought that she was out for a morning jaunt around the shore, but how wrong he was. She was heading directly to India, and there was no way he would follow her across the ocean. He didn't care enough to exert that much energy over her anymore. She gave him ten minutes tops before he grew bored.

Pax concentrated to increase her speed as much as possible, letting out a yell to channel more energy into her flight. If only she could get her teleportation to work, she could be with her father in the Himalayas instantaneously. But she had not perfected the technique, and she didn't want to risk landing somewhere halfway between her current position and her destination. It would mess up her sense of direction and she might become lost. It was better just to fly west for a few hours. Once she reached Sakra's Point, she would be safe. Getting home was a different story—maybe she could take a plane, or wait until her energy had replenished.

An hour passed, and Pax could still feel the familiar life force in pursuit behind her. *Will he really chase me around the globe? How many times?* Pax couldn't help but smile at his persistence as she made her body more rigid and streamlined in order to speed up, slicing her body through the air like a hot knife through butter. She could feel Thornton slipping away behind her. *Yes, I'm losing him. He's a good distance behind me. He may have been doing this his whole life, but so have I.*

When another hour passed, and Pax began to

grow tired, she began to feel worried. Her exhaustion was not of the body since flying did not require the movement of any limbs, but of the mind. The prolonged and controlled levitation of flight tired the mind in the sense of concentrating on something extremely hard, and just needing to lie down to rest one's eyes for a few minutes. Of course, the wind whipping into her eyes did not facilitate keeping them open. An involuntary thought clawed its way into her mind. *If I grow too tired and fall, at least he's nearby to catch me. He's stronger than I am, and he could carry…* Pax immediately swore at herself. She would not allow herself to depend on him! She would not ask anything of him ever again; she would never accept anything. She would happily plunge down into the ocean and drown if her energy gave out rather than clutch his treacherous hand. *I know that it's wrong to be so prideful, but Vincent always said that pride is paramount.* Of course, this was dramatic. She had flown larger distances than this in the past, but usually not at this breakneck speed. A frown settled on her face as she felt him gaining on her.

Her anger at the thought of needing Thornton and fear at the concept of confronting him gave her a double burst of pep and an idea. It was only the ocean which was making her uncomfortable, and if she could return to flying above land she would feel stronger. She could always visit her father another day when she wasn't being pursued. Maybe with an airplane. Turning her flight path suddenly southward, Pax changed her direction in an attempt to confuse her unwelcome travel companion. He probably knew she was headed to India, and thought to intercept her—but if she changed her destination, then perhaps he would give up the chase.

Curving her flight path, Pax headed southeast back to the Americas. Hopefully, it would take Thornton a while to realize she was not on the normal path, and a while longer to locate her. Flying at her current speed, which was several times greater than before, she reached the mainland in about an hour. That was when she realized that her pursuer was still behind her. Her change in direction hadn't dissuaded him, but she felt more at ease now that she was above the continent. She could fly down at any point and lose herself in a city.

Pax enjoyed the wind tossing around her black hair wildly. For the first time, she was grateful that she had sliced off all of her hair; it certainly made visibility easier. She wanted so much to enjoy the scenery below as she flew, but needed to concentrate on evading her hunter. *This is actually kind of thrilling,* she thought to herself. *I like the fact that he can't catch up with me, but the longer the chase goes on… the more I start to wish he would catch me. Stupid Pax! That will only cause a huge fight, verbally and probably physically since lately you have zero control. It will just be a lot of unnecessary pain for both of you. However, fighting can be a nice way to let off steam. I always grow so much stronger and discover more of my power after a really heated emotional spat.*

She didn't quite know where she was—probably over Ecuador or Peru. As she gazed at the lush forests memories came rushing back to her. Not too long ago Thornton and Pax might have flown around the globe like this a bit more leisurely, and stopped in random countries to explore the culture, cuisine, and landscape. They would often stop to stay at a hotel or inn and make love in the most exotic possible locations—oftentimes, in the remote outdoors. They had a gigantic map on the wall at Pax's condominium in the city where they placed thumbtacks on all the places where they'd had sex. It was a private joke they enjoyed, and they could point at a thumbtack and reminisce. They had been trying to cover as much of the globe as possible in their spare time, and it was easy when they could fly for free anywhere they wanted, both in and out of planes. Sometimes Thornton had taken Pax along on his business trips all over the world.

But nothing could compare to the greatest trip they had taken together. Shortly after Pax's mother had died, Thornton had offered to take her along on the final test run of a Kalgren Tech spaceship. Pax had been extremely depressed and skipping most of her classes. Although Mrs. Rose Kalgren had not approved of allowing a fourteen-year-old into space due to issues with bone density, Pax could not turn down the once-in-a-lifetime opportunity to leave the planet's atmosphere. She had begged Thornton to sneak her on the ship, and the summer they'd spent in space together had been the highlight of her entire life.

Thornton had probably saved her life with that gift.

There was nothing quite like floating around the planet to give a girl perspective. In later years, they had often joked that it was too bad Pax had been so young while they had been testing the ship, or they could have put thumbtacks on a map of the solar system. They had often dreamed of going back someday and making up for those lost thumbtacks. Maybe on their honeymoon. Thinking of all these memories left a taste in her mouth that could only be defined as bittersweet. She couldn't help it; her heart ached. *Who's going to do all that with you now, Thornton? Who's going to make a future with you that can rival our history? Why didn't you think about what you were throwing away?*

She wrangled all of her focus into the thrill of the flight; she felt the energy rushing through the channels of her body and the blood pumping through her veins. She might not be Para, but even so, there was something valuable in her ability. As she experienced the perfect natural adrenaline and endorphin high, her ego was boosted as well. *I know that I'm one in a million. Heck! I'm probably the strongest girl on this planet right now, so that's one in 6 billion-ish. Not that it's the only reason I'm special. Just nice to mention. I'm also a very good person until someone pisses me off and I explode. Find another like me, Thorn! Find someone better, someone more perfectly matched! Find her, I dare you!*

His life force was growing stronger and closer. Was he really managing to catch up? She looked over her shoulder, something she knew she should never do in any race or chase, and sure enough she saw the little blip of red light in the distance. *Damn. He assumed Ruby Form. That's drastic, and I should do the same—but it will take everything out of me, and I will probably have to sleep for days!* She looked behind again and he was close enough for her to make out the shape of his body. *Screw it. I'm a Burnson, and I'm going to push myself to the limit.* She clenched both of her fists and released a guttural scream as she altered the source of her *prana*, turning her normally transparent energy vibrantly red. This drove her body's output of energy dangerously close to the maximum. She nearly fell out of the sky as the heat and flame of her own insides consumed her.

Choosing to use the technique colloquially coined 'Ruby Form' meant willingly succumbing to a fever of a thousand degrees. This was the price one paid to exist in the heightened state of consciousness for a few minutes; it was one not many devas could afford to pay. An additional challenge was containing most of the power and heat inside the body so that one's clothing did not burn to cinders. Only a few descendants of demigods could sustain the state, and Thornton's father had been the one who prepared and trained Pax to withstand and master Ruby Form when she turned eighteen. He had also been the one who warned her never to use the technique unless she was desperate. *Push it, Pax, push it.* And she was desperate.

Why on earth is he following me? He doesn't want me; he wants to have sex with Para. And a bazillion other women. Not me. So why is he chasing me? Probably only because I'm running away. She considered trying her teleportation trick to send her body instantly back to Vincent, or possibly to her father. But she knew she would not be able to successfully accomplish the task; she was too focused on Thornton, who was exuding massive amounts of energy very nearby. She might just screw up and teleport directly beside him. She had managed to teleport to Amara that one time, but at the moment she couldn't find Amara's life signature whatsoever… it was too weak from halfway across the world. She couldn't concentrate enough and relax enough to teleport. The only thing to do was keep flying. For how long, though? How long until one of them ran out of energy, or until he caught her? She suddenly realized that she was no longer over

South America. The landscape was all white.

Antarctica was beautiful.

What the hell! In the moment she had been distracted by the scenery, two small mountains of ice had begun barreling toward her from either side to intercept her path. She instinctively slowed down to dodge being crushed between the gigantic chunks of landscape. That was a mistake. In a second she was caught in a death-grip, with her arms held fast against her sides.

"Gotcha!" he said, laughing. The worst part was that his laugh made her want to smile too—the vigorous chase had made her body hum with excitement and energy, and her mind was calmed. She had almost forgotten the reason she'd been running away. Almost. The hurt and betrayal of the past months almost disappeared, and crushed in the vice of his arms she almost felt like nothing at all had gone wrong. Almost.

"You cheated," she mumbled into his chest as the boulders crashed into each other inches away from them.

"All's fair, sweetheart."

He turned his body to shield her from the shower of debris. When the crash had ended, she realized that he was being playful with her. He wasn't allowed to do that. Not anymore. Not after what he'd done. She began struggling, but his grip was more unyielding than being the meat in an ice sandwich. She regretfully wished she had been the latter.

"Release me, Thornton. I told you to stay away."

"It's unreasonable to expect me to obey that command forever. I gave you time to cool down, hot stuff, and… hey! Paxie, where's all your beautiful hair?"

"Don't call me that," she said, grinding her teeth together. The fact that he could restrain her while casually examining her haircut enraged her. A high-pitched noise began ringing in her head. She fought to maintain control of her life force. Thornton might be comfortable in Ruby Form, but it was killing Pax.

"I need to talk to you," he was saying when she could hear again. "This isn't how I planned it. I was thinking of running into you 'unexpectedly' at the Kalgren compound. But when you took off flying, I knew that I couldn't be casual and smooth about this. It's now or never. Will you just listen for a moment? Don't I deserve that much, after all these years?"

Her heartbeat began to quicken without her permission, and a little butterfly in her gut seemed to begin fluttering its wings hopefully. She immediately crushed it. She knew that it was mainly the result of his proximity: hormones and such. *If I didn't have proof, hard evidence of him cheating, I would fall for this. I still might fall for this. Do I love him that much? That I'd put it behind me? No. Get a hold of yourself, Pax Burnson! Visualize and remember what you saw.* In perfect clarity, she could feel her arms filled with warm paper bags holding several Styrofoam containers of takeout food. She remembered balancing the bags on her knee in order to push the buttons to his private elevator. She remembered kicking the door to his office open and seeing glimpses of a grey pinstriped blazer and red hair. And skin. Lots of creamy white skin. She remembered staring disbelievingly at the naked thighs which were wrapped around *her* Thorn as she crushed the takeout food in her arms.

"I can't believe you followed me here." Pax tried to escape again, but his grip was stronger than steel. Stronger than titanium, stronger than tungsten. The red energy still surrounded him, imbuing him with exorbitant amounts of power.

"To every corner of the omniverse, remember?"

Their sweet old jokes were suddenly sour. Her own red energy was fading fast, and she needed to break free and get away before she lost consciousness. She thrashed wildly, delivering multiple head-butts to his neck and chin, but she didn't have enough leverage to faze him and he still held onto her securely. She tried to release fire from her hands and mouth to scald him, but his body was crushed tightly against hers and the attacks scorched her face and arms as well. While in Ruby Form, the burns could hardly be felt and she worried about causing permanent scarring. She had garnered enough scars as a result of her own recklessness. She tried to bring up her knees up against his midsection to force some space between them, but he just brought his own knee up in between hers and forced her knees to the side of his body.

This motion, a form of grappling in midair, resulted in the rough grinding of their bodies together. She could feel his warmth and hardness being mashed against her as she fought to resist his grip. She dug her teeth into her bottom lip as she fought. He was becoming aroused as they wrestled, and this in turn had the same effect on her. She could feel the clammy sweat dripping off his face, and the moisture soaking the fabric over his chest. The scent of him was too familiar to find unpleasant. *Stay cool, Pax. This isn't a game. This isn't supposed to be fun.* But she loved fighting too much that she couldn't help but enjoy the tussle. She couldn't help feeling a thrill from the challenge.

Pax was so focused on the specifics of combat that she forgot the reason she was trying to get away. She became lost in grunting as she slammed her kneecaps into his thighs. She became lost in the taste of him as she sunk her teeth into his jaw and carnally tried to rip the bone out of his face. She became lost in the pain as she tried to flex her shoulders backwards until she felt like her spine was going to break. She did not even notice how seamless the transition was from fighting to free herself to struggling to touch him and grow closer to him. She did not even notice when her chest began heaving with deep breaths for a different reason than exertion. She did not notice when she finally lay limply against him and clung to his waist, rubbing her lips against his neck. She was hardly surprised by his fingers entangling in her short hair, and his other hand slipping into the waistband of her jeans to rest comfortably on her bare bottom. It was too natural to fall back into this.

"Thorn," she whispered, in a pleading voice that was more recognizable to him. Gone was her fake formal address using his full name. Gone was the stiff, standoffish façade of being a stranger. She had easily melted in his arms, just as they had both expected. Pax felt his lips against her temple, and then against her eyes. There was no need for words. Both devas could feel in the quiet humming of their once fierce red energy that they had missed each other gravely—their bodies were pining for the other's touch. Pax's mind was so blown, so clouded with such a fuzzy mist, that she could only think about how much she needed to remove her clothing. At the back of her mind, a thought seemed to float to the surface like a solitary message-in-a-bottle bobbing in a vast sea. The note inside was a reminder of why she could *not* allow herself to succumb to her lover's charms, as much as she wanted to drown in him. As much as she wanted to feel him inside of her without delay.

I can't believe that I still want him after all this. I am the weakest woman who ever lived, she thought in exasperation. *Thorn, why do you always have an erection? Did you follow me around the globe just to torture me with that thing? I know; your penis is beautiful. It's an enchanting shade of pink and so silky to the touch. Not to mention the cute blonde curls at its base, so perfect for nuzzling. It's the fairytale cock of dreams. You're probably the only man on earth who has a beautiful penis, because frankly, penises are weird looking. I've seen plenty in the hospital, and of course they're usually injured or diseased (why else would they be showing them to me in the hospital?) but regardless of that, they're all funny and odd. I think yours would look great even if it were injured or diseased. Which it probably will be soon, if you keep up the lifestyle! Syphilis, I hope. Except for the fact that demigods are immune to infection. Damn. How could I have almost forgotten?*

This has been an odd mental soliloquy. I think that keeping my energy red for this long is driving me insane. I should focus all my attention on breaking free and kicking your ass now. You cheated on me, you man-whore. Those blonde curlies were supposed to be for my eyes only. So stop pressing your junk against me!

Fueled by that thought, Pax rammed her knee up

into Thornton's groin. When he began whimpering, her lips curled deviously. A small wave of pity ran through her, but it was easily overshadowed by amusement. *How does it feel to have a demigoddess in Ruby Form bust your balls?*

"Cheap shot, Paxie," he said, growling from low in his throat.

"Let me go. I'll do it again, but harder."

"You wouldn't," he said, wincing. "You enjoy the talents of Mini-Thorn far too much to unman me. Besides, if you injure me too badly you won't be able to have my babies."

"Yeah. 'Cause in some universe, that's still on the table." Pax released a burst of rage-born energy she brought up her knee with full force into his groin, but he blocked her by twisting his body to use his own knee. He laughed then, hooking his legs around one of her thighs so that he had both her arms and her legs locked firmly.

"I'm sorry. That was pretty inappropriate considering the circumstances," he admitted with a smile. "It's just the kind of thing I would have said to you a few months ago, you know?"

"I think the fact that I'm repeatedly kicking you in the balls indicates that things have significantly changed between us."

"I've known you since the day you were born," Thornton reminded her. "A short hiatus does not *significantly change* as much as you think."

"No, but the reason for that hiatus does. Thorn, I swear I'll do something drastic…"

"Everything you do is drastic. It's what I love most about you. So quit fussing and listen to what I have to say."

Pax snarled as she tried to yank free. She managed to slip an arm out of his hold and concentrated all of her life force into her fist, imagining that it weighed several tons and was as dense as iron before she swung to hit him in the face. She hoped that the punch would knock him out, or at least give him enough pain and shock to release her, but he was only momentarily dazed. He promptly re-pinned her hand firmly behind her back. She made a sound of exasperation as she channeled all her power to her knees, desperately kicking him with force that would have dented concrete. It didn't even leave a mark. She could not imagine how furious she had previously been in order to harm him—at the moment, she could not seem to access her power. She was draining fast.

Even as her stores of energy diminished, Pax felt the delight of rivalry reviving her determination. She hated being at a stalemate, and it drove her to fight more creatively. Her legs were free, and she entangled her limbs with his, using her flexibility and strength to try and break his legs. This had always been the nature of their communication. Pax and Thornton had always been physical and aggressive with each other, and that always found its way into the other aspects of their life as well. They couldn't deny their violent deva heritage. Pax couldn't deny that having her legs wrapped around him made her yearn for other activities.

Ugh. Bad thoughts, Pax. Bad thoughts. Get away from him! If only I were fused with Amara right now, this wouldn't be bothering me quite so much… I think. Time for a new strategy!

Pax abruptly spun around so that they were

upside-down. He was strong, but she was determined and clever. If she couldn't get out of his grip with brute force… well, Antarctica was only a few thousand feet below. Pax began to fly, diving headfirst into the large icy continent, with Thornton still attached to her.

"You think smashing me into a glacier is going to help this situation?" asked Thornton loudly to be heard over the whistle of the wind as they both barreled down head first.

"Absolutely."

The theory is this: maybe grinding both of our heads into a glacier at an extremely high speed will take my mind off you grinding your body against me. And hopefully, once your head is smashed open and your juicy grey matter is spilled out on the ground, you'll quit doing that and leave me alone. Pax gritted her teeth together and closed her eyes before the collision came. She felt a second of almost-nauseating fear; the feeling right before a rollercoaster plummets vertically downward from a considerable height. A moment of pause. Then it came, and it was sharp, blinding pain exploding through her head and entire body. Her entire nervous system was jarred by the impact.

The only comfort was that Thornton was getting the worst of it because he was taller than she. His head acted as an icebreaker first. It was petrifying, and she might have instinctively grabbed Thornton and clung to him tightly, if not for two important factors: one, she couldn't move her arms because he held them locked tightly to her sides, and two, the only reason she was doing this in the first place was to use the ice to break him *off* her. Holding on tighter would not help the situation in the least, even if it were possible.

Thornton had been using his own energy to try to pull up so that they didn't hit the ice, but Pax's momentum had been strong. The only change he was able to make was after the initial impact. He was able to shift their path so that they moved horizontally within the ice, just under the surface. After a few miles, they eventually broke out of the surface again and went sliding along the top until Thornton used his energy to forcefully stop.

Both Pax and Thornton had torn their clothing badly—she only just noticed that he had been wearing a rather nice suit. It had probably been expensive. She felt a pang of regret thinking, *I'll have to replace… stop! That's girlfriend thinking. You're not his woman anymore.* There were bloody scrapes along both of their arms and backs, and bruises were visible everywhere skin was exposed. Pax panted as she lay on the ice in the aftermath of the crash. She had been hoping that one of them (preferably Thornton) would be knocked unconscious, but unfortunately they were both fine. Even after having their heads rip through several football fields worth of solid ice. They both seemed only a little dazed.

Perhaps dazed was enough. Pax decided to take advantage of the dizziness she could see on Thornton's face as she made one last ditch effort to break free. He anticipated her movements from the resolve in her eyes, and he tightened his grip on her. She growled, twisting and bringing her knee up hard into his ribcage, and the two of them grappled on the ice for several minutes, turning over and over as one would gain the advantage, only to lose it again.

Finally, fed up with the fighting, Thornton slammed Pax's body down hard into the ice, and placed his own body weight on top of her. They were both panting and breathing hard from the effort, and she could feel his chest constricting and expanding quickly against hers. Blood from his forehead dripped down onto her own forehead and slid into her dark hair. They stared at each other, one set of steely blue eyes into a darker pair. Both of their eyes were impeded by a foggy film of translucent red energy. Pax felt a bit sorry to see just how bruised his head was, but she knew he could handle much more abuse. After a few moments, Thornton smiled.

"I'm not sure the penguins will appreciate the renovations."

Pax tried to resist. She tried to hold onto her anger. But her lips were already smiling without her permission. She simply couldn't help it. *My sweet Thorn.*

"Now can we talk?" he pleaded. The blood tracing patterns down his face made him look so pathetic. She felt the urge to take care of him, to heal the injuries she had given to him once again. Was it the woman in her, or the doctor? He wanted to talk, and she should listen to what he had to say. She couldn't possibly say no to those pleading aqua eyes.

"No," she croaked, and she dug inside herself, searching for more *prana.* She was ready for another round of fighting to get away from him, and possibly some more head-bashing into ice.

He sighed, as though he were very tired. "Look, Pax. I've been trying this life-without-you thing. I don't like it so much."

Could have fooled Para. "Drink, women, freedom: what's not to love?"

"Cool down, hot stuff." He moved his face very close to hers so that their noses touched. "I made a mistake, and I need to tell you why…"

"You don't understand, do you? I don't want to think about it. I don't want to remember. I don't want to be angry anymore."

"I wish I could go back in time and change what happened," Thornton said. "I tried. There's an incantation, and if I had the power to invoke it, I would. I lie awake every night thinking about it."

"I have a hard time believing there's anything you can't do."

"If I bugged my dad or Ash to help me, I could probably manage to make it work—but I don't want others to have to clean up my mess. So I guess all I can do is explain. Maybe it will make things right and you can stand to be around me again…"

"No. If you ever loved me, even in the least, please stay away from me. Stop bringing up the subject. We can't spend time together anymore." *Not in this body, not in this mind, at least. I just can't bear it.*

Fresh waves of pain were exploding in her chest at the reminders of his infidelity. Even though she had seen a great number of chests cut open to expose beating hearts, and even though she knew that the heart was just an organ made of muscle tissue… she felt suddenly very aware of hers. All the poems, all the songs, and all the stupid sappy movies made sense, because the emotions *did* really concentrate there. It must even really be possible to die of a broken heart, for the pain in her heart was greater than the pain in her head. And her head had just smashed into a glacier.

"Pax," he said softly, "I do love you."

And the pain intensified tenfold. *Of all the attacks I've ever seen and borne, and of all the godlike destruction I have witnessed and caused, this takes the cake. Thorn wins the trophy of most lethal.* Pulling her left hand free, she moved it down to her abdomen and placed the fingers firmly against her solar plexus. She tried to follow with her right hand in the correct formation to attempt teleporting away, but before she could touch her stomach, Thornton grabbed her wrist and slammed her hand into the ice above her head.

"Don't go," he said softly. He lowered his lips close to hers so that his warm breath caressed her lips. Visibly. It was rather cold that particular day in Antarctica. This made the warmth of his threatening kiss even more welcome to her body, while being *completely* unwelcome to her mind. *You have got to be kidding me. He's not really going to do this.* Pax's eyes darted to his lips and back to his eyes with alarm.

Yep, he did it.

His lips had descended on hers with soft wet warmth, pressing together the final part of their bodies that needed to be touching. The kiss sucked away her energy, rapidly reducing her strength. As he moved his lips against hers, kissing first her bottom and then her top lip, she felt her *prana* retreat somewhere far away where it couldn't be reached, almost completely disappearing. The red energy that had surrounded her dissipated, and her short black tresses fell limp and flat against the watery ice. She expected unconsciousness to take her, but unfortunately, she remained awake.

She prayed for a miracle. Ideally, the miracle would consist of her body morphing completely into ice and becoming one with the glacier beneath her. For that was the only way that she could resist moving her lips in response against his. Her rebellious body was disobeying her commands. She was allowing herself to be kissed, and soon she was kissing back, savoring the taste of him. The sweaty, bloody, manly taste of him.

Disappear. Disappear. I need to not *be me any longer. Para… I need to be Para. She would never feel so defeated and ashamed. Would she?*

Thornton allowed his own energy to be calmed as well, slipping out of Ruby Form. This meant that he knew she was no longer struggling to get away from him. She was submissive; she was his again. *I'm sorry, Pax. I'm so sorry,* he said telepathically. *Forgive me?* Without intending to, her arms snaked around his shoulders so that she could cling to him, and she gave the tiniest of nods without detaching their lips. He kept a small aura of energy around them to keep them warm as he continued to devour her mouth with hungry kisses. It had been too long. The warmth generated by their bodies had melted some of the ice around where they lay, and Pax was almost immersed in a small pool of water. Thornton lifted his mouth from her now swollen and pink lips to gaze down at her body ardently. Her tattered clothes were soaked and adhering to her in a very enticing manner.

He brushed his thumb over the exposed patches of skin. "I don't think we have a thumbtack in Antarctica," he mused in a breathy voice before returning his mouth to hers. His hands were moving to the buttons on her blouse. For the first time since they'd been in the neighborhood, she suddenly felt the coldness of the ice against her skin, and it pierced right through her. It was, in fact, pretty cold.

One button.

If I know my Thorn, he'll have my clothes off in an instant and then there's no going back. It's just so natural, how can I fight it? I need to fight it, but my body is staging a mutiny against me. I wish someone would come and save me from this… save me from my own weakness. I do so love it when he does that to my neck.

Two buttons.

I guess there are no chances that anyone will walk by, considering this continent is uninhabited. Why did I have to fly in this direction? I should have stayed close to the equator. China would have been nice. And at least I would have been warm while miserable.

Three buttons.

Am I going to allow myself to be used? Probably. So help me, my body remembers things that my mind has forced itself to forget. I won't be able to look at myself in the mirror ever again. Maybe someone will come to check on us. Vincent? Papa? Ash? Maybe someone will notice the fluctuations in our life forces and realizing that we were fighting, they will come to see if we're okay.

Four buttons.

This is ridiculous. My shirt is torn to pieces anyway; why bother with the buttons? Just rip it off me like you always do, Thorn. And like you probably do to all your other women. No. What am I doing?

"Stop. Stop, Thorn. Please."

Pax placed her hands on her chest, trying futilely to hold the pieces of her blouse together. Telling him to stop was something she had never, ever done. Not once in the past decade. She was usually starting things, and begging for more. It was hard to play this harsh new role.

"I can't stop," Thornton groaned, grinding his body against hers to show her. He pressed his lips against her neck. "God, Pax. I need you so badly…"

She felt the ache in her womb respond to his words. She needed him too. Her body urged her to give in, to relax and let it be. To allow herself to gain and receive pleasure from the man she loved. The needy parts of her mind and spirit also begged her to let things continue—they knew that it would somehow feel reassured once it was over. It would make her forget everything for a few minutes, and she could move on… they could go back to the way things used to be. She wouldn't be alone anymore. She didn't have to say or do anything; she could just relax and let him heal all her hurts, and make it all better.

But her pride said no.

"Thorn… it's over." The effort it took to resist sent tears sliding out of the outer corners of her eyes, soaking her already blood-soaked temples. "It's over, for good. You know that I can't forget. I loved you. I do love you with all my heart, but you *cheated* on me. You were with another woman, and you'll just do it again. Please, just leave me alone."

He looked at her with surprise, moving a thumb to her lashes. "You're crying? You, *Pax?* Not blowing me up, but crying?"

"Does it give you satisfaction? To see me belittled and broken? To know that you have power over me, that you can affect me so greatly? Congrats."

The pool of water was growing too deep, and Thornton gently cradled Pax in his arms and flew her onto the solid ice. He held her close, against his chest. "Why do you think I'm such a monster? I could never gain pleasure from your suffering. I haven't seen you cry since… since your mom..."

The memory triggered a sob and another vehement outburst. "Soak it up! Cherish the moment! Take a fucking picture, because you won't see it happen ever again. Now please go away!"

"And leave you crying on a glacier in the middle of Sakra-knows-where?"

"Yes. Sakra does know, so I'll be fine. Please go."

"I'm not going anywhere, hot stuff." Thornton sighed, kissing her forehead. As the tears froze on her cheeks, he carefully wiped them away from her skin. She moved her head to the side angrily to avoid even that tiniest of touch—as though it burned her. She looked off into the distance and still prayed that someone would come. She felt so weak. So very helpless. She, *Pax!* She was still in his arms, which meant she hadn't won yet. *Isn't anyone sensing our* prana*? Doesn't anyone care that we've been fighting and… why couldn't you just show up and save me, Papa? Like you always did when I was little. Right at the moment things were about to get dangerous, you'd always be there.*

Thornton kissed her tears away gently, murmuring sweet nothings. She didn't hear any of them until this sentence:

"Pax, you need to know this: that woman you saw in my office…"

Something snapped in her. This was it. This was

the doorway to her strength. The doorway to the power released by her insane, violent, female deva rage. Deep in her center it awakened and exploded in an instant, flooding her consciousness. She didn't need anyone to come and save her.

Like an intergalactic shampoo commercial, her limp hair began to glow and lift off the ground, engorged with pure red energy. Eyes that had been dull and lifeless a moment before were now filled with electric golden passion. Vivid visuals of Thornton putting his lips on Para's shoulder the night before came to her. She saw his body moving on top of the pinstripe suited redhead as he unapologetically pounded his hips against her. Images of him with his face glued to the woman's offensive neck polluted her brain. Now, using those same lips to kiss her! To kiss *her!*

She sobbed, her small hands condensing into even smaller into solid, airtight fists. In perfect, powerful form she smashed her knuckles into Thornton's mouth with all the strength in her body. He rolled away from her, clutching his bleeding lips in shock.

"How *could* you?" she yelled, blinking away tears of rage as she leapt on him and began to pummel his face for all she was worth. Thornton needed to assume Ruby Form again in order to defend himself. He managed to block most of her blows at first, but as the fight carried on her increasing frenzied mania proved too much. After a time he was overpowered, for his own energy seemed to be fading while Pax's was seemingly unlimited, flowing forth from an ethereal source.

Her wrath took her from one attack to another seamlessly for over an hour, and she found herself hovering in the air high above him and chucking beams of *prana* down toward him in rapid succession. The heat from the explosions melted the ice around him, making a large watery crater that she hoped would be his grave.

"…And I *don't care…*"

She used her hands to dislodge a frozen fragment of the landscape and send the giant chunks of ice hurtling down into the wounded man.

"…If the fucking penguins…"

Concentrating mildly and twisting her fingers, she broke the top off a mountain and retreated upwards so that she would have room to crush it down on Thornton repeatedly.

"…*Hate* the renovations!"

Finding this weapon satisfactory, she slammed the same heavy mountaintop down on him again and again. Her power swept her into delirium as she continued fighting frantically. It was like this, with Pax in this blind fury, that their fathers found them.

"I *told* her to wait until lunchtime," remarked Vincent, who did care enough about his son's life enough to show up after all. "This is worse than before."

Raymond had simply stared in open-eyed disbelief, not even recognizing his daughter. The rich red glow around her concealed her face and body from view, and her features were transformed with madness. "Is that really Paxie? What's gotten into her?"

Vincent's eyes shifted to the left as they observed Raymond callously. "Why don't you go back to India and leave *me* to be the primary father figure for the girl: what's the worst that could happen? She could turn out like this?"

Frowning, Raymond examined his daughter's life force. "She isn't like this. Her *prana* is all fragmented." The dark haired man stared with uncomprehending wide eyes as his only daughter tried her best to obliterate Thornton with thousands of tons of ice and rock. Having noticed the intensity of the fight while meditating in India, he had flown toward the crisis as fast as possible, and Vincent had done the same. He knew Pax had a temper and every time she got herself into a fight it was not necessarily an emergency… but *this* time, Raymond's fatherly instinct made him feel he was needed. What concerned him most about the sight was the change in his daughter's appearance.

"Where's all her hair?" Raymond asked. "I thought Paxie loved having long…"

"You idiot! Your daughter is killing my son and you want to talk about her haircut?" Vincent turned to the side and spat. "For the record, I've been telling her to cut her hair for years. Long hair just gets in a warrior's way and…"

Raymond growled. "What happened, Vince?"

Vincent folded his arms as though he were casually watching a display of fireworks. "She caught my son growing familiar with another woman's genitals. She fried the woman and then let loose on Thornton. Asher and I stopped her before any serious harm could be done, mainly to keep anyone at the compound from seeing them use their powers. Out here it's not much of an issue that anyone might see."

"No," said Raymond, processing the information and shaking his head. "Are you trying to tell me that Pax killed someone? That's impossible. In the first place,

Thorn would never do that to Pax. He loves her. There must be some mistake."

"You've been in India for a really long time."

Deciding that the battle had come to a critical point, Vincent moved forward to interrupt and terminate the fight. It was a dark violence which had overcome Pax and allowed her to conquer a fighter who was more experienced and much stronger than she. Her energy had always been greatly tied to her emotions, and Thornton had certainly evoked the wrong ones. It wasn't until she had her father's arms protectively around her did the fires within subside into tranquility.

Although Raymond's arms were powerful, he didn't restrain her forcefully as Thornton had done to try to *make* her listen to his sorry excuses. Instead, Raymond held her gently, with understanding and love, in the tender way that only a father can hold his child. Even when that child has murder in her eyes. This peaceful, caring approach melted through her wrath and exposed her hurt.

She collapsed against Raymond sobbing. She clung to him tightly, inwardly begging to be taken back in time to when she was a little girl and crying in her father's arms wasn't humiliating. And to cry in front of Vincent! She begged to be taken back in time to before she'd fallen in love with Thornton and apparently kissed goodbye to her sanity. Maybe she could manage to travel back… but no, it was too difficult. Since she couldn't be taken back in time, she would have to settle for being taken home. *Will you come home with me, papa? Just for a little while?*

I will, Paxie. But you can't keep your old man in the dark.

I need to know what's going on with you. Promise you'll tell me?

Yes, papa… everything's just gone horribly wrong.

After using his mind to dig his son out of the debris, Vincent sighed. He tossed the trashed boy over his shoulder for the second time that month, and bid goodbye to the Burnsons. After a moment's hesitation he turned around to address Pax directly.

"A word of advice, girl. Thorn is my son I am well aware of his flaws. He wronged you, and you have every right to be infuriated. That is righteous deva rage." Vincent's brow creased as he continued. "You can't keep letting this anger consume you. I've been down that path and it doesn't end well. He is not worth your time, energy, or suffering. Find a stronger and more honorable warrior to be your mate."

Pax and Raymond looked at Vincent in speechless surprise. It was rare to see him exhibiting such concern. Rarer still to see him belittle his own offspring in favor of a Burnson. Vincent turned to fly away but Raymond shouted to stop him.

"Vince!" Raymond yelled. "You're wrong. Thorn is a good man, I know he is! He may be misguided at times, and he may screw up… but we all do. I'm sure that there's a reasonable explanation for these unpleasant incidents."

"I know my son better than you do. I can give you the reasonable explanation: he is, quite simply, what you humans call a 'dickwad.'"

Pax felt a small laugh bubble up in her throat, which was still rather sore from screaming. She felt suddenly very blessed to have two such men as her father and Vincent in her life. She realized that part of the pain in losing Thornton had been losing the hope of officially belonging to his amazing family. It had been a treasured dream of hers to someday call his parents and sister in-laws. Now she realized that she hadn't lost them. She still could sit with the Kalgrens at the breakfast table on any given day, just like she had earlier that morning. They always had been and always would be her family, regardless of her connection to Thornton. This thought gave her great strength.

"I will take your words to heart, Vince," said Pax, releasing her father and wiping the blood and tears from her face in attempt at dignity before the Prince of Devas. "Thank you for your advice. Could you please give Thorn a message for me when he wakes up? Tell him we already had a thumbtack on Antarctica anyway."

Chapter 11: What Raymond Knew

Pax had passed out from exhaustion somewhere between Panama and Belize.

Now Raymond, having carefully removed the torn pieces of fabric which had clung to her body, gently swabbed the bruises with antiseptic. He had carried her home to the family manor in Burnson Grove. It was a quiet house tucked away in a secluded clearing in the middle of a massive redwood forest. His small mother stood in the doorframe, with her fingers interlocked near her lips in a prayerful position.

"She was using Ruby Form?" Amelia Burnson asked with a furrowed brow. "Good heavens. She swore she wouldn't..."

"It was like she was possessed. I've never seen her like that," Raymond admitted. "Has she seemed troubled? Did you try speaking with her?"

"Honey, I haven't seen Pax in over a month. She has a condo in the city where she stays most of the time with Thorn. Either there or at the Kalgren Compound. She did come home really upset a while ago... but before I could find out what was wrong, she took off." Amelia pulled her lips into a thin line as she stared at her son. "I knew something was wrong when I found all her hair in the trash—I knew it was serious, but what could I do? I don't have your father's talents—I'm just a regular woman. I tried calling but she wouldn't answer her phone."

"I'm sorry. I should have been here." Raymond

closed his eyes and shook his head.

"Is she going to be okay?" Amelia asked, her eyes quickly scanning the comatose girl on the bed.

"Pax is made of tough stuff, mom. A few scrapes and bruises could never break a Burnson."

"Oh, Ray," Amelia said, turning around swiftly so that her son could not see the emotion on her face. He still heard it in her wavering voice. "Couldn't you have come home to visit without someone needing to be mortally wounded?"

"I can't stand being in this house," Raymond said quietly. "It reminds me too much of her."

"It's been over ten years."

"It feels like just yesterday. How can I stay in the Grove, knowing this is where Bridget lived and died?"

"I have the same pain of loss for your father," Amelia said, her back still turned. "But did it ever stop me from taking care of you and your brother? Sakra knows I still take care of Ash even though he's 37. Pax may act tough and independent, but she *needs* us. Specifically, she needs you. You're her father, and you're the son of a deva. She needs to be closer to her roots than her human grandmother can provide."

"But Ash is…"

"…a pathetic replacement for you," Amelia finished, leaving the doorway. "I'm going to prepare dinner."

As Amelia's footsteps creaked on the old stairs, Raymond turned to gaze at his daughter. "I thought things were fine, Paxie. I wish you would have told me before it got to this point." He sighed. "I know I've been distant in many ways. It's my fault that you feel you can't talk to me… but you're still my little girl."

* * *

Amara glanced up at the imposing old house as she parked in the driveway of Burnson Grove. The isolated Victorian mansion contrasted sharply with the modern style and congested urban setting of the Kalgren Compound. She used to love this house and look forward to tasting Grandma Amelia's cooking when she visited with her mother. Now, she could not help hating the beautiful building a little because of its association with Asher. She had called ahead, and she knew that he was not at home, but she still felt queasy as she pushed open her car door and took a deep breath.

Shaking out her hands and shoulders, and leaning her head back to arrange her layered blonde hair, she marched forward to climb the steps. She pressed her French-manicured index finger down on the doorbell. Hearing no response in a few seconds, she pressed it again.

Raymond answered the door a moment later, and quickly ushered her inside. "Thanks for coming over, Amara."

"Is she okay?" The blonde woman played with the hem of her blouse anxiously.

"She's going to be fine," Raymond said with a reassuring smile. "What about your brother?"

"He's awful. He looks like a train hit him, followed by a plane, and then a steamroller."

"He probably would have been better off if they had."

Amara sighed, reaching up to fiddle with her earrings. "It hurts me to see things like this between them. Thanksgiving and Christmas were really lovely—it's too bad you missed it. Just a few months ago, we were all really happy."

"I know," Raymond said, moving over to the sofa. He lowered himself slowly, and allowed his eyes to settle on a random point on the wall. He stared at it thoughtfully for several moments. "It was only about three months ago that Thorn came to speak to me."

Amara glanced at the wall to see if there was something of interest there. Seeing nothing, she turned back to Pax's father. "He visited you in India? What did my doofus brother want? Raymond?"

Raymond looked at her in surprise. He had drifted off into his own world and had almost forgotten Amara's presence. "Yes. I probably shouldn't be sharing this information, as obviously things didn't go as planned. Thorn asked for my daughter's hand in marriage."

"What?" Amara shrieked, stumbling backwards as if she had been struck. "You've got to be kidding!"

"He was on business in the area. He came to visit me at Sakra's Point and he spent the day training and meditating with me. I spent the day teasing him about how weak he'd gotten from sitting behind a desk all day." Raymond shook his head, looking up at Amara with confusion. "Finally, at the end of the day he revealed the real reason he had come. He showed me the ring—he'd had it custom made for Pax. He told me he intended to do it sometime before her twenty-seventh birthday. He was just waiting for the right moment."

"I can't believe that," Amara said. She had reached out to place her palm against the nearest piece of furniture for support. "My brother really asked you… I didn't know!"

"He didn't tell anyone except for me," Raymond said with a weak smile. "He said he wanted for it to be a surprise."

"Then how could he *do* this to her?" Amara asked, her voice rising in volume.

"I don't know, Amara. But I do know that he was serious about Pax, and he has always been serious about her. Hell, I trusted him to babysit her when…" Raymond hesitated, returning his eyes to the wall. "When Bridget and I needed a date night away from our screaming, troublemaking toddler, Thorn was the one person I trusted to keep Pax from burning our house down. Literally. I trusted him more than my own brother—and I still do! He loves Pax just as much as I loved my wife, and I can see it in his eyes…"

"Raymond, you have no clue what you're saying. You haven't been around. You haven't seen…"

"I don't need to see your little squabbles to know the truth of the matter. Something is *wrong* here, Amara. Possibly supernaturally wrong. I would appreciate it if you spoke to your brother and tried to find out exactly what happened, and exactly why he did whatever Pax thinks he did."

"She doesn't *think* he did it, she *saw* him!" Amara moved forward in frustration. She was gesturing wildly to emphasize her every word. "I *cannot* believe you're defending Thorn in this! If my angelic brother does something wrong, why must it mean there is some kind of evil influencing him?"

"I just believe that..."

"Raymond, I don't want to talk about Thorn anymore. I'm not responsible for my brother's actions. In fact, after what he has done I would like to disown him. I'm here to see Paxie."

Raymond nodded numbly, and continued staring at the wall. "She's upstairs."

Amara turned to leave the room, and immediately saw that in the adjacent corridor there was a family portrait. The beautiful actress Bridget Burnson was smiling a true Hollywood smile as she held her young daughter and stood proudly beside her handsome husband. Amara turned back to see Raymond still staring in an almost catatonic state—he had been looking directly *through* the wall. The flesh-and-blood man looked sad and broken; he was nothing like the animated fellow in the briarwood frame. Amara's grim expression softened as she was suffused with guilt for being upset with Raymond.

"I'm sorry," Amara said to her friend's father. "I just don't think that anything I say to my brother will help this situation. Please don't worry about Paxie. She has an amazing father—she hardly has any use for a husband. Especially one as mediocre as my brother would have been."

"Will you keep an eye on her for me?" Raymond asked quietly.

Amara's lips curled. Her own father had asked the same thing of Pax. "Of course I will, Ray." Suddenly disturbed by how much Raymond looked like his younger brother, she had to turn away. She swallowed her saliva. "In fact, Pax and I were thinking of taking a… vacation of sorts."

"Vacation?"

"Yes. One of those all-inclusive things, you know." Amara declined to mention that the vacation destination was in another dimension. "Just to blow off some steam and get away."

"Sure, Mara. That sounds like a good idea."

It was obvious that Raymond was upset and hardly paying attention. He was so distracted that she probably could have asked for permission for Pax to become a porn star and he would have agreed. This thought plastered a complete smile on her face as she left the room. Heading up the stairs, Amara found it strange that she still remembered which steps to skip because they creaked. How many thousands of times had she climbed these stairs in her life? How many hundreds of times had she climbed them specifically to sneak into Asher's room in the middle of the night?

Shuddering at the memory, she rebelliously stepped on the creaky step before the landing. She did this to demonstrate to herself that she didn't care anymore. Crossing the hallway to Pax's room, she let herself in without knocking and closed the door behind her. Amara observed the dark-haired woman lying unconscious on her old bed, clad only in her beige underclothes and beige bandages. A mischievous glint made its way into the blonde woman's pale blue irises.

Reaching into her purse, Amara fished out what appeared to be a tube of lipstick. Cautiously approaching the sleeping Pax, she pressed a button on the cylinder before holding it above her friend's swollen purplish eyelids. Amara waited for a moment, gently waving the small gadget back and forth over the unconscious woman's face. She smiled when she saw the rows of eyelashes parting to reveal puzzled dark eyes.

Pax batted her friend's hand away from her face before sitting up and clutching her head. She groaned and rubbed her eyes, only to find that her eyes were ultra-sensitive. "What is this? A hangover? How many gallons did I drink?"

"I'm a genius," exclaimed Amara, flipping the cylindrical device off. "No drinking, silly. You were fighting with my brother. Maybe more than fighting considering you're just in your bra and panties. Cute matching set, by the way."

Pax's hands moved over her body and she glanced down to assess the multitude of bruises and scrapes. *Did I...? No.* She remembered the morning's events and cringed. "Thorn said he had something he wanted to tell me, but then… ah, forget it. What's that in your hand?"

"This is my newest invention!" Amara said proudly. "It releases constant waves of a synthetic stimulant which causes your body to produce certain hormones. When I noticed the guys using energy and warmth to seduce women, it gave me an idea—what if I made a device which specifically targeted receptors in the brain? So I did some research, and came up with this gadget which could emulate the sensations of…"

"It looks like a tube of lipstick."

"I wanted it to be portable so we could take it on our dates. Speaking of which, we have a date with Ash in a few hours and you need to get yourself healed up."

"Why?" Pax had returned her face to her pillow,

adding to the brownish bloodstains which marred the white fabric. "Do I have to?"

"Yes. You promised," Amara said with a pout. "I really want to experiment with my new toy. It should make us give off pheromones as if we're ovulating, which is supposed to be subliminally irresistible to a…"

"I don't feel very fertile right now," Pax mumbled.

"Aw, come on! In preliminary tests my simulator heightens oxytocin (the 'cuddle hormone') along with vasopressin and some other stuff—I have no clue what they all do, but I'm hoping they do good, sexy things."

"So what effect do you think it will it have on the guys?"

"It should… well, I'm not sure *exactly*. The idea is that it will cause their bodies to physiologically respond in a way that makes them feel as though they are madly in love with Para. It's my version of revenge for their energy tricks, with an effective scientific twist. I'm not even sure whether to call it the 'simulator' since it emits synthetic hormones, or the 'stimulator' since that's what it does to the body."

"You're crazy," said Pax, opening one bruised eye, "but it could be fun. Let's give it a shot."

"It works at least in a general way, trust me. I am *such* a genius. Do you think that if I gave the prototype to my mom and brother, they would consider selling it? I could make a fortune from this invention if it works."

"You really are Rose's daughter. Capitalism is in your blood." Pax's lips stretched in a small sardonic smile. "Just don't go telling your brother all our secrets yet."

"Good point. Well, enough about my job. I know

it bores you." Amara frowned, placing her hands on her hips. "Pax Burnson! You get a vial of Sakra's water right now and heal that face of yours. Para is *not* going on a date with Asher looking like a trailer park whore!"

Pax recoiled from the insult and reached up to run her hands over her face. "Is it really that bad?"

"Worse! It looks like your abusive drunk husband just got bailed out of prison, and he took a baseball bat to your nose," scolded Amara. When she saw that this description had coaxed a smile out of her friend, she relaxed. "Fix yourself up. I'll be downstairs in the car waiting."

"Yes, ma'am." Pax tossed the covers off her legs and stood up, moving to the mirror to check out the damage. She groaned as she fingered a gash on her temple. *She wasn't kidding about the baseball bat. 'Crowbar' might have been more accurate. Definitely not sexy.*

"Were you thinking something about a crowbar?" Amara asked, narrowing her eyes. "Or was that just me imagining your face getting pummeled with various weapons?"

Pax chuckled. "Go downstairs! I'll be ready in a sec." She began to rummage through her drawers for clothing.

"Okay, Paxie. See you soon! Don't forget to bring some naughty clothes!" said Amara, opening the door and turning to leave the room.

She ran smack into what felt like a solid wall.

Amara cursed, putting a hand out to steady herself. "I'm so sorry, Ray…"

She stopped mid-word because her hand and eyes had settled upon the ultra-soft deep burgundy cashmere of a sweater she remembered buying. It had cost $149.99. Instantly, the strong-yet-gentle hands on her waist which had steadied her from falling unleashed an attack of panic inside her.

Maybe he gave Raymond the sweater? Yes, of course, that explains it… and Raymond must be wearing his cologne too. Amara didn't think to sense for his energy as she slowly, fearfully moved her face upwards. It wasn't Raymond.

"Hi," he said softly.

Her stomach exploded into terror and dread. *Hi? Hi! How do guys do that? How do they have the ability to see their old lover and not care? And act cool and casual like everything's fine?*

He was gazing down at her with familiar warm chocolate eyes. Were his fingers tightening around her waist? Was he inhaling her scent? *Alright. Maybe not so casual. Maybe he's just reacting to the effects of the stimulator... simulator. At least my invention works… but I have to get out of here.*

Amara ripped herself away from him. She fought the urge to grasp the wall for support as she straightened and walked away from him wordlessly.

"Amara?" he asked. There was a note of surprise in his voice at her cold treatment of him. Why did he expect more?

She paused, turning to throw a callous and appraising glance over her shoulder. Asher's face looked… hurt? She never could stand to see him hurt… maybe she *should* say hi.

Her lips parted slightly, as though she intended to speak… but no sound was emitted. *If I do say something, it had better be meaningful and epic and… to hell with it.* Amara closed her lips. She turned back around abruptly, and marched determinedly down the stairs. *I can't fuck you up like Pax did to Thorn. But even if I could, I wouldn't. What's the point? It's unsatisfying. Meaningless physical violence. What I want is to fuck you over.*

She had a date to prepare for.

Asher stared after her retreating form in silence for a moment. He then shook his head to clear his thoughts. Amara had every right to ignore him like that, and to be as insensitive as she wished. He'd left her in the worst possible way.

Pushing those thoughts out of his mind, he extended his hand to push the door to Pax's room open. He winced at the sight which greeted him.

"Eek! Pax, you're naked!"

Pax, who had been in the process of pulling a t-shirt over her head, froze. She still had the t-shirt wrapped around her arms and head, and was still clad only in her underwear below that.

"Ever heard of knocking, Uncle Asshole?" she mumbled from under the fabric as she blushed and struggled to pull it down over herself without ripping it. She inwardly wondered why she was blushing at a family member seeing her almost-nude, but then again… things had changed, and she did kind-of have a date with this family member in a few hours.

"Sorry, cupcake. Whoa! Why are you so bruised up? You're bleeding from everywhere!"

"Uh. Shouldn't you have commented on the injuries before the nudity?" The shirt had finally been pulled down and it revealed Pax's piercing glare of death.

Asher's hands went up in a gesture of surrender and he paled, "I'm sorry, Paxie. I'm a guy, and I saw boobs and went into shock. I still have a hard time remembering that you own a pair… Yikes!"

Asher ducked as a small piece of furniture went flying his way. "Pax! I'm just kidding. What happened to you?"

"This morning, your good friend Thornton Kalgren tried to have… *a conversation* with me."

"I always told that guy he shouldn't mess with you. After all, you were named after the goddess of peace…"

Pax sighed at her uncle's private joke for her. It was the same silly one he'd been telling her since she'd been old enough to smack him. She pulled on a pair of jeans as he finished the worn-out joke.

"…and it was sarcasm."

"That still hasn't become funny, Uncle Ash," she said, pushing past him. "Now if you'll excuse me, I have to fix my face and book a vacation."

"Paxie, don't want to hang out with your old uncle? Don't even have a few minutes to catch up?" he asked her retreating form. She turned back briefly. She felt a wave of sadness at the broken relationship, for when she looked at Asher she felt none of that innocent childish love that made her want to hug him endlessly and beg him for ice-cream. No, she felt mostly anger tinged with disappointment and disillusionment. One of her fairytale heroes had turned out to be a villain.

"Not for you," she answered. "Not anymore. Maybe someday if I can look at you again without feeling upset about what you did to Mara."

Asher remained silent as he watched her walk

away.

*　　*　　*

With a duffle bag hung over her shoulder, Pax made her way to the library. She moved to the hollow book where she knew the vials of Sakra's water were kept. When she reached up to remove it from the shelf, she heard a throat being cleared. Turning, Pax saw her father standing in the doorway.

"Papa. I only need a few drops," she told him, feeling like a guilty child who had been caught stealing.

"You don't need any drops. Sit down and give me your hands."

"You learned how to heal?" she asked as she followed his instructions and moved to a sofa.

"Yes." He sat across from her, and took both of her hands in his. "Sakra taught me some basic healing along with many other techniques. You'd be surprised what you can pick up living as a monk for a decade."

Pax closed her eyes as she felt her father's strong hands tighten around her palms. A cooling sensation swept over her body, easily erasing all the toxins and inflammation. It was the purest wind and freshest summer rain all rolled up into one revitalizing touch. It reminded Pax of being healed by Sakra himself long ago—she smiled, remembering how the loving energy seemed to have healed her soul as well. The feeling of love was even more powerful when coming from her father. Pax opened her eyes and was surprised when she saw her own bruises and gashes appearing on Raymond's face.

"Papa!" she said, pulling her hands away frantically. "You didn't say you would be transferring my injuries to *you!*"

"I heal faster than you," he said as he fingered the new wounds on his face. "Unfortunately, I can't heal as Sakra does without there being a price. This is the price."

Pax felt guilt and horror replace the sensation of weightlessness. "If I had known I would have never…"

"Hush. It's a father's duty to take on the pain of his daughter," Raymond said with a smile. He reached out and ruffled her hair as if she were ten years old. "I can't get over the new 'do. Do you want to talk about what happened, Paxie?"

"No," she said softly. She rose to her feet. "Amara's waiting in the car. I should probably go."

Raymond cleared his throat. "I called your work to tell them that you might not be coming in for a few days because you were injured. They told me you hadn't been to the hospital in months."

"Yes, papa." Pax felt her guilt increase and she rubbed her upper arms idly. "I'm sorry. In my defense, I haven't really been 'working' there—just volunteering. As you know, mom left with me a pretty substantial inheritance and I don't really need money."

"So you have chosen to waste your days away doing what exactly? You're certainly not helping people anymore. In fact, it looks like you're doing precisely the opposite of what your grandma raised you to do. The opposite of what it means to be a Burnson. Have you considered Grandma Amelia's feelings in all this?"

Pax released a gigantic gush of air from her lungs.

Raymond knew that familial duty was her soft spot, and he was striking it hard. "Papa, of course. I just didn't think it would be safe for me to enter an operating room lately. I promise I'll get back to being myself soon…"

"Pax, I'm very disappointed with how vengeful you're becoming."

"So am I," she answered. Feeling remorse congesting her chest worse than pneumonia would have, Pax turned away abruptly. "I really should go. Mara's waiting outside."

"Vincent told me that you killed a woman, Pax."

The dark-haired woman stopped moving towards the door. She suddenly noticed that there was a small fire lit behind the screen of the library hearth. Her face wrinkled with emotion as memories of her mother reading to her by that fireplace assaulted her mind. She closed her eyes tightly. As much as she loved Burnson Grove, she despised it doubly.

"Don't you feel you should be held accountable for your actions, young lady?"

When Pax was able to speak, her voice was a whisper. "What are you talking about, Papa?"

"You don't know?"

Her breaths were shallow. She wanted to know, but she was also afraid to know. Was it possible to hate herself more than she already did? Was it possible to feel more uncomfortable in her own skin? *Para,* she thought to herself weakly. *I need to be Para right now. I need to stay Para, for it seems that this woman named Pax has ruined her life beyond repair. I need a different name and a different face. I need to get away from my family so that I can no longer disappoint them.*

"Vincent said that you caught Thorn with another woman, and you burnt her to a crisp. Is this true, Pax?"

She whirled around, and looked into her father's dark eyes pleadingly. "I don't remember. I think—I think it's true. I blacked out. There's a fuzzy memory, as though it might have been a dream. Sometimes I see my hands doing things, and they're not attached to the rest of me. I have nightmares, and… I don't know what happened. I'm so sorry, Papa. I promised I would never…"

"Shhh, Pax." Raymond said, rising to his feet and crossing the room. He pulled his daughter into a hug. "It's not your fault, darling. In moments of great injustice, the goddess in you will take over. It's easy to be blinded by her wrath--I could have prevented this. If anything, it's more my fault than anything."

"What do you mean?" Pax asked. The world was spinning at this new information, and she was gripping her father's arms tightly. She blinked several times to clear her double vision. "What do you mean?"

"I was the one who chose to prevent you from knowing your power. I decided to forbid you from practicing and gaining control of your abilities—I thought that the amount of goddess in you was small enough that if we ignored its presence, it would remain dormant."

"Dormant?" Pax repeated. "But it was the biggest part of my life, and the attribute which defined me! Grandpa would teach me a little more about my powers every day when he was alive. And mother learned ancient languages to read every book she could find…"

"I know, and I was wrong to try to turn it off like

a switch after it was so deeply ingrained in you. I just saw that Amara didn't care about her powers much, and I figured that you could forget and be a normal girl." Raymond's mouth drew into a fine line. "I just wanted you to have a normal childhood."

"My childhood ended the day I saw my mother's body," Pax answered. "I was forced to be an adult at fourteen, and I tried to do everything you needed me to do. I tried to do everything I could to make you stay, but you left anyway."

"Paxie, do you want to know the real reason I left?" Raymond asked. "I wanted to prevent you from doing exactly what you've done. I never wanted to you to become a killer."

"And I would have been a killer if you had stayed?" she asked incredulously. Tears were springing to her eyes. "If anything I wouldn't have thrown myself at Thorn so hard—I wouldn't have needed him so badly, because I could have looked up to *you* and depended on *you.* That's all I ever wanted, Papa."

"Listen to me, Pax," Raymond said firmly, gripping the girl's shoulders. "I have something important to tell you."

She nodded, unable to speak. She wished for the ground to open up and swallow her whole.

"You need to know exactly how Bridget died."

Pax sighed. "I've heard the cautionary tale. My mother was meddling with forces far greater…"

"No, darling." Raymond released Pax and moved over to the fireplace. He placed his elbow on the mantel tilted his head towards the ground, closing his eyes. "Your mother didn't kill herself trying to use magick.

She was murdered."

Pax stared at the man unblinkingly.

"I didn't tell you because I didn't want you to get angry and do something vindictive. We are devas, and we have a responsibility to be better than that. Nothing can be solved by this whole eye-for-an-eye...."

"What killed her?" Pax asked hoarsely.

"You can *never* take any action on this information."

"What killed her?" Pax demanded again.

Raymond sighed, leaning his forehead against the mantelpiece. "An emissary of the Asura. An energy-sucking creature called a vetala."

"You mean the same type of thing that has been visiting me in my nightmares? You mean the same type of thing I mentioned to you, and you said it was nothing?" Pax's voice was rising as she spoke.

"Paxie..."

"You shouldn't have lied to me. You thought that if I didn't know I would somehow be a better person? Well, I'm sorry to break it to you, Father. You might have let those things kill my grandpa and my mom, but I won't sit quietly and..."

"Pax!" Raymond yelled sternly. "You can't go up against the Asura. There are too many of them, and each one of them is dozens of times stronger than you are. Stronger than I am! The best defense is to stay hidden and go on with your life."

"Wow," Pax muttered as she grabbed her duffle bag and turned to leave. "Well, don't worry about that. I don't have much of a life left to go on with."

"You can walk away from me," her father said in a

tired voice. "That's fine, I understand. I walked away from you when you needed me most. But don't walk away from Thornton."

Pax paused. She pressed her lips together tightly, drawing them between her teeth.

"Please, Pax," Raymond said humbly. "Even if you and I can't fix our broken relationship, I implore you to give Thorn a second chance. I'm not even sure what you saw was real…"

She dug her nails into her palms. If there was anything she wanted to believe, it was this. If there was anything she could not allow herself to believe, it was this. Pax did not understand why it felt like her father was suddenly not on her side.

"Has the boy ever given you a reason to doubt him?" Raymond asked.

"No," Pax said in a voice that was barely audible.

"There are many people out there who would seek to manipulate one as powerful as you are," Raymond said. "What you saw—everything you see from now on. You must take special care to make sure it's real before taking action."

"It was real," Pax said, "but why would you believe the word of a murderess? I love you, Papa, but I need to go."

Feeling like the old Burnson house was suffocating her, Pax ran from the room. She was at Amara's side in under a second.

"There you are, slowpoke!" The blonde woman chucked her car keys at her friend and headed for the passenger side.

Pax swallowed as she caught the jangling metal

pieces. "Mara… can you drive today?"

Amara's brow instantly creased. "Whoa. Okay, what's eating you up, girlfriend?"

"I don't want to talk about it." Pax lightly tossed the keys back at her friend with an underhanded swing. She suddenly felt the need to overcompensate her every motion, and be as gentle and careful as possible.

"You might as well spill. I'm your partner in crime, remember?"

Pax climbed into the passenger seat and waited for the car's wheels to begin turning before she spoke. When she was in a moving vehicle, she always felt a little bit safer. "Apparently, I killed the woman I saw your brother with."

"Karina Allbright?"

Pax's head snapped around to look at Amara. "You knew her name? Why did you say that! I don't want to know her name!"

"Relax. I did some research on her. She was the head of a rival company and she recently disappeared. No body was found, and now I know why."

"God," Pax murmured, resting her head against the back of the seat. "I never thought it was possible to forget my own actions. Did I really kill her? I must have. Good Sakra..."

"When you can disintegrate someone with a thought, it's easy for murder to be little more than a… passing thought." Amara chuckled at her little joke, and seeing her friend's glare, cleared her throat. "Sorry, but I can't say I'm mourning the chick. I had actually put in a call with Layla Solyst, our good friend in law enforcement—if Karina Allbright lived, I was going to ruin her life the good old-fashioned legal way. Fabricate crimes and put her behind bars for a while in a maximum security prison."

"Really?" Pax asked. "You were going to do that for me… and Layla agreed to help?"

"No one messes with my best friend," Amara said in a grave tone.

Pax smiled weakly. "Mara, I don't know if this is possible… but do you think you can work on a way for us to stay joined as Para for longer than thirty minutes?"

"I thought you'd never ask!" Amara answered. "Already on it. I can bring the science, but I'm going to need you to investigate the old books. I can't read those old languages, and I don't even know how to use magick to translate them."

"I'll work on it," Pax said. "But I don't think there's any magick that can join two bodies forever."

"Then we'll create a way," Amara said. She glanced at the Burnson home in her rearview mirror, and thought she saw the movement in the curtains of Asher's bedroom window. "Frankly, I'm sick of being myself too."

Chapter 12: Sidekick and Housewife

When Rose heard about the day's events she had grabbed Thornton by the ear and yanked him out of bed. "I don't care how badly hurt you are!" she had said, wagging a finger at him sternly. "You're not getting to skip work because of it."

Now Thornton stared at the paperwork before him, his head throbbing painfully and his eyesight blurred. It wasn't so much the physical pain as the humiliation of defeat which dizzied him—and not just the physical defeat.

Where is that damned stapler? Thornton was throwing open every one of the drawers in his desk and rummaging madly through them. When he found the stapler, he realized that he did not have all the files he required. Cursing, he stood up and walked over to his filing cabinet and began to rummage wildly. His fingers touched an object which made him pause. A deep frown transformed his features.

His desk phone rang and snapped him out of his stupor. He moved over to the desk in an instant and jammed his finger down on the phone, causing the plastic to crack.

"Thornton Kalgren speaking."

"Hey, man. Have you set up your date with the sexy doctor yet?"

"Date? She hates me and tried to kill me, why would she date me again?"

"Kill...?" Asher's familiar voice was confused.

“I'm not talking about Pax. I meant Medea.”

"Oh. No, I haven't."

"Great! Well, I hope you don't mind if I go first."

"Go ahead."

"By the way, bro… what did you do to my niece? I saw her naked earlier and she was bruised from head to toe."

"Why the *hell* were you looking at her when she was naked?"

“Relax… whoa, what are you, jealous? It was an accident; I just walked in on her like that. Oh, Amara was there too.”

"Was she naked as well?" asked Thornton in confusion. “Er… is there something between the girls? Is that why Pax won’t give me the time of day? Are they experimenting with being lesbians? Because that won’t last.”

“What! No. Amara had her clothes on. Lesbians? You're kidding right?”

"Well, they are practically living together these days…"

There was an awkward silence on the line.

“Anyway," said Asher, clearing his throat, “about Medea. I'm thinking of taking her to the beach. She said she likes beaches when I asked her about her fantasies, so I figured why not? Plus I'll get to see her in a bikini.”

“Good plan. Better than what I had in mind.”

“I know. So I just wanted to warn you, she is probably going to fall madly in love and lust with me and not even bother going out with you.”

Thornton frowned, rubbing his aching brows with his thumb and forefinger. “Yeah, you’re probably right.

I'm not that great with women."

"Huh? You were all gung-ho for this little tournament yesterday. Where'd your competitive spirit go?"

"I think I left it in Antarctica."

"What?"

"Nothing. Never mind. Yeah, Ash. I'll take her on a date too, and we'll see who she chooses. I'll do my best to impress her."

"Cheer up, bro! It'll be fun. Just like old times. We'll even make a bet out of it."

"Yeah. Sure."

* * *

Asher stood barefoot in the sand, gazing out at the horizon as his music player pumped lyrics into his ears. His date was late, but he didn't really notice. His mind was elsewhere. He kept glancing to the north, his eyes following the gently curving shoreline. His mind continued to follow the shore far beyond the point where it disappeared from view. He saw the great cliffs which would swell the landscape in about fifty miles, he saw the aerial view of well-maintained gardens and forest, and he saw the scattering of unique, breathtaking mansions. He swallowed back a lump in his throat as a memory came rushing back to him, provoked by the tune serenading him from his earphones.

He held an information brochure and was scanning through the pictures casually while following her through the massive rooms.

She turned to him, pale blue eyes alight with excitement. "What do you think, Ash?"

A few weeks before she had signed a solid contract for her first invention, and even though she had made the deal under Kalgren Tech, she had dealt with every aspect of it herself. As all patents were in her name, she had received a juicy check and would continue to receive numerous papers with impressive numbers on them.

"Well, it's a lovely home. In a lovely neighborhood," said Asher, slipping his arm around Amara's waist and looking at the real estate agent squarely, "but are there schools nearby? My fiancée and I want to have children. Soon."

"Ah... I think so, sir," said the real estate agent as he nervously searched the map.

Beside him, Amara had buried her face into Asher's shoulder to conceal her giggles at his playful lying. Whenever she reacted like this, it just egged him on. He couldn't help continuing.

"Well, it's important. We're going to start working on it as soon as we buy the house, so I need to know if this is going to be the right neighborhood in which to raise our... eight kids once they're born. We might have one in the oven already, right sweetie?"

Asher affectionately patted Amara's stomach and she promptly paled, then blushed, and then began to cough violently to conceal her laughter. She snaked her fingers around Asher and pinched his butt hard to let him know that he was going too far. His ridiculous joke would probably be in the news the next morning with the way gossip spread about the Kalgrens.

The poor real estate agent had dropped his glasses on the countertop in surprise and was now fumbling for them madly. He had been showing Amara and Asher around for most of the day and Asher had been doing his best to make him as uncomfortable as possible.

The two had enjoyed pretending to be a couple long before

they had actually considered the idea of being together. Asher would defend Amara from the gold-digging, lecherous hounds that seemed to be stalking her at every corner by assuming the role of the big strong boyfriend. Perhaps it had been their play-acting which had led so easily into reality. Now they were play-acting that they were married or engaged whenever they went out shopping or anywhere they could make a silly spectacle. Would they someday turn that into reality too?

"Can you just give me a few minutes to look at it again?" Amara had asked the realtor.

"Of course, Miss Kalgren! Take as long as you'd like. I'll be out in the car."

Amara had walked from room to room as if in a daze. She appraised the crown moldings on the ceilings and ran her fingers over the dark marble countertops. She glanced out at the ocean view from each room. She stood over the bathroom sinks and tried to imagine herself brushing her teeth, applying makeup, and generally living in the home. It was a huge step. She had never lived away from her parents, and wasn't even really sure that she wanted to. Although she loved the idea of owning property and being independent, she loved Vincent and Rose far too much to leave them. Asher followed her, as usual, hypnotized by the sway of her hips. Whenever she'd stop to review an aspect of the home or to mumble pros and cons to herself, he couldn't resist the opportunity to touch her hair and caress her back while she was distracted.

Eventually she found herself in the bedroom, walking around in circles with her hands on her hips and trying to imagine what the room would look like with furniture. "What do you think, Ash?" she asked in a hesitant voice. "Is this me? If I lived here would you come and visit me sometimes?"

"I'm not sure," he had answered mischievously, approaching her. "Let's feel out the vibe of this place."

"Ash!" she'd protested, laughing as he advanced to hastily smash his lips against hers. He lifted her against him and pulled her legs up around him, making her red skirt ride up as he pushed her back against the glass panel which made up the bedroom wall.

"Someone could see!" she'd protested pulling her mouth from his and glancing over her shoulder. There were a few boats out on the water, and anyone with decent eyesight or binoculars would have had a spectacular view of her bare bottom pressed up against the glass.

"Then let's give them something to talk about," he'd said, holding her up against the glass with one hand and fumbling to open his zipper with the other. He moved quickly, and using one finger he yanked her thong down and ripped it off her.

She'd inhaled sharply as he positioned himself at her entrance, raking his swollen member back and forth along her flesh. "Ash…" She hadn't been expecting it, and her body hadn't been fully ready—but when Asher was this close, her blood intuitively began pumping to all the right areas. Her insides grew moist and ready for him almost instantaneously. She gasped as he entered her, closing her eyes and clinging to his shoulders for dear life. He felt too large at first, but her body had quickly adjusted and welcomed him. He'd thrust his full length in and out of her quickly, forcing her body to slam again and again into the cool glass.

Just when he felt her body shuddering and approaching orgasm, he stopped, holding her close and kissing her deeply. "Let's see… where will you put the bed?"

"You dork," she mumbled, entangling her fingers in his dark hair.

He carried her, with her legs still wrapped around him, over to the floor in the center of the room. He laid her down gently before picking up where he'd left off. With her blonde curls spilled out all around her, Amara moaned, her back arching off the ground as she became lost in bliss. Her fingers dug into Asher's neck and shoulders as she braced herself against the pain and pleasure of his glorious lovemaking.

He loved the way that her body shook in his arms when she had an orgasm, and he loved the way she screamed his name. He waited until he felt her release, the tension in her body dissipating into softness, before he allowed his own seed to gush out inside of her. Panting, he held her close for a few moments. He kissed her temple lovingly.

"Guess the house didn't shake too *badly. I approve."*

"I like it," said Amara, breathlessly. "I really like it. The house, I mean."

"Will you let me stay here with you sometimes, Mara?" he'd asked, suddenly shy as he stood up and helped her off the ground. He fixed her disheveled clothing, tugging her skirt back down into place before zipping himself back up.

"Of course," she'd said, looking away to conceal her flushed cheeks. "Isn't that why you came along with me? Because it's important that you like it too… since you'll be staying with me sometimes."

"I thought I came along to see if the walls could handle my powerful thrusting."

"You goof!" she'd scolded him, laughing as she picked up her ripped thong from the floor and shoved it into her purse for safekeeping. It was designer—she'd sew it back together later.

"I don't know why you bother wearing underwear at all," he'd said grinning.

"And I don't understand why you don't!" she'd countered before turning around to glance at the room once more. "That might have been slightly better with a bed."

"Doubtful," he said.

Could I really live here? *She asked him telepathically. Asher approached and hugged her from behind, kissing her neck and gently swaying her from side to side.*

Can you imagine me making love to you here a thousand more times? *He asked her in return.*

"Only a thousand!" she had complained. "I would have thought the son of a demigod had more mileage left in him."

"I do. I'll make love to you all day, every day, until I can't get it up any longer. Or until it falls off."

"That's better." Amara said with a wink. She took a deep breath. "Okay! Let's go purchase this thing."

As the song on his music player finished, Asher's memory faded and he was summoned back to reality by the waves lapping at his toes. *Just how many hundreds of spoken and unspoken promises have I broken?* Asher remembered waking up with a clammy layer of sweat gluing his skin to Amara's in the summer. He remembered the soft fabric of her warm nightgown in the winter, and her small arms draped across his chest. He hadn't known it would be so difficult, so insanely difficult, to sleep alone again. He had taken her proximity and her love for granted. He had not even realized how deeply he'd grown connected to her, and he felt like a fool and a failure needing to live at home with his mother again.

Although Asher loved his mother, Amelia's company did not compare to the casual freedom he had experienced with Amara. He felt lost without her. The number one oversight he had made was underestimating the value of Amara's friendship. The young woman seemed to have been born under a lucky star, and while he was near her he could feel the glow of the spotlight.

Now that there was distance between them, Asher could admit to himself that it wasn't just her name and heritage that made her special. Amara Kalgren would have been the same intelligent, successful woman whether she had been born a Kalgren or not. Asher wondered if he could say the same for her older brother.

As another tune began to play, another melancholy rock ballad, more memories returned to Asher with an unwelcome intensity. He saw his good friend, Thornton. An angry, extremely pissed off Thornton who sat with his head in his hands in his ransacked, blown-up office.

"Are you mad, Ash? I am not *going to apologize! How can that little bitch not trust me? Fuck her! Do you hear me, man? Fuck her! I don't give a rat's ass if I was wrong. I don't give a flying fuck if this ruins everything!"*

"For Sakra's sake, calm down… she saw what she saw and overreacted. Are you telling me you wouldn't have gone nuts if you'd seen her with another man? Seriously, Thorn, get it together. You love Pax, and this isn't you."

"No! Obviously I don't love her or I wouldn't have done this. Who the fuck are you to tell me who I am?" Blue fire seemed to be flashing in Thornton's eyes, but there was also desperation. "I'm not a fucking pussy-whipped weakling like you! If Mara snapped her fingers you'd go running like a fucking golden retriever, wouldn't you?" Thornton whistled and patted his lap, "Here boy! Come get it, Ash. Sex and food! That's all it takes to control a pussy like you."

Asher visibly flinched. "You're way out of line, man… what's wrong with you?"

"What's wrong with me? What the fuck is wrong with you! I'm a descendant of the royal deva bloodline and I'll be damned to

hell if some woman is going to fuck with my head like this! Control me *like this."*

"Thorn…"

"Here!" Thornton used his foot to sift through the embers of what had been his desk. Finding a small, singed velvet box, he chucked it at his friend. "If you want to play these stupid women's games, you go and do it. Take the damned ring and go propose to my sister. Sakra knows I don't need that thing anymore. You go and be a pussy. I'm done."

Thornton had stormed out of the office, and for some reason, Asher did not feel angry at his friend. He felt mostly sad and guilty. He felt as though he'd done something wrong. Asher looked at the small charred box between his thumb and forefinger which Thornton had so rudely flung at his head. Dusting off some cinders, he opened the box and peeked inside at the brilliant diamond. How he would have loved to give something like this to Amara! His eyes immediately narrowed and he closed the box. No. She deserved more than a castaway ring originally intended for his niece. She deserved a ring chosen specially, specifically for her.

She was a Kalgren. She was the princess of devas, and she deserved a ring fit to grace the hand of a princess. Asher was just a poor boy from the forest, living in Amara's magnificent house. He had nothing to give. He could never afford a ring like this! Growing increasingly depressed, he wondered how much had Thornton spent on the piece. Tens of thousands? Hundreds of thousands? Or possibly even millions, knowing how Thornton liked to go all out. Asher gulped. He knew he'd never be able to afford that much. He couldn't afford anything, and had no ambition to do so… Amara deserved someone who could. Someone who gave back at least as much as he took.

Asher felt the weight of his friend's ever-present shadow on him as he stared at the scorched box. He felt helpless. Thornton had always been better than Asher in every way. He'd flaunted his one year of additional age, his greater strength, his endless amount of money, and the fact that he could have any woman he wanted. When Asher had been younger, it hadn't bothered him much. While his father had been alive, he had been too good-natured to notice his friend's competitive condescension. As he'd grown older, he'd found that it did get under his skin more than he'd ever admit to anyone. More than anything, he just wanted Thornton's respect. As time progressed, he felt uncomfortable playing sidekick to an impressive alpha male; he wanted to be a man who could stand on his own feet, but somehow this could never be. Every time he tried, he seemed to land flat on his ass—humiliated and belittled. And now, in this moment of brutal, honest anger, Thornton had revealed that he considered Asher to be the lowest possible form of man. The blonde businessman saw him as a "pussy-whipped weakling." Was he really so worthless?

Sitting for a moment and fingering the box, Asher considered the past few years. What had he done to deserve his friend's condescension? The answer was simple: nothing. He had done nothing, and accomplished nothing. He had devoted himself to making Amara happy, and he had found a simple kind of happiness in just being with her. He didn't know how to do more—although he had inherited divine powers, he had not inherited the empire to go with them. Asher had become something of a house-husband, supporting the brilliant young scientist as she tried to bring life to the mechanisms she envisioned in her mind's eye. He had been obsessed with her imagination and dedication to her job, and enraptured by the playful passion with which she loved him. Life had been perfect.

But now he saw that he had trapped himself in playing second fiddle to yet another Kalgren sibling. He was 37 years old, and little more than a housewife for Amara. Meanwhile, he was sidekick to her brother—the man he had always considered his own brother, and the man who would someday legally become his brother. Unless he stopped it. Asher clenched the box tightly in his hand, feeling it heat up as his passion spread out of his fingers in the form of prana. *He did not wear gloves like his niece, because his father had taught him to have much more control than the young girl possessed. He was supposed to teach his niece all he knew! Asher looked around at the destruction Pax had caused, and felt guilty for neglecting the poor young woman who was his actual blood relative. His* actual *older brother's daughter, whom he should have been protecting from harm. He should have been protecting Pax from herself.*

Ash nodded, making a firm decision. He would not become a slave and helpmate to the Kalgrens, despite how powerful and prominent their family was in the world. The Burnsons were a proud and strong lineage as well—he could find his own path. He would break away from the siblings. Somehow. Asher moved to the cabinet in the corner of the corner-office which had sustained the least amount of damage, and tucked the ring box away behind dozens of files. Someday, when his friend cooled down, he'd probably want it again. Asher had no need of it; would never have any need of it.

As the burning office faded from his mind with a cool ocean breeze, Asher frowned as he stared out at the water. He wondered how many of his decisions were made solely on his own desires. How many were rash and hot-headed, intended just to prove points or to make impressions? Amara had been *his* happiness. She'd had nothing to do with Thornton and his selfish slipups; she'd been his and his alone. They'd existed in their own little world, far away from everyone else, happy on the edge of the ocean. Yes, happy. But had she really been happy with him? Even though he could offer her nothing? No. She couldn't have been. She was accustomed to luxury, and he couldn't even afford to buy her gifts regularly.

But why had she seemed so devastated when he'd left? Had it only been pride, or had she really been as wounded as he felt? Why had she been so cold to him earlier at his mother's house? Had she really loved him, flaws and all? Poverty, low self-esteem, and all? It was impossible.

Asher shook his head to clear the thoughts. Seeing Amara again had simply hurt too much. He did not even know why he was standing here on the beach, trying to appreciate the beauty of what was spread out before him and only seeing the past. Why did he always feel the need to prove his masculinity to Thornton? He wondered if he really wanted Medea or if she just served as the trophy for another competition between the two men. It had gotten to the point that Asher truly had no idea of what he wanted. He just went with the flow, wanting whatever he believed he should want. Whatever Thornton believed a man should want. Doing whatever made a man a man.

Asher felt more sea winds ruffle his hair and was startled when two warm hands slowly slid around his waist. Small, slender arms had encircled him. He felt a warm body, including two soft-but-firm mounds of flesh pressed against his back. His heartbeat quickened.

Mara? This was his first thought as he looked down at those hands, his eyes clouded with emotion. He violently reached up to yank his headphones off.

"Hey, handsome," a familiar voice murmured

against his back.

A few strands of long hair danced over his shoulder in the wind, illuminated and almost translucent in the fading sunlight. *Mara!* He thought again, completely elated. He fully intended to turn around, take her up in his arms and never let her go again. He would beg and plead and cry for her forgiveness. He would do anything.

Just as long as she never looked at him again the way she had that afternoon.

He turned around in her arms, a massive smile on his face—a smile which disappeared as soon as he saw the girl's face. It wasn't Amara. Of course it wasn't! He'd abandoned his love, and he had planned to meet with this woman here and now. Why was he expecting a miracle?

"Were you expecting someone else?" asked Para in surprise. Of course, she had heard his thoughts, and had heard him call Amara's name in his mind.

"No, no. I'm happy to see you, Medea," he said, sighing and offering her his arm to stroll along the beach. "I've just been lost in thought. It's been a long day." Asher still looked out at the waves blindly. *It's been a long few weeks… since I left her,* he added inwardly to himself. *Get a hold of yourself, Ash Burnson. You made your bed, now lie in it. Move on; seduce the woman you intend to seduce for the hell of it.*

Para strolled alongside Asher, glancing at his face curiously as she read his thoughts. She squeezed his hand and stopped their stroll by asking softly, "What's wrong?"

"I… I ran into my ex-girlfriend today," Asher

found himself saying, without intending to. He scowled at himself. *Well, that's not how you seduce a woman. Great job, idiot.*

Actually, sweetie, I ran into you. Para tried to conceal her smile. "What happened? Did you realize you're not over her?"

Over her! Does this girl even know who Amara is? You don't get over someone like Amara Kalgren. You try your best to convince yourself there's another reason to live—and fail miserably. Asher cleared his throat before speaking. "The way she looked at me… I can't describe it. I guess it made me wonder if I'm really a good person."

"Why would you question that?" Para asked, extremely curious to hear his answer.

"My dad was this… war hero, of sorts. Everyone loved him, and he was just the most noble and downright *godly* person you can imagine. I look a lot like him… but the truth is, on the inside, I'm nothing like that. Also, my brother is a *monk*. That's not a metaphor—when his wife died he abandoned society to go to India and become a *monk*. Everyone in my family is so pure and perfect, and I just can't even attempt to fill their shoes much less make my own."

Para sighed. "Do you realize you have been more honest and open with me in the past… one minute and forty seconds than you have been in all the time I have known you?"

Asher shrugged. "I guess it's tough for me to be myself around Thorn sometimes. He brings out the best and the worst in me."

"I know that feeling," she responded quietly. Para reached out on an impulse and gave Asher a small hug in an attempt to comfort him. She rested her cheek against his chest. *Oh, Ash… why haven't you said such things to us? Why did you need to spill your heart out to a complete stranger? Well… he did ask Pax to talk this morning, and she did cruelly brush him off. I'm a bad niece…*

"I hardly know you, Ash Burnson, but I think you're being too hard on yourself. Only a good person has such doubts about their own virtues," said Para softly. *A good person who does terrible things. I hope you feel sorry, and I hope you beat yourself up about it. You ruined the life we had together, you ruined everything… and you broke my heart.*

"You couldn't possibly understand," he said, but he hugged her back, slightly comforted by her words and embrace. "You haven't met my family."

"What about that violent niece of yours?" she suggested. *There's one Burnson you'll agree isn't pure and perfect: me.*

Asher smiled sadly. "Even Paxie. She may be aggressive, but inside she's as good as gold if you get to know her. And I really let her down in the past few years. I could have been this cool uncle, a good role model, but I just… she always seemed more mature and grown-up than me. I never realized she needed my guidance until it was too late."

"I'm sure there's nothing you could have done," Para said.

"No. There was lots." Asher glanced out at the water again. *Pax never would have killed that woman if I had trained her properly.* "But the truth is, she's still better than me. She fights for what she believes in. Me? I don't even know what I believe in. And even if I did know, I don't think I'd be strong enough to fight for it. I'd let it pass me by."

She leaned back and looked at him with surprise. Who knew Asher had so much turmoil beneath that sweet, seemingly unperturbed surface? Maybe she hadn't been as sensitive a girlfriend as she should have been. *But of course you'd fight, Ash. It's who you are; you have fire deva blood in you. You went up against the Asura when my grandpa died and you were just a teenager. You survived the Spiritual Vector Zone, and a whole host of villainous creatures… you've always fought to protect those you love. What has made you feel so insecure?*

Asher gave Para a small smile and took her hand, linking his fingers with hers and beginning to walk along the beach again. He gazed off into the distance, still imagining Amara's house. *All I know is that I was so happy with her. Happier than any man ever has the right to be. And I didn't deserve that. She deserved so much better than a poor, stupid boy from the wilderness. I'm nothing.*

Para stopped walking again, listening to his thoughts, and feeling chills run through her. She stared down at their feet—both of them were barefoot in the sand. *Asher… why do you get to decide what I deserve? I loved you, and I wanted you. Sakra, if only I'd known the way you felt! If only I could have read your mind sooner and eased your every apprehension and doubt…*

"Medea, can I ask for your professional advice on something?" asked Asher awkwardly, staring down at his feet and wiggling his toes in the sand. "It's a weird question, but I think a doctor would know the answer."

"Sure."

"Is it possible for women who weren't lesbians before to suddenly become lesbians? Like if something really bad happened, if they were mistreated by men?"

"Um, why do you ask?" Para chuckled, looking at him curiously to try to figure out where this was going. "That's a tough question. There are both genetic and environmental factors."

"Well, Thornton said that my niece and his sister might be lesbians."

"What!" screeched Para, falling over. She lay sprawled, half in the sand, half in the water. She felt an explosion of giggles consume her, and she couldn't suppress them.

"Medea! Are you okay?" asked Asher, falling to his knees at her side.

"Yes, I just stumbled," she said, between giggles. "I'm so clumsy."

"You have such a lovely laugh," said Asher, smiling and leaning close to her.

He studied Para's face intently, brushing his thumb along the line of her chin. *It doesn't really matter if Amara's turned into a lesbian or not. I ruined everything as permanently as I could manage. Seize the fucking moment, Ash. Here's a beautiful girl, right in front of you. An incredibly beautiful girl. She's not Amara, but whatever. It will piss Thorn off if she chooses me instead of him, and that's worth something at least. It's for the best in the long run. I don't deserve anything more than loneliness.*

Para looked up at Asher frantically, fear dancing in her midnight blue eyes. *No… if you really don't want this, don't do it! Just turn around and forget these damn games, and I will too. We'll just go back to the way it used to be. We'll just be happy together.*

It's finished with Mara forever, thought Asher with

determination. *I did the nastiest, foulest thing thinkable to make sure of it. She hates me; I could feel the ice in her glare. So, let me kiss this woman to solidify that. Let me finally pass that point of no return, where I hate myself so much that I wouldn't even be able to condone begging Amara for forgiveness. I deserve worse than that evil look she gave me. Far worse. Here goes. No return.*

Para leaned backwards, shocked to hear these thoughts. *No! Don't solidify. You mean, you haven't kissed any other women? You haven't slept with a dozen other women? You haven't cheated on me like Thorn did to Pax? But why all the flirting in the clubs? Why, Ash, why?*

"Medea," Asher was saying as he leaned in towards her and cradled her face in his hands. "There's something I've wanted to do since I first saw you. I know we hardly know each other… but for two strangers to kiss on the beach in the sunset is hardly a crime."

God, you look so much like her, he thought as he moved forward and dipped his chin to place his lips against hers. He kissed her gently and probed her lips with his tongue until they became soft and parted. *And you even taste a bit like her, if I just close my eyes and imagine…*

Para wrapped her arms around Asher's neck and she threw her body against his in response to his warm kiss. *Asher, it's me, it's me! Please, let's just forget about all this and just go home. I'll tell you who I am and we can forget about this ridiculous charade…*

Shut up, Amara. Seriously, I'm not going to let you take over Para and screw up our game. Why? Simply because of this: these are Asher's private thoughts we're hearing. He doesn't mean for them to be public, and maybe even he himself will not acknowledge them. Don't forget he's my uncle and I love him too, and I want nothing more than for both of you to be together and happy. But unless *he publicly and* openly *makes an apology to you; unless he comes out with all this, then I won't allow you to be hurt again. I won't allow* you *to be the first to make a move toward him. Does that make sense?*

Yes. Fine.

Let's look on the bright side. At least his rebound woman is you.

Pax, can you save the lecture for a time when we're not *kissing Ash? Seriously, I can't concentrate on a damn thing you're thinking. This is… so… good…*

It's not bad.

Not bad? Like you've had better. My brother is an office nerd and I bet he can't kiss for beans.

Don't even go there! Thorn has magic lips.

Ha! Wait until you see what else Asher can do with his mouth.

Para ripped her justifiably-schizophrenic self away from Asher and moved away, smiling coyly. She was wearing a white summer dress over a crimson red bikini, and she pulled the dress off and tossed it into the sand. She opened her small purse and pulled out two decorative chopsticks which she deftly used to tame her wild hair into a makeshift bun. Before closing her purse, she also discreetly activated her lipstick-looking simulator to see if it would have any discernable effect on Asher. *No time like the present for testing products.* She tied the small purse to her hip with her bikini string.

Para walked into the water, checking the time on her watch. She turned around once the water had reached her thighs and smiled. "Asher, want to know a secret about me?" she teased in a playful voice, cupping the water with her hands and splashing herself.

"What's that, Medea?" he asked, already following her and gazing hungrily at her radiant exposed flesh.

"I'm part-mermaid," she said with a wink, before disappearing under the waves. She swam just under the surface for a few seconds before coming up for air. Asher was already swimming beside her and she laughed.

"There's a little sand bar we can rest on not too far from here. See it?" He pointed while treading water.

"Yep. Race you there!" Para dived under the water again and swam at what she believed was a human speed, but still pretty fast. Asher obviously was trying to do the same. It was a double deception. He let her reach the sand bar just before he did.

"Wow! You really are part-mermaid," he said with a smile, crawling over to where she lay on the sand and positioning himself next to her.

She grinned, squeezing the water out of her hair. Although she was a strong swimmer, the sea was not her element in the least. It terrified her, and she would sooner dive into a burning blaze than into a seemingly-tranquil lake. "I bet you let me win," she teased, running her finger over his dripping wet chest.

Asher couldn't resist gazing down at her body. *Sakra, this woman is incredible. Just looking at her gets me so hard. She must work out, because that's some serious muscle! Her body actually reminds me so much of Pax's… I want to rip off that bikini-top and replace it with my mouth. Whoa! Weird sequence of thoughts, Ash. It's just that Pax was the last female I saw unclothed, and that's why I must be comparing her body to Medea's body. What delicious breasts. Her nipples are erect, they're just begging for my attention… and once I get her wet enough, I can make my way between her legs. Slowly, Asher. Slowly.*

While Asher struggled with his thoughts of desire, Para couldn't help blushing as she listened in on them. *What kind of asinine thoughts go through a man's brain? Sakra. He recognized my body as his niece's and he* still *wants to eat me out! Ewww… ohhhh. That is nice. I wonder if the simulator's working?*

Asher had begun to kiss and nibble on her neck and collarbone, working his way down to the exposed flesh of her breasts. He used his thumbs to massage circles around her nipples through the triangular pieces of fabric that formed her bikini. She gasped as he used his finger to shift her bikini top aside, and promptly captured her left nipple in his mouth. He began to suck and nibble ravenously on her breast, and Para felt the sensations spread through her deliciously. She couldn't resist moaning and writhing under his hot tongue.

She had thought that knowing what he was about to do would make her less affected, but it was not so. It only added to the anticipation. Perhaps the most exciting part of all this was that he didn't know who she was. Para's fingers found their way into Asher's hair and she found herself gripping his scalp a bit too forcefully as her body ached with pleasure. She felt herself losing control over suppressing her life force as she relaxed—she fought to regain focus so that her energy didn't spike upward dangerously. A red, fiery glow suddenly surrounding her would be too suspicious. She tried to relax her grip on his hair.

"God, Ash…" she found herself gasping as he

moved his lips to her other breast, leaving the other one exposed and so sensitive that even the cool breeze stimulated it tantalizingly. He moved his hand down to her stomach. He placed the palm of his hand flat against her abdomen, directly over her womb, and released a small but warm river of pure energy into her body. As his life force mingled with her own and spread through the channels around the organs responsible for reproduction she felt her body reacting independently—she felt her muscles constricting in a powerful spontaneous orgasm.

During the moment of her release she almost forgot to suppress her energy, but she was barely able to maintain control and prevent her body from bursting into flame. Her chest heaved with her deep breaths, and she hoped that Asher hadn't noticed her orgasm—it was a bit embarrassing that she was able to climax so quickly. But then, he was very skilled and had pushed all the right buttons. He had attacked her from the *inside*. She saw him smirking, and she knew that he knew. He must have felt the muscles in her stomach contract, and he must have noticed the small spike in her *prana*, regardless of how she tried to restrain herself.

And he wasn't even close to being finished. He moved his lips back to kiss hers and slowly slid the hand which rested on her abdomen lower, and lower yet. He cupped his hand over the flesh between her legs, rubbing gently through the thin fabric of her bikini for a moment. She opened her mouth to protest, but he had already begun moving his fingers under her bikini and sliding them along the moist folds of skin there.

He plunged two fingers inside of her at once,

making Para gasp in surprise. He immediately withdrew the fingers, glistening with moisture. He ran them lightly along her stomach and over her breasts before bringing the fingers to his lips and placing them in his mouth.

"You taste too good," he said gruffly, moving his lips down to kiss her mouth again, and enjoying the thought that she might taste herself on him. *Rice pudding with a sprinkle of nutmeg meets crème brûlée. No, vanilla pudding meets lychee jello meets almond ice-cream meets… Amara. Sweet, juicy, tasty Amara. Why can't I stop thinking of Amara? Even at a moment like this? Especially at a moment like this. This girl is driving me crazy. Her smell and her taste… it's all too divine. I want a better taste of her nectar.*

He broke his lips away from hers and began to drag his face down her body, his barely-there stubble grazing against her flesh in a scintillating manner. He moved his face over her bellybutton, and finally he used his shoulders to roughly nudge her legs apart, and push the bikini bottom aside to take in the view of her moist, swollen vulva, and her delectable bottom covered in sand. She was completely turned on and ready for him. He smiled up at her before lowering his face to her body.

Oh, yes. Please, Ash. Please just use those gorgeous lips and suck…

Her watch beeped, bringing her back to reality.

"Wait!" she said, gasping and crawling backwards in the sand before he could make contact with her. There were only seven minutes left in her union.

He frowned, crawling forward to chase after his retreating meal. *The little wench wants to play hard to get now? Now, after I've gotten her dripping wet and she's been moaning like mad?*

"Ash, this is going a bit too fast for me," she forced herself to say, even though she was dying to completely finish what they'd started. Completely. Her cheeks were rosy and her breaths were short and quick.

"Too fast?" he repeated dumbly. "But I've been taking my time to get you warmed up…"

"No!" she said, straightening her bikini over the parts that were exposed. "I don't mean physically. This was just supposed to be a casual get-to-know-you date. We weren't supposed to get so carried away!"

"But now that we know we have chemistry," said Asher, crawling over her and gazing down at her hotly. "Wouldn't it be nice to keep going?"

"Chemistry!" she exclaimed. *It's just the chemistry*. Realizing that all of this must be the effect of her new gadget causing an insane influx of arousal-hormones, Para reached down to her purse to turn it off. Her hand was seized by Asher. The dark-haired man smirked and guided her wrist down to the front of his swimming shorts where his burning-hot manhood spoke to her of his arousal more than his words ever could. There was so much heat being emitted from his member that she didn't have to worry about the heat of her own hands. Wouldn't this burn a human woman? She gulped, and moved her hand over the engorged organ, unable to resist stroking it to feel its size.

"Medea," he whispered, leaning close to her ear. "Wouldn't you like me to put that in you? I promise it will be the best thing you've ever felt in your life."

She then abruptly stopped caressing him and pulled away. The same hand that had been timidly giving him pleasure a second ago suddenly swung into his face and connected in a firm slap. His head swung to the side with the force of the slap, but mainly from surprise. Para had restrained most of the force which she yearned to put into the smack. Her cheeks burned with embarrassment. Mainly because she did want him, very badly. She needed to turn off that damned simulator, now. She could hardly think straight.

"You ought to be ashamed," she said, standing up. She was about to open her purse to find the simulator, but her watch beeped again. Five minutes. That was hardly enough time to swim back to shore and get to a safe distance before her body separated into two.

Asher rubbed his cheek as he stood up, surprised that he had even been able to *feel* the slap of a human. He looked at her angry eyes, her tousled hair, and her trembling body swathed in a thin film of sand and he only felt his arousal grow, and the ache in his groin intensify. He ran a hand through his hair in frustration.

"This was supposed to be innocent," she accused. "I haven't even gone out on my date with Thorn yet. If you were trying to force me to decide that I wanted to see you instead of him, this wasn't the way to do it. All I learned about you today is that you're dominated by sexual impulses."

Para wanted to get away from the situation as dramatically as possible. She had lifted her feet a few inches off the ground and was about to fly away before she remembered that she was not supposed to be a deva and mentally smacked herself. She was too shaken to think! It looked as though Asher was so distraught from sexual aggravation that he hadn't noticed her blunder.

She slowly descended back onto the sand and ran towards the water.

"I don't want to see you ever again, Asher," she said, sending him the exact same disappointed look that Amara had given him earlier that morning before plunging herself into the waves and swimming for shore. She tried to swim at a normal speed while still making sure she'd get away in time for the body-separation, but when she was almost at the shore she felt a strong hand wrap around her ankle and pull her back down. She felt herself being dragged under the water until she was completely submerged. She flailed her arms wildly, splashing in a moment of panic. Para *hated* the water. She turned to view her attacker nervously.

Would she have to fight and display her strength, possibly revealing her identity? Or would she be detained long enough for the merger to wear off, thereby revealing her identity anyway? Time was running out.

Chapter 13: A Stimulating Simulator

Para struggled as she felt herself being tugged down to the seabed. When she felt the sand against her side she rolled onto her back and tried to see through the disturbed and darkening waves of water. Two strong arms descended on either side of her shoulders.

Asher was hovering above her, holding her fast underwater, and staring at her intently. There was a strange lusty look in his eyes which worried Para. She still hadn't turned off the simulator, but she imagined that the effect of its stimulating waves and any released pheromones would be dulled underwater. This was the issue with using a piece of technology that hadn't been beta-tested in all kinds of environments—but Amara had always enjoyed doing her own beta-testing.

Medea, can you hear me? He spoke telepathically.

She didn't want to respond with her mind to reveal that she knew how, so she merely nodded, looking at him with surprise. Asher ran his finger along her cheek, as though memorizing her features.

I'm so sorry for rushing you. I didn't mean to cause you discomfort or anxiety. You know, men and women are really different when it comes to these things.

Para looked at her watch and saw that there were less than two minutes remaining. She put her hand over her mouth as though she were in need of air. Asher gently removed her hand and lowered his face down to kiss her, giving her the air from his own lungs. He then continued to kiss her for several seconds until she broke free and ducked under his arms, swimming for the surface.

She ran toward her discarded clothing on the beach, and he followed her.

"Medea, please give me a chance to make it up to you. I don't know what came over me, but I really have never felt such a lack of control!"

"You are not a gentleman, Asher Burnson!" As she said this, she silently congratulated herself on technology well-built. *Now that's a stimulating simulator.* She picked up her white dress and tugged it down over her body as she turned to run away from the beach. Her body would split apart in only a few seconds, and she needed to get away before Asher learned he had been intimate with his niece and ex-girlfriend.

He blurred in front of her placing his hands on her arms almost obsessively. She glared at him, wondering why he was being so careless with their family secrets and powers.

"Tell me you didn't feel that! You didn't feel more connected and deeply attracted to me than you've ever felt to anyone?" Asher asked, dripping wet and looking absolutely wretched. *I lost Amara forever. I even drove Paxie away! Please let me keep a small portion of this woman's respect. I can't lose Medea too, before I've even had her. What's wrong with me? Why do I have to be such a moron?*

He's trying to use me to replace us, thought Para sadly. Her heart went out to Asher—Pax felt regret for being cold to her uncle, and Amara yearned for her love. *Don't worry, Ash. Things will be right again soon. Oh, great. Wasn't the whole point of all this to make him suffer? Now that he is suffering I can't bear it! I suppose he has been suffering all along. I just didn't know. And I suppose there's no way to make someone you love suffer without hurting yourself in the process.*

The watch began beeping frantically. One minute remaining.

"I have to go now, Ash." She fished in her purse to find her device and end the emission of stimulating waves. That would help to clear the raging hormones.

"You can't deny that there's a powerful connection between us. I've never felt this way about someone that I've just met. I think there's something far greater at work here… like destiny."

Para resisted the urge to make a gagging sound or to laugh hysterically, and she simply smiled and nodded. *That's the oxytocin and vasopressin talking. There is something greater at work here: Science and Revenge. Also, that connection you feel might be the fact that I'm two of the people closest to you, with whom you have pre-established connections.* Para felt the strong urge to grin and punch Asher hard in the shoulder, a classic gesture of affection from his niece, but she restrained herself and remembered the ploy.

"I agree, Ash," she said, sighing deeply. "This *is* a powerful connection. I'm just… scared. Things are moving too fast for me. Physical intimacy isn't something I take lightly. I need to be assured that our connection is a lasting one first. I don't want to give myself to you and then find that it didn't mean anything to you, and have you just… walk away from me." *Again. You asshole.*

"I would never do something like that," said Asher, swallowing at the lie and painful memory of Amara's hysteria when he'd done exactly that to her.

"I'm sure you wouldn't. I knew you were a noble guy. Just like your father who you mentioned earlier, I'm sure," said Para, giving Asher a gentle hug and a small sarcastic peck on the cheek. If a peck on the cheek could be sarcastic. . Her watch beeped thirty seconds. "I need to go."

"Just promise me I'll see you again!" he said, putting his arms around her and hugging her tightly.

"I…" Para was frozen with the need to bolt, and the need to deepen into the hug. Asher always had given the very best hugs. This was something that every part of Para agreed on. How could she pull away from a comfy hug like this in thirty seconds?

Asher spoke stubbornly. "I won't let you go unless you promise this isn't the last time I'll see you."

My guy. My dorky, lovable guy. "Of course you'll see me again!" she said with a laugh. She ripped herself from him and began jogging away. *I can't be detained any longer. I may have to teleport… and the technique might fail. I might teleport to Thorn and divide in front of him. That would be stupid. Very stupid.*

Para increased the speed of her run, nervously looking at her watch. Ten seconds. Her heartbeat raced as she glanced back and saw Asher waving at her. *Nine.* She waved back to be polite, when all she really wanted to do was allow her body to burst into flame and blast away at a supersonic speed. *Eight.* She ran as believably quickly as she could. *Seven. Six. Please let him not follow me.* Finally, she was able to duck behind a hot dog stand and out of Asher's sight. *Five. Four.* Para moved so quickly that she was imperceptible to the naked eye, and was several blocks away and standing beside her car in less than a second. *Three.* She dove into the vehicle and immediately started driving away, before she'd even had a chance to put her shoes back on. *One.*

This time, she was driving when her body tore itself apart. The car swerved uncontrollably into oncoming traffic, and Pax had to quickly correct the steering before they crashed. Taking a deep breath, Pax reached up to adjust the rearview mirror which had been knocked out of place by Amara's shoulder. She paused with her hand poised halfway to the glass when she saw a flash of sharp white teeth.

Jerking her head back over her shoulder to look in the backseat, she saw a shadowy figure lurking there, and staring at her with ravenous red eyes. She recognized the blood and saliva dripping from its teeth, and over its chin. She knew she should use her powers to defend herself, but she was too frozen with fear.

"Pax, pay attention to the road!"

At the sound of Amara's shrill voice, the creature disappeared. The dark-haired woman turned around dutifully to correct the steering once again. "Mara, did you see…" Pax glanced into the rearview mirror furtively. There was nothing there. The hallucination had probably been some sort of symptom of her mind and body splitting apart. She swallowed the saliva which had been gathering in her own mouth. "Never mind."

Amara groaned and lowered her chin to her chest shamefully. "I have no self-control when it comes to that man!"

"No kidding," said Pax, fanning herself with one hand and driving with the other. "*That* wasn't part of the plan. I really had to struggle to get control over Para a few times. You even nearly told him our identities!"

"I couldn't help myself, Paxie!" Amara's voice was a mournful whine. "I love him so much, and he's so sad. I miss the way things were between us." The blonde woman ran her fingers through her hair, which caused a small shower of sand and water to fall onto the seat of the car. "But in my defense, some of that desire was artificially awakened."

"Sure. It's either that or you're the horniest woman alive, and making me suffer the same feelings while merged with you!"

"Sorry," said Amara blushing, "maybe it's a bit of both. If I ever send that product for mass production, I'll tone it down significantly. I'll make it give off only trace amounts of stimulants instead of overdosing the user with high-powered aphrodisiacs."

They stopped at a red light and Pax suddenly grinned and looked over at her friend.

"Isn't it disturbing to know how much Ash thinks about food during sexual activity?" Pax put on her best Asher-voice and imitated her uncle. "Rice pudding, almond ice-cream, crème brûlée. Yum, yum!"

Amara giggled. "I didn't know he did that before today."

"What else don't we know?" Pax wondered, thinking about Thornton. She thought about her mother. She glanced into the rearview mirror again, but there was nothing in the backseat.

"Asher doesn't just think about food. He also thinks about me," Amara said with a little smile. "I won't lie—I get a kick out of hearing him think about me when he's with 'another girl.'"

"It's only fun because the other girl *is* you."

"Just you wait. I bet my brother thinks about paperwork."

"Ha! I never gave him time to think during moments like those. I kept him too occupied," said Pax, winking and accelerating hard with her still-bare foot as the light turned green.

"Well, you wouldn't know because you can't read minds," said Amara, placing her arms behind her head in a cocky manner. She gazed smugly at the oceanfront scenery they were passing. "I love this technique. It's so very useful. You have to help me develop it!"

"Alright. What am I thinking now?" asked Pax as she made a right turn.

"You're thinking…" Amara examined her closely for a minute, and was unable to get any reading whatsoever. She concentrated and closed her eyes and still heard nothing. She frowned—why was it so easy to do it as Para? She then observed her friend's body language, noticing how tensely the dark-haired woman was staring forward and how rigidly she sat. Amara began to giggle profusely. "You're thinking how embarrassed you are that you got so turned on by your uncle!"

"I am *not!*" said Pax, blushing fiercely. She hadn't been thinking about that; she had been thinking about her hallucinations, but she was still greatly embarrassed by the thought. "That wasn't me. That was *Para,* and it was *completely* your fault! I was just feeling *your* thoughts and *your* emotions. You should thank me for being such a good friend and going along with this instead of accusing me of such depraved thoughts!"

"Maaaaybe," Amara said teasingly. "But then why is it still affecting you now? I can't read your thoughts, but I can see that you're still just as hot and bothered about the whole thing as I am. I bet you can't wait to get home and get into the shower!"

"Your fault," mumbled Pax, her cheeks flushing even darker. Even though she and Amara had made a pact not to ever blame each other for Para's behavior, she couldn't help it in this instance.

"Not totally my fault, Miss Burnson. Remember when Ash put Para's hand on his sausage? Well, I remember feeling a very small amount of curiosity. Now tell me Pax, why would I feel curious about something I already know so well?"

Pax slammed on the brakes. She grabbed a bottle of water and uncorked it before leaning back and proceeding to pour the contents of the bottle onto her face.

"I blame your damned invention for this, Amara!" she shouted.

"Yes!" squealed Amara, pumping her fist victoriously.

"This whole Para situation is messing with my brain. I swear, each time we break apart, there's something of you left inside me! It's changing my physical makeup and the way I think. I'm not the same as I was before." Pax began to grumble in a low voice. "Just wait and see how I get you back for this! Wait until our date with Thorn! You'll see."

"Aw. Paxie's embarrassed for wanting to take a closer look at the *family jewels*?" said Amara, grinning. "You know, in some cultures it might be considered acceptable to… ouch! Ow, ow, ow! Pax, stop, stop! Don't hurt me! Calm down. I'm just teasing you because I love you."

A bright yellow aura had formed around Pax as she growled at Amara. "I did this to help you!"

"Paaaaaxie!" whined Amara, tugging on her friend's sleeve. "This is what friends do. They tease. I was just kidding around."

"And now you're manipulating me with the cute routine the same way you manipulate your father! And your brother! And my uncle! Do you think I'll fall for your manipulation?"

"Fine, fine! I'll stop."

They drove on in silence for a few minutes before Pax began to chuckle, and then launched into a fit of laughter that resembled a seizure. Amara looked over at her and was about to enquire what was behind the laughter when she understood. She couldn't read thoughts in this state, but she could read Pax. Seeing the serious woman in such throes of humor was contagious, and Amara also began to giggle.

Lesbians! They really thought we were lesbians? Pax couldn't speak over body-rocking spasms of laughter. She clutched her sides and the car swerved out of the lane again. She corrected the steering clumsily with her mind.

Well, at least they have no clue what our real *activities are,* thought Amara smugly. *When we're through with them they're going to* wish *that we were lesbians.*

Chapter 14: Exiled from Pax

"So, Thorn, want to hear about how my date went?"

"No, not really." Thornton balanced the phone on his shoulder as he placed his signature mindlessly on the papers piled high on his desk.

"What's wrong with you, man? Forgot to take your PMS medication?"

"Quit it, Ash. I'm just really not in the mood." Thornton sighed as he fished around for the stapler that he was constantly losing.

"Don't worry," said the cheerful voice on the other end of the line. "I can get you in the mood. I know exactly what you want and I'm going to give it to you. Lots of it!"

"Uh, Ash?" The confused look on Thornton's face was replaced by a startled one as a knock sounded on his office window. He didn't have time to stand up before Asher let himself in, carrying several bags of takeout food which smelled heavenly. The dark-haired man closed his flip phone and shoved it back into its holster on his hip with a big smile.

"I figured out the reason you've been so grumpy lately. Pax always used to treat you with a midmorning snack around this time, and without her tender loving care, you've been practically starving!"

"That's not all she used to treat me with," mumbled Thornton.

"I draw the line there, man. Have some pork fried

rice!"

Thornton glanced up at the insignia on the paper bag and frowned. "Did you have to get it from the Hakka place?"

"They make the best food," Asher said as he unloaded the Styrofoam containers.

Thornton closed his eyes. "I can't. I can't eat that stuff anymore. Please take it away."

"Are you sure?" Asher asked with his mouth already full. "Pork chops, man! To *die* for."

Thornton used his telekinetic powers to savagely fling all of food through the window. "I can't."

"Hey! I'm poor, remember? Purchasing food is actually a luxury for me."

"Sorry, Ash." Thornton immediately reached into his back pocket and began peeling bills out of his wallet. "I'm just kind of upset lately."

"No problem," Asher said, taking the bills from his friend with a grin. He stuffed them in his pocket and tilted his head towards the window to indicate the Styrofoam containers bobbing in midair. "I caught the food anyway."

Thornton smiled. "It's nice to have a friend like you who can put up with my temper. Anyone else would go running."

"Well, you may be difficult, but you're still honorable. When we were kids and you destroyed something that belonged to me, you would always replace it with something way better. I trust you."

"Thanks, Ash." The blonde man began strumming his fingers on his desk with a forlorn look on his face. "I found the ring yesterday. You left it in my filing cabinet."

Asher nodded, sitting on the edge of his friend's desk and tearing the meat off a chicken wing which he had floated back to his mouth. Thornton studied him for a second, leaning back in his chair. His eyes drifted to the window. "I realize that I lost my sanity for a while after Pax caught me with that girl. I took out my anger on you more than anyone else. I said really terrible things, but I didn't mean any of it. I just couldn't believe that my life was falling apart so quickly. I really lost it."

Asher chewed and swallowed. "I know. That's in the past now anyway. Let's not bring it up anymore. You did what you did, and I did what I did. Let's just move on and have fun. You should set up your date with Medea!"

"Dammit. I don't want Medea, Asher!" Thornton slammed his fist down on the desk.

Asher watched his friend warily, and shoved the food aside. "What do you want?"

Thornton looked up at his friend with misery etched in every contour of his face. "What do you think? I want… oh, Sakra. I can't even say it."

Asher stared at him. He tried to sense his friend's *prana* for his emotions and felt… despair? He chewed his lip, identifying with the feeling well. Why was Thornton telling him this? Ah. He wanted permission. He wanted absolution. "Thorn, you know that you can have anything in the world."

A small spark of hope seemed to bring life into Thornton's aqua eyes. The blonde man seemed ready to thank his friend for his forgiveness, but Asher kept speaking. "You've been hearing that since you were born, hearing that the world is yours. It's totally true; you are not only a prince among devas, but you're a prince among humans too, in a way. You inherited the leadership of one of the world's biggest corporations… you *can* in fact, have *anything* you desire on the planet."

Thornton rose to his feet, feeling inspired by the younger man's words. Asher had always looked up to him, making him feel greater than he was. His pride and vigor came rushing back to him. It was true. He wasn't just an ordinary man, and he'd very much needed to be reminded of that. He wanted to hug his friend for his kindness and compassion when he most needed it.

"Thanks, Ash. I really…"

"Except Pax."

His smile faded and his hopes receded. "What?"

"Not her. Not ever again. You could have a dozen women in your bed in a few minutes if you really wanted. Just walk through the office and ask them. Heck, I'll ask them for you. There are women literally camping out on the doorstep of the Kalgren Compound 24/7 for a chance at the richest blonde, blue-eyed bachelor around. You're a cliché."

"But…"

"But they're not Paxie?" mocked Asher in a whimpering voice. "No shit, Sherlock. You're just going to have to get your kicks out of the dozens of other women around, human or not."

"Not for kicks…"

"Yup. Why do you think I'm here? I know that Pax has been your best friend for over the past decade, ever since her mom died and you took her on that crazy trip. But you and I had decades of friendship before that. So here I am, the original Burnson best friend, the replacement, to cheer you up with Chinese food and keep you from having an emo-tantrum."

Thornton resisted the urge to retaliate. "I really appreciate that you've been there for me, Ash. But it's not quite the same. She's…"

"I know who she is! I know she's more educated and interesting than I am, with a vagina to boot. But you should have thought of that before." Asher was unusually serious. "Why do you want her back all of a sudden? After all the nightclubs, and all the crazy binge-drinking extravaganzas? Is it because she no longer wants you? She's not playing hard to get, Thorn. She *is* impossible for you to get. Everyone knows that you cheated on her, including my brother. Well, Raymond doesn't really want to believe it. He believes in you, for some reason."

"And you don't?"

"What is there to believe in? You admitted to me you cheated. You're like a brother to me… closer than my own brother in most ways. But have you seen Pax lately? She looks like the walking dead, and she won't even give me the time of day. You took her from me. *You turned her against me.*"

Asher bit his lip after he said this. He knew that it wasn't totally his friend's fault—his own actions had played a huge role in causing Pax to become estranged from him, but he couldn't help lashing out with blame. It was a reflex, even though he knew it wouldn't assuage his own guilt, but only make it worse. He still couldn't stop.

"You didn't just break her heart. You broke apart

my family! A family that was already torn apart by tragedy. After my dad, and Bridget…" Asher shook his head. "Did you think that just because Pax is used to losing everyone she loves, it would be easy on her?"

"Ash," Thornton said, closing his eyes in pain. His friend *never* grew angry with him. Thornton could have done the most despicable things imaginable, and Asher would have always been there by his side, supporting him and having his back. Always. No matter what. It seemed this was changing.

"And she loved you most of all," Asher said, suddenly understanding his niece a little more. "That's why this was the worst loss she has ever suffered…"

"Don't say that," Thornton snapped.

"You know it's true. She was so depressed, but you helped her past it—she grew from a miserable young girl into a loving, happy woman. You took such good care of her when she was in college, but now she's regressing. She's worse than when Bridget died. She's not just in despair, but she's *vengeful.* I hardly recognize her! She's been a lot of things, but never vengeful." Asher lifted himself off the edge of the desk, levitating in midair. "You have to stop chasing her. Forget Raymond… he's an idealistic idiot and he doesn't know you like I do. But I'm putting *my* foot down. I don't want you going near Paxie anymore. Fuck *anyone* you want. I don't care! Fuck the whole world, literally! But not her, not anymore."

"How can you say that? She's everything to me."

"Ha! No one means anything to you except yourself! I've known you since we were kids, and I know this more than anyone. You only ever think of yourself.

Even at 39, you're not ready to really love another person. I guess I'm not either, but at least I'm man enough to admit it. I'm man enough not to chase after your sister when I know I am not good enough for her. I won't hurt her again."

Thornton looked up at his friend miserably. "You don't understand. I may seem like I have it all because I have money and a good family. But I'd sacrifice everything for Pax. I *need* her."

"No, you need to get laid."

"Ash, do you remember the day Pax was born? Bridget and Raymond let us into the room to see her, and that tiny baby tossed a fireball at me. She hadn't even opened her eyes yet or made a single noise, and she tossed a fireball at me. Wasn't that the most adorable thing in the world?"

Asher restrained himself from smiling at the fond memory. Instead, he scowled. "Let me tell you something about people in the world who *aren't* you. We don't always get what we want. Regardless of how much we want it, and how much we sacrifice."

Thornton stopped protesting and remained silent. Asher immediately felt guilty for being too mean and tried to lessen the blow. "Look, if you don't want to date the generic fangirls who are obsessed with you, go after Medea. She's not just another random woman; she's special. I'm not really sure if she likes me yet, but she promised you a date. So do yourself and Pax a favor and *move on.*"

Thornton stared at his friend without really seeing him. His hand went to his neck and he pulled off his tie and shrugged his shoulders out of his blazer. "There's something I need to do."

Thornton knew he needed to talk to the one person who still believed in him. He blasted through the window leaving a bluish trail of *prana* behind him. Asher frowned.

"He didn't even try the chicken wings! Oh, well. More for me."

*　　　*　　　*

The tension between the two men was thick.

Amelia poured a steaming hot cup of tea for their guest before sitting beside her eldest son and looking up at Thornton. "Well, sweetie. What did you come here to tell us?" she asked in a friendly manner.

Thornton took the tiny teacup into his hands and stared at it for a moment before sipping it.

"It's about Pax…"

"Oh, Thorn. It was probably something silly, wasn't it?" Amelia smiled nervously. "I know my granddaughter isn't perfect. She's always had a temper and at times she can be completely irrational."

Raymond stared at Thornton, his lips tightly sealed. Thornton glanced from Amelia to Raymond, trying to find the words. "Pax wasn't irrational," Thornton said, gazing down at his tea.

"Nonsense!" said Amelia with a laugh. "Nearly killing you is very irrational. But that's the deva temper for you—I can assure you she doesn't get that from *my* side of the family. You really don't have to defend her, dear. We know Paxie can be pretty immature. She overreacts to just the slightest thing sometimes."

"She didn't overreact," said Thornton softly.

"Let me guess: she probably found some lipstick on your shirt?" offered Amelia.

Thornton shook his head.

"Did one of your crazy stalkers call her and profess love for you? Try to threaten her?"

Thornton shook his head again.

Amelia smiled. "Well, do tell what happened, my boy! What sent her off the deep end? Did she find someone's phone number in your wallet? A receipt for going to a strip club? A photograph of you with another girl? What was it?"

Thornton stared at Amelia, unable to speak. He had known the old woman's kindness since he was a boy. At first she had just been "Asher's mom" but she had quickly grown to feel more like his own adopted mother; he couldn't believe she was making excuses for him. He couldn't believe that the Burnsons thought Pax had acted out of unfounded jealousy. He couldn't believe that they thought so highly of him. They had all trusted him so much, and he had disappointed them.

Raymond continued observing Thornton and waiting for him to come clean and explain the situation. There must be an explanation. Why else would he be here? There was an awkward moment of silence as Thornton examined his teacup. It was suddenly the most interesting porcelain receptacle in the world.

"Thorn." This was Raymond speaking finally, and the eyes of the two men met. "I have always loved you as a dear friend, and as a member of the family. When you were a toddler, you were always underfoot with my little brother, and it was hard to think of Ash without thinking of you. You two were more inseparable than twins. You certainly caused enough trouble to be related," said Raymond with a chuckle. He sipped his own tea. "After my wife died, you really stepped up to help me take care of my little girl. I'm ashamed to say that you did more than I could do—and a few months ago when you told me the big news, I couldn't have been happier. You must know, Thorn—there's no one I could be more honored to have as my son-in-law. There's no one else I could possibly trust more with my daughter."

Raymond swallowed and looked at his friend directly as he spoke. "I knew that you always have and always would do everything in your power to take care of Paxie and keep her safe from harm. I know that there's some mistake here, and that you didn't really…"

Thornton felt tears slip from his eyes.

It all sunk in. It fully hit him for the first time. Asher was right. He hadn't just betrayed Pax; he had betrayed her family. The family who had been his second family since his birth. He had betrayed everyone. He had lashed out at Asher and hurt him, and probably helped along the destruction of his sister's relationship. Raymond had been his mentor; someone Thornton admired with every ounce of his being. The dark-haired monk was a better, kinder version of his own dad; Vincent was powerful, but without humanity or compassion. If only Thornton could have foreseen this moment when he had made that fateful decision, he never would have chosen to go down this path. But it had all happened so fast…

"I'm so sorry, Raymond."

Amelia and Raymond shared a glance. It was a knowing glance that only a mother and son could share, and one that communicated volumes without the need for speech or gesture. Amelia's lips became firmly set in anger, but she still couldn't bear to see Thornton upset. She went over to the blonde man and put her arms around him in a tender embrace.

He couldn't believe this: the Burnsons were still showing him such care and kindness after what he'd done. It had always been their way. He didn't deserve it. This brought more tears, and Thornton soaked Amelia's shoulder, finding comfort in the closeness of her energy and her scent, both so similar to Pax's.

Amelia stroked his back in a motherly fashion, and when his shaking subsided she held him at an arm's length and dotted his tears away with a handkerchief. Then she spoke, her voice as cold as ice:

"I think you should get the fuck out of our home."

Thornton blinked. One moment Amelia was kind and gentle, the next moment she was a raging she-demon. Just like Pax. The Burnson women were in a league of their own.

"Mother," scolded Raymond in a tone of warning. He didn't want Amelia to be rude to Thornton, but Raymond was having trouble controlling his own anger. Even as he spoke the teacups were rattling on the coffee table. Books were falling off the bookshelves as the ground vibrated as he fought against his increasing *prana.* Waves of heat swept off the powerful man, washing over Amelia and Thornton as though they had just stopped out into the sunshine on a brutal August day.

"What she means to say…" began Raymond, slowly and carefully. His voice was so artificially calm that it frightened Thornton. "...Is that we would both be very happy if you would *please* leave our home."

Thornton couldn't help but listen to that authoritative voice. It was so steady and decidedly hostile that he felt his blood freeze. His circulation had surely stopped. He remembered that Raymond was at least as powerful as his own father. Thornton struggled to stand, feeling the prickling chills run through his body. In a zombie-like state, he turned to head for the door.

Amelia followed him and stepped outside. "Don't you dare go anywhere *near* my granddaughter again. Do you understand me, Thornton Kalgren?"

Thornton nodded, speaking in a cracked whisper. "Yes, Amelia."

"She deserved better than this!" Amelia hissed. She advanced on Thornton and shoved her finger in his face. "You babysat her. You were there through the worst of it, when Kaden died. You knew what a good-hearted and brilliant kid she was, and you knew the woman she could become! You knew Bridget—do you remember Bridget?"

"Yes, ma'am."

"How do you think Paxie's mother would feel if she were alive today?" Amelia asked, her eyes tearing up. "If that poor woman, Sakra bless her soul, knew the way you had treated her daughter…"

Thornton felt as if the world was collapsing around him. He felt the urge to get as far away as possible and bury his head in the sand.

"…She would surely strangle you with her bare

hands," Amelia finished. "Your life has been blessed. Natural physical strength and a fortune to inherit—amazing parents like Rose and Vince. But hear me now, boy. Despite all of your physical strength, on the inside you are pathetically weak. Physical might does *not* equate strong character, young man!"

Amelia turned around and marched back into the house, slamming the door behind her.

Ouch. There could have been no greater insult to a deva than to call him weak on so many levels. Amelia knew this, having been married to one of the greatest devas who had ever lived. The worst part was that Thornton knew in his heart that it was true.

Asher had been right, of course. There was no longer any chance for him with Pax. No one in her family welcomed him any longer. He had to move on. He had to force himself to move on. And there was only one possible way he could think of doing that.

As he took off into the sky he gazed behind him at the manor of Burnson Grove and the beautiful forests and rivers of the landscape. He had so many memories in these woodlands. From his earliest childhood he had escaped here to spend time with the Burnsons. These people were far more than just family friends and far more than just family—they were ingrained deeply in his soul, and part of his very foundation. Thornton had to look away to stop the pain he felt at being exiled from Burnson Grove. Exiled from Pax.

He wondered why he had even travelled to speak to her family. What had he intended to explain? Now it was eternally finalized. He wondered if he could use his magick to move through other planes of existence; could he take Pax and chose to pursue a different life? They could be reborn again hundreds of years in the past or future—he could alter the very fabric of time. But he had a hunch that he would still be forbidden from seeing her again. For Raymond could follow him to any world and any time period. Raymond and Vincent had already lived countless lives under countless names, and such feats were nothing to them.

Amelia was right. Thornton was weak. Even as a deva, his power was insignificant—for if he possessed any real power, he would not have allowed Pax to slip away. The sinking feeling in his stomach intensified as he stared blankly into the sky ahead. He pulled his cell phone out of his pocket and dialed a number. He had to force himself to go through the motions of moving on, or he never would.

Chapter 15: In Pure Starlight

Thornton waited by the fountain in the city's largest downtown mall, checking his watch sporadically. He only had a forty-five minute lunch break before an important meeting, and had requested to meet with his new lady-friend for a casual noontime date in the mall. It was something to take his mind off Pax.

He saw her approaching from a distance, and he took in her unusual pink and black summer dress. It was a type of style he had never seen before, and it looked like a melee of two different garments. *Mara would dig this girl,* he thought to himself. The indigo-haired beauty always seemed rather trendy and fashion-forward. Her smile was what caught him off-guard. She looked so cool and confident that she made him feel a touch nervous. There was something uncanny about her; she was definitely special.

The smile on her face led him to imagine he had seen it before. It reminded him of someone. His mother? The inane thought made him smile. The young trainee doctor looked nothing like Rose Kalgren.

"Good afternoon, Medea," he said giving her a small hug.

"Hello, Thorn," she said brushing her deep indigo locks out of her eyes. "It's good to see you again. I'm curious about why you wanted to meet here."

"Well," he said, leaning close to her while speaking in a low tone as though conspiring. "I happen to know one of the most closely kept secrets on the planet."

Para felt a shiver of excitement at his words, even though she was certain she knew all of his secrets. She gazed at him attentively and curiously before moving her lips to brush his ear. "I promise I won't tell."

Thornton smiled handsomely, taking her hand and guiding her through the mall, "They just opened up a new shop. They serve the very best ice-cream in the universe. I'm not kidding."

Para smiled. She did love ice-cream. She murmured a challenge as she followed him. "I've had some pretty great ice-cream in my lifetime. That's a lofty claim!"

When they reached the little shop, which was adorably named *Intergalactic Ice-Cream* and decorated with space-themed decorations, Para was seized with a childlike delight. She ran to the glass and gazed through at the flavors. They were about thirty in total, and all named astronomically, for example, "Venus Vanilla," "Asteroid Apple," and "Supernova Strawberry."

"Whoa!" she exclaimed. "This is amazing. What a selection!"

"What would you like, Medea?" he asked, feeling a smile take over his face at her reaction. Her sexy smirk and elegant confidence had instantly disappeared and had been replaced by an incredibly sweet innocence. He felt more attracted to her than ever before. She was acting so much like… a Burnson!

"One of each!" she blurted out instantly, her eyes big and round as she stared at the rainbow assortment of colors.

"I'll have one of each," Thornton told the shopkeeper as though it were the most natural thing in the world.

The shopkeeper stared for a moment in confusion. He dropped his ice-cream scooper. Thornton frowned at the reaction. Then he realized what he had asked for. He slowly turned back to the girl who was still staring through the glass with excitement.

"Uh, Medea?" he asked, his face contorting into weird shapes. She turned back to look at him curiously.

"What's wrong, Thorn?"

"You want one of… each?"

"Peach!" she corrected hastily, feeling a rush of terrified dismay at her forgetful mistake. "I said 'peach,' Thorn. I simply love peach!"

He nodded, relieved. And also not-so-relieved, because frankly, he had really wanted to try one of each. Para glanced back over her shoulder at the display, silently praying that there *was* a peach flavour. Then she saw it, and breathed a sigh of relief. *Pluto Peach! Thank Sakra.*

Once the shopkeeper had scooped their small single scoops, and Thornton had paid, the couple began strolling around the mall while licking their respective cones. Para's stomach growled at her angrily. A deva having an ice cream cone for lunch was the rough equivalent of a human having a lollipop. At least they were suffering together. It was the price of dating supposed-humans. They chatted for a while, making small talk, before Thornton asked the fateful question. The one question that had the power to divide Para in two more efficiently than a chainsaw.

"So, Medea, would you like to do some shopping?"

"YesNo!" said Para, nearly coughing from the effort it took to twist her tongue simultaneously into the shapes her mind was commanding her to. She also had a small spasm in her shoulders as a mini-war raged inside her brain and nervous system. It was lucky that she was made of two demigoddesses and not any robotic Kalgren-Tech elements, for the question pushed all of her capacities into conflicting overload. If she were mechanical she would have surely short-circuited and perhaps combusted into a million pieces and died on the spot.

"Did you just say 'yes' and 'no' at the same time?" asked Thornton, raising an eyebrow. An ancient chord was struck in his memory at the sound of her dual voice and he turned to her with a serious look on his face. He couldn't quite put his finger on it…

"I said 'yes!' Someone behind me said 'no.' You must be hearing things, silly." Para clutched his arm and smiled cheerfully. Thornton shrugged and brushed it off as nothing.

Good grief! That really hurt. My brain hurts. Why couldn't I just say no?!

Pax, I'm a type of warrior too, and this *is* my *battlefield. I'm steering this ship until further notice. I believe it was Sun Tzu who wrote in such detail why it is important to know your terrain.*

Damn you, Amara Kalgren! You can't apply The Art of War *to a shopping mall. I won't allow this.*

"Great! I'll take you on a little shopping spree. Buy anything you want, anything your heart desires," said Thornton, squeezing the hand of the merged woman.

Para almost squealed in delight, but then a very contrasting serious look came over her face. "Thorn, I won't have that. I don't want to spend your money, and there isn't anything I really need."

"Whoa! Now you're sounding *exactly* like my ex-girlfriend!" said Thornton in surprise. "I thought there was only one woman on earth who didn't love shopping."

"I guess there are two of us," said Para with a nervous laugh.

See, Pax! Shut your fat mouth before you blow our cover. Jeez!

"Hmm. Very strange. This is an interesting phenomenon," Thornton joked as he put his face very close to Para's and poked her nose. "Are you sure Pax isn't in there somewhere?"

Para whirled around to hide her sudden hyperventilation and her eyes bugging out. *Damn it!* When she turned around an instant later she had regained composure completely and wore a classic angry-female look on her face. One that made Thornton gulp, because he had often seen it on the face of his mother.

"Well, I never! Why do you want to spend time with me if all you want to talk about is your ex-girlfriend? Pax this, Pax that! If you are so obsessed with her, why don't you go and be with her instead of me?" Para whirled back around and began to march off, silently congratulating herself on being such a great actress. *3… 2… 1…*

"Medea, wait!" exclaimed Thornton, catching up and gently circling her waist with his arm. "I apologize for mentioning Pax so much, but I was in a relationship with her for years and before that she was my friend for as long as she has been alive. To be perfectly honest, I don't have many connections with human beings, period. I spend most of my time in the office and the rest of my time… doing traditional family-stuff with my dad. Pax is one of the only people I can relate to. One of the only people I really know. Forgive my lack of manners."

This is what he said. Para could hear what he actually was thinking: *I wish I* could *go and be with her instead of you, even though you are a mind-boggling beauty… but she hates me for what I've done to her. And her family hates me even more. So, right now, this stupid game and this bet with Asher is all I have going for me other than working myself into oblivion. And maybe I can find some comfort in you.*

Para's face softened after hearing his words and thoughts. *Thorn is talking and thinking about me enough to scare any woman away. He's only here because he's lonely… because I abandoned him. Poor guy…*

"If you prefer we can go for a walk in a nearby park, or grab a bite to eat. Whatever you like, let's just spend some time together," said Thornton with his classic charming smile.

"Well, there is *one* store in this mall that I have been dying to check out," said Para, her face lighting up. *Come along and buy me things, big brother!*

Para slipped her hand under his arm and led him to her favorite store in the mall, Isadora's Intimates.

"Mr. Kalgren!" exclaimed the shop owner excitedly upon recognizing her newest client. She wore a gaudy nametag declaring her to be *Madame Isadora* and spoke in a thick accent. "I presume you are here to pick up the shipment your sister ordered? It just arrived this morning!"

"No, I'm not. We're just browsing." *Really, like I'd fetch Amara's bras like some kind of delivery boy.*

Para cleared her throat and looked at Thornton with a sweet and confused glance. "I thought you were a kind and caring brother?"

Thornton mentally cursed. "On second thought, I will pick up the package for her."

Mara, you weasel! Para mentally scolded herself, but with affection.

"You're so sweet, Thorn!" said Para, sending him a false but admiring smile. "I always did think you could tell the most about a man from seeing how much he cares for his family."

Thornton grumbled softly to himself while thinking, *If only she knew how little my sister cares for me. How she goes to all possible lengths to avoid me. Especially lately.*

You know deep down I love you, Thornie-poo, especially when you buy me things! This is so much fun, Pax.

Not for me. Let's get to the good part already.

Thornton thought to himself as he accepted the package, *I guess I could stop by Amara's house later... but if Raymond senses my energy near to Pax he'll probably show up with guns blazing. I'll just leave it in her room at the Compound for whenever she comes home.*

"Ah," said Madame Isadora. "Can I interest the lady in some fine lingerie? Our undergarments are the very best, imported from Italy and France! They are guaranteed to add spice to the bedroom."

Thornton glanced around the store aimlessly. *I wonder what Pax would look like in that red and black corset. But she'd never wear something like that.*

"Oooh," said Para, pointing at the garment that first caught his eye. "I think I would like to try on that corset."

"That one is a piece of art, my dear! It will complement your figure and complexion very well. Why! You have almost the exact same body size as Miss Kalgren, just with a bit more muscle on you. Your complexion is just a few shades darker than hers. Let me select a few more pieces for you to try. Your lover is gorgeous, Mr. Kalgren. She is breathtaking!"

Para genuinely blushed as she made her way into the private changing area of the store. It was the first time in her short life of a scant few half-an-hour periods that she had been complimented by a woman. She heard Thornton think about correcting the woman's "lover" remark and then changing his mind.

Madame Isadora ushered them into a very posh private room and bowed politely. "Please take your time. I hope that you will find everything comfortable."

She then left and closed the door behind her. The changing area of the store was part of the reason Amara loved the place so much. It consisted of several small private rooms, each of them cylindrical in shape, with walls were covered in mirrors for viewing every angle. Couples could go into the rooms and there was a little cushioned bench for the man, and a screen door for the woman to change behind. Amara had many fond memories with Asher in those changing rooms.

There was no way a man could sit in a small private room with a woman changing into imported lingerie and not jump her bones. *Amara, this is ridiculous,* thought Para as she shrugged out of her clothing and pulled on the tiny black lacy panties that went with the corset. There was also a little toile skirt which barely covered her bottom.

Really? Then why do your thoughts sound so excited. You little vixen, you're getting aroused from just feeling the clothing against you! Here, let me do up these clasps and you can take over from here. Should we turn on the simulator?

Hell no! I do not need that thing messing with my head right now. Our head, that is. Amara, is it really wise to reveal so much of Para's body? Her body looks so much like mine. I don't want to give it away. Thornton knows *what I look like…*

Quit stressing and seduce the man already, sheesh. I'm letting you blend with my skin for a disguise, so at least do what we planned and entertain me! Para slipped on the black heeled sandals she had been wearing before.

She took a deep breath and stepped out from behind the screen door. "Do you like it, Thornton?"

He looked up at the woman who smiled somewhat nervously as she wore an impossibly alluring garment over an unbelievable body. He scanned from her toes to calves and thighs to hips before looking up slowly and settling on her eyes. She was a fantasy. He stood up quite suddenly.

"Medea, you look…" he was at a loss for words. He suddenly felt insecure, and realized that he had not *really* spoken to a strange woman with the intent of being with her in well over ten years. All he knew was that he was moving forward, and his hands were extending towards the dark-haired woman as though he were magnetized. His hands slipped around her body gently, stroking the perfect hourglass figure accentuated by the corset. He let his fingers drift from her ribcage down into the deep dip at her waist, and out over her hips, then back up. He caressed her sides like this absentmindedly for a moment.

"You look..." *Almost as beautiful as Pax.* "Beautiful."

Para smiled at him amorously, but little did he know that it was the unspoken compliment in his mind which warmed her heart. The words which he could not speak, for fear of offending her. They were in no possible way true in the factual sense—both Para and Thornton knew this. Para was mysterious and strikingly beautiful while, in comparison, Pax was a plain and simple girl. But with beauty being in the eye of the beholder, the fact that Thornton felt plain Pax was lovelier than the radiant Para meant a lot to her. Was Para herself offended? Not in the least.

He moved his hand up to cup her chin, and brushed his thumb along her jaw. He searched her indigo eyes, as though the answers to every mystery of life lay within their hue. They were so deeply midnight blue that he felt the same sensation he felt when looking up at the starry night sky. Respect, admiration, awe, and yet familiarity. He could get lost in such eyes, the same way he could get lost in watching the heavens. He imagined that there was just as much mystery and wonder within this woman as there was beyond the stars and in distant galaxies. He had seen a bit of that, once.

He let his fingers drift back into the hair at the nape of her neck, and lightly caress her scalp. He ran his fingers through her hair, or at least through a few inches of it. She closed her eyes for a few seconds, savoring the sensation, but she opened them again to watch him as his hands drifted down her back and rested again at her waist. In the corset her waist was so small that his large hands almost encircled her completely.

Fuelled by raw desire and naïve wonder, Thornton tightened his grip around her waist and slowly drew her body close so that it was pressed flush against his. He felt her breasts press against his chest and her hips press against his own hips. Her arms naturally moved up along his arms, and circled behind his neck, until the two were wrapped up in one another.

Their energy mixed and hummed around them as the passion mounted, neither of them noticing the transparent white aura. Thornton inhaled the scent of her skin, moving his hands slowly over her back. He mused at how easily a tug of his fingers could rip the garments apart, and expose her bare flesh to him completely. He could throw her down on the floor and have her right there in the dressing room. He would definitely make her scream, but he could clamp a hand over her mouth to muffle it.

Para heard these thoughts of his and felt shivers of fear and currents of delicious electricity run through her. She could experience every facet of his feeling through his thoughts and his radiating energy. Even without the mystical and spiritual connection to his psyche to gauge and share his arousal, she could see the desire in the hard glint of his sapphire eyes. She was lost as she stared into their depths, and she couldn't help leaning in closer to him.

She is magnificent. Magnificent. I must have her. I have to remember to be gentle so I don't destroy her body… she isn't Pax.

Para couldn't help smiling. The fact that Thornton

was thinking of dominating her made her grow extremely aroused, and she could feel the moisture beginning to gather at the junction of her thighs. *No, I'm not Pax. I'm stronger. Destroy me, Thornton, just try it. Take my body just like you want to.*

All this tension and their lips had not even met yet. The two just continued to gaze at each other, as though they were afraid to unleash whatever torrents could result from that amalgamation of flesh. It would be an entirely different kind of amalgamation than Para already was. Thornton wondered to himself why he was afraid and he wondered why she looked so confident, why she was smiling. He briefly envisioned Pax's face with the same expression on it.

He's so much more cautious and refined than Asher, Para thought to herself. *This is why I love him. He's measured and meticulous—he makes each breath and each millisecond count. He doesn't treat the female body greedily, as a delicious thing to devour—no! Thorn considers it a sacred thing to worship. And he worships so well.* Para finally became the aggressor and closed the distance between them. She tugged his head down so that his face met hers, capturing his lips in their second first kiss.

Despite the massive yearning in both devas, the kiss was restrained and chaste. It was hesitant and wary as though their lips were testing and analyzing. It tasted like the few seconds before an explosion. The rumbling in the ground before a cataclysm. And cherries.

Perhaps it was the extraordinary coincidence of the manner in which their bodies and lips met, or perhaps it was the unusual combination of their thoughts and feelings when it occurred, but both of their minds were catapulted back in time about twelve years, to a hauntingly vivid memory. It is possible the memory belonged to Thornton and Para was only sharing in it because of her ability to read minds. It is also possible that the magic of the moment invoked the same memory in both of them. For whatever reason, it flooded their consciousness completely.

Pax was leaning her chin on her forearms, with her forehead lightly resting on the glass window. She gazed off into space, focusing on the growing star in the distance that she knew was their own dear Sun. She had been staying like this for hours each night and she barely slept.

"Bree. Bree. Pax require rest for maximum function."

"Shhh, Bree," she whispered to the little robot puppy. In an attempt to cheer Pax up after the death of her mother, Rose Kalgren had given her a special prototype of a puppy with artificial intelligence. At first, Pax had considered the gift retarded, but she had quickly begun taking the small robot everywhere with her. She had named it Briar, which was similar to her mother's name, but also followed the Kalgren theme. Pax pressed a finger to her lips, although she knew the robot could not process the action. "Thorn is sleeping. I know I should be too, but I have too much on my mind."

Little did she know that Thornton wasn't sleeping. He watched her from the bed on the opposite side of the room, as he often did. Their trip was nearly over, and while the initial excitement of being in space had kept Pax constantly buzzing with nosy questions, the thrill had quickly died down to normalcy. He couldn't ignore Pax's quiet and solemn vigil. The girl had been so loud and obnoxious before her mother had passed away—almost to the point of being a spoiled brat. Since then, she had been transformed into a silent and pensive creature. Seeing her like this scared him more than just a little.

"Bree. Bree. Pax miss home?"

Pax turned to look at her soccer-ball sized companion. She smiled and reached her arms out to embrace the puppy. She pulled the little machine close to her chest.

"Oh, Bree," she said. "Yes and no. It's too much to explain."

Thornton swallowed back a lump of emotion as he watched her. In the night, when she took off her tomboyish ponytail and let her hair down, when she put on those adorable red pajamas, she transformed into such a soft and vulnerable creature. And unbelievably wise beyond her years.

How many times he'd listened to her whispering to Bree in the dark, and how many times he'd wanted to go to her! To speak with her, to console her. It was lonely and disconcerting to be out here in space. Too lonely for a young girl who was growing and discovering life, and full of questions and new thoughts and ideas, too lonely for her to be conversing only with an inadequate piece of artificial intelligence. He wanted to give her the human companionship she needed and deserved.

Now they were so close to home, and this celestial voyage was almost over. It had only been a test run, but Pax's childlike wonder had turned it into an adventure. Now, they would return to their ordinary lives. He would go back to working his mind numb at the office, and she would go back to preschool, or kindergarten or something of the sort. He watched her silently stare out into the night, and he corrected himself mentally that she was actually in high school. She had grown up so quickly, right under his nose, and he had hardly noticed. What he did notice was that she possessed knowledge and insight (and strength of course) far beyond most of the people he worked with in the office.

"I don't really belong there, Bree," she admitted so quietly

that Thornton would not have heard if not for superhuman senses.

This was the last straw. He forcefully shoved himself off his mattress and crossed the room to Pax's hammock, sitting beside her.

She was startled and let go of Briar, turning to look at Thornton with surprise. "Sorry, Thorn. Didn't mean to wake you. I'll keep it down."

"I'm not an old man—you don't have to be quiet so I can sleep. What's wrong?"

She looked at him, her large dark eyes shining in the soft bluish starlight from the window. This might be one of the last times he ever saw her face like that, he realized. On earth there were so many forms of artificial light that it was blinding. Pure starlight was a very rare circumstance.

She had not responded, but she blinked, staring at him curiously. Was she observing his face in the same way?

"Pax? We'll be home soon. Won't you be happy to see your dad again? And Uncle Ash? Grandma Amelia?"

"I am happy," she said breathlessly, before closing her eyes and letting a small smile touch her lips. Thornton observed the girl with wonder, almost feeling as though she were suddenly a stranger. She seemed to transform into someone he barely knew in the starlight.

"Paxie?" he asked again softly, resisting the urge to move closer to her, or to reach out and hug her. He knew those things were innocent friendly gestures he had made countless times before, but somehow the lighting and the moment felt too uncertain.

She opened her eyes and twisted her mouth to the side. "You know, I exist only in liminality."

Thornton was floored. Wasn't she fourteen? How did she even know what that word meant? Her black hair had such a strange metallic quality in this ambience. He did reach out and touch her hair then, tucking it behind her ear. He had to make sure that she was really human, and not one of his mother's perfect robots.

"What do you mean?" he inquired, prodding her to continue.

She smiled weakly. "I don't want to bore you with my trivial teenage troubles."

"Pax," he said with a low threatening growl, almost demanding that she continue. How dare she open up to Briar but not to him? Thornton glared angrily at the innocent puppy.

Pax looked surprised at his demanding tone. Thornton was rarely anything but gentle. "Well, I don't fit in very well with the humans on earth. Even if I wasn't a freak, I would still be considered a freak."

"Ah, your abilities are making it tough for you to fit in? Ash and I had the same trouble, but we had each other. Luckily, you have Mara!"

"No, I don't. Mara has a new clique of rich, fashionable friends. They suit her more than I do. She's hardly said a word to me in years."

"That little bi… um, bigot. I'll speak to her when we get home."

"No. I don't want her pity and fake friendship. Besides, I am not interested in wasting my time on superficial things like clothes and makeup. Before mom…" Pax hesitated. It was still too fresh to talk about it casually. "I used to spend all my time reading up on ancient magick and practicing my powers. Even then, Amara was all about the fashion magazines. Now, I read mostly about biology and anatomy. Grandma Amelia wants me to be a doctor."

"Wow! I didn't know you were considering that."

Pax shrugged. "It's not really a passion or anything. I

figure that I might as well try to make Grandma happy. I miss practicing. I crave it so badly, and I've tried to fill the hole with a social life, but you should see how badly I fail. I've gone out on a few dates..."

"You're too young to be dating!"

Pax's shoulders moved in a silent chuckle as she looked at him in a way that made him know that she thought otherwise. "My strength scares them away, along with my burning hands. Boys are terrified of me, girls even worse. I have no friends. I'm not really great at being human. Neither am I fully a deva. To powerful warriors like Vincent and my dad, even to you and Ash... I'm pretty much worthless."

"You could never be worthless to us, Pax! We all love you."

"Oh, please!" she held up her hand to silence him. "I have never been treated as though I was a real *deva, and you know it. I'm neither human nor goddess, just hovering somewhere between. I'm not a child, nor am I totally an adult. And worst of all..." She looked at him with embarrassment as she said this next part. "I'm not feminine, nor am I masculine. I'm not ugly, but I'm not beautiful either. I wish I could be more like Amara. How could anyone ever want to be with* me*?"*

Thornton looked at her in surprise as she turned away from him and forced a light laugh to ease her distress from the moment of honesty. He studied the tension in the muscles of her face and her downcast eyes. He felt himself moving and speaking before he had given it any thought.

"Paxie," he said gently, guiding her chin so he could look into her eyes. "I will give you my honest opinion. Right now, as I look at you in the starlight, to me, you are absolutely perfect."

"Oh, please," she said again, reflexively.

"I mean it," he said, taking her hands. He began to remove

her gloves; she tried to resist at first, but then complied once she remembered who he was. When her palms were naked, he pressed his palms against hers, demonstrating that he could handle the heat easily. He could see the discomfort she felt in touching the skin of another person, and he moved her hand up to press it firmly against his cheek. "Look, Pax. You can't hurt me. I'm not afraid. I know exactly who you are; all of your strength and vulnerability, all of your humanity and your deva abilities, I understand it all completely. All of your innocence and wisdom, your femininity and that tomboy streak; everything about you is perfect. To me, you are the most beautiful creature that could possibly exist."

Pax stared at him with eyes wide in astonishment and almost disbelief to hear Thornton speaking to her like this. His words, his touch, they were comforting and kind—but there was something more than that. They were romantic. She studied his face, trying to understand where this speech and these emotions had come from. Was he just pitying her because of her mother's death?

"I promise you someday you won't feel as insecure," Thornton said. He moved his thumb over the palm of her hand. "This will all pass soon. The situations will be the same, but you will accept them much more than you do now. You'll grow to be more comfortable with yourself and in your own skin before you realize it's even happening."

"Thank you, Thorn," she whispered, gazing at him gratefully as she mentally committed his words to memory. Someday when she felt alone and inadequate again, she'd remember that Thornton had thought she was perfect in the pure starlight. But it was likely that it ended there.

Thornton glanced down at the robotic puppy which was staring at them with something resembling curiosity. He frowned and telekinetically tossed the puppy across the room, just in case his mother had installed a camera somewhere on the makeshift beast. Returning his attention to Pax, he could see that she was mulling over his unexpected words. This was the first serious conversation they'd had in years. Hesitantly, he closed the distance between them, and slipped his arm around her waist. He smiled down at her as their noses almost touched and spoke as softly as possible.

"You asked how could anyone want to be with you? Well, I want to be with you. If you'd like that. Heck, even if you wouldn't I'm going to try to win your heart anyway, and maybe I'll change your mind."

Pax seemed frozen in shock. "Why?" she asked.

Thornton laughed. "Lots of reasons. But you're only fourteen and you're already exactly the kind of smart, serious woman that I've been searching for. If you continue growing at this rate, you're going to blow my mind. And of course, you're a goddess."

"Only like a quarter or a sixteenth," she said modestly, to offset the embarrassment of receiving all these compliments at once.

"It doesn't matter. You've done more with the power you possess than people with twenty times the power have managed to do. You've studied and worked hard to improve yourself. You're a pretty impressive kid, Paxie."

She finally smiled at this. She squeezed his hands thankfully, finally allowing herself to believe that he was telling the truth. "You're not so bad yourself, Mr. Kalgren."

He chuckled at the way she mockingly emphasized his name to highlight his age. "Someday, when you're a little bit older, you and I are going to be together. As a couple. Once you're legal for me to pursue down on the planet Earth, I'm going to have you as my own, Paxie. For keeps. And I'll never let you go."

He was so bold and decisive. Pax stared at him wordlessly for a few minutes. She felt as though she were in some kind of surreal dream. What fourteen-year-old girl having a quiet and sad moment alone on a spaceship suddenly had a heroic prince come and say the most uplifting and romantic things possible to her? Life was full of surprises. She'd seen a lot of strange things from strange perspectives since they'd left the planet's atmosphere, but this surprised her the most. In a good way. My sweet Thorn, *she thought before a smile transformed her lips. She tried her best to keep the smile from being too large.*

He seemed uncomfortable with her lack of response, and he spoke again. "I never told you this before because I didn't want to seem like a creepy old man. I mean, 28 isn't that old, but I know I must seem ancient to you. Once you graduate the difference will seem smaller—and plus we have those nifty extended lifespans. I didn't want to freak you out by telling you I was interested, but I just know that someday things will be like this. I won't stop you from dating those human boys your age. Heck, I'll probably keep dating supermodels to keep up appearances. I just thought it was a good time to tell you that there's someone who definitely wants to be with you someday. I won't interfere with your freedom for many years."

"My freedom!" Pax exclaimed. She abruptly ripped her hand away from his and hit him in the face. "Don't you dare!"

Thornton was immediately and worried that he had said too much, too soon. "Pax…"

"Don't you dare date those stupid supermodels!" she said with a frown. "You can't say things like this to me and go back to acting like nothing happened. I'll never be free again."

"Paxie, listen…"

"It's too late, Thorn. The truth is, I always hoped… I always fantasized you'd someday see me this way, but I always thought it would be impossible. Every time I looked at you, my whole life, I have hoped for this. And from now on, every time I

look at you, I'll remember you said it was possible. It's too late to go back. I'm already yours."

Thornton stared in amazement for a moment. "Really, Paxie?" When she nodded, he couldn't stop himself from running his fingers over her face, trying to capture how it looked in the starlight for memory. They might never have an excuse to test a spaceship again. He moved his fingers back to stroking her metallic hair, and she closed her eyes at the sensation. He loved the fact that she had accepted his words. The idea had been floating around in his mind for so long. She would be his someday. He wanted nothing more. Someday when it was permissible, when it was acceptable.

"Thorn," she said coyly, opening her eyes. She'd gestured outside the spaceship. "We're not on Earth right now. I'm legal out here."

He laughed, before he saw she was serious. "Pax," he said with a small warning in his voice, but she was already grasping the front of his pajamas and pulling him close. "But you're still a citizen of…"

His meager attempt at protest was hushed by her aggression as her lips smashed against his. Her lips were soft and supple, and they tasted like cherries. He had basically given her permission, given her an idea of his feelings and intentions. How could he expect a take-action girl like Pax to sit still on information like that? The kiss was chaste and tentative, for she was young and inexperienced, but it was also forceful and demanding, for she was a deva. It was wonderfully liminal, just like her. He found himself putting his arms around her small body and deepening the kiss. Underneath her oversized pajamas her waist was incredibly tiny and he loved the feel of her against him.

He couldn't believe he was kissing Pax. Not in five or six years like he'd planned, but now. *He was kissing fourteen-year-*

old Pax. And it felt… completely natural. Okay, and a bit forbidden. But other than the fact that Pax's father would murder him if he knew, and Asher would probably almost-murder him, it felt like home. The spectacular view of the stars only added to the mood, and to the dangerous thrill.

Thornton let himself become lost in kissing her, and only when she began to moan softly against his mouth did he realize that he had begun to use his tongue to explore her lips and to tangle with her own tongue a bit too passionately. His arms also held her body too tightly against his own and Pax was responding too fiercely, practically climbing on top of him, and making her hammock sway.

He held her away from him then, suddenly feeling his cheeks redden at what they'd done. It was definitely too much, too fast. He calmed his breathing and tried to focus. Even the slightest, most innocent of touches…

He glanced behind him to make sure that Briar hadn't caught the kiss on camera. Pax noticed his action and giggled softly. He turned back to her, and couldn't resist giving her one more gentle, soft kiss on the lips. She quieted down and just stared at him lovingly. He stared back, feeling his own heart soaring. There were a million reasons why he shouldn't be kissing Pax, but he knew that it was right. Her acceptance of his affections and her enthusiastic response told him that someday they would have something special together.

He couldn't wait until that day. Seriously. A mental clock had established itself in his head, called the "Countdown to Pax Turning 18 Clock." For years to come this clock would jump to the forefront of his mind every time he looked at a calendar. And then soon it would be replaced by the "Countdown to Pax Finishing College Clock," but he didn't anticipate that at this point. Both clocks, and what they represented would be violated many times anyway.

He broke their silent staring by asking her, "Do you think you can get some rest now?"

She nodded. He smiled, lifting himself off the hammock and into the air, but she stopped him from flying away by tugging his pajama sleeve and looking at him with those pleading puppy-dog eyes. She was still young enough for them to have a 100% success rate. He understood what she was requesting, and with another glance at their robotic puppy chaperone, he crawled into the hammock with her and pulled her against him so her head rested on his chest.

"Thorn," she had said softly, glancing back through the window. "I sometimes get a bad feeling. Like people aren't telling me everything about my mom. You would tell me if the adults were concealing things from my kiddie ears, right?"

"Of course. Consider me an infiltrating ally among the grownups."

She nodded, unconvinced, but smiled and snuggled closer against him. Within a few minutes she was asleep. Thornton imagined that he should leave and return to his bed, but he couldn't move. It was too comfortable. Besides, he knew she would just wake up and continue to stay up for the rest of the night, and he would stay up watching her. Teenagers had an unlimited supply of energy, but Thornton was 28, and even though he was a deva, he couldn't get by without sleep for days on end like Pax did. He would stay. It was the first time he'd ever held her as she slept, and the first real quality sleep they'd both gotten in days.

Thornton snapped out of the memory suddenly, and was transported back to earth, to a tiny mirrored changing room where a beautiful woman in lingerie had her lips pressed against his and her body wrapped around his in an extremely erotic manner. And all he could think of was Pax. And his first first kiss with her.

What the hell am I doing? Thornton removed his lips from Para's. *I promised Pax I would never let her go. Do I really care what Amelia said? Am I going to let her stop me from trying to win Pax back? This is larger than some stupid mistake. This is my life. Her life, our life.*

And I'm in a dressing room with some girl I barely know in lingerie. Thornton pulled away from Para forcefully and moved to sit on the little bench, resting his face in his hands. "God," he said, the words muffled by his hands. "What am I doing?" *But Pax won't let me near her. But Pax still loves me, and if I'm persistent enough she'll crack! She has to…*

Meanwhile, Para had stumbled backwards, shaking at what she had experienced from invading his mind. She held onto the screen door for support. Para blinked back tears at the memory she shared with him. Tears partly caused by Pax's own emotions at the memory and Amara's emotions at seeing that moment for the first time. It was the first time tears had become acquainted with Para's eyes, but they did not fall. She willed them away before they could completely be gathered.

She turned to look at Thornton, her eyes clouded with antique emotions. She saw him again through the rose-colored glasses of a fourteen-year-old girl, and *he* was perfect. He was her answer to everything, the solution to every problem. He was the kind of big brother she could look up to and respect. He was someone who was always there to step in and fight for her when the battle got too rough. He was the kind-hearted and gentle boy she had grown up with.

And he really still loves me. He remembers our first kiss so fondly. I can feel that it still means something to him. Goodness, he's so sad. What did grandma say to him? When did he speak to her? Para moved towards him, feeling the strong urge to either caress him with her fingertips or tackle him with a gigantic hug. She wanted nothing more than to throw her arms around him and tell him the truth. *I'll tell him I'm Pax. That I do love him and will listen to him and we'll fix things.* She stepped forward.

"Thorn, I'm..." *No, Pax. No! He cheated on you. We have no guarantee he won't cheat on you again! Just because it sounds like he misses you and regrets what he did... who can say that once he has you again he won't go back to his old careless ways. We need to teach him a lesson first.*

Besides, look. Para turned to face the mirror. Her reflection stunned her—her exotic features and knee-length wavy midnight blue hair. *You're not Pax. You're Para. You were born to create the ultimate seduction and test him. Screw with his brain a little. You haven't learned all you need to learn. Don't throw in the towel yet.*

"I'm so sorry, Medea," said Thornton. He was digging his fingers through his blonde hair as though he had lost something important and it was buried in his scalp. "It's just that... when I kissed you, I remembered something I'd almost forgotten. Something that happened a very long time ago."

Para still gazed into the mirror, but she shifted her eyes to glance at Thornton' reflection. He looked torn.

"I can't do this," he groaned. *This is by choice. This is me kissing another woman because I want to, not because circumstances forced me to. Not because I was conned into it by extortion. I can't, because this would* actually *be cheating on Pax. And Pax is still mine. I don't care if she tells me a thousand times that it's "over." What kind of bullshit is that?*

Extortion? she wondered to herself. *Is that what he meant to tell me? Was he… blackmailed?*

Thornton looked up to see Medea looking at him with a very strange and soft look on her face. She looked hurt. *And I don't care what her grandmother and father say, or even what Asher says. Pax belongs to me. I promised her I wouldn't let her go. You don't say things like that to a young girl and suddenly change your mind one day.*

He moved towards Para and cupped her face gently in his hands.

"I am unbelievably attracted to you, Medea. But you couldn't understand. No one can." Thornton placed his hands on her shoulders, looking into her sweet face passionately. He let the smallest of smiles overtake his face before speaking.

"When you fall in love with someone in pure starlight… that love lasts forever."

"Thorn," Para whispered. *You dork.*

He kissed her forehead, a brotherly kiss. "Thank you for reminding me. I've decided to do something stupid, and I'll probably get myself killed. If I survive, I'll call you. I'll probably need medical attention."

Thornton quickly exited the room, and Para stared after him, smiling. *My sweet Thorn.*

She leaned against the screen door with a dreamy look on her face. She allowed her body to relax completely as a whimsical smile transformed her features, and she imagined that everything might be okay again someday.

He returned after a moment, and removed a credit card from his blazer, placing it in her hands. "I almost forgot I promised you a shopping spree! Go and buy some shoes and jewelry or whatever. There's 10K on there."

With that he winked and left again.

Love you, brother! thought Para, lifting the plastic American Express triumphantly. Thornton had often given Amara this card to shop with when she was younger. She glanced at her watch and saw that she still had ten minutes remaining of fusion. *Just enough time to do some rapid shopping.*

Hell no! There's only one kind of shopping we're doing. Para immediately began to undo the clasps of the corset. She looked at herself in the mirror and paused.

If he could choose the distant memory of a fourteen-year-old miserable, boyish girl in oversized pajamas over the gorgeous flesh-and-blood woman in fine lingerie he held in his arms… well if that's not love, I don't know what is! Personally, I'd go with me.

Thanks a lot. Thinking about me like that really helps my self-esteem! I'm in here too, you know.

Sorry, Pax. That was a cute memory. Sorry that I neglected you in high school. Also, I can't believe you tried to rape my brother when you were fourteen.

Hey! It wasn't like that. Much.

And you wished you could be more like me? Aww, Paxie, that's so sweet.

Can you blame me? You're drop dead gorgeous and have always had guys falling at your feet.

Maybe, but I wished I could be more like you.

Really?

Are you kidding? You're bold, you're bad, you're fierce. You traveled into space!

Well, look! thought Para, pointing at the mirror

smugly. *I guess both of our wishes came true. In a kick-ass and unexpected way! Here we are.*

The merged girl laughed lightly, running her hands over her body. *That's true. She's the best of us both. The perfect woman.*

But I'm glad she has my *breasts,* Para thought, cupping the lovely mounds of flesh proudly.

Suddenly one of her hands left a breast and smacked herself in the face. *Your breasts? These are obviously* mine.

Ow! That hurt. That wasn't a very sane thing to do, considering I just smacked myself. Anyway. Now there's something that this perfect (crazy) woman wants… no, needs. *And if I don't satisfy this need I'm going to go bananas, throw a tantrum, and blow up this shopping mall.*

Para quickly slipped out of the remaining garments and into her own clothing before leaving the dressing room. She handed the corset to Madame Isadora who placed it in a bag and handed it back to her.

"Mr. Kalgren paid for it," she said with a smile.

"How thoughtful of him," said Para.

"He just added it to his sister's bill. You should really be thanking Miss Kalgren."

Para scowled in a rather terrifying manner. "Wonderful! Who needs enemies when you have *family*."

She marched out of the store, leaving the shop owner very confused. She walked directly to the ice cream shop and slammed her hands down on the countertop, speaking very slowly to the shopkeeper.

"One. Of. Each. Please."

Chapter 16: You Omnipotent Folks

In retrospect, ordering that much ice-cream had been greedy and unladylike. As Para shoveled the sugary confection into her mouth, she squinted at her phone which was constantly ringing. Thornton was calling Pax every few seconds. Impressed and slightly upset by his persistence, she considered increasing her consumption to be the best solution to her conflicted feelings. Para didn't have to wait for the frozen delicacies to melt, for as soon as the scoops neared her tongue they became liquid. At this rate, she was able to guzzle the dairy products down like a creamy milkshake. Kids sitting nearby glanced at her with a combination of suspicion and jealousy. Para smiled at them smugly. When her watch beeped, she licked her sticky-fingers, and decided to finish the rest of her scoops in solitude.

Balancing shopping bags and frozen goodies in one arm, Para strolled away from the food court and headed towards the women's restroom. She waited by the sink for all the women to leave before locking the door to ensure her privacy. There were only a few minutes remaining in her union, and she climbed onto the counter housing the sinks and leaned her head against the mirror as she nursed her final ice-cream cone. It was mint-chocolate chip, and she had saved the best for last; Pax loved mint while Amara preferred chocolate.

In her other hand, she received a text message: *Pax, please pick up. It's urgent.* She rolled her eyes and muttered, "Urgent, my foot." But part of her really wanted to pick up the phone. After the memory-inducing kiss, everything she had pushed to the back of her mind was rushing to the forefront with full intensity. Para banged the side of her head against the mirror lightly, causing cracks to run through the entire panel. "Whoops," she whispered to herself, but she didn't move from the spot where she sat.

Para's eyes darted to the west. *Mara, can you feel him flying around searching for me? He just left your house and now he's at my condo. I haven't been to my condo in ages—not since the incident. He paid for half of it, you know. Maybe I should speak to him. Maybe once I separate, I will teleport over to Thorn…*

Her mind immediately interrupted itself. *Wait a moment, Paxie. Need I remind you why we risked everything to join ourselves as one person? For vengeance. He cheated on you.*

But he was thinking something about extortion. What if there were circumstances…

You and I both know that Kalgren Tech spares no expense in hiring the best lawyers. People in positions of power are constantly threatened. Come on! How many times have people tried to kidnap me? *If it weren't for your uncle, I'd be in a body bag at the bottom of some river. Thorn has been running the company for long enough to know how to deal with situations like that.*

We don't even know what the whole situation was! Para straightened her posture abruptly as she tried to consider the possibilities. *I was a shitty girlfriend, and I didn't let him explain it to me. I just flew off the handle and went ballistic. I gave him life-threatening injuries and more problems to deal with when he probably needed me for support.*

Don't you dare think like this, Para chastised herself. She wasn't quite sure which half was speaking, or whether it was the union of her halves speaking. Her mind was a mess of voices. *There is no good reason for someone to cheat. No excusable reason. Thorn is a charmer. He'll say the right thing and put his hands in the right places, and poof! All is forgiven. Then, one day, another busty redhead walks into his office intending to blackmail him by revealing one of the fifty apocalyptic mistakes he makes in an average day, and instead of calling a lawyer he unzips his pants.*

She sighed and let her head drop against the mirror again. The cracks along the glass intensified. "I destroy everything I touch," Para said as she stared at the splintered glass. Her watch beeped to indicate that there was less than a minute remaining of her union. More than anything, she didn't want to separate. There was always an awful feeling of withdrawal and loneliness when she was in her original bodies. Para drew her knees up to her chest and hugged them, as though if she tried to hold herself together physically, it would prevent her spirit from ripping in two.

"Please," she said to no one in particular. She looked up at the fluorescent bathroom ceiling-lights. "Please let me live for longer than thirty minutes. I'm whole this way. I'm still sad and confused, but not to the same degree—I am a single person with clarity, purpose, and strength. Every horrible thing is easier to handle."

She closed her eyes, dreading the sound of her watch beeping again. When it came, it was accompanied by the vibrating of her cell phone as Thornton called. Her eyelids parted only just enough to read his name on her phone. "Please," she said again. "Sakra, if you're listening. You omnipotent folks can do just about anything. So bend the rules of this magick and let me stay Para Kalson. One fully-functioning, fully-*together* deva woman is better than two broken-hearted, useless, mostly-human girls. Right?"

Her watch beeped again, indicating thirty seconds. She sighed. "I'm waiting for that miracle. Any time now. Thirty seconds, universe. That's the magic number—I live for glorious bite-sized chunks of thirty minutes at a time, so let's use the next thirty seconds to work a miracle and make my existence permanent…"

Para was distracted by a disturbance in the air near her. Her dark indigo hair was ruffled as though someone had walked by, but no one was present. "Hello?" she called out, her voice echoing through the vacant restroom stalls. The lights in the bathroom began to flicker. Para's hands tightened around her knees as she glanced up at the lightshow curiously. There was a sound at the door, as though someone was trying to enter the locked room. Clanging sounds reverberated in the vents.

"Hello?" she asked again, sitting up and tossing her legs off the side of the counter. She stuffed her phone into her purse. "Is someone there?" There was the low drone of some sort of electric surge an instant before the room was plunged into pitch darkness. Para's watch beeped to indicate that there were only ten seconds remaining in her merger. "Great," she said aloud, "just what I need to…" She paused in her ranting as a chill settled in the air around her neck and shoulders. She reached up to touch her gooseflesh and found that the hairs on the back of her neck were standing up.

Her body sensed the trouble before she did. *Something's wrong here,* she realized as she peered through the darkness cautiously. As her watch began beeping faster, Para noticed a strange green glow reflected in the creases of the mirror she had shattered. The broken glass was amplifying and distorting an inhuman figure. Para gasped when dozens of bloodshot eyes became visible in the shards of the mirror. A split second later, they were gone. Her watch began to frantically remind her that she was about to divide just as the green glow intensified. Para raised her arms to cover her face as an icy wind suddenly swept across the room, making her hair billow up madly.

She felt massive frozen hands with sharp fingernails dig into shoulders, and another pair of burning hands on her waist. Finally, a third pair of hands clamped down on her hips and sent a potent electrical surge through her entire body. She screamed at the dizzying pain. In that moment, her body separated from itself.

The piercing shriek which hung in the air was not her own. As it faded away, Pax groped for its source blindly. "Mara!" she shouted, trying to touch the woman who had been part of her a moment ago. *"Mara!"*

Pax used her hands to create a giant flame which she cast before her like a torch. She knew that the blonde woman should not be more than a few feet away from her, but the room was empty. In their fleeting instant of vulnerability as their bodies divided, Amara Kalgren had been taken.

The lights turned back on. "Dammit! Fuck!" Pax continued to curse as she tossed her flame at the already-destroyed mirror. Her indistinct reflection began to melt. She instinctively knew that she had to find her friend, and fast. Someone or something had known precisely when to attack the girls, and this meant that they were being watched. It meant that her hallucinations of beasts in the backseat and creatures hovering over her at night might not have been figments of her imagination. Pax had to grasp the countertop with both hands to brace herself as she thought of her mother's dead body. Feeling nausea churn the dairy products in her stomach, Pax tried to push the images from her mind.

Pax wanted to run to her father for help, but she was still upset about his lies. She wanted to run to Vincent for help, but she had promised the man that no harm would come to his daughter and he would be murderous. She had to do it on her own. Pax tried to replay the events leading up to Amara's abduction in her mind. She was not even sure whether there had been one creature or several in the bathroom stall. It had all been a hazy blur of mirrored green smoke. Pax grabbed her purse and shopping bags, moving to the door, bursting through the narrow sheet of wood without bothering to unlock it first. She ignored the several women who had been impatiently waiting outside to use the facilities as she levitated off the ground and flew past them in a blur.

Moving at lightning speeds, Pax swept through the mall and alighted on top of the glass roof of the shopping mall. She dropped her bags in a discreet place on the roof so that she could close her eyes and scan the surrounding area for Amara. The girl's life force was nowhere to be found. *Come on. Concentrate, Pax.* The dark haired woman lifted her fingers to plug her ears to drown out the whirr of downtown traffic. She tried to focus on searching with her heart and mind, using her interior senses to see deeper than the superficial world around her. When she felt a blip in the distance, to the northeast, she nodded slightly.

Here goes nothing, she thought to herself as she removed her hands from her ears and pressed them to her abdomen. As the teleportation initiated, Pax felt her body dematerializing to weightlessness. She concentrated on Amara's life force and imagined the woman's pale blue irises. She hoped that she would see her friend's face the next time she opened her eyes.

When her body felt solid again, the incessant city sounds had disappeared. She inhaled and found a change in the consistency of the atmosphere. There was less oxygen. Pax tentatively allowed her eyelids to separate, and she was met by the precise pair of pale blue eyes she had been imagining—but they didn't belong to the right Kalgren. Pax immediately stumbled backwards, horrified that she had teleported inches away from Thornton. He reached out to catch her because he had been standing at the sharp edge of a mountaintop.

"Just the girl I've been looking for," he said as he pulled her away from the vast drop.

"Please, not now," she whispered as she tried to pry his arms away from her. Her high heels skimmed the edge as she struggled to push away from him, sending small rocks tumbling down below.

"I've been calling you," he said, before glancing down at her clothes. "Going somewhere nice?"

Pax froze, seized by the fear that he would recognize Para's clothing, but when she looked down she was wearing her own simple, black long-sleeved dress. The more feminine and alluring half of the garment had disappeared with Amara's hopefully still-living body. She looked back up at Thornton's familiar face. There were all kinds of reasons she should bolt away and get back to finding Amara, but she somehow felt comfort in the sight of him and could not look away.

"I really screwed up this time, Thorn," she said softly.

He recognized the serious note in her voice and released her arms. She levitated slightly and lowered herself a few feet away from him on the rocky terrain. Looking around, she recognized the lofty location. "This is where we used to come and meditate when I was in high school," she said in wonder as she stared down at the forested landscape through the thin, wispy layer of clouds.

"It was one of your favorite places," Thornton said, studying her face. "I've been searching for you everywhere. I really need to talk to you. Pax… what's wrong?"

She realized that she had turned to observe him, and was gazing a bit too fixedly. Pax was considering telling him about Amara and enlisting his help. But how could she tell him that she had allowed his sister to be taken from right under her nose? She could not explain without mentioning Para and their joined bodies. Even if she tried to conceal the details, inconsistencies would be found out and their union would be discovered. If she revealed their secret, Amara would be upset. Both girls were heavily emotionally invested in the ploy, however ridiculous it seemed now that her friend's life could be in danger. Pax shut her eyes tightly, knowing that she had to find her friend alone.

"You're worrying me, Paxie," Thornton said in a low voice. "I can tell by the look on your face that something serious has happened. Tell me how I can help." When she didn't respond, but just continued staring at him, he pressed again. "I know you better than anyone, and I know that you're upset. Let me help."

"If I did something really horrible and unforgiveable, would you still love me?" Pax found herself asking.

"Always."

She nodded, satisfied with the answer. "Thanks. Really appreciate it." She moved her hands to connect her fingertips against her abdomen. The last thing she saw was Thornton's arms reaching out towards her as her body faded from that moment in time and space.

"Pax, wait…"

Her teleportation swept her away from his grasp. When she was whole again she fell to her knees, overcome with dizziness. She blinked to clear her vision and saw that it was night. There were large white bones bathed in moonlight all around her. *Where am I?* she wondered to herself as she struggled to rise to her feet. She recognized the sleek formations which tapered to a point as tusks which had once belonged to elephants.

"Mara?" she called out feebly. Hearing the pathetic sound of her own voice echoing through the natural graveyard, she cleared her throat and yelled louder. "Mara!" Her teleporting was not only inaccurate and faulty, but it sapped her strength. Amara was evidently not in this location or anywhere nearby. *I teleported to her once before, and I did it while barely concentrating. Why can't I do it again?* Pax moved her hands to her stomach, creating the shape of a heart around her bellybutton and initiating a new teleport.

Pax was suddenly in a crowded sports bar. She frowned at the noise and scanned the room. "Amara!" she shouted. A few men turned to look at her, but most of the bar ignored her. She gritted her teeth together tightly. Walking up to the bar, Pax reached out and grabbed the front of the shirt of the bartender. "Did you see a blonde woman in here a few minutes ago?" she demanded.

"Whoa! Baby, this ain't the kinda joint where you find *any* women. Are you lost?"

"Dammit. Dammit!" Pax reached out and grabbed the nearest glass of whiskey right out of a man's hand and drank it in a single gulp before trying to teleport again. *This had better work,* she thought to herself as she fixed her hands together just below her ribcage. Her back and shoulders had broken out into sweat, and the heat of fear was traveling throughout her body. What if she never found Amara? A pulsating migraine was beating the insides of her skull as she attempted the challenging technique again. And again.

Dozens of scenic empty landscapes, and dozens of crowed cities later, Pax finally found herself collapsing, dizzy and disoriented in the middle of a desert. She had no idea for how many hours she had been popping all over the planet, screaming Amara's name until her throat was sore. "Dammit," she whispered hoarsely to herself one final time. She stared up at the sun, and watched through blurred vision as the orange sphere divided itself into two suns. She peered curiously at the warped image of two distinct balls of fire. She imagined that each orb was the eye of a mother tigress in the sky who roared down at her to open her own eyes.

That's it, she thought to herself. *One sun became two suns. Just like Para dividing in two. When we disconnect, there's still something of Para left in both of us. We're changed somehow. Amara's energy won't feel exactly the same as I remember, because she's stronger—there's more goddess in her. The particles in the blood that Rose always talks about—there should be some residue of Para's blood in both me and Amara. If I try to search the unique signature of my own prana, and isolate the change in myself, maybe I can lock on to the feeling of the new energy and find her…*

It occurred to Pax, as she closed her eyes and tried to focus, that Amara was being intentionally concealed with magick. She realized that whoever had taken her friend was not just another kidnapper after a generous Kalgren ransom, and not just another beastie in the night after a juicy meal. This was part of a sophisticated plan by a complex enemy. *Asura,* Pax thought as she placed her hands over her chest and tried to gauge the feel of her own energy. She remembered the demon that had sunk its claws into her chest during the nightmare. *It's the Asura.*

Once she memorized what her own power felt like, Pax gathered up the last bit of her resolve and tried to teleport away from the desert. Nothing happened. "Come on!" she said, looking down at her fingers splayed against her abdomen. *"Work!"* When she did not manage to budge from the spot, Pax felt helplessness begin to truly saturate her veins. She regretted not telling her father, Vincent, or even Thornton that Amara had been taken.

She had placed her friend's life in jeopardy just to conceal their secret. For the sake of Para's games, she had sacrificed Amara. Shame and remorse joined the helplessness as Pax dug her hands into the hot sand on either side of her body. She stared up at the two suns through eyes blurred with tears. "Take me to her!" she shouted hoarsely before slamming a hand down on her chest brutally.

Pax found herself disappearing again, and felt the familiar sickening zephyr of weightlessness. She let herself go completely and trusted that she would be taken to her friend. When she was solid again, she abruptly found that everything around her was not. Again, there was a change in the consistency of the atmosphere, but this time, there was not less oxygen. There was no oxygen. Thick, dark yellow clouds seemed to be suffocating her with a foul scent. Pax was falling rapidly through the noxious fog and was too exhausted to levitate and catch herself. As the heat increased, she felt the fabric of her black dress melting and simmering against her skin.

She opened her mouth wide and tried to gasp for breath, but her lungs were filled with the poisonous yellow filth. Her eyes watered and burned as she blinked away the acidic gases. "Mara," she wheezed. But she was pretty sure that her friend wasn't here either. In fact, she was pretty sure that she had royally screwed up and teleported clean off the planet. It certainly didn't smell anything like Kansas. Her last thought before losing consciousness in the middle of her whirlwind, breakneck fall, was that she should have told Thornton she loved him too instead of trying to be tough.

Chapter 17: Create One Beautiful Thing

A woman with long white hair sat atop a white horse, staring down at Pax with dismay. She was blindingly beautiful, and when she spoke, her voice was so ridiculously sweet that Pax wondered if she had bells on her fingers and toes.

"Child, you don't need oxygen. Breathe with your blood."

Although feverish and possibly delirious, Pax followed this advice to the best of her ability. She relaxed and allowed her *prana* to draw energy from the ground, from the air, and from the world around her. The temperature was intensely hot and Pax groaned as she shifted her position on the ground. While it felt like every bone in her body had been broken from the fall, the heat was so penetrating that she was sure it was melting the marrow inside those already crushed bones. As quickly as sweat could appear on her skin, it instantly evaporated. She squinted and saw that behind the gorgeous white-haired woman, the sky was the color of dark mustard.

"Are you a deva?" Pax asked.

"Something like that," the woman answered.

As Pax examined the stately woman, she felt a small twinge of nostalgia for her own long hair. It was impossible to look upon the woman's silver tresses without feeling a touch of jealousy. Even so, the mustard-colored sky was the real party piece. "Are we on…" Pax hesitated. She had been into space before, but it still sounded ridiculous to say it out loud. "Are we on Venus, and if so, how is it possible that you're riding a horse?"

The woman laughed, and it sounded like a peal of bells. "There is no horse. You see with your eyes, child. I imagined someone would have taught you to see the world more deeply. I can choose to appear in any form I wish, and the horse is merely an extension of my energy. A fashion accessory, if you will."

"Using a horse as a fashion accessory," Pax mused with lifted eyebrows. *Well, Amara would dig that.*

"I can wear a different body, if you prefer. The person you most wish to see, perhaps?" The woman smiled, and with a shimmer, the horse faded from under her body. As she levitated slowly to the ground, her silver hair began to darken and curl softly around her shoulders. Her pale face became infused with lifelike color. Soon, she was smiling sweetly from pink lips and the darkest blue eyes, in a face that Pax recognized well.

"Mom?" Pax said as she quickly scrambled to rise from the ground. Only then did Pax realize that her clothes had mostly melted from her body, and there were only black clumps of liquefied synthetic fibers clinging to her skin in various places. However, the vision of the woman before her was so heartening that she didn't care. Logically, she knew that the form-shifting creature was not her mother, but it did not deter her from eagerly approaching the figure.

"Dear child," said the apparition of Bridget Burnson as it reached out to take her daughter's hands. "Welcome to Ishtar."

"My mother was human," Pax said, trying to shake

away the foolish emotions. "She could never have survived in these conditions."

"Yes. Bridget Burnson only used rudimentary magick under the supervision of her husband to further her career. What a great beauty she was," said the woman, touching her own face, "much like her daughter would be if she cared about her appearance."

Pax was surprised by how much the apparition sounded like a chastising mother. "Well, I don't."

"Of course not, dear," said Bridget, moving closer and stroking Pax's short locks. "You're a tomboy through and through. But you can't fool me; I know you miss your hair." As the woman ran her fingers across Pax's scalp, the black tendrils began to glow like fire and lengthen. In a few seconds, Pax's hair had returned to its original length around her waist.

Pax sighed blissfully and moved her head from side to side, testing the comfortable weight. She laughed, feeling suddenly herself again; it was as though her hair had not only lengthened, but she had grown several inches and become somehow greater. She suddenly realized that this was a distraction from her purpose and her eyes narrowed. While Pax did feel thankful for the return of her hair, her intimidation at the casual show of the woman's power was far greater than her pleasure. "Please, ma'am. I am looking for my friend Amara Kalgren. Have you seen her?"

"One of the Kalgren devas. Have you two girls been getting yourself into trouble?" Bridget asked with a smile. "Let me help you find your friend, Pax Burnson. Something tells me that she is closer than you think."

Pax felt comfort and relief wash over her. She

wondered what degree of that comfort was due to her mother's image, at which she could not seem to stop staring. When the woman extended her arm, Pax took it eagerly. "Thank you so much for your help," she said sincerely as they began walking. "I'm not sure, but I think Amara was taken by some kind of glowing green creature. Does anything like that live around here?"

"Dear child, look around." The woman gestured to the landscape graciously. "Nothing lives here except for the beings I have created specifically for these conditions. Is that not the task of a goddess? To create that which others cannot conceive? My children would be frozen solid in the temperatures of Earth, but here, they are comfortable." The woman glanced sideways at Pax with a small smile. "Are you comfortable, darling?"

Pax had been gazing a bit rudely at the profile of her mother's face. She realized for the first time that it was kind of creepy to allow this woman to wear her mother's body like an ornament. She looked away. "It's only about eight hundred degrees. I'm comfortable, but I wish I had dressed for the weather," Pax said softly, glancing down at the remnants of her destroyed outfit.

The woman laughed again, producing the same achingly melodious sound. "That is easily remedied." She waved her fingers ever so slightly, and Pax felt a refreshing coolness envelop and caress her body. It felt divine and pleasant, and was so sudden that it caused her to sharply inhale a gulp of carbon dioxide. Looking down, Pax saw that she had been garbed in a white dress made of something like silk. The fabric was so light that it was almost transparent. "Is that better?" the woman asked.

"Yes," Pax answered politely as they continued walking. She was still embarrassed at being so uncovered, but the garment did provide some modesty along with relief from the blistering temperatures. Although the woman was being extremely kind, Pax felt a bit distrustful about her intentions. "I'm sorry, ma'am, but are you sure Amara is nearby?"

"Yes, child. Do not worry. Your friend is safe."

Pax felt a sick sensation in her gut. She wouldn't believe it until she saw Amara. "I don't even know who you are. Why are you helping me?"

"I knew your grandfather," the woman said, patting Pax's arm. "Kaden Burnson. What a man! If ever there was a god to be loved and feared… but I never did understand why he chose to live among humans. What a disappointment."

"What do you mean?" Pax asked.

"You Burnsons and Kalgrens forsook the old ways, you know. But I suppose the old ways are meant to be forsaken. Personally, I didn't leave Earth until my husband forsook *me.*"

"Your husband?"

"He was a deva. *The* deva. He placed perverse constraints on my abilities." The woman turned to Pax and raised her chin proudly, almost regally. "My personal motto has always been to create one beautiful thing every day. What is the point of having celestial powers if we are restricted from using them?"

Pax nodded, thinking of her father. She thought of Raymond's lies, meant to stop her from developing familiarity with her heritage. "I understand that," she said, "but sometimes people who love us may restrain us for our own benefit."

"Is that what they call it?" the woman asked with a laugh. "Darling, the only reason to keep someone else down is so that you can remain above them. There is never any harm or danger in allowing someone to grow and learn about their natural abilities. There is, however, tragedy in scaring a person into submission and forcing them to walk a mediocre path far from their deepest inclinations."

Pax forgot how to breathe with her blood for a second, and her body began shutting down on her. She had to concentrate to focus on drawing energy from the ground and very heat which was suffocating her. "You know too much about me," Pax said finally, when her brain stopped aching from the lack of oxygen. "Have you been watching me?"

"I can read your thoughts, child. Is that so farfetched?" The woman smiled. "It seems to me you have some experience with that sort of thing. As I scan your mind, I see a great many similarities between you and me."

You're a fat, hideous, disgusting cow. Pax thought, just to test whether the woman was really a true telepath. When there was no reaction, Pax's suspicions grew. *I'm about to strangle you, crush your head with rocks, and then… uh, rape you, because I'm actually a transvestite truck driver from Arkansas?* When Pax saw that the woman had absolutely no reaction to any of these outlandish and shocking thoughts, she had her answer.

Instead of saying any of those things, Pax asked, "How are we similar?"

The woman's face remained completely serene.

"Like you, I possess power, although my foolish husband tells me I must conceal it. I delight in using my power. It is who I am."

"I haven't used my powers as much as you think," Pax said. She was growing upset, and wanted to see evidence of Amara's safety as soon as possible.

"Yet, you are greater than a human. You have the fire of life in your blood. Tell me, how can they expect us to bottle ourselves up and waste our lives away being mundane?" The beautiful woman's eyes narrowed in anger. "We are so obviously special, and we should be allowed to express that."

"I agree," Pax said, "but my mother was human, and I am mostly human."

"Child, tell me you don't get a thrill from being able to stand on the surface of Venus. It's positively torrid but it barely bothers you. I can't say the same for your little friend. Can you imagine how the delicate-but-stylish Miss Kalgren would fare in these conditions?"

"Where is she?" Pax asked sternly. "Please take me to her. She's not strong enough…"

"And whose fault is that? By pretending to be human, Miss Kalgren has become as weak as any human. You know the laws of nature. The strong succeed and the weak perish."

Pax stopped moving, standing completely still. "What do you want from me?" she asked abruptly. "I'm listening."

"It's simple, Pax. I want you to see the possibilities that stretch before us." As the woman spoke, she raised her arms before her. The ground began to tremble with the onset of an earthquake. Pax levitated off the ground to prevent her body from being agitated and tossed around. A pointed black object began to rise from the dark soil at a rapid rate. As the woman wearing Bridget Burnson's body lifted her hands, it became evident that a structure was emerging from the surface. Pax recognized it to be a palace. It seemed to be made from a dark kind of steel.

Pax was filled with a simultaneous anxiety and anticipation. Even the rumbling of the ground caused a thrill in her gut, and the ascending palace filled her with wonder.

"It's gorgeous," Pax said, once the terrain ceased trembling.

"Thank you," the woman said proudly. "It took me more than a day to create this. I call it the Palace of Ishtar. It remains hidden beneath the ground to protect it from those who would seek to harm me. A woman must protect that which she owns."

"I'm impressed," Pax said, trying to gain control of the naked astonishment splayed across her facial features. "I'm really just… blown away."

The woman smiled graciously. "I want to be a different kind of ruler here than I was on Earth. Sakra is such a foolish man. He observes everything from his little temple in the mountains, but what does he really do?"

Pax froze. Even in temperatures exponentially hotter than the most brutal desert on earth, she managed to feel her blood run cold. "You're Sakra's wife. That's who you are."

"Yes—you should have been able to gather that by now. I am Suja, Queen of the Asura." The woman's body began to transform once more, and Bridget Burnson's dark hair swept into the classy blonde French twist worn by the scientist Rose Kalgren. Her dark eyes transitioned to pale blue effortlessly, and all of her new features looked at Pax as kindly as Amara's mother truly would have. "I would reveal myself to you in my true form, but I fear that I have long since forgotten what that even was."

Pax's pupils had dilated, and her mind swam wildly as she processed this information. Sakra's wife was a supremely powerful being. She was sure that there was some formal way to address the woman, but all she could think of saying was, "It's nice to meet you." She mentally slapped herself for how retarded she felt this sounded, and tried to cover up by asking the important question. "Is Amara in the palace?"

"Yes, of course. Why do you think I brought you here?" The Asura woman smiled with Rose Kalgren's classic witty and mischievous smile. "There's a bit of air conditioning inside. And oxygen, if you like that sort of thing."

"Thank god," Pax said.

"Why, you're very welcome."

Chapter 18: Palace of Ishtar

"There's nothing here," Pax said as they walked through the palace.

"You're still seeing with your eyes," Suja remarked. "If you relax and allow yourself to believe what your intuition already knows, you will be able to perceive the presence of my army."

Pax tried to do as the woman recommended, but could just barely sense that anything living was in the castle. She did, however, sense Amara. "I haven't practiced nearly enough," she told Suja apologetically.

"I can teach you all you've missed and more," Suja said. "You just have to open yourself to me and have faith. I know you don't trust me yet, and that is wise. I am a stranger, and although I have always been on your side, I am a highborn Asura woman by birth."

"You're very understanding," Pax said. "Thanks for being so candid."

"I'm selfish in the end, my dear. As all living things must be. I only wish to gain your favor so you will assist me. I only strive to be honest so that I may retain your respect."

"How can I assist you?" Pax asked. "I'll do whatever I can."

"Really, darling?" A smile transformed Suja's features. "I am so pleased to hear you say that. All I want is for you to be my ally. All I want is for you to rule!"

"Rule what?" Pax asked.

"Earth of course," Suja answered. "I rather like it here in Ishtar. I'm a solitary woman, and I enjoy warm places with little oxygen. But if you wish, I can give you Earth."

"Sakra rules Earth," Pax answered nervously.

"No, he observes Earth. He's a pathetic shrimp who should never have been appointed Lord of Devas. Your lives are all little more than a soap opera to that self-righteous, so-called god." Suja's voice was bitter when she spoke of her husband. "Also, he's getting fat."

"Really? I thought he was a skinny little guy."

"He was. But underneath those embroidered golden brocade robes, there is a definite potbelly starting to appear. I just can't believe how flabby his arms are getting. I swear, Pax. He won't even shapeshift into a body that doesn't have man-boobs. It's humiliating."

"I'm… sorry," Pax said slowly, a bit perplexed, "but what did Sakra *do?*"

"I would prefer not to discuss that. Let's just say we had a final difference of opinions. He upset me so much that I couldn't watch him blinking without wanting to disembowel him. So I left." Suja reached up to finger Rose Kalgren's sophisticated blonde bun. "But all that is behind me now. Will you help me overthrow him, and retake the highest temple of Earth?"

"I'm not sure I can," Pax answered cautiously.

"With my training, you will be capable. Your father is Sakra's prime bodyguard, and he won't stop you." Suja placed both hands on Pax's shoulders. "It's what you were meant to do, child. You were meant to rule!"

She's insane, Pax realized. *Do I try to placate her until I get Amara back and betray her later? That could be dangerous. Should I just tell her that I'm not the person she's looking for? Even though she's mad, I still admire her for some reason. I should be honest.*

"Suja, I am not capable of overthrowing Sakra. Even if I could, I wouldn't know how to rule as the god of gods. I'm just a human girl. I'm flattered that you see this great potential in me, but I'm not as strong as you think."

The woman wearing Rose Kalgren's body pulled away abruptly. Her hair became white again, and it lengthened until it touched the floor. She began levitating off the ground, until she was suspended in the center of the great hall. Her snowy hair had lengthened as she rose, and it was still sweeping the floor. "I expected that you would say that, Pax Burnson. Allow me to change your mind."

Extending an arm, Suja used her finger to touch the corner of a geometrical shape which had not been previously visible. Pax watched in awe as a pyramid made of thick transparent glass became visible, suspended in the center of the room. There was a woman concealed within the glass, and Pax knew it was Amara.

"Let me present my bargaining chip," Suja said with a gesture. "The helpless Kalgren girl."

Pax sighed, allowing her shoulders to fall. "Seriously? You seemed so cool about five minutes ago." She gestured at the glass pyramid. "This? This is just *tacky* second-rate villain stuff."

Suja laughed, and the sound was still magical. Her hair began to glow and twist, rapidly braid itself. Pax had to leap back to avoid being struck by the ropelike collection of strands. "If I am so second-rate, it will be easy to defeat me, fire deva. Here is your task: overpower the monster and liberate the princess."

"This isn't a game!" Pax yelled as she levitated off the ground. "This isn't a homework assignment; my friend's life is at stake. Release her. I *will* wreck you if you don't let her go *now.*"

"There's that confidence you were pretending not to have a mere minute ago!" Suja said triumphantly. "There's that capacity for violence, that lust for vengeance and justice. Show me your true nature, little one."

Pax cracked her neck and rolled her shoulders to loosen them. "In ten seconds I want you to remember that you asked for it." Tossing her head back, Pax reached deep inside herself and allowed the flames of Ruby Form to consume and transform her body. She formed a precise and economical plan of attack. She would rush at the glass pyramid and shatter it, retrieving Amara. Then she would unleash a stream of blue-hot flames from her hand which would temporarily blind Suja, allowing her to teleport away and escape. She had no hopes of actually killing the Asura woman, but if she could get home, she believed that the woman would not follow. Suja would not risk facing Raymond and Vincent.

"Let her try," Suja spoke softly to a being which Pax could not see. With the woman's obvious madness, Pax doubted that anything was even there, and continued to release her latent goddess. *How's this for dormant, Father?* Her thoughts were filled with arrogance and anger.

When Pax felt fully charged with adrenaline and the natural firepower of her *prana*, she extended her fist and charged the pyramid. She unleashed an earsplitting battle cry as she imagined her clenched hand having the density and mass of a small star. She channeled all the power she could grasp and all the energy she could access into the two inches across her knuckles before she smashed her hand into the bottom of the glass pyramid. Pax expected the material to crumble beneath her blow, but she was shocked when she instead struck a rock-solid, unyielding wall. The force of her own strike traveled through her own arm, and Pax screamed in excruciating pain as the limb fell limply against her side. She had shattered her own bones.

Pax clutched her dead arm in disbelief as tears clouded her eyes. She tried to move her bloody fingers, but they lay disabled against her thigh. "Damnation!" Pax whispered as she stared at the unaffected pyramid. There was a new spot of blood on the bottom of the structure, but there was otherwise not even the tiniest of cracks in the material. She turned to Suja, panting heavily in pain. "You're using magick to fortify the glass," she said weakly. "I should have known."

Suja clucked her tongue. "Glass? It's not glass, child. That was a miscalculation on your part."

"What is it?" Pax said, massaging her arm and trying to regain feeling in the immobilized limb. She was still in denial of the fact that the arm was gone. Her stomach contorted in knots. "That stuff can't be... diamond?"

"Honey," Suja said with a laugh. "You should see

the look on your face. You really did believe that the Asura queen, wife of Lord Sakra for a thousand years, was a second-rate, *tacky* villain. If I had other invincible friends to join me for fine beverages, we would surely be laughing about this until all the planets had circled the sun."

"It's diamond," Pax said, staring at the transparent material encasing Amara. She saw that her blow had caused at least some vibration in the structure, and Amara was stirring awake. "For Sakra's sake. You trapped her in a diamond pyramid."

"No," Suja said, laughing even louder. "It's not an element found on Earth. You don't have a name for it, but we call it fjuyen. It's harvested from the center of a white dwarf star, and it's far *harder* than diamond, my dear. Who's tacky now?"

Amara was no longer unconscious, and was beating her hands futilely against the insides of the fjuyen pyramid. "Pax!" she screamed, but her voice was muffled. She pressed her face close to the translucent walls to peer through the material. *Paxie! Where am I?*

You don't want to know, Pax answered. As she gritted her teeth against the blinding pain in her arm, she realized that she had been defeated. At least for the time being. "Okay, Suja. You win and I'm yours. Just please have mercy on Amara and send her home to Earth. Then I'll do whatever you command."

"I have a better idea," Suja said. "I'm going to punish you for a little while. Just so you learn the price of calling me names and underestimating me. Obake! Seize her."

Pax screamed when she felt claws dig into her

good arm, and into her waist. Although she could not see the beings surrounding her, she remembered the familiar feel of the claws from the demons in her dream. She felt her body slammed roughly against the black metal walls of the palace. She heard the sound of cackling as the invisible demons raked their claws all over her body.

What the hell is happening, Pax? Amara's voice shrieked into her brain. Pax closed her eyes and swallowed, unable to respond.

"Now, now, boys," Suja said disapprovingly. "A little hospitality for the young lady?"

The claws stopped roaming abruptly, but Pax remained firmly clamped against the wall at her neck and waist. "Just let Amara go," Pax pleaded. "Then you can let a giant invisible octopus rape me for all I care."

Suja giggled in delight. "Oh, darling, don't tempt me. I have plenty of room in my home for new pets." The white haired woman floated toward the fjuyen pyramid and placed a hand on the surface. "Triangles are extremely strong shapes. I find them stunning, really. You know, since I left my husband—I have created one beautiful thing each day. What have you done since your deva betrayed you, Pax Burnson? What have you done except rot?"

Pax could not answer. She drew her eyebrows together, and could only think of Para.

"Exactly. You have done nothing. Your merger with Amara, you consider that significant? Ha! So you created a woman. A goddess more powerful than yourself—but she has a weakness. She can only live for thirty minutes at a time." Suja smiled. "You should know this, Pax. A being is the sum of all their weakness and strengths. It's like a ledger calculating net worth: your debts are subtracted from your assets. If your weakness is greater than your strength, you are the sum of both qualities. You have deceived yourself into thinking Para is greater than you are—that was a mistake."

The sound of Amara's muffled screams were heard as the clear pyramid began to fill with a neon green substance. The blonde woman struggled and thrashed her arms wildly before the green substance had completely covered her from head to toe. Pax tried to see what was happening, but only knew that her friend was in great distress.

They're worms! Get them off, please! Oh my god, they're eating my skin! Pax was powerless as the thousands of tiny green worms crawled all over Amara's pink designer dress. The insects twisted themselves right through the fabric and burrowed down into her flesh. Several seconds passed while Amara violently scratched at herself and suffered from spasms which caused her body to bang against the insides of the pyramid. She released several bloodcurdling screams. *Ash,* she mentally moaned. *Where are you? Help me, Ash.*

Pax frowned when she heard her friend call for her uncle. She knew Amara was buckling under the stress of the situation. The blonde woman was too delicate for this type of trauma, and Pax was filled with guilt for putting her in harm's way

"Do you see these little diggers, Pax? They are sucking her energy as fast as she can gather it. They are depleting her life force. In effect, I have turned her into my own little deva-battery." Suja smiled. "If only Mrs.

Rose Kalgren knew that the solution to renewable green energy was not in one of her laboratory creations, but in her own daughter's blood."

"Why are you doing this?" Pax asked with a frown. "What do you need her energy for?"

"I don't really need it, but it sure is fun to watch those worms wiggle into her body. Look at how she squirms! Those adorable green critters are latching themselves onto her blood cells and transforming pure *prana* into electricity I suppose I could use her energy to power the planet, but there's nothing on the planet that needs power.. I just hate to waste good electricity, don't you?"

Suja twitched her finger, causing a narrow wire to extend from the pyramid to Pax's neck. The dark-haired woman's eyes widened as electricity traveled along the wire and began to prickle her skin. At first it was a prickle, but then she found her limbs involuntary quivering. Then her head violently jerked against the wall behind her, and she lost all control of her senses. There was only pain. Pax became vaguely aware of foam leaving her mouth and dribbling down her chin.

"You're a deva," Suja said, as she turned her back and swept away from the room. "You can handle a few hours of being tortured by your own friend's life force. Amara's energy isn't strong enough to kill you, but it should sting a little. It should sting at least as much as it wounded me when you called me second-rate. Obake guards! See that she does not escape. If she tries, you have my permission to rough her up as much as you like. I'm going to take a nice long bubble bath. I might even catch up on some reading. Bye, Pax." Suja waved and was about to leave, when Pax screamed.

"Wait!" Pax shouted at the top of her lungs. The Asura woman turned back, startled that Pax was even able to form a coherent word. Pax moaned, and ripping her good arm away from its invisible restrains, she wiped the foam from her chin. She struggled to straighten her posture and stared directly at her captor. "I'm not second-rate either," Pax whispered.

"Oh?" Suja asked. "I would love a demonstration."

Pax began to laugh. At first it was a small chuckle, but it soon became a hysterical roar. The electricity was still feeding into her neck, but the force of the glowing red aura around her caused the wire to tremble.

"Obake! Restrain her!" Suja shouted to her guards.

In her hysteria, Pax could suddenly see the silhouettes of the guards around her. She saw their claws reaching for her skin and let out a piecing scream, causing the wire around her neck to break and the guards to be flung away. She looked out across the room, and suddenly realized that there were hundreds of other Obake guards standing at attention and ready to attack her. She glared at Suja, holding her good arm out defensively to keep the guards at bay with her *prana.*

"I'm sorry for whatever Sakra did to you. Your palace is amazing and when I arrived here, I thought you were wonderful. But now, after what you've done to Amara? You're not going to get away with this. You're going to suffer," Pax promised. "Your power is great, and your reach is immense, but you made one grave mistake. When you reached for me, you overextended yourself."

"What a moving speech," Suja responded, clapping gracefully. "I guess we'll just have to see if you can actually follow through with all those grandiose and pompous claims."

"I can."

Pax glanced up at the fjuyen pyramid, and made a split-second decision. She knew she wouldn't be able to rescue Amara on her own. Not without her arm, and with her body close to the point of collapse. With a desperate internal plea for strength, she pressed her good hand against her solar plexus. *Please,* she thought as she tried to initiate the transference, *please.* She exerted more and more energy, pushing herself harder until there was unbearable pain in her body. Pax waited for her technique to commence for what felt like an eternity. It was really just a fraction of a second. Even that delay was far too long in such a situation, and Pax was relieved by the sensation of weightlessness as her body began to dematerialize. She had been able to generate just enough energy to teleport away.

Chapter 19: Removing His Glasses

Pax found herself stumbling against one of the wooden posts at the foot of Thornton's bed. She inhaled her familiar earthly air and the saturation of oxygen entering her body was blissful. She wrapped her good arm around the wooden post and pressed her forehead against the carved patterns as her chest heaved with her ragged gasps.

Thornton stirred under his blanket at the sound of the noise.

"Thorn," she croaked out. Hearing the pathetic sound of her own voice, she wheezed a few more times to try and regain her voice. The last teleportation had sapped everything out of her. She clung feebly to the bedpost to keep herself upright. Casting her eyes on Thornton's sleeping figure, she felt reassured that he was nearby. When she breathed, the familiar scent of him and his bedroom comforted her senses, and she knew that no further harm would come to her. It should have surprised her that even after everything that had happened, she still felt safest in this place above all others; but she was far too tired to be surprised.

I need your help, she said into his mind.

Paxie? Even his telepathic voice was groggy. He reached out an arm as if he expected her to be beside him in bed; upon finding nothing, he frowned and sat up abruptly. The blanket fell from his chiseled chest into his lap, and he reached up to try to arrange his tousled blonde hair. *What's going on? I've been looking for you.*

I'm here now, she answered wordlessly. There was something about communicating telepathically that was more intimate and exciting than a whisper. Or perhaps it was the sight of his bare torso that was affecting her, causing her body to respond even though it was trashed. Pax turned away and spoke out loud: "I was too proud to accept your help earlier, but I can't do this on my own. I need you." She used as stern a voice as she could muster, trying to override and erase the intimacy of being in his bedroom again.

"Your hair is back," he observed as he rubbed his eyes and looked up at her. She had forgotten this fact and she nodded wearily. Thornton cleared his throat and stretched out to grasp a cardboard box lying on his night table. "I have a present for you. I wanted to give it to you earlier, but…"

"There's no time to…"

"Please open it, Pax."

She swallowed as she used her good arm to lift the lid from the box. When she saw the robotic metal dog, her eyes flooded with tears. "Bree," she said softly. She immediately lifted the dog to her chest, and clutched it tightly.

"I haven't activated her, but…"

"Thorn, I need your help right now," Pax said. A tear splashed from her eye down onto the mechanical puppy. "There's danger. We have to fight."

"You're wounded," he suddenly noticed. He moved closer to examine her limp arm and his eyes widened when he felt all the spots in which the bone had been splintered. "Good Sakra, Pax! Where on earth have you been?"

"Not Earth. Sakra's wife," she said softly, feeling fatigue lower her eyelids. "Fight her."

"I'm not strong enough to take on Suja," Thornton said. He noticed that Pax was falling asleep on her feet and reached up to take the mechanical puppy from her arms. "You could have gone to Raymond or my dad for help. They're both stronger than I am. Why did you come to me?"

"I don't know," she answered, hesitating. She noticed that she was no longer holding Briar several seconds after the dog had been taken from her arms. She tried to focus on Thornton's face in the darkness. "You've always been there when I needed you."

"I always will be," he said. "Paxie, you need to know…"

"May I lie down here for a sec?" she asked. She was already keeling over, and the top half of her collapsed lifelessly on the bed.

"What kind of a question is that?" he asked, reaching down to grasp her waist and drag the rest of her onto the bed as well. "You've only slept beside me thousands of times." He positioned her unconscious head on the pillow beside him. Moving to his night table again, he opened the top drawer and pulled out a vial of Sakra's water. He used his thumb to part her lips slightly and trickled several drops of the healing fluid into her mouth. Once the bottle was emptied, he tossed it away and moved to her side, slipping his arm around her ribcage to hold her. He pressed his forehead against her shoulder and entangled his leg around hers. "I missed you, Paxie."

* * *

Pax bolted upright violently, looking around in a terrified panic.

Thornton rubbed his nose where her shoulder had clipped him in her vigorous motion. "What's wrong?" he mumbled sleepily.

"I can't believe I fell asleep!" Pax yelled, furious with herself.

"It was only for a few minutes," he told her.

"Why didn't you wake me?" she asked, turning to him angrily.

"You were tired and wounded, as though you'd been fighting." He raised himself up onto his elbow to study her in the dim lighting. "Your arm was crushed, and you were bleeding all over like you were shredded by claws."

She reached up to feel her arm and was happy to see that it had healed—Thornton had taken care of her like she knew he would. "We have to get going *now*," she said fiercely, trying to overcompensate for the fact that all she wanted to do was lie down again. Her body and mind were both shot. "That's the first time I slept without nightmares since…" Pax put her face in her hands.

"Me too," he said softly, reaching up to stroke her newly-lengthened hair. "I promise you that we'll have many more restful, dreamless nights as soon as I do whatever you need me to do."

Pax nodded, feeling her sense of purpose return. "Mara is being held captive by the Asura and a small army of creatures called Obake in a pyramid-prison made from a substance harder than diamond. On Venus."

Thornton began to chuckle. When his hilarity evolved into a full-fledged laugh, he was abruptly halted by the force of a full-powered, burning-hot slap across his face. He saw the literal fire in her eyes, and swallowed. "Okay. So, you're not joking. Venus?" Thornton pushed himself upright and levitated to the ground. "I'll have to tell Father."

"No," she pleaded. "It's my fault. He'll kill me."

"How is it your fault?" he asked.

"I used powerful magicks and attracted the attention of the Queen of the Asura."

"What were you doing?"

She hesitated. "I was trying to hurt you."

Thornton smiled. "You already have. You don't have to trap me in lava at the earth's core or turn me into a cockroach to get back at me. It hurts badly enough when you avoid me."

"Very good to know. So what can we do about Amara?"

"Do we need a ship? Because Kalgren Tech just sold the newest model of…"

"No. We need to get over there *now*. I have to teleport us."

"Okay. Well, I've got a book on my desk, and a few more hidden in the safe behind the Cézanne."

"I hate that painting," Pax said, dragging herself from the bed and moving to sit on his ergonomic office chair. She looked down at the tome that lay open. She ran her fingers over the ancient writing, using her *prana* to translate the Sumerian script. "A treatise on inducing an individual to forget… Thorn!"

"Sorry. Just some light reading," he said, clearing his throat as he turned the dial on his safe.

"Were you going to use this on me?" Pax asked as she hastily turned to other bookmarked pages. She found more perception-altering techniques and turned to him suspiciously.

"I'm not sure," he answered honestly as he pulled a few books out of the safe. He sent her a sheepish and apologetic shrug. "But I was considering it. I'm not sure how far I was willing to go to get you back… Pax, are you smiling?"

"No," she said, turning away rapidly to conceal the small smirk which she couldn't keep from her face. "This is messed up. But it *is* kind of… sweet."

"You find it sweet that I was considering rearranging your brain to make you love me again?" he asked with a frown.

She released a small chortle. "Well, if anything, it's passionate. But right now we need to be passionate about getting Amara home safely."

"Right. Little sis is in distress, as usual." He approached the desk and deposited several giant books on the polished mahogany surface. "I'm not sure how much of this I can actually manage to *do* successfully. The collection isn't as impressive as yours, but you better believe that if a demigod ever imagined a creative way to use his powers as a weapon to cause suffering and mayhem, it's in here." Thornton pressed his index finger down on one particular volume.

"Good," Pax said, staring at the book. "It's what

we're best at, after all. There are hundreds, maybe thousands of invisible Obake guards. Suja created them to be extremely cold blooded creatures which would freeze at the temperature of the planet Earth. So… do you think there's a recipe somewhere for an instant ice age?"

"Whoa. That's serious stuff, Paxie." He was frowning thoughtfully.

"We need serious. We need deadly."

"That's my girl." Thornton lifted his glasses from his desk and slid them onto his nose. He began scanning pages rapidly. He suddenly glanced up at her body. "Uh, you'd better put something else on."

"Why?" she said, looking down. When she saw what she was wearing, her cheeks reddened.

"I don't know how you feel about doing battle in a transparent nightgown," he said with a smirk, "but personally, I will find it distracting."

"It doesn't matter," she said. "Most fabrics won't be able to sustain the heat on Venus."

"Don't you have an aramid vest somewhere around here?" he asked.

Pax drew her eyebrows together. She moved over to his dresser and opened one of the drawers where she used to keep her own clothing. She dug through to the bottom and found the old training vest she had used when she first learned Ruby Form. "You still have all my clothes here," she said softly.

"I wasn't about to get rid of them anytime soon." A mischievous sheen came into his blue eyes. "Unless you gained a few pounds and wanted to bring some new stuff over."

Pax rolled her eyes and closed the drawer abruptly. She opened a drawer containing Thornton's clothes and withdrew one of his old t-shirts. She tugged the garment over her head before returning to the desk. "Let's get to work." She sat down and extended her fingers, creating a black glow around the tomes. Using her energy to absorb the information was a physically grueling method when she was already exhausted, but far faster than reading. "This is going to be the hardest thing I've ever done," she suddenly realized as the difficulty of the incantations registered in her mind.

Thornton squeezed her shoulder reassuringly. "We'll do it together, Pax. I need you to tell me everything you can remember about the place Amara is being held."

*   *   *

"It's more reasonable if we do it this way," Thornton argued, sitting on the ground and pouring metallic sand around himself. "I'm not powerful enough to plunge the whole planet into a deep freeze, and nothing like that is recorded here anyway. I imagine that the last time someone used power like that was 20,000 years ago, and it was probably a group of pureblooded gods. I plan to create a concentrated blizzard for an area roughly the size of a city, and intensify it as much as I possibly can. Will that work?"

"I hope so," Pax said. "I just need a decent window to break Amara free. I'm not even sure how I'm going to manage that."

"There won't be much of a window, I'm afraid."

Thornton used both hands to smooth his blonde hair, a nervous habit. He immediately placed his hands down over the metal dust and began to release a stream of vivid blue *prana* into the metal. "I'll create a bubble with several miles radius, but I'll have to constantly feed my energy into the atmosphere to sustain the artificial temperature. It's a heavy-duty task, Paxie. It will take all my concentration and power, and I'll probably only manage to hold it for a minute. Then you will have to use your relocation technique to teleport us the hell out of there. No room for failures, okay?"

"Okay," she answered. "What do we do about the Asura woman, Suja?"

"I don't know," Thornton said. "Let's get Mara home first, and worry about her later. It seems like her main goal was to separate you from us and attract you to her side—so if she sees that you've still got backup, and you march in there with an army, maybe it will dissuade her from attacking us any further."

Pax smiled. "Are you my army?"

"Always."

Pax lowered her eyes to gaze at the blue *prana* circle. She chewed on her lip for a second. "I'm really upset with you, Thorn."

"I know."

"Sorry for beating the crap out of you a whole bunch of times."

Thornton smiled. "Stop distracting me now. This is the part where I need to focus."

"Okay. Thanks for being on my side again."

"Pax, you're my best friend. Nothing else matters." Thornton reached up with one hand, removing his glasses from his face and handing them to her. She took the metal frame and quickly returned it to his desk as he began to chant in Sumerian. The turquoise colored energy continued to pour forth from his hands, creating a chill in the room.

Pax returned to kneel before him, spellbound as his eyes glowed blue to match the *prana* leaving his body. The tone in his voice as he chanted was raw and precise, and it sent a chill through her to witness him being so authoritative and focused.

He was never like this at the office. Thornton was always tense and high-strung when surrounded by piles of paperwork, and he always gave the impression of someone wanting to curl up into a ball and die. His classic office-posture was to sit with his head in his hands. It was part of the reason that she had tried to visit him as often as possible, and bring him food to cheer him up. He hated his job as much as she hated the hospital—they both had chosen their work to please their families, but it was far worse for Thornton. The reputation of his family's company depended on him.

The cyan swirls of *prana* which rose from the circle tossed cool waves of air around them. Pax gazed in admiration as Thornton's blonde hair wafted back from his forehead, blowing wildly in the breeze. His voice grew louder as the incantation became more challenging. His arms began to shake and a vein visibly pulsated in his forehead. As he gritted his teeth and struggled with the technique, the muscles in his arms and neck grew taut with his determination.

This was the man she had fallen in love with. Pax swallowed, swept away in the aura of masculinity that she felt in his energy as it closed in all around her. Without thinking, she reached across the circle and grasped his hands, feeding her own prana into the incantation with him. He did not pause in his chanting, but locked his eyes with hers and tightened his grip on her hands. Their fingers interlaced; his icy cold digits linking between her burning fingertips and finally descending to touch her palms.

Shivers ran through her, and not because of the temperature or the energy. Pax realized as she stared into his luminous eyes that she was not touching him to help out with the incantation. She was using the magick as an excuse to touch him. Watching him practice was a spiritual experience; the dominance in his voice as he chanted was hypnotic. He was completely in his element, and his element was power.

Whenever Thornton removed his glasses, her body began to hum with excitement. It usually meant that impressive events were about to go down, and this time was no exception.

Teleport us now! One minute, Pax. The shield is about to go up, and that's all the time you'll have.

I'm used to working with budgeted time, she responded as she released one of his hands and touched it to her own solar plexus.

Chapter 20: Inside this Body

When they arrived on Venus, Pax was pleasantly surprised by her own good aim. They arrived directly in the large room of the palace where Amara was being held prisoner. She immediately moved away from Thornton and flew to the fjuyen pyramid. There was still a neon green glow visible over Amara's body.

I'm back, Mara. Are you hanging in there?

Ash? The telepathic voice was feeble.

Pax placed her hand on the transparent fjuyen material. *No, it's me. Your big brother's here and we're going to bust you out!*

Where's Ash? Amara asked wretchedly. *I need him.*

Ignoring this because she did not quite know how to respond, Pax focused her energy on breaking apart the pyramid prison. *Just hang in there, Mara. I'll get you out.* Channeling her *prana* to what she believed was the weakest point of the structure, Pax tried to use her mind to force a crack in the fjuyen. *Harder than diamond, my ass!* She summoned every ounce of grit she possessed.

Pax suddenly felt sharp Obake claws rip across her thigh, and she levitated away from the pyramid in surprise. She turned back to observe Thornton as the blonde man struggled to hold up the shield.

"What's wrong?" she asked him. "Isn't it working?"

Thornton growled as a pair of claws slashed across his own chest. "It's not activated yet. I can't get it to work."

"Do you need my help?" she asked, already flying

back down to him.

"No!" he shouted. "If you waste all your energy on the shield then you'll pass out and we won't be able to free Mara and teleport back. It'll be a waste."

"Try harder," she encouraged. "You can do it."

"No, I can't. I'm sorry, Pax. I can't manage to control the shape of the shield and fill it with enough *prana* at the same time."

She moved to dodge an Obake that she could sense was moving to attack her. "Let me help a little…"

"We have to go back to Earth and get a new strategy," Thornton said.

"Thorn! Your sister is going nuts up there," Pax said frantically. "She has energy sucking bugs digging into her skin and we can't leave her trapped in that pyramid for even an hour more…"

"She's safe, Pax. She's not going to be killed…"

"But she's scared!" Pax insisted. "She's not tough like us. She keeps calling me Ash and I know there's a family resemblance but do I look like a retarded, macho, nincompoop, freak of…"

"What did you say?"

Pax dodged another invisible beast, realizing that she was learning to see them better without actually seeing them. "That I'm not a retarded, macho, nincompoop…"

"Ash!" Thornton said abruptly. "Get Ash now!"

"Are you serious?" she asked. She felt that he was about to be attacked, and she dove forward, grabbing an invisible clawed Obake hand before it connected with Thornton's face. She reached out and twisted the creature's head sharply, killing it instantly.

"Thanks. I can't put up the shield on my own," Thornton gasped. Every inch of his skin was moistened with sweat, and his blonde hair was sticking to his forehead and cheeks. "It's harder than I anticipated. You have to get Ash."

"Why?" she yelled, as she continued to fight the Obake around them.

"There's a coalescence technique," Thornton said, struggling to control the icy blue energy around him. "Ash and I can join our bodies together and it will increase our power by at least ten times. We should be able to manage this then."

Pax paused in her fighting, turning to look at Thornton nervously. So he was aware of the coalescence technique. An Obake used her moment of distraction to slash her across the stomach, and she screamed. In rage, she lashed out and shoved her own hand completely through the creature's stomach. She was almost sure that she broke a nail on its spine. "I can't leave you unprotected!" Pax said. "There are too many of these things."

The muscles in Thornton's arms strained to hold up the portion of the shield he had already erected. "Just go! I'll be fine. *Hurry,* Pax!"

She nodded quickly and moved her hand to her bleeding stomach. "Be safe," she whispered as her body disappeared. Thornton returned his attention to the shield, concentrating to keep it from dissipating. At the same time, he could sense the Obake creatures closing in around him. His eyes drifted back and forth from invisible being to invisible being. When they lunged at him, he tried to divide a portion of his prana into fighting them, but there were too many. He was able to deflect some of the blows, while several claws sneaked past his defenses to slice at his body.

"Enough!" commanded a white-haired woman as she glided into the room. "A handsome visitor is so rare in these parts. Let us not shred him like mozzarella."

Thornton groaned at this analogy. "You'll find my texture is closer to tough beef."

"Thorn, dear boy! How good to see you again," Suja remarked.

"Again? We haven't been introduced," Thornton said. He knew that he needed to stall for time until Pax returned, and gods and goddess loved to waste time on big ceremonious introductions. He nervously glanced up at the pyramid holding his sister.

"How rude of me to forget to welcome you to the Palace of Ishtar," Suja said. She curtsied slightly to Thornton, and as her head lowered, her hair began to change color once more. The white tendrils snaked and writhed until they became ginger-dyed waves. When she looked up again, her clothes began transforming from stately, flowing robes into a professional pinstriped business suit. She ran her tongue along her top lip almost hungrily as she toyed with her new red hair.

"Perhaps you remember me like this?" she purred. "The last time we met, I was inside this body. And so were you."

*   *   *

When Pax completed her teleport to Earth, she found herself standing before the strongest life force on the planet. She considered asking him for help, but he sneered at her and seemed prepared to toss a handful of popcorn into her face.

"Girl, the humans are all abuzz about this phenomenon called 'game night.' I have placed bets on this spectacle and if you don't quit blocking the television, I will destroy you."

"Sorry, Vince."

What a serious man, she thought to herself. *I shouldn't bother him.* Covering her wounds with her hands, she began teleporting to Asher. Of course, she failed again.

Times Square. Elephant Graveyard. Sahara Desert. Each time she botched the technique, she grew more and more frustrated. Finally, Pax found herself standing on the edge of an extremely high skyscraper. She was about to try teleporting again when she heard a voice behind her.

"What's up, cupcake?"

"Ash!" she said, pivoting in midair. Her eyes widened when she saw that her uncle was leaning against the railing and smoking. "Are you *smoking?* Forget it, explain later. Amara's in trouble."

"Sorry," he said, dropping his cigarette and crushing it under his shoe sheepishly. "What's going on? Pax! What the hell happened to your stomach?"

"Would you risk your life to save Mara?"

His eyes narrowed. "In a heartbeat."

"Great. Let's go."

"Wha—"

When Pax grabbed her uncle and initiated the relocation technique, she clenched her eyes tightly and hoped it would work. She focused on the distant feeling of Thornton's shield, and his weakening energy signal. When she was able to open her eyes again, she saw that Amara's pyramid was inches away from her nose. She breathed in relief and released her uncle.

Asher fell a few feet before catching himself, shocked at being suddenly dematerialized. He reached out and touched the fjuyen pyramid tentatively. *Mara?* he asked in confusion.

Ash, she moaned. *They're eating my life away…*

Meanwhile, Pax was staring down at the scene unfolding below them. She noticed that Suja had changed form, and the particular form was causing her blood to boil.

"Perhaps you remember me like this?" Suja was saying in a seductive voice. "The last time we met, I was inside this body. And so were you."

"Karina?" Thornton asked furiously.

"Mmm," she responded, walking up to him. Her patent leather heels clinked on the floor as she approached him and dragged a fingernail over his chest. "So you do remember."

"You did this?" Pax asked. She didn't wait for an answer before her body burst into flames hotter than Venus. "*You* did this!"

Suja smiled deviously as she glanced back over her shoulder. She continued to stroke Thornton's chest possessively. "Did what? Had some fun with your lover? Sure. If either of you had looked deeper than the surface, you would have been able to tell I was hitching a ride in that pathetic human's body."

"So I didn't actually kill someone?" Pax asked as

she advanced on the woman. "You just made everyone think I was a murderer?"

"No, you *totally* killed her," Suja said cheerfully. "I hightailed it out of her body before you attacked her. I prefer to make love, not war."

Pax raised a hand to launch a fireball at Suja's face, and the woman pursed her lips, blowing a gust of prana forth which turned the fireball into red feathers. "That wasn't nice, Pax. In fact, I'm starting to think you're not a nice girl. Poor Karina Allbright had a major crush on Thorn. She was jealous of you, and just wanted *one* night when she could feel…"

"Shut up!" Pax shouted, clenching her fists to her sides. The flames consuming her body swept out several feet around her.

Pax! Thornton yelled telepathically. *She's distracting you from Mara. Direct your anger at the pyramid.* When Pax nodded, he changed the channel of his thoughts and focused on his dark-haired friend. Ash*! Get down here and join your body with mine so that I can put up this shield.*

Asher had been staring through the transparent pyramid in horror. "She hates bugs," he whispered.

Ash! Thornton's voice bellowed into his brain. *Coalescence technique, now!*

Coming. The slightly younger man flew down to his friend and touched his fingertips to Thornton's. *I'm not sure if I remember how to do this, buddy. It's been a long while.*

You have to remember. My sister needs us.

Asher nodded and closed his eyes as he began releasing his energy. *Be in me. Be of me. Be with me. Only but fragments, let us be whole.* He had almost allowed the magenta glow to cover Thornton's arms when Suja began shouting orders to her Obake.

"Stop them!" Suja barked at her invisible guards. They immediately advanced on Asher, attacking him from behind with weapons instead of their claws.

Asher swiveled and caught an invisible sword in his hand. "I don't think so," he said, ripping the weapon away from the invisible guard and impaling the creature's head with the blunt end. Asher lifted both hands and released an acidic dark orange wave which melted the Obake advancing on him.

You have to join with me now, *Ash,* Thornton was demanding. *I'm about to lose the shield.*

Nodding, Asher turned and clenched his friend's hands and let out a yell as he surrendered the form of his body completely. *Seamlessly we unite, soul to soul; my heart is half yours this half hour.* His energy rushed out in the color of magenta, surrounding Thornton and finally transforming the two men in a blinding white, iridescent inferno.

Even Suja lifted her arm to shield her eyes from the overwhelming luminosity. The mighty woman cursed under her breath when she sensed the power increase the deva men had undergone.

Pax had never been on the outside of a bodily fusion. When the magenta glow gave away to a pure white glare, she felt the pain of sharp arrows stabbing through her eyeballs and she hadn't even been looking directly at the men. She had been studying the fjuyen pyramid and trying to determine how to break Amara out, but the light reflected sharply off the surface of the foreign substance. Pax had to close her eyes, and she imagined the center of the white dwarf star from which the mineral had been extracted. Surely there was a way to cut the fjuyen if Suja had forced it into the shape of a pyramid?

"Wow," Suja said when the light finally died down and one man was left standing where two had previously stood. "Wow. And I thought they were attractive *before.*"

With an introduction like this, Pax could not resist stealing a glance down over her shoulder to behold the merger of Thornton and Asher. Her eyes widened as she observed the shoulder-length indigo locks that framed the man's chiseled face. His eyes were of deepest midnight-sapphire, almost identical to Para's ethereal coloring. Pax was unable to resist allowing her eyes to travel down over the man's body hungrily, and she found every aspect of him to be angular and pleasing.

"Wow," breathed Pax, as she looked at the merger of Thornton and Asher. "Wow, guys. You just became, like, muscle-magazine buff."

"How do you like *this* mozzarella, baby?" the colossal man asked with a hostile leer. "I am Ashton, a fucking raw filet mignon. Sink your teeth in me, woman. Chances are you'll choke." His voice was deep and filled with foreboding. Pax shivered, realizing that she did not know this man. There was no familiarity in the metallic tone of his voice, and she hoped he was still on her side.

Ashton frowned at Pax from under thick dark eyebrows as he pumped his massive arms to either side of his body. A freezing cold wind swept through the palace, along with a pale blue glow. "The shield is up. The Obake guards are frozen. Break Amara free now."

"Right," Pax said, as she flew up to the pyramid. She pressed both hands against what she believed was the weakest part of the pyramid. She searched her mind for wisdom on how to break or dissolve an element that had never had been studied by man. *Mara! How do I get you out of there?* Pax asked. Her friend's knowledge of chemistry and science was vast.

Get them off me. Ash. Please, Ash.

"Dammit," Pax said, realizing that her friend was too traumatized to be of any use. "If my thoughts can travel through the substance..." Pax tried to focus on creating heat inside the pyramid to expand the air on the inside, and force the structure to break apart. When Amara began to scream, Pax realized that she couldn't heat the insides of the pyramid without frying her friend. Anyway, the material was from the core of a star! Heat was not the answer, although it was Pax's strength. She began to try to emulate the acidic attack that Asher had used a moment before, but she felt a soft hand suddenly grasp her by the throat.

"Things could have been different between us, sweetie," Suja said as she crushed Pax's windpipe beneath her fingers. "We could have been friends."

Pax gasped for air desperately before she remembered—she didn't need oxygen. Drawing her energy from the world around her, she reached out and grabbed Suja's wrist. Her hand burned through the Asura woman's skin until she felt carpal bones. Pax looked into the woman's eyes before grabbing the wire that had been used to harm her earlier. She grabbed the wire and wrapped it around Suja's wounded wrist. The Asura woman began to scream as the electricity from Amara's energy caused her body to spasm wildly.

Ashton's unfamiliar voice echoed in her mind. *I*

can only hold this shield for about thirty seconds, Pax. You need to get a move on.

I don't know what to do, she told him. *Do you have any ideas on how to break a substance harder than diamond?*

You probably can't break it. So find another way to get her out!

I could try teleporting into the pyramid…

No! Ashton commanded fiercely. *You are inept with that skill, and if you drain your energy trying you won't be able to take us home. We'll die here.*

Suja ripped the wire from her wrist, and clutched the wound with annoyance. "We don't have to fight," the goddess said softly. "Children, with my guidance don't you see what an unstoppable force we would be together? I can free Amara and we could work together to create something instead of all this destruction."

"Free Amara," Ashton said. "Then I'm yours to command."

"Pax said the same thing earlier," Suja mused. "How loyal you all are! That I would have three devas enslaved to me just for the freedom of that pipsqueak? It baffles reason."

"Will you do it or not?" Ashton asked.

"That depends," Suja said. "Will you be my champion and help me conquer the Earth? If I can find a way to keep you joined as one, will you rule at my side as my King?"

"It would be my pleasure, Suja," Ashton said with a grin. "Free Amara and you've got yourself a deal. We can begin right away."

"No!" Pax yelled. "But Thorn…"

"I'm not Thorn," Ashton said. "I'm exponentially

stronger. Instead of running a stupid tech company, I should be running the whole fucking world."

Pax felt physically ill as Suja laughed. "Then let's seal the deal, young man." The Asura woman extended her hand toward Amara's prison and the fjuyen pyramid disappeared. When the blonde woman began falling, Pax moved forward to catch her friend's limp body. She began to scratch off the energy sucking worms, as Amara whimpered in her arms.

"You can take her away," Suja said to Pax, gesturing in dismissal. "I'm done with you two."

Pax nodded slightly, but looked up at Ashton in confusion. *Thorn…*

Get out while you can, Pax. Before she changes her mind. The shield is going down any minute now. I'm nearly depleted.

Do you really want to stay with her?

I want for you and Mara to be safe. I said what I needed to say.

I'm not leaving you, Pax told him mentally. Throwing Amara over her shoulder, Pax flew towards Ashton as fast as she could, intending to grab him and teleport all of them home.

Suja blocked her path. "Excuse me?" the woman said. "You need to go, and you can't take my stuff."

"Actually, ma'am, he's my stuff," Pax told her.

"Ask him," Suja said. "He wants to join forces with me and take over Earth."

"I don't want to join forces," Ashton said through gritted teeth. "I want this miserable fiscal year to be over! I want a good night's sleep! I want my mother and my accountants to stop bothering me, and I want my girlfriend back!"

"So modest," Suja said with a sigh. "I hate modesty. But I hate *liars* more than anything!" Suja flung her hand out at Ashton, causing the air around him to cackle with electricity. Ashton screamed in pain.

"Pax! You need to go!" Ashton shouted, as he fell to his knees. Sweat was pouring down his face and his shirt was soaked. "I'm sorry." The deva man's arms fell, releasing the shield. His face tumbled forward, colliding with the ground as he collapsed.

As the shield disappeared around them, Pax flew to Ashton's side. She deposited Amara beside the unconscious man, and Amara stirred awake just as the Obake began to defrost and attack them. Pax turned rapidly to defend her friends against the invisible foes.

"Wow! He is totally ripped," Amara said as she stared at the comatose body on the ground beside her. "What a cutie. I'm completely over Ash! Who is *he?*"

Pax sighed as she hacked apart three Obake guards with their own weapons. "You're hopeless. How can a technological genius be such a total imbecile?"

When Pax had cleared the immediate attackers and was turning to grab her friends and teleport away, Suja abruptly materialized in her path. "Darling, I'm so sorry. I'm afraid I cannot allow any of you to leave. This kind of insult cannot go unpunished."

"Suja, Suja, Suja," Pax murmured, as a smile overtook her face. "Remember when I said that reaching for me was a mistake? Reaching for him was an even bigger one. He belongs to *us.*" Pax telekinetically flung the Asura woman clean across the room, placing her own body between her friends and the Obake guards.

"Guards! Don't let her touch them," Suja

commanded. "She cannot leave this palace!"

Pax snorted. "Actually, I can." She glared across the room into Suja's eyes, and she thought about her mother. She thought about her grandfather. Every dark part of her life had been caused by the Asura. This woman was the enemy, regardless of her sweet voice and beautiful appearance. This woman could have been directly responsible for her mother's death. It was that thought which helped Pax realize what she needed to do. Suja was still wearing the body of Karina Allbright, and as Pax stared at the woman's pinstriped business suit, she realized that Suja was responsible for corrupting Thornton and breaking her heart. She had surely used magick to ruin Pax's life. It was that thought which gave Pax the strength to do what she needed to do.

Plug your ears, she told Amara mentally. The dark-haired woman threw her arms up over her head and curled her spine backwards, letting out an ear-piercing scream. A stream of red energy shot out of her mouth like the eruption of a volcano, filling the room like freshly spewed lava. It headed directly for Suja, whose eyes widened.

The Asura woman's kindly voice entered Pax's mind. *If I'm going down, then I'm taking you with me, child.* The goddess raised both of her hands and retaliated by sending a green substance into the lava. Pax grasped that it was radioactive, for she saw that as soon as the green fluid touched the lava, it caused combustion. She realized that the whole palace, possibly the whole continent, was going to explode with the force of her own volcano meeting Suja's nuclear bomb.

She turned to Amara fearfully as the explosion

instantaneously engulfed the room. Even though the blonde woman had forced her index fingers into her ears, blood still ran down her cheeks from the thunderous sounds raping her eardrums. The woman's frightened pale blue eyes were the last sight Pax saw before the heat and force of the explosion collided with her back.

Chapter 21: Let's Go Home

Groaning, Pax tried to move her fingers. They were caked with dried blood and glued to the open gashes along her abdomen. She winced as she pulled her hand away from the wounds, causing them to begin bleeding again. She placed her hand beside her, and felt the most welcome texture she had ever felt in her life; it was the moisture of morning dewdrops on grass.

Pax released a laugh as she rolled over, pressing both of her hands into the grass, along with her face. The grass was sweet-smelling and it felt like home. Sitting up quickly, she looked around and saw that Amara and the boys were lying unconscious just a few feet away. She must have been able to reflexively initiate one final teleport just as the nuclear explosion had tossed her against her friends. Because their bodies had been in contact, they had come with her. She laughed at this amazing luck and turned her face skyward. The first rays of dawn were just beginning to break the horizons, and it was the perfect sight to welcome her home.

Why does it always have to be just *in the nick of time?* she wondered to herself. *I would experience much less of the heart-stopping stress that causes me to lose five years of my life if I could save my friends, say, with a few minutes of time to spare.* Her moment of happiness had segued directly into cynicism and she pulled herself to her feet. Looking down at the claw marks and wounds all over her body, she knew that her friends would need immediate medical attention.

Turning to Thornton and Asher, Pax saw that the boys had separated. This meant that she had probably been unconscious for longer than thirty minutes. She smiled and nudged Asher with her foot.

"Hey. Uncle Asshole."

Asher groaned as the prodding foot roused him from his sleep. He rubbed his aching head. "Paxie. What gives?"

"Thanks for helping to save Mara."

"You kind of clued me in at the last minute there, cupcake. Next time someone I love is in mortal danger, can you include me as part of the initial rescue party?"

She hesitated, surprised at his casual use of the word. "I wasn't sure whether you cared."

"Are you kidding me?" Asher asked, rising to his feet angrily. He swayed for a moment, slightly dizzy. "This is serious stuff, Pax! You better be careful before you go practicing dangerous techniques and get us all involved in…"

"I know about mom," Pax said softly. "Why didn't you tell me?"

"What about Bridget?" Asher asked, rubbing his head again and grunting.

"That it was the Asura who killed her? That it wasn't an accident because she was trying to practice?"

Asher's face froze. "It was?" He sighed and reached out to hug his niece gently. "I swear, kiddo, I didn't know."

Pax hugged back, feeling forgiveness creep into her skull. It seemed her uncle was innocent—in this at least.

"Hey," Thornton said, pulling his head off the

ground. "Are we alive?"

Smiling, Pax ripped herself away from her uncle and moved to the ground to hug Thornton. She hugged him a bit too fiercely, causing many of their wounds to be rammed together, and they instantly recoiled.

"Ow," Pax whimpered, clutching her stomach.

Thornton groaned, running his fingers over the claw marks in his chest. "Yep. That pain means I'm alive."

"Do you think Suja is dead?" Pax asked as she pressed her hand down on the deep gashes to stop the bleeding. "That was a pretty big explosion."

"No kidding," Asher said. "We all need to get some vials of Sakra's water. Pax, the skin of your back is totally burned off. It's really gross looking."

"Thanks, Ash," she said with a grimace. His mention of the wounds brought them to the forefront of her mind and somehow made them hurt more.

"She's still alive," Thornton said, staring up at the sky. "I'm pretty sure that explosion wouldn't kill a goddess of her level. It may slow her down for a while."

"She's going to be angry with me for destroying her home," Pax said softly. "We should talk to Sakra—he's the one she's really angry with. They're having marital problems, obviously."

Amara stirred then, pulling herself from the ground. She immediately twitched and moved her hands over her body to check for worms. "Oh god, oh god! Please tell me those things are gone."

Asher laughed. "Yep. No more slimy green critters."

"Do not laugh at me!" she warned him. "Those

weren't regular bugs. They were energy-sucking *space bugs,* Ash. I'm going to have nightmares about it forever."

Pax suddenly emitted a giant yawn. "Nightmares sound wonderful right about now. I'm so tired I could sleep right here in the grass."

"Don't do that," Thornton said with a smile. "Let's go home."

The four devas suddenly looked at each other awkwardly. An unspoken question hung in the air: who would go home with whom? Pax looked at the blonde man with a touch of hope on her face. She wanted nothing more than to forget the misery of the past few months and go home with her lover. She had only slept in his arms for about five minutes, and she dreadfully longed to lie in bed next to him for the next five *days.* The fighting, frequent teleportation, and excessive expenditure of energy had left her exhausted.

Suja revealing herself as the source of his duplicity had definitely changed Pax's perspective. While she still felt crunchy about the situation with Thornton, she was willing to make steps towards forgiveness. Suja's magick was powerful, and her manipulation was legendary; it was not completely Thornton's fault. Pax truly felt she would be able to let go of the feelings of betrayal… someday.

But when Amara lifted her eyes to look at Asher, the dark-haired man turned away. Amara's lips parted and she was about to speak, but she could read in his body language that anything she requested would be rejected. Suja was not responsible for their relationship problems. Amara sunk her teeth into her bottom lip to stop it from quivering. She crawled in the grass over to Pax's side and took her friend's hand. "Take me home, Paxie," she whispered. She sounded more defeated and miserable than when she had been trapped in the pyramid.

Pax glanced at her uncle with disappointment before nodding. "We should probably go to the compound and tell Vincent about what happened. His football game is probably over by now. Your dad will protect you better than I can, Mara. Right after he slices my scalp off, that is."

Thornton stepped forward. "I'll go with Ash to the grove. I can tell Raymond what happened. If he doesn't cut any important parts of me off for going near Pax, that is."

Pax nodded at the boys and commenced the teleport. She expected to land directly in front of Vincent, but she found that she was suddenly sitting in a few inches of muddy swamp-water. Amara began to cry.

"Your dress was already ruined," Pax told her.

"Paxie, he barely spoke to me. I was hurt and scared, and he didn't even care."

"He does care," Pax answered. "He risked his life to save you. If you could hear his thoughts, you would know that he cares. He told me he cares."

"But it doesn't matter. He's not here with me right now, and I *need* him."

"I'm sorry. I know." Pax hugged her friend and allowed Amara to cry into her shoulder. She sighed and rubbed her friend's back. "It's going to be okay. I'll help do whatever makes you feel better. We still have Para, and they don't know about her…"

"Forget it," Amara whispered. "Nothing can make me feel better. He's just so… indifferent."

"I really don't believe he's like that on the inside," Pax said. "He's just troubled."

"By what? What's troubling him? Did Suja do something? Is there someone else? Why doesn't he want to be with me? It doesn't make sense, Paxie."

"Shh, Mara. It's okay."

The blonde woman was inconsolable as she sobbed into her friend's bloody clothes. Pax could not say or do anything but remain still and hold Amara as she cried.

Pax. Thornton's voice said into her mind. *Stay with me tonight?*

Yes, please, she answered instantly. *Once I put your sister to bed. She's really shaken up.*

Have my parents look after her. You were a real heroine today, and I want to make sure you get some of that deep, dreamless sleep I promised you.

Pax felt guilty that she should be happy while her friend was not, but she smiled against Amara's shoulder. For the first time in months, she could not wait to get home. For the first time in months, she felt like she actually had a home.

* * *

Wearing a loose cotton dress, Pax exited Amara's room with a replacement phone in her hand. Having lost her phone sometime early during her teleportation failures, Amara had insisted that she get a new one before doing anything else; even before healing her wounds. As Pax caught up on her text messages, she was interrupted by a firm hand on her shoulder.

"Girl," said Vincent angrily. Pax cringed, awaiting her sentence. She was surprised when the man paused and relaxed his death-grip on her shoulder. "You did well today. But next time something of this magnitude happens, I expect you will inform me."

"Yes, sir."

"There's one more thing. You know when I said there was only one rule for all devas to remember? I lied."

"Why am I not surprised to hear that?" she asked. "First my dad, and now you."

He ignored this. "The other rule is even more ancient than the first. We had hoped you would never need to know it, as every parent foolishly wishes and expects that the younger generation will not have to face the same troubles that we did."

"What is it?" she asked, fearing what her mentor would say.

"Si vis pacem, para bellum."

Pax used her prana to translate the Latin in her mind. She looked at him in surprise and spoke the words out loud, just to hear them a second time in English.

"If you wish for peace, prepare for war."

Chapter 22: Deep, Dreamless Sleep

Thornton had left Burnson Grove only after explaining the details to Raymond several times. The older man had healed Thornton's wounds and requested that he look after Pax before mysteriously taking off. Raymond and Amelia seemed to have completely forgotten about everything that had happened before at the mention of Suja.

Now, Thornton was returning to his bedroom, where he could feel Pax's life force waiting for him. He temporarily assumed Ruby Form to increase his speed. When he finally entered the room, he calmed his flaming *prana* and stood quietly by the bed, listening to her breathing. She was lying on top of the blankets and resting on her side, since her stomach and back were both wounded. Thornton felt guilty that he had no more vials of Sakra's water remaining. He levitated into the bed beside her carefully so that he wouldn't wake her, and placed his hand gently on her hip.

Pax immediately woke up and turned to face him. "Thorn," she said softly. She moved a hand to cup his face for a moment before sliding her hands behind his neck and tangling her fingers in his blonde hair. She wanted to crush her mouth against his, but she felt the need to apologize. "I'm so…"

"Shhh," he said, pressing his lips against her chin. He kissed the corner of her nose, followed by the corner of her mouth. He circled her lips with kisses. He finally pulled her bottom lip into his mouth and gently nibbled on her skin. *You don't need to say anything.*

He caressed her hip and slid his hand over her thigh, but he felt her body jerk when his fingers came into contact with several deep cuts. *You got some battle wounds, hot stuff. Let me clean those for you.* He ran his fingers lightly along the cuts in her leg, using his *prana* to create a heat which would burn any bacteria out of the wounds. Pax exhaled slowly at the sensation.

You should probably get looked after, Pax. We have doctors on staff in the K.T. infirmary. You should get stitches…

Screw that, she told him, rubbing her cheek against his stubble. It was driving her crazy that his fingers were so close to her skin without actually touching her. She clasped his hand and pressed his fingers against her wounded thigh. *I heal fast. I'm strong.*

I know, he said. He kissed her nose gently. *But you still need to sleep.*

I don't feel like sleeping right now, she told him, scooting closer to his body. She pressed her lips against his, but he immediately pulled away.

Pax, he said with a warning tone in his telepathic voice. *You are covered in claw marks, and you have serious burns from that explosion. You're exhausted from teleporting and…*

Excited from a good fight, she finished with a smile. She lifted his hand to her face and wrapped her lips around the tip of his index finger. *Missing you like crazy.* She gently sucked on his finger, running her tongue along the ridges of his nails. *Feeling glad to be alive.* She kissed down the length of his finger, allowing her lips to settle against his palm. *Wanting to make up for lost time.* She released a warm breath of *prana* into the center of his palm, allowing her warmth to travel through him to the deepest reaches of his body. Pax looked into his blue eyes mischievously.

Thornton stared with growing arousal as she kissed, nibbled and suckled at his hands. He finally caught both of her wrists and held them above her head to forcefully restrain her. *Doesn't change the fact that you're wounded. Come on, Pax. We'll have plenty of time when you're better.*

She smiled and snaked her leg around his body. *I'm not a patient girl.*

Your dad would kill me. He would kill me and mutilate my corpse.

Please, Thorn, she begged, pressing her lips against his again. She closed her eyes and poured all of her pent-up desire into a sweet-tasting stream of *prana* she released into his mouth. *The cuts and bruises just make things more interesting. It's been so long and I want you so badly...*

He didn't need another word of encouragement as he grabbed her hips and lifted her on top of him. He grasped the back of her head as he smashed his mouth against hers greedily. *Pax Burnson, you drive me utterly insane.*

*　　*　　*

Despite her wounds, Pax was experiencing what was possibly the most blissful sleep of her entire life when a familiar melodious voice clawed its way into her consciousness. She stirred against Thornton, hating to be disturbed from her warm and comfortable spot.

"Hello, Pax. I thought we should talk."

Pax sat up abruptly, gasping and reaching to her

side to wake Thornton. Her hand went directly through him. Frowning, she noticed that there was a copy of herself still lying in the bed. She was not corporeal.

"You're dreaming, darling." The woman appeared sitting in a pale white lotus flower, completely naked except for golden strings of jewelry around her neck and hips.

"I see you're decked out in more ridiculous fashion accessories," Pax said.

"Yes," Suja said softly. "You destroyed my beautiful palace, so I thought I would console myself with a pretty flower and some necklaces."

"I hope you're feeling really consoled."

"Oh, I am," Suja said, running her fingers along the length of her golden necklaces. She smiled. "There's no use in holding a grudge. I want you to know that I see a lot of myself in you, Pax. There's a lot we could learn from each other. I could show you true power, and you could teach me to be a good person—and learn this thing you call forgiveness. You're the kind of woman I would value having as a friend."

"You used my closest friend like poker chips. Sure, let's be best buds," Pax said sarcastically.

"You have spunk, child. But you also have more than that." Suja's flower floated closer to the bed and she stared at the girl curiously. "It's impossible, you know. What you did should not have been doable. You don't have enough deva blood coursing through your veins to launch an attack like that. You were magnificent! A sweet little volcano. How did you do it?"

"My Grandpa Kaden always said I had a lot of heart."

"Heart. Yes, that you certainly do," said the Asura queen. She smiled and transformed back into Pax's mother. The lotus blossom beneath her morphed into a fluffy angelic cloud. "Do you know how your grandfather died, Pax? My husband was negotiating to end the war between the Asuras and devas, and Vincent Kalgren offered up Kaden as a sacrifice."

"Are you trying to turn me against Vincent now?" Pax asked, frowning. "He's like a second father to me, so good luck with that."

"I'm just telling you the truth, child. You have been lied to so much by all the men around you, and I want you to know that when you decide you would prefer to be enlightened and liberated, I will be waiting for you."

"Thanks. I'll be in touch."

Suja clucked her tongue disapprovingly. "You needn't use that sardonic tone with me. I have your best interests in mind. I feel your power is going to waste being joined with such inferior companions. Don't you ever feel like the Kalgren girl is holding you back?"

"Yes," Pax responded honestly, "but she's my friend. I'll always be loyal to her."

"But she's so weak. She's so… blonde."

Pax sighed. "If you're not going to attack me again, can I get back to sleep?"

"Of course, dear," Suja said, floating away. "Let me know if you ever would like a friend who can challenge you and bring out the brilliant colors of your potential that you would otherwise never fathom. Not even in a dream like this one. Goodnight, Pax."

"Goodnight," Pax said, bewildered by the concept

of wishing a good night to someone with whom she had just waged a small war. Shrugging, Pax nestled back down beside Thornton. She was sinking back into the comfort of dreamlessness when the lyrical voice whispered into her ear:

I didn't use magick to seduce him, you know. There was no godly or mystical power at work when he betrayed you. I merely entered the human woman's body and watched from her eyes—a front row seat to the fall of the Kalgren prince. I thought you should be aware. Sweet dreams.

Pax tried to continue resting and ignore this voice, but after several minutes of going over this information, her eyes slowly opened. She was unable to close them again.

"Dammit," Pax said softly. Thornton's muscular arm was wrapped protectively around her, and she reached down and brushed her palm across the golden hairs on his skin. She never wanted to move from that spot. She also wanted to get as far away as possible. She wanted to know, but she also could not bear to know. There was a high probability that Suja was making it all up, but there was also a high probability that she was completely correct. Pax's mind could not stop racing with the heaviness of the bad memories. She saw the woman in his office again, and ran over the scene in her mind. She felt his hand slipping up Para's skirt. She felt him kissing Para in the dressing room.

Grasping his arm gently, she lifted it so she could slip out from underneath his embrace. She levitated off the bed and moved across the room to get her purse.

"Where are you going?" Thornton asked sleepily.

"Bathroom," she said as she duly changed

direction. She had been heading to the window.

Run, said a little voice inside her head. *Run as fast as you can.* She frowned at the voice. *But I'm happy here. For the first time in weeks, I'm happy.* Her head ached as it spent several minutes at war with itself. *There's only me in this body! I shouldn't be so confused.* She opened the medicine cabinet to check for painkillers, but there were none. She picked her purse off the countertop and began rummaging through it for any sort of pharmaceutical relief. Surely there were still some of the sedatives she had used to weaken Para? She found the little pillbox and hastily swallowed a heavy sedative. Miserably, she prayed it would help her get back to sleep. As she returned the pillbox to her messy purse, she was distracted by her phone lighting up amongst the mayhem of small but useful items.

Withdrawing the new machine, she found a text message from Thornton which simply said: *Hi.*

Pax smiled suspiciously, thinking that it was kind of clingy for Thornton to be texting her only a moment second after she exited the room. A second text messaged arrived while she still stared at the phone in puzzlement: *How was your day, Medea?* Her smile disappeared. The text hadn't been sent to her.

He was messaging Para.

Reaching out to pick up the phone tentatively, Pax frowned. She stared at the letters in disbelief. She bolted to the bathroom door and flung it open, half expecting to see Thornton lying peacefully asleep and Suja or some other demon messing with his phone. But to her dismay, Thornton was sitting up with his phone in his hands, awaiting a reply.

"What are you doing?" she asked him sharply.

"Just texting a friend," he answered, putting his phone aside a bit too quickly. He patted the empty space beside him. "Come back to bed, hot stuff."

Pax's tongue moved. Her first instinct was to ask whether it was a male or female friend to test his honesty—but she immediately pressed her lips together. *Pride. Have a little pride, Pax.* She moved back into the bathroom and looked at herself in the mirror with determination. *I won't let him turn me into a nagging, jealous, distrustful woman.* She hastily shoved her phone and sedatives back into her purse.

He hasn't learned anything. He hasn't suffered. He'll do it again in the future. He'll do it once a week. He hasn't even told me about Para—there could be other women in the future and I would never know about them because I wouldn't be lucky enough to be *them. What am I doing here? Why did I fall back into this so easily?*

"Where are you going?" he asked as she headed for the window.

"I don't know."

"Pax. What's going on?"

"I… I might drive around for a while," she answered.

"Let me come with you," he said, sitting up. "Antarctica, Venus, anywhere. To every corner of the omniverse."

She hesitated. "No. I need some time alone to think."

"You're not coming back, are you?" There was a frantic look in his eyes. "Pax, don't leave me. You can't…"

"Shhh," she said, crossing the room and pushing him back down onto his pillow. She smiled and leaned forward to press her lips to his forehead. "You're everything to me," she said against his skin. She simultaneously released a wave of prana with her breath, amplifying the sedative she had just ingested and using it to tranquilize him. Once he was knocked out, she pulled away from him. For several minutes, she sat on the side of his bed looking down at him.

She reached out and grasped his hand, squeezing it gently before she fled from the room.

Chapter 23: Beloved Metal Box

Pax pushed on the door to enter the Burnson Grove home, but before it was even fully open, her grandmother was pulling her into a hug.

"I'm so glad you're okay, sweetie," Amelia was saying. "Thorn and Ash told us everything. Your father felt so horrible and he's gone back to India to speak to Sakra and get some healing water. He'll be back before morning. You have to talk to him—poor Raymond feels so guilty. He thinks that his friendship with Sakra is what caused Suja's anger and…"

"Grandma," Pax said gently. "I really don't want to talk about the fight right now, if that's alright with you."

"Sure. Of course, sweetie—would you like some tea?"

"No, thanks. I just need to lie down." Pax forced a weak smile and moved into the house, but she paused at the foot of the stairs. "Grandma. What should I do about Thorn?"

"What do you mean, dear?"

"I am kind of… scared." It was hard for her to admit such a thing. "Do you think I should try to get past this and be with him again?"

Amelia was silent in consideration for a moment. "He's a good boy," she said finally, "but you deserve better. You deserve the best."

"There isn't anyone else," Pax said.

"Do you mean devas? Well, that may be true. I

know there are only a few devas and their children left in the world. But honey, there are worthy human men out there…"

"No. I didn't ask about other men. I didn't ask about humans or devas," Pax said, turning to look at Amelia desperately. "I asked about Thorn. It's him or no one."

"Darling, you're a young woman with your whole life ahead of you," Amelia said with a small smile. "You shouldn't shut yourself down to the world just because of one bad experience. Why, did you know that a co-worker of yours named Michael calls the house positively every single day to check on you? Sweetie, you should be open to…"

"Sorry, Grandma. I need to lie down." Pax tried to keep the anger from her voice. She moved so quickly that her body was a blur as it travelled up the stairs and entered her room. Once there, she shut the door behind her and began to pace. Even though her power was spent, she could not force herself to lie down. Her head ached more than her open wounds. Pax considered chewing her nails to ease her stress, but she had never found that habit enticing. Dragging herself over to her bed, she positioned herself horizontally.

She lay on her scorched back and levitated off the bed until her nose touched the ceiling. Finally she lowered herself until her hair began to pool on her pillow. Pax repeated the procedure of vertical pacing before she abruptly dropped herself back to the bed. "Ow," she muttered. She reached over to her night table drawers, and pulled out an old photo album. She turned onto her side and began to flip through the photos. They were mostly kiddie birthday photos where her mom had been present. The Burnson family had stopped taking photos regularly after the death of Bridget Burnson.

Pax barely had any recollection of most of the images, but she drank up the images of her mother's smiling face. *I wish you were here right now, mom. I wish I could talk to you about this.* She began searching photos for the Kalgrens. In every photo where Bridget was pictured with Thornton in the frame, Pax tried to search her mother's face for approval or disdain. *Give me a sign, mom. Tell me what to do.* She fingered the photos desperately, using her *prana* to try and determine the opinions of a dead woman.

When Pax started thinking about calling upon Suja and asking the demon woman to assume her mother's form just so she could feel a sense of comfort, she knew that she had ventured too far from reason. Abruptly closing the photo album and stuffing it in her drawer, Pax exited her room through the window. She flew through the night sky drowsily, with her eyes closed half the time. Luckily, her route was a familiar one that she could navigate without vision.

When her feet finally touched down on the ground, she was at Amara's oceanfront home where her jeep was parked in the driveway. Pax felt a smile come to her lips as she put her arms around the car and pressed her cheek to the glass fondly.

"It's just me and you now, old friend," Pax told her beloved metal box on wheels. "Let's get the hell out of here!" She was digging into her purse for her keys when she noticed that a light was on in Amara's house. It was her master bedroom. *That's odd. I thought Mara was staying under her father's watch at the Kalgren Compound.*

Pax levitated up to the window, and could not see inside due to the curtains. She lifted the latch and slid open the window so that she could crawl inside. When she saw a familiar dark head of hair peek out from Amara's bed, she frowned.

"Ash! What the hell are you doing here?"

"Hey, cupcake," he responded in an empty voice. "I couldn't sleep."

Pax was about to scold the man, but she didn't have the heart. "Same here," she responded, moving to sit beside her uncle.

"Seeing Amara hurt like that… it was a really big shock," he admitted. "It scared the bejesus out of me."

"Ash, you idiot. Amara isn't physically hurt. She had a few creepy-crawlies dig into her skin and steal her energy, but do you know what's really got her upset? The fact that you didn't care. You saw she was shaking and scared and you just stood there. You didn't even go to her and comfort her."

"I couldn't, Paxie. I made a decision and I need to be firm." His face was miserable as he stared forward blankly.

"So even in a life or death situation, you can't show her a little human kindness?" Pax demanded.

"We're not human," Asher responded automatically. Then he realized how foolish he sounded. "Look, I helped, didn't I? You showed up out of the blue on my favorite skyscraper and interrupted my perfectly relaxing smoke. I dropped everything and went to freaking Venus with you to help save Amara! So quit judging my words, and judge my actions."

"I don't even know you anymore," Pax said.

"That makes two of us. I am only your uncle when you need something from me, Pax. We used to be close. We used to be family. But frankly I don't know why you're here right now talking to me instead of with Thorn or Mara."

"I guess we're both closer to the Kalgrens than we are to each other."

They were quiet for a period before Asher spoke. "It doesn't matter, Paxie. Nothing matters as long as you girls are safe."

Pax laughed as Asher tried to tousle her hair playfully as though she were twelve. "Does Mara know you're in her bed?" Pax asked.

"No," Asher said. "Please don't tell her. I just can't sleep anywhere else. I've been living here for five years, you know."

"If you ask, Mara would probably let you stay in one of her other rooms," Pax suggested. "There's plenty of room in the house. It's just a bit odd that you're sleeping *in her bed.*"

"I know. I'm a loser," Asher admitted easily. "Keep this secret for me, cupcake?"

Pax's heart always melted when her uncle was modest and self-effacing. "Fine."

"Thanks, Paxie. You're my favorite niece."

She smiled at the lame old joke. "I'm still your only niece, Uncle Ash."

The touching family moment was interrupted by Pax's phone ringing. She felt a pang of fear, praying that it would not be another text or call for Para. When she uneasily withdrew the phone from her purse, she saw that it wasn't who she expected.

"Thorn wants a booty call?" Asher guessed with a grin.

Pax hit the dark-haired man in the shoulder. "It's Layla Solyst."

"The earth deva's wife?"

"Yeah," Pax said, sending her uncle a puzzled look. "I'll just let it go to voicemail."

"Doesn't she have kids?" Asher asked. "Maybe they need you to teleport over there and help out in some kind of crisis. It could be Suja. Us devas gotta stick together!"

When the phone rang again, Pax nodded. "She's double-calling. That means it's an emergency." She answered the call and pressed the phone to her ear. "Hi Layla. What's up?"

"Paxie!" came the earsplitting shriek from the other end of the line. "I just saw the news! Good Sakra, I am so sorry sweetie. I had no idea things were this bad."

Pax winced and moved the phone a few inches away from her ear so that the loud voice wouldn't damage her hearing. "What's going on?" she asked.

"Mara called me a while ago and asked me to do some investigating for her, so I've been loosely keeping tabs on the situation. But Paxie, you poor thing! I just woke up to feed the baby and turned on the news and saw *her!* Do you want to meet up and talk about it?"

Asher could also hear Layla's voice. When Pax looked at him with confusion, he grabbed the television remote and turned on Amara's giant flat screen TV. When he flipped to a news channel, Pax wrinkled her nose at the sight of a segment on her mother's death, complete with crime scene photos.

"Layla, you called just to tell me that some idiot has a new conspiracy theory about my mother's death? Dear Sakra! I don't want to listen to this garbage."

As Pax's finger moved to hang up the call, Layla's voice could be heard screeching, "No! Go to channel six. Channel six!"

Pax exhaled loudly and rolled her eyes at Asher who shrugged and compliantly switched the channel. Then they saw her. Pax stared at the television in dumbfounded shock while Asher also gawked.

"Sweet Sakra," whispered Pax. "She's beautiful."

"I know, darling. I'm so sorry," crooned Layla Solyst from the other end of the line. "She's a definite fifteen out of ten. You don't deserve this public humiliation."

Asher and Pax stared at the TV for a few more moments. It was the first time that Pax had seen pictures and videos of Para. She couldn't help admiring the woman's flawless grace as she glided through the mall on Thornton's arm with her unusual dress and ultra-long hair. When the news program filled the entire television with a still shot of Para's face, she noticed the way her makeup accentuated the softness of her lips and hardness of her striking eyes.

"Whoa," said Asher as a picture flashed on screen of Para caught in a romantic embrace with Thornton. He was whispering something in her ear as she smiled. Several more pictures of compromising, incriminating positions flashed across the screen.

"Oh, Paxie! Please tell me you've left that cheating

scum for good!" begged Layla from the other end of the line. "I can hardly believe what I'm seeing. That shameless creep! I'm happy I dumped him while you were still in diapers."

Pax finally recovered from her daze and smiled. "Thanks for your concern, Lay. Yeah, I left him. Don't worry about me, I'll be fine."

"Do you need me to come over?" Layla asked.

"No, no. I'll be just fine! Say hello to the babies for me, okay?"

"Paxie, are you sure…"

Pax hung up and stuffed the phone back in her purse. She made a mental note to never answer her phone again.

"Who is this new mystery mistress?" the news report was asking, and Asher finally had the presence of mind to shut off the television.

"Paxie, that girl doesn't mean anything to him," Asher said quickly. "I'm actually dating her—in fact, they were just talking. It was completely innocent. Thorn's a good guy, and he loves you…"

"Why are you lying for him?" Pax asked. "Why are you trying to cover for him?"

Asher paused. "I don't know. He's my best friend."

"I guess our loyalty to the Kalgrens will always supersede our loyalty to each other, right Ash?" Pax smiled cynically. "I need to go."

"Wait, Pax," Asher began, but the woman had already shot downstairs like a lightning bolt, and he could hear the sound of her Jeep's engine starting. He considered chasing after her to defend his friend and try to clean up Thornton's mess, but he quickly remembered that he wasn't completely on his friend's side.

He had forbidden Thornton from seeing Pax, and even though it had been revealed that Suja had influenced his friend, it did not explain or justify his behavior after the situation. Asher shook his head, surrendering. He had his own mess to wallow in. Sometimes it was satisfying to do something one was good at, and he was definitely good at wallowing.

Asher lay back down on the bed and closed his eyes to sense for Amara's life force. *She'll be happier this way,* he told himself. He focused on her energy, meditating to carefully watch over her from afar. He could sense that she was in her old room at the Kalgren Compound. She did not seem to be sleeping. She seemed restless and, well, sad. He couldn't help thinking that Pax had been right, and he should be comforting her. *No. She'll be happier this way eventually. I know I did the right thing.*

He continued to focus on her *prana* until he felt himself nodding off. He fought to stay awake.

His last barely coherent thought before he drifted off to sleep was of Amara, and a few words seemed to appear in his mind out of the blue. He clumsily processed them, not sure if they were from an outside source or distortions of his own thoughts. He was too tired to make sense of it:

You're wrong. I only wanted you.

Chapter 24: Not Really Happening

"Agh! What is that!" growled Pax as she snapped awake with a start. Her cell phone had vibrated so much that it had crawled along the leather seat of the car, slowly, like scorpion poised to sting. When it touched one of the gashes in her wounded thigh, it had caused her to leap in surprise and hit her head on the car roof as she was snapped out of her slumber.

Pax looked up at the roof which now had a small dent in it and cursed. She ran the back of her hand over her eyes. Pax frowned down at her small rectangular attacker with infinite malice. *I will never answer my phone again,* she reminded herself. Nevertheless, she could not resist reading the name of the person who had caused this disruption.

After a moment's consideration, she answered the call reluctantly. "Hello?" she said, still groggy.

"Pax! This is Michael calling."

"Good morning, Dr. Winters. How may I help you?"

"I'm sorry to call at this hour, Pax. Believe me, I wouldn't have bothered you if it weren't a serious life or death situation."

She sighed. "You work in a *hospital.* It's always life or death. What makes this time different?"

"I think your… special abilities might be of service to helping this patient."

"How?"

"Well, we have something of a situation in

neurosurgery. We just put a patient under…"

"No. Do not tell me that you found another 'anomaly,'" Pax said with a groan.

"Unfortunately, that's what happened. We opened up the skull and…"

"You know that there's no such thing as an 'anomaly,' right? It's just your freaking staff not preparing properly."

Michael Winters cleared his throat. "Yes, well, that's why I need you. I've seen what you can do with your hands, Pax. Get those pretty little fingers into neurosurgery, stat."

Pax was about to protest, but she just groaned. "Fine, Winters."

She turned her key in the ignition to start her jeep. The radio immediately turned on, and Pax was startled by the discussion on the morning show.

"… the daughter of the late Hollywood actress, Bridget Burnson, for five years. Here's a picture of her, Fred. Pretty plain lookin' girl, huh?"

"Oh, Sakra. Seriously?" Pax asked the radio. "You're going to do this to me before I've even had coffee?"

"Yeah, Jimmy. There's no resemblance whatsoever between the Burnson girl and his new sexy mystery woman. I can see why he upgraded."

"No resemblance? *No resemblance?*" Pax asked the radio, staring at the station number angrily. "She *is* me, for Sakra's sake!"

"Can you blame the guy? He has enough money to do anything he wants. The Burnson girl is just dried up. I think last week's leftovers in my fridge look more appealing!"

"It's a disguise," Pax mumbled. "I'm like Clark Kent, and they don't know that I'm actually a cool superhuman type-thing."

"I hear you, Jimmy. There are rumors she even cut off all her hair! She probably looks worse than this photo. Who can blame Mr. Kalgren for wanting to wake up beside someone who looks like a woman? I know I…"

Pax reached out and switched off the radio. "Dammit. This is unhealthy. I can't listen to this. Stupid morning shows!"

As she drove along, she nibbled on her bottom lip nervously. *Maybe I can throw myself into my work,* she thought to herself. *They always need help at the hospital. I could volunteer every day. I can work inhuman hours until I don't have time to generate a single original thought. Maybe through my productivity and contribution to the world through the hospital, I can redeem myself and find meaning in life again.*

*   *   *

Pax had entered the hospital staff area and pulled her scrubs on quickly over her normal clothing, thinking how surprised she was that everyone was being so nice to her. At least four people had asked her about her health and well-being on her way to the staff area. It seemed that she had been missed while away and that people had been concerned about the "injuries" she'd sustained which her father had fabricated. Well, not really fabricated, as she had been injured, but of course, she had been healed and injured so many times since then that she had forgotten which particular injuries they meant. She still had some serious lesions and second-degree burns she could have showed off, but they might be difficult to explain. Regardless, the concern was nice.

It was almost a welcoming feeling, Pax thought as she read the charts of the patient she was about to operate on. She walked briskly toward the neurosurgery wing of the hospital as she scanned through the files and the imaging from the scans.

She stopped abruptly when she saw someone blocking her path. She looked up and saw a nurse with a chestnut brown braid.

"Dr. Burnson, I brewed some fresh coffee for you." The girl smiled and handed Pax the mug. "Just the way you like it—black with no sugar. Welcome back!"

Pax studied the woman's face for a moment to judge whether she was sincere.

"Thank you, Cassidy," said Pax with a professional smile as she took the coffee and sipped it. It was actually good. Someone had done something considerate for her. She felt very well-received back at work. There really was a place for her here.

"Dr. Burnson, can I interest you in a newspaper?"

"Thanks, Cassidy, but I don't really have time to read it. I am needed in neurosurgery and I should probably finish reviewing the patient's charts."

The nurse forcefully placed the newspaper in the crook of Pax's arm and gave her a sweet smile.

"Trust me, Dr. Burnson. It's a great read.' The brunette winked before traipsing off.

Pax frowned at her retreating form and looked down at the paper. In huge print, a headline jumped out at her:

CEO of Kalgren Technology Cheats on Long Time Girlfriend

Single women everywhere can rejoice, for the handsome blonde businessman is single again! After years of waiting for this moment, Thornton Kalgren may finally be returning to his playboy ways.

Pax didn't even notice that the ceramic cup she had been holding was now in pieces and that she was standing in a small pool of coffee. *It's official. This day is not really happening. I'm in some kind of alternate-reality nightmare punishment.* Her eyes skimmed the article even though she didn't really want to keep reading. Pax was shocked to learn that the column continued inside the paper. *Not happening. This is not happening.* How could anyone have so much to say on such a subject? She furiously flipped through the paper, completely forgetting that a patient was in neurosurgery with his brain exposed, in desperate need of her medical attention.

There it was. In full color, a candid photo of Thornton holding Para and kissing her cheek.

...a mysterious woman that no one has been able to identify. It is uncanny how much her body and features resemble Miss Burnson, suggesting that Mr. Kalgren does indeed have a "type." Who is this gorgeous goddess with hair that falls down to her knees? No one knows.

Pax studied the picture and fought back the urge to have a temper tantrum right there in the middle of the hospital. *So now there* is *a resemblance between us? Make up your minds people!* Pax calmed herself to avoid the paroxysm, for she knew the precision which so many doctors were taking right now in their surgeries and didn't want to cause a small earthquake.

"Pax?" asked a familiar voice. She looked up and saw Dr. Winters standing rather close. He'd obviously noticed the picture on the newspaper and the crushed coffee cup in her hands.

"I'm sorry, Dr. Winters…"

"It's alright, Paxie. If you aren't in any condition to go into the operating room right now, I understand. We all know about what happened with Mr. Kalgren…"

Oh! So that's *why they've all been so nice to me. Did he just call me Paxie?* Pax felt a twitch of rage as her fellow doctor placed a hand "comfortingly" on her back. *I see what this is. This is the reason I was called into work. Single men everywhere rejoice? Bridget Burnson's heiress is back on the market? He had better be careful, I'm* this *close.*

"I'm fine. What's the situation Dr. Winters?"

"Please, why won't you call me Michael?" asked the other doctor, gently prying the pieces of ceramic away from Pax's clenched fist. "We just need you to get in there and remove a tumor with these beautiful steady fingers of yours."

Pax frowned as the man made a motion as though he were going to kiss her hand. She jerked her hand away in disgust and slapped the newspaper into his hands before briskly walking away. *He didn't really need me. Anyone could have done this.* She just wanted to do the surgery and get back to her jeep. She didn't know if she could last another *minute* in this dimension, with *these* people.

She understood Suja. She wanted to get away from the hospital, away from the city, and away from all of humanity. She almost felt regret for destroying Ishtar, because it was the kind of remote place she wished she could stay.

*　　　*　　　*

Pax had been driving for days, and she was not even sure which country she was in. She had crossed the border back and forth between Canada and the U.S. several times. She played music at the maximum volume in the small chamber, and endeavored to completely block recent events out of her mind.

She often reflected, as she tried to keep from melting her steering wheel, that she was back at square one. Nothing had changed, and she hadn't learned anything. The whole experiment with Para had only left her with a greater hole in her heart, and feeling like a more incomplete and inadequate person. The situation with Suja had left her questioning her own allegiances and purpose. Pax often remembered Suja's words, and felt like a waste of space for not doing more with her life. She also felt distanced from her family.

All she could successfully manage to do was escape.

She was actively engaged in escaping when something unexpected appeared in her path. Pax squinted, seeing a strange object in the middle of the road up ahead. She switched lanes to avoid it, and saw that the object moved into her lane—it was some kind of animal. Tapping the brakes to slow down as she approached, Pax was surprised when her headlights glinted off the creature, and it had long wavy blonde hair.

A woman? Amara.

Pax frowned. She did not want to talk to anyone. She tried to drive around Amara, but the woman moved into her path again. Pax had to swerve violently and found herself driving into a ditch to avoid her friend. The car careened into a tree, but Pax lifted her hand to telekinetically stop the vehicle from crashing a moment before impact.

"What's the big idea?" Pax asked, climbing out of the Jeep and slamming the door. She hadn't even been aware that Amara had learned to fly. She marched over to the highway and stood across from the blonde woman, holding her hands at her sides and feeling strangely like they were about to have a showdown in an old western film.

"Why did you leave without telling me?" Amara asked.

"Your brother…"

"I know! I get the text messages too, remember? I've been trying to reach you!"

"I've been avoiding the world."

"You could do so more effectively," Amara said through clenched teeth. "I need to get out of this place right now."

"Fine." Pax turned her head slightly and used her mind to lift her Jeep back onto the road. "Where do you want to go?"

"No. Not anywhere around here."

"Off the continent then?" Pax placed her hands on her hips. "Let me guess. You need a lift to go shopping in Paris to keep up with the season."

"Why are you being so cruel?" Amara asked, stepping forward angrily. "I need your help, Paxie. I need to train. I want to grow stronger so that I can use my telepathy, and so that I can't get taken prisoner again. You could also benefit from improving your relocation technique."

A car began to approach in the distance, and Pax flung her hand out to slow it down. "What do you want from me?"

"I want us to get the hell out of this dimension. I want to go to the Pseudosphere."

Pax blinked. "For real?"

"Yes. I've decided. I don't care how difficult it is. I need the change, and I need the challenge. I need to do something crazy."

"Mara," Pax said softly. "The vector zone is worlds apart from shopping in Paris. We could die."

"I know. When I told you I'd sacrifice anything and everything, I wasn't kidding."

"We might be in there for years," Pax reminded her. "It will only be days on the outside, but there's a chance we could go insane and be trapped there forever."

"I'm sick of being hurt and vulnerable, Pax!" Amara screamed. Her face was determined and there was a frantic tone in her high-pitched yell. "Do you have any clue how I felt when I was trapped in that pyramid? I don't want to be in danger anymore. I want to *be* the danger, and together, we're definitely dangerous. I want to be Para."

Pax smiled. "Okay."

"Okay?" Amara asked for confirmation.

"Yeah." Pax nodded slowly, accepting every facet and consequence of the decision as she spoke the word again decisively: "Okay."

Chapter 25: A Twisted Path

Sakra stood with his back turned to the two determined women clad in aramid armor. His hands rested loosely at the sides of his robes as he stood in motionless silence. Neither Pax nor Amara spoke as they waited for the hallowed Lord of the Devas to pass his judgment.

"After observing your recent activity," the man said quietly, "I have had to reconsider my decision to allow you girls to enter the vector zone."

"Reconsider?" Pax asked in a cautious tone.

"As you know, the portal to the Spiritual Pseudosphere leads to a dangerous dimension. The world on the other side of the door was created by ancient gods, tens of thousands of years ago. They were much more powerful than even the strongest of us. Only in times of dire need should access be granted to this realm, when earthly gods need to strengthen themselves to defend against wrongdoers and threats to the peace."

"We're aware of this Sakra," Amara said politely, "but don't you think…"

"I am very disappointed in you girls." Sakra clasped his hands behind his back, causing his wide embroidered sleeves to create a V-shape at the base of his spine. "You have chosen to direct your time, energy, and knowledge to scheme against two of our strongest warriors. I thought that you both knew better. I thought that you both had seen enough suffering to not to wish anguish upon others! Especially upon those whom you love: your own family members!"

Amara and Pax shared a look of defeat. They were duly humbled and humiliated before the great demigod. Amara dropped the heavy duffle bag she carried and sighed. She had really been looking forward to the escape. "I'm sorry if our actions have offended you, Sakra. They were just foolish games, and I am willing to give them up forever if you let us leave the dimension."

Pax nervously adjusted the straps of her own luggage which dug into the flesh of both her shoulders. She gazed off the edge of the mountain temple down at the Earth far below. She really did not want to return to her insipid and increasingly meaningless daily life. When Amara had stepped in front of her car with the proposition, it had felt like she had been offered salvation. It was not just the concept of leaving Earth which appealed to her; it was the concept of leaving her mundane, earthly self behind. Each time she had ventured beyond the planet's atmosphere, she had discovered a greater value in herself than she had previously known. It was all a matter of perspective. Pax had always needed to be on the outside in order to more successfully peer in—and now she needed it desperately.

No escape could be as thorough as the vector zone. No excursion could be as taxing. Pax closed her eyes tightly, feeling a bit like her passport had just been declined at a border crossing. The image of the white-haired goddess Suja came to her mind. She considered contacting the woman and taking up her offer of overthrowing Sakra just so she could access… she stopped the thoughts before they could be completed. The demigod standing before her was a good friend of her father's, and he had not, in fact, gotten fat.

Pax bowed her head slightly. "We know that we've been acting in unorthodox ways with respect to the deva code."

"Who told you that?" Sakra asked curtly. He was still facing away from the women.

"Well, my father always says that devas have certain responsibilities," Pax answered.

"Phooey," Sakra said, lifting his hand and waving it in dismissal. "Raymond has always been so solemn. Most of my 'training' him consists of trying to get the boy to loosen up and quit going on and on about his fictional responsibilities."

Pax smiled at this apt description of her father. "Sakra, if you wish for us to stop using the coalescence technique…"

"Nonsense!" said Sakra, turning around and cracking a large grin. "It's very entertaining to watch."

Pax and Amara glanced at each other in surprise.

Sakra frowned. "My wife thinks I'm uptight and incompetent, but she's wrong. I believe in observing others and allowing them freedom to pursue their own proclivities. Suja believes in controlling them to her own purposes. She has good intentions for the most part."

Amara's pale cheeks had flushed and she had begun chewing on her lip compulsively. "Sakra, do you intend to tell the others about Para?"

"Of course not. It's not like those boys don't deserve it. You should have seen the trouble they used to cause when they were kids! Gosh." Sakra laughed and waggled his finger kindly. "If you had let me finish speaking, you would have learned that after my extremely careful reconsideration, I have decided that I *will* open the portal to the vector zone. I want you both to know that I am very proud of you girls for finding motivation in your emotions to push yourself to grow stronger."

Pax released the breath she had been holding. "Don't scare me like that!"

"Couldn't resist," said the demigod with a wicked shrug. "I don't get much company up here at the Point."

Amara was beaming. "Thank you, Sakra! You won't regret this; we won't abuse the privilege."

"Good child, why not? The privilege is going to abuse the stuffing out of you. It is not going to be a pleasant adventure by any means. But you know this. I just have a few pieces of advice before you continue. Regarding coalescence: not much is known about the process and its long term effects, but from what I can discern, it creates strong changes in the patterns of thought of the individuals using the technique. The constant switching back and forth from one identity to another may result in severe mental illness. It will most certainly change who you both are."

Sakra's voice took on a serious tone of warning. "If you girls practice coalescence on a daily basis for all the years you spend in the vector zone, you will emerge with your souls changed permanently. There's a little bit of Ashton in both Thornton and Asher at all times. Already, there's a little bit of Para in both of you at all times."

"We know, Sakra," said Amara with a smile.

"You know?"

"It has similar side effects to being in a

relationship," explained Amara. "A person always becomes what they spend the most time with; it's unavoidable to pick up aspects of your surroundings. Husbands and wives, even roommates pick up each other's habits because they live in such close proximity. Of course it's intensified when you're spending time in the same body. There's no greater proximity than that! We didn't even need to be demigods to figure that much out."

"Ah, yes. You girls are very sharp," said Sakra as he looked at them both with concern. "Are you truly ready for how much this will change you? You won't be the same girls when you leave that zone."

"Sakra," said Pax softly. "Even if we didn't merge our bodies in there, we'd still be different people upon our exit. Years of intense training in the Pseudosphere aren't easy, as far as I've heard from my family and friends. The whole point of the experience is to emerge an improved person."

"Yes, this is true. It is very challenging to survive in such maddening conditions, but I'm confident you are both mentally capable." Sakra lifted one of his embroidered sleeves as he scratched his head. "If, by some chance, you still hold a grudge against the boys when you exit, I have a suggestion."

"I'm all ears," said Amara, cheerfully having picked up her duffle bag again.

"I think you have a very interesting plan to hurt Thorn and Ash, but perhaps you should consider this: instead of using Para to create and destroy a love to hurt them both, you could use Para to destroy a solid connection that already exists in their lives. Target the strongest, deepest love in both of their hearts. The friendship that they both have depended on practically since birth."

Pax clenched her fist around the strap of her luggage as she listened, spellbound.

"Take away the love of the first person they each cared for who didn't belong to their family. *Each other.* If you can drive a wedge *between* Thorn and Ash their suffering will be extraordinary. You two have found strength in each other during this difficult time. Similarly, those two have always found strength in each other and their friendship. If you can make them angry with each other, then you will be literally ripping apart the fabric of their beings. You will be causing pain not only to both men, but to the part of Ashton which still lives in both of them, and depends on their love for each other."

There was a brief silence as the girls processed the words. Amara finally spoke. "That almost sounds too harsh, Sakra. We wanted to harm them, but… why are you telling us this?"

Pax nodded. "You just said that you were disappointed that we wished to cause suffering, and now you are helping us. Giving us ideas on how to do it better? Why?"

"That's a complex answer. You girls have been forced to walk down a twisted path. It might have been easier to walk the direct path, but nevertheless... all paths end up in the same destination. Pax, my wife surely told you her philosophy about creation, but every god worth his salt knows this: destruction is a necessary thing. True creation comes from the ashes of the greatest destruction." Sakra smiled and extended his right hand, spinning a silver ball of prana on his palm. "I can foresee that the damage caused by your scheming will eventually lead to a brighter future, one filled with more understanding and wisdom on both of your parts. After the cataclysm, there is a deeper contentment. Even Thorn and Ash will be the better for what they learn from all this. Learning cannot happen without pain."

Sakra smiled as the silver ball in his palm became narrow at its center, creating the shape of an hourglass. "Vincent has surely told you his philosophy about the golden rule of devas. But his royal ancestors distorted it from the original inscription: *pain* is paramount. Pain is the harbinger of truth."

The silver hourglass in his palm melted down into dust. Sakra extended his palm to the side, and allowed the dust to travel into the air, and spin in an oval shape. The air in the center of the oval became darker. "You're both good girls. You wouldn't have wished to cause harm unless you had been harmed. It's a natural human and godly reaction. And through that suffering comes insight. Sometimes the twisted path is the better choice."

Pax was suddenly overcome with optimism. She moved forward boldly and hugged the Lord of the Devas. "Thank you for everything, Sakra. Even gods need their gods, and I'm so happy you're the one who guides us all. I am so grateful that you took care of my father after my mother's passing."

"It has been an honor, child. Raymond is a good man."

Amara was studying the silver dust spinning around the dark oval; it seemed to be a portal to another place. "Does lead to the vector zone?" she asked.

"No," Sakra answered. "I will open *that* portal once you both say goodbye to your parents."

The girls looked at each other anxiously.

"We were hoping to sneak away quietly," Amara admitted. "We didn't tell them we were leaving."

"Ah, but I did," said Sakra with a grin. "I summoned them and they will step through this portal momentarily. Raymond would kill me if I didn't tell him his little girl was about to leave the dimension."

"Dammit. You were stalling us!" Pax accused. "You gave us this whole godly philosophy lecture just to stall us."

"Guilty as charged. You can thank me later." Sakra winked. "After a few months of solitude in oblivion, you'll be glad you got to hug your parents one last time before entering that place."

Chapter 26: More Vastly Infinite

The Burnsons and Kalgrens, summoned by the Lord of the Devas, had stepped through the portal and arrived at Sakra's Point. Many of them had not been to the mountaintop temple in many years, and Asher moved to the corner to look at the view below quietly. Raymond immediately moved to his friend's side and began consulting Sakra about changes which had been made to the vector zone since it had last been used.

Thornton stood with his arms crossed, clad in his typical tailored business suit. While everyone else chatted around them, he stared directly at Pax. *You were going to leave without telling me?*

I'm sorry, she said looking away. *I wish he hadn't told you. You would never have noticed that I was gone. It's only for a few days.*

You are out of your mind, Pax. I notice every minute that you're gone. Thornton's lips were pulled tightly into a thin line, and he was evidently upset. *What was that last week? Just a one night stand or ex-sex? Did you need a release after the big battle, and I was just there? You said you were going out for a drive and you never came back.*

I basically haven't stopped driving since that night, Pax explained as she looked off into the clouds below. *Mara jumped in front of my car with the idea to go to the vector zone, and I agreed.*

Thornton's voice in her mind was pained. *Paxie. Why won't you even look at me?*

"I'm fascinated with the science of the vector

zone," Rose Kalgren was saying to Amelia. "I mean, not just the actual realm, but can you imagine the mechanics of opening that portal? I've been drawing up schematics to try and explain this, but it's simply mindboggling!"

"Do you think you could open the portal?" Amelia asked nervously. "I mean, if something happened to Sakra in the next few days, would the girls be trapped?"

"Ladies, I have lived for hundreds of years. Nothing is going to happen to me in the next week!" Sakra assured them with a chuckle.

"But with your wife's new vendetta…" Rose said skeptically.

"Raymond and I will take turns defending the skinny man," said Vincent gruffly.

Sakra snorted, as though the Lord of Devas needed defense. "How comforting," he said, but he was grateful for their concern. His skills lay mostly in healing and using his mind, but Vincent and Raymond knew how to channel their powers into brute strength.

"I'll go to the vector zone too," Thornton announced suddenly. He reached up to rip his navy blue tie from his neck, and shrugged his suit jacket off his shoulders. "I can help protect the girls."

We need to do this on our own, Pax told him telepathically. She still could not meet his eyes, for she *did* want him to come along. She had always enjoyed traveling with Thornton, and it would be uplifting to have him beside her in the Pseudosphere.

I always said I'd go everywhere with you, he reminded her. *To every corner of the omniverse.*

"You can't take a week off work!" Rose Kalgren reminded her son. "Who's going to go to the meetings?

I'm not doing it. I'm retired. Why doesn't Ash go?"

"No!" Amara said a bit too quickly. Asher turned around at the mention of his name. *Pax, say something! Don't let her force him.*

"I don't need my uncle chaperoning my field trip," Pax said.

Sakra cleared his throat. "Unfortunately, I cannot condone more than two people occupying the Pseudosphere at once. It has never been done before—and Thorn and Ash have already passed their trials."

"How long will they be in there for?" Asher asked, turning back to stare at the view. "When Thorn and I went, we stayed for two years, but it was only two days on the outside."

"Ah, but you were very young then. The girls will be able to handle more rigorous training. I anticipate that they will be locked in the room for at least five days."

"Five days!" Amelia shrieked. "That's five years of their lives!"

"My good woman, have you forgotten? When they exit, they will not have physically aged at all," Sakra explained, in a calm voice meant to soothe Pax's grandmother. "I know it has been several decades since anyone has used the Pseudosphere, so perhaps I should refresh your memory on its properties."

Sakra released a stream of purple prana from his hands, which quickly formed the shape of a cube. "Upon entering the vector zone, the girls will emerge into a very small room, the shape of this cube. This will be the only safe area, meant for resting. As you can see, there six sides to this cube—four walls and a floor and a ceiling."

"That seems basic," Amelia remarked.

"Yes, except that the room floats in nothingness," Sakra said, using his other hand to create a dark fog around the cube. He pointed and several bright yellow squares appeared in each larger square. "There are six doors in the room. One on each wall, and one on the floor and the ceiling. The portals lead out to six different trials. Six different realms of hell, one might say. Only when the girls can withstand the hardships beyond each of the six doors will they be allowed to return to this dimension."

"It's extreme," Raymond said softly. "I still have nightmares, and it's been over thirty years since I set foot there."

Amelia's face displayed worry, and she rubbed her son's shoulder. "Maybe the girls shouldn't go."

"It's a worthwhile and necessary experience," Vincent said firmly.

"The whole point of the Spiritual Pseudosphere is purification," Sakra said. "It is similar to the human concept of fasting. The girls will have to live as the old gods did, without food or water and often without air or rest. It is our attachment to worldly needs that make us weak. Once we learn to survive on the *prana* inside instead of on energy from exterior sources, we purge the human weakness out of us and make room for unadulterated power."

"That's all very interesting," said Rose Kalgren, who was furiously scribbling in a notebook. "So would you say that the room is floating in infinite three-dimensional hyperbolic space?"

"Not quite, Rose." Sakra frowned, thinking of how to phrase his explanation. "I would call it two-dimensional, on a constant curvature. Fundamentally, one could describe the Pseudosphere to be more *vastly* infinite than other planes of existence."

"More vastly infinite?" Asher asked in confusion.

"That makes perfect sense," said Rose Kalgren, making a quick sketch. She held it out to Asher. "Here's a rough diagram to explain what he means."

Asher squinted at the scrawled circles and lines and still could not understand. "O…kay…"

Thornton grinned and slapped his friend on the back. "Don't worry about it, buddy."

"Paxie," Amelia said anxiously. "Are you sure you want to go, sweetie?"'"

"Grandma, I *need* to go," Pax responded. She moved forward to give the old woman a gentle hug.

"Please be careful. Don't push yourself too hard," Amelia said tearfully. "Your Grandpa Kaden would be so proud of you."

Pax nodded at the old woman before turning to her father. Raymond didn't say anything, but he held out his arms to her. She smiled and let her father envelop her in a giant bear hug. She could feel the unconditional love in his embrace. He did not question her decision or try to change her mind. He respected her choice and supported her, and that was what she most desperately needed. She rested her cheek against his chest in contentment, thankful that Sakra had called her family and not just let her escape quietly in the night. It made her little quest feel more official and righteous when it had previously felt like a frantic escape.

Rose put her notepad away and moved forward to stroke her own daughter's hair fondly. "Honey, I know you'll be fine. You deserve an adventure."

"Thanks, mom," said Amara with a smile. "When I get back we can start planning the charity ball."

Vincent was noticing that his daughter was clad in aramid armor. She usually wore trendy and impractical garments, but for the first time in possibly her entire life, she was dressed for battle. Unbeknownst to Vincent, a strange light had come into his eyes. "Amara. It pleases me to see you're finally taking your heritage seriously," he said brusquely. "If you practice diligently, you will see great improvements in your life." Vincent would never betray the enormity of his fatherly joy. He glanced over at Pax and noticed that she was also wearing the heavy fabric. She normally dressed as casually as possible, often practicing in jeans and a t-shirt. Vincent realized that something crucial had changed about the young women.

It must have been their recent battle with Suja. They were suddenly driven and dogged, and he had not even needed to push them and be as strict as he had been with Thornton and Asher. Their youthful enthusiasm was a formidable sight which he had long forgotten, reminding him of his own formative years, and his good friend Kaden who had been a formative influence. The two men had constantly challenged and pushed each other to new heights of skill, and as he looked at Pax's face, he could see a shadow of her grandfather's spirit. It swelled his heart to witness this again.

Although Kaden Burnson was gone, and many devas of old had perished in the wars with the Asura, their old traditions were being carried on in these young hybrids. Of course, one could not have discovered Vincent's nostalgia from glancing at his stoic face as he made eye contact with Pax. He inclined his head to the left.

"Girl. A word."

He instantly blasted off into the sky a few miles away from everyone. Pax pulled away from Raymond and quickly followed her mentor. When the two left all the others to an awkward silence, Amara wondered to herself what her father and friend were discussing. She glanced after their trails of prana, hoping that their discussion would not result in a more challenging training regimen. She knew that it almost certainly would.

"Why are you going?"

Amara flinched to find that Asher had approached her and was standing not far away. When she turned to face him, she felt a pang in her heart at the lost expression of his chocolate-brown eyes. His sad face was framed by messy dark locks of bed-hair. She lowered her eyes so that she would not have to look directly at him, and of course, her eyes settled on the contours of his chest muscles beneath his taupe cashmere sweater. Why was he still wearing the clothes she had bought for him? Didn't he own anything else? She knew that she couldn't gaze wordlessly forever with their families watching. She titled her chin up a little before responding as curtly and succinctly as possible.

"To practice."

Asher's arm drifted up as his fingers settled against the back of his neck to scratch absently as confusion displayed across his face. "But you can practice here," he said softly

Clenching her fists, Amara glared at him. Everyone around could feel the tension fizzing in the air as the two silently locked eyes. Rose lifted her eyebrows in confusion at the strange interaction, realizing that volumes were being communicated that no one but the former couple understood. She also knew that at the core of the matter, and regardless of their current conflicts, these two loved each other.

Amara did not trust herself to speak, fearing she'd either say something too callous or too friendly. She only continued to glower and silently prayed for Pax to return and remove her from the spotlight. Unfortunately, Pax would not return before Asher opened his mouth again:

"You're not strong enough to deal with the conditions in there, Mara. You shouldn't go."

"Don't you *dare* tell me what to do," Amara snapped, her brows furrowing.

"I know you," Asher said, moving forward hesitantly. "You can't even tolerate a camping trip."

"Who *likes* getting eaten alive by mosquitoes?" she asked stubbornly.

"I've been to the vector zone, Mara. There are things far worse than mosquitoes. Far worse than those worms Suja used on you. You're going to spend every day crying to return…"

"I will *not!*" Amara shouted. A red aura of *prana* flashed around her as she felt bile rise from her gut. "You're not part of my life anymore, so don't get involved!"

Vincent and Pax returned instantly at the signals

they felt and stood beside Amara. Vincent scowled at the man who had upset his daughter. "What the hell is going on?"

"Open the portal, Sakra!" Amara commanded. "Please. I want to go now."

"Sure," said the demigod. He began releasing his prana into the shape of a hexagon on the ground. "One weeklong all-inclusive trip to hell coming right up!"

Vincent looked at Pax intently. "Remember what I told you, girl."

"I won't disappoint you, sir." Pax said this with a respectful lowering of her chin. The girls picked up their duffle bags and stepped away from their families. They turned and headed for the hexagonal portal Sakra was preparing.

"Wait a moment," Thornton said forcefully. "Don't open the portal yet."

"It will take me a few minutes, son. I might as well get started," the god explained.

"I need to talk to Pax privately," Thornton said.

"We can talk later," Pax said, "when I return."

"Wow," Thornton said in a low voice. He moved across the temple floor, materializing directly in her path. "Could you try to be any more coldhearted, fire goddess? You're going to be gone for *years*. You didn't even bid me goodbye personally. You exchanged more words with *my father* than with me!"

"She considers me to be of consequence," Vincent said smugly.

"Shut up, Dad!" Thornton said fiercely.

"You will not speak to me in that..."

"Listen, Father. This is between me and my

woman. Please shut your mouth and stop acting like all hemispheres, biospheres, and pseudospheres revolve around you."

"Your woman?" Pax asked sarcastically.

"Yeah," Thornton said, glaring at her. "I'm not going to take this kind of treatment sitting down, Pax. You know how shitty it feels when your dad leaves you and runs away to the other side of the world when things get difficult for him?"

Pax nodded slowly, glancing at Raymond.

"I'm not going to let you do the same thing to me. Not without addressing our problems like mature adults and getting everything out in the open first."

"I don't want to," she said. "You're free to do as you please; just leave me out of it."

"This isn't like you," he said. "You have always fought with me about everything. So attack me. Tell me all the reasons you're upset and let me apologize."

"Would you feel like I was paying more attention to you if I hit you in the face?" she asked.

"It would be progress," he answered, offering his cheek. Pax turned away and crossed her arms.

"God, Pax!" Asher said with a groan. "Just hear him out to save us all from listening to his begging."

"Okay," Pax said softly. She dropped her duffle bags abruptly. "Talk, Thorn. You have one minute."

Chapter 27: The Tigress Eye

"Well, let me start with this," Thornton said. "I betrayed your trust by being with another woman, and it wasn't because of magick or mystical manipulation. It wasn't Suja's fault. I was blackmailed."

All eyes were fixed unwaveringly on him, except for those belonging to Pax. She stared at the tiled floor so that she wouldn't meet his gaze.

Amara sent her friend telepathic messages of encouragement. *Be strong, Pax. Whatever he says, we're just going to head into the Pseudosphere and put this world behind us, got it?*

"Young man!" said Rose Kalgren, placing her hands on her hips. "What are you talking about?"

"I took an illegal shortcut. Karina Allbright was spying on me and threatened to expose everything with a press release. The evidence was solid, and it would have cost the company hundreds of millions. It would have sunk Kalgren Tech completely. I would have gone to jail, along with many of my best employees. That snake of a woman said she would make it all go away if I…" Thornton hesitated. "Pax, I was just so overwhelmed…"

Pax stared down at Thornton's black socks. They seemed to be some sort of cotton-poly blend.

"How could you, Thorn?" Rose was saying, almost at the point of tears. "What were you thinking?"

"He *wasn't* thinking!" Amelia hissed. "He has zero honor and he is not worthy of my granddaughter."

"No. He does have honor," Amara said, suddenly

feeling defensive of her brother. "He was trying to protect our family and save mom's company. We *are* Kalgren Tech and Thorn has more responsibilities than any of us. Frankly, I would have done the same thing."

"Really?" Asher asked.

"Yes. And I would have enjoyed it, and I wouldn't have apologized," Amara said with emphasis.

Vincent shook his head. "You're mistaken, Amara. You would not have done something so foolish because you possess a functional brain. You see, I'm pretty sure your mother was drinking and smoking heavily during your brother's gestation and…"

"Don't pin this on me," Rose said angrily. "You're the one with the inhuman sperm!"

"Conflict is healthy," Sakra said in his sagacious way. "My temple is private, and I encourage you to argue all you wish. By the way, the portal is now open. The moment anyone stands on it, they will be transported to the vector zone."

Pax immediately began moving toward the portal but Thornton grabbed her arm. He looked at her pleadingly. "Don't go without saying something to me, Paxie."

"Let her go, boy," Vincent commanded. "I care nothing for Kalgren Technology and the foolish monetary ambitions of this family. I come from a lineage which is far greater than a multinational corporation. We are devas, and we follow a code separate from those of humans. We respect each other and we are faithful to those who are faithful to us. I am ashamed to call you my son."

Thornton's face was stricken, and his grip on Pax's

arm loosened. Her insides ached at the sight of the pain on his face, and she reached out to clasp his hand. She turned to their gathered family members, and knew that she had to speak on his behalf.

"Please don't be upset with him," Pax said, gently imploring the Kalgrens and Burnsons. She scanned her mind quickly for any way to turn everyone's hatred away from Thornton. "I am not sure if all of you know this, but I made a much bigger mistake than he did."

Amelia scoffed. "Darling, I doubt there is anything you could do…"

"I killed Karina Allbright," Pax said to her grandmother, causing the old woman to gasp in shock. "I don't even remember doing it, but apparently after I saw her with Thorn, I incinerated her body."

There was a silence in the temple. Rose Kalgren stared unblinkingly in surprise while Amelia tried to restrain her tears. "Paxie!" the old woman moaned.

"And by every rule we have, that was unacceptable," Raymond said grimly. "We raised you better than that, Pax."

"He's right, girl! You can be such a damned fool," Vincent said, crossing his arms with a sneer. "You should have *at least* tortured her first."

All eyes turned to glare at Vincent.

"What?" he asked, with a scowl more profound than the one which usually graced his face. "First of all, my son should have killed the woman straightaway when she threatened him. No one blackmails my boy! Secondly, Pax was far too lenient for a deva. I would have pulled out each of her fingernails, followed by her teeth and hair. Over the course of several days, I would have removed eyeballs, lungs, or kidneys, depending on my mood. It is thrilling to see how many parts you can remove before…"

"Vince," Rose said in a low voice.

"And of course, instead of incinerating her all at once, you could burn holes through her flesh a little at a time, and enjoy listening to the sound of…"

"Vince!" Rose shouted. When she had her husband's attention, she cleared her throat. "Don't say those types of things in front of the children."

"Why not? The devas of old had specific methods of exacting vengeance…"

Rose glared at her husband to silence him before turning to her son. "Thorn, sweetie. You should have called me to help deal with the situation. And Pax, your reaction… my goodness! The both of you."

"Yeah," Pax said softly. "I never want it to happen again. I believe that if I practice constantly in the vector zone, I will learn to control my abilities and prevent a repeat of the situation. No one has punished me for my actions, so I need to punish myself. I can't think of a better sentence than the Pseudosphere."

"You shouldn't have to punish yourself because *I* hurt you," Thornton said. "You should punish me. I deserve it—but don't avoid me, Pax. We've been through too much together for you to turn your back on me."

"We'll talk when I return," she said again, moving to the glowing portal.

"Wait, wait. There's one more thing," Thornton said. He reached into his pocket and pulled out a little black box. "This is yours."

She stared down at the black box blankly. "What is…"

"I know you'll be in there for a while, Paxie. I want you to think about forgiving me. I want you to think about giving me a second chance. When you get out, I'll be waiting." When she did not respond, he placed his fingers under her chin and lifted her face so that her pained onyx eyes met his cloudy blue ones. "Say you'll think about it?"

"About what?" she whispered.

Thornton withdrew his fingers from her chin and slid his hand down to grasp hers. He placed the velvet box in the palm of her hand and closed her fingers around it. Pax could hear her own heartbeat pounding loudly in her ears.

"It's all wrong, I know. I was waiting and waiting for the right moment, and I let a hundred amazing moments pass by because I always felt that a better moment was right around the corner." Thornton paused, taking a deep breath. "I always felt that way with you. Like every day could only get better. "

Pax could see the shine of moisture in his eyes, and knew that he was close to tears. "Thorn," she whispered, "please, don't…"

"I must. I have to do this now—before you go. Pax, you need to know that I'm serious about fixing things."

"Shh, Thorn. I know." She reached up and touched his face as she struggled to hold back her own tears. "Don't say anything more. Please."

"I want us to be married," he said. "And I want you to fry me like extra-crispy bacon if I ever hurt you again."

Pax could not resist a smile. This was all the encouragement he needed to reach out and snap open the velvet box, revealing a massive brilliant-cut orange diamond. In the lighting, it glinted the color of flame. Even Amara, who owned plenty of jewelry, had a small seizure when she saw the ring he had chosen. *Holy fuck, Pax! Do you know what diamond that is? The Tigress Eye! It used to belong to the empress of…*

Shut up, Amara. I can't think.

What is there to think about? He's my big brother. I know how you feel…

Shut up! Pax could not concentrate as Thornton's fingers grazed hers. He was gingerly sliding the ring onto her finger. The huge round-shaped orange stone was set in the middle of a row of smaller diamonds. She suddenly felt dizzy and completely unsure of whether it was euphoria or fear that flooded her chest.

"Should I get down on my knees?" Thornton asked with a smile.

"If you do that I will murder you," she said quickly, her cheeks flushing. *Pride,* she reminded herself, *pride is paramount. Stay strong, Pax.* She lifted her eyes to examine his face. It was unbearable to look directly at him, for his sweet sapphire eyes pulled her in magnetically. She felt powerless; it was in her blood. Every drop of her deva blood, and every drop of her human blood called out for him against the logical wishes of her mind. She blinked away tears as her insides warred.

"When you come back," Thornton said, moving forward and slipping his hands around her waist, "I could prepare a ship for that trip we always planned to take."

"You're impossible," she said. Pax bit her lip and waged a war against her brimming tear ducts. She had spent years dreaming of a honeymoon in space with the man standing before her. It was where their romance had begun, and it was the most romantic venue possible to celebrate their marriage. Without Thornton, the fantasy would not be possible—it would not even be desirable. There was no one else. She felt somewhat imprisoned by the intensity of his gaze, and forced herself to look away.

Pax was surprised to see that there were other people present in the temple. She blinked, seeing how her friends and family members stood as frozen as statues. When she searched the faces of her father and grandmother for strength, she only saw her own confusion mirrored back at her. There was a definite hint of expectation there as well, especially in her Uncle Asher's smile. Ripping her eyes away from her relatives, she turned to Rose and Vincent. The Kalgrens also seemed torn between anger and hope. Pax was drowning, and could not remember the reasons she had wished to escape. There was only all-consuming optimism. She frantically searched her mind for a fragment of reason or rope of reality which she could clutch to keep afloat.

She looked down at the ring and felt heat spread through her with the overwhelming emotions. Tears pinched and stung the back of her eyes. She returned her gaze to Thornton, feeling her strength completely sapped. All of her defenses had doubts were crumbling.

A response came to her lips before she could contain the words.

"Thornton Kalgren," she said softly. "You drive me fucking insane."

"Good," he said with a smile. "I think that means you like me."

The confidence on his lips was irresistible. She moved forward and pressed her mouth against his smirk to taste his conviction. As she wrapped her arms around his neck and felt the warmth of his chest even through her armor, it occurred to her that he knew. He knew that she had already forgiven him. He knew that she always would. He knew that she was putty in his capable hands, which had naturally moved to her lower back.

Amara sighed at the sight of this movie-worthy kiss. She didn't know whether she should feel upset that Pax had caved so easily, or overjoyed that her best friend would soon be her sister. She knew that what she did feel was jealousy that her friend would have a happy ending while she could not. Amara was inwardly bemoaning the situation and obvious change of plans when the dark-haired woman stopped kissing her brother and stooped to pick up her travel bags.

Let's go, Mara. Pax said telepathically.

Feeling her thin blonde eyebrows knit together, Amara responded in bewilderment. *I understand if you want to abandon this Para thing and return to him. I'm fine with that. If you want to cancel the training, that's cool. I know you love him. There's no way I could refuse if I were in your shoes.*

Are you kidding? What am I, a doormat? Pax glanced at Sakra whose face bore a soft unreadable expression. Her eyes then fell upon Amara. *I'm not going to abandon you. We began walking down the twisted path together, and I'm not taking any shortcuts. This doesn't feel right. Not here, not now, and not like this. I want to continue following this warped highway and find out where it leads. Let's stick to it until the end.*

Paxie, if we enter that zone we'll be stuck there for years and years. Can you handle being away from him for so long? Don't you want to be close to him now that you're engaged, and things are going to be right again?

Since when am I engaged? I didn't say yes, did I?

Pax! You smooched him!

A flicker of mirth tickled Pax's skin into creases at the corner of her eyes and lips. *I promised you we'd go. We're going. Even if I do agree to marry him, I'd like for him to suffer for a few days while awaiting my decision.*

That's my girl, thought Amara with pleased relief. *I was worried I'd lost you.*

Never. Pax turned to look at Vincent. Strength poured into her from his eyes. She remembered the words he had spoken to her in private. Finally, she turned back to Thornton and rubbed his arm gently.

"Give me a few years to think about it," she said with a sly smile. "I'll let you know when I return to this dimension."

"No, you should tell us now, Pax," Vincent advised. "I'm sure my wife and Amelia would love to begin planning a big expensive wedding. How much do you think it will cost, Rose?"

"Oh, I don't know! A few million at least. I'll have to start immediately with the…"

Vincent cocked his thumb in the direction of his wife. "See this, Pax? This is the appropriate enthusiastic female response to the concept of a wedding. Even a wedding that seemed ridiculous a few minutes ago because the bride and groom have recently committed murder and adultery, respectively."

"Vincent, I said that I…"

"No, Pax. You should do it. Marry my son. Just be aware that once you get fat and pregnant he's going to go and fuck a dozen other women like all human scum tend to do."

Pax's eyes snapped open wide in horror at Vincent's words. She placed a hand on her chest weakly. She knew that Vincent was just trying to push her buttons, but it was working. The man knew exactly where to attack her.

Thornton, however, was not amused. He turned angrily and shouted. "Father! I am not like that! You *know* me."

"I know that your decision-making originates from the organ dangling between your legs."

As soon as these words left Vincent's mouth, a sickening crack was heard and the man was sent reeling. Thornton had launched his knuckles into his father's face.

"Stop it, you two! Vince, have you been watching my soap operas again?" asked Rose, shaking her head. "These men! My goodness."

Vincent growled and picked himself off the floor. Thornton advanced on him with his *prana* flashing dangerously, and his fists ready for more action.

"Stop it," said Pax quietly. "Stop it. Vincent may be vulgar and have no manners, but he is not totally wrong. I'm sure you've all seen the news recently."

Thornton paused and turned to her in confusion

for a moment before understanding dawned on him. *Medea.*

"She's just a business contact, Pax," Thornton said quickly. "It was just the media twisting…"

Pax smiled. He was blatantly lying, and she would have believed him otherwise. She turned to Amara, sending her a victorious look which somehow carried undertones of defeat. The blonde woman shook her head in disbelief.

"You always have an explanation, don't you, big brother?" asked Amara, picking up her duffle bag and moving towards the glowing portal. "I'm ashamed to call you family. If it weren't for the superhuman abilities, I would swear that you had to be adopted."

"Why is my own family against me?" Thornton asked angrily. "Mara, you should give me the benefit of the…"

"Uh huh," she said, giving him a scowl almost identical to her father's. "Though I have to hand it to you. Nice strategy! Proposing to Pax as she's about to enter a collection of hell dimensions and conditions which are known to induce *insanity*. She would have to be insane to accept you!"

Amara continued, placing her hands on her hips to echo her mother's earlier pose. "Not to mention the fact that there will be no men in this dimension. I bet you're expecting that when Pax leaves the vector zone after years of harsh training and being totally man-starved she's going to be desperate and run right back into your arms!" The blonde woman chuckled and stepped onto the portal. The glow began to consume her legs. "Think again! For your information, I've invented some really powerful goddess-grade vibrators, so don't think she'll have any need of you. Goodbye everyone. Sakra, please send us away."

The small Indian man cleared his throat to alleviate the awkward moment. "I bless you in your journeys, children. May you find all you seek and more in the Pseudosphere." With a flourish, Amara and Pax found themselves suddenly separated from their shocked and blushing family members.

Amara pumped her fist triumphantly at the stylish exit. "Damn! There are few pleasures in life greater than telling off my big brother. The looks on all of their faces!"

Meanwhile, Pax had collapsed to the floor and was sitting and staring at her ring. "It's paramount," she told herself. "Pride is paramount. I had to be tough and refuse."

"Honey," Amara said. "That's not pride. That's self-respect."

What if I lose everything because of my foolish pride? Pax asked herself. She allowed her tears to flow freely, and at the same time she suddenly found herself laughing. "Goddess-grade vibrators? What the hell?"

Amara crouched down too, grinning and rubbing her friend's arm. "Sorry. It was the best I could come up with on short notice."

"Mara," said Pax weakly, displaying her hand. "Look at this thing."

"I know," Amara said gravely, "I know."

"I act like this super tough girl all the time, but I always knew it would be him. And when the moment came, and he was finally saying the words… everything was wrong." Pax moved the hand with the ring on it to her chest, and clenched it there. "It wasn't the way I had pictured it. I was… ashamed."

"It was a pretty disappointing proposal," Amara agreed.

"Not just the proposal, but what it meant underneath. I swear, a few months ago I would have said 'yes' on the spot. I *want to* underneath it all," Pax mumbled in a daze. "What if I lost the chance forever? What if I screwed it up?"

"Twelve years together and adventures on other planets. A temporary delay in response isn't going to screw all of that up."

"What have I done? I should have agreed. The shame would have disappeared eventually. I would have been happy to be his wife."

"Maybe you still will be someday. You've got plenty of time to consider it, and when we leave maybe you'll become my sister-in-law!"

"You'll have to talk me out of it." Pax suddenly smiled. "Hey, did you really invent goddess-grade vibrators?"

"Well, no. I mainly said it for the shock value."

Pax let out another burst of laughter and rapidly bounced up into a standing position. She took a good look around at the cubic rest area of the Pseudosphere for the first time. The walls were, in fact, purple. The doors in the walls were bright yellow. Pax moved over to one of the doors and yanked it open. She immediately recoiled from what she saw.

It looked like the darkest reaches of hell during a lightning storm.

White-hot flames filled the area, licking at the open door with a menacing crackle. Swallowing back her fear, Pax boldly stepped through the door. Immediately, the atmosphere transformed around her, and the black sky began to pelt rocks of hail down on her head. She gritted her teeth and turned to Amara.

"Come on in! The weather's fine."

Amara stood with her duffle bag at her feet and her mouth slightly open. "Are you fucking kidding me?"

"I didn't come here to goof off, Mara. Let's get started."

"I'd like to get settled in first," the blonde woman said with a gulp. "Maybe you could wait for me to unpack my toothbrush?"

Pax turned her face up to the black sky and laughed as the boulders of hail rained down on her. Amara's mouth suddenly went very dry to see her friend enjoying the violent assault as though it were a fresh summer rain. Had Pax lost her mind? No. This was the true, uninhibited Pax.

"Can we use coalescence now?" Amara asked meekly, hoping to take advantage of the other woman's strength and boldness.

"No," Pax responded. "I want to see what you're made of, Blondie."

Amara raised her eyebrows. She noticed the sudden change in Pax's voice as she turned and walked out into the opaque black area of the vector zone. Amara watched through the doorway nervously, knowing that Pax had flipped the switch and was now in training mode. Amara moved forward slowly, expecting the worst.

Pax placed her hands on her armor-swathed hips and looked over her shoulder with a superior smirk. "I can't believe what a pitiful excuse for a deva you are, Amara Kalgren. With such an amazing warrior for a father, you would think the daughter would have a backbone."

"The whole taunting thing isn't really necessary."

"Of course not. Because you're brave enough to step through that doorway without being coaxed like a terrified child?" Pax tilted her head back and snorted. The white flames licked around her body, reflecting off her armor. "You're such a failure as a deva. You're older than I am with purer bloodlines, and you've wasted all your free time on improving your wardrobe instead of your mind and body."

"Pax, please stop that. I'm going to enter the room in a second. I just need to prepare myself."

"Why are you even here, Amara?" Pax snarled as she assumed Ruby Form. "Suja was right when she said that you were holding me back. I'd gain more from practicing with dirt."

"Okay, hot stuff. I know you want to get started, but you need to bear with me…"

Pax smiled. "You don't deserve a deva man. You *never* deserved my uncle. He was right to leave you."

"Going too far!" Amara said. "That isn't going to help me get stronger. That's going to make me sit and cry."

"You know who would be a great match for you? Some pencil neck, needle dick weakling with credit cards who can take you shopping."

"You bitch!" shouted Amara, clenching her fists

and sprinting away from the resting area of the vector zone. As soon as her feet hit the white flames of the Pseudosphere, she fell flat on her face.

"Oh my god, Pax! I can't move!" Amara exclaimed as she tried to get up. Her limbs felt like lead. The white flames scorched her face as she tried to pull herself off the blazing ground. "Help me, please!"

Pax's face wrinkled in surprise. "Um…" She reached up to scratch her head, in much the same gesture her uncle used when puzzled. Was this a battle strategy? Making her feel sorry and enlisting her help to catch her off guard and attack? "I'm not falling for that, Amara. We have trials to complete, and this is one of them. Come on, get up. Let's get moving. "

"Pax, I'm serious. This gravity is insane. My body feels like it weighs a thousand pounds."

Pax hadn't noticed this and she tried jumping up and down a few times. "I guess I do feel a bit heavier than normal. But it's not enough to really make a difference."

"It makes a difference *to me!"* Amara screamed.

"How are we going practice anything if you can't move? I guess I'm just going to stand here and insult you until you can get over here and punch me in the face for it."

"Pax! My dad told you to take care of me," complained Amara, wiping beads of sweat from her forehead. It was painful even trying to stand. She began to try to turn around and begin inching back to the rest area.

"When Vincent tells you to 'take care' of someone, this is what he means. Did you think he meant I was supposed to put you to sit on my lap and spoon-feed you while reading children's stories?" Pax used her telekinesis to fling Amara away from the door. She slammed the door shut, and the door promptly disappeared. Amara moaned when she saw this happen.

Pax laughed as she approached the golden-haired girl who lay sprawled on the floor. She stood with her black armored boots inches away from her face. "Get up! Get up and prove to me you're a fucking goddess. Show me the strength of your bloodline."

Amara stared at the pointed tips of Pax's boots, through eyes blurred with tears. *This is going to be a very long vacation. Next time I'll just spring for the Bahamas instead.*

ABOUT THE AUTHOR

Nadia Scrieva was born and raised in Toronto, Canada, where she grew very strong from carrying heavy bags filled with books back and forth from the library. She attended the University of Toronto, graduating with a B.A. in English and Anthropology. She likes knives. Her writing always features powerful females and (mostly) honorable male characters.

The author loves receiving feedback from readers, so do not hesitate to contact her with any of your comments or even just to say hello.

www.NadiaScrieva.com

13433915R00199

Made in the USA
Charleston, SC
10 July 2012